Praise for *End of Active Service*

"Brilliantly captures the peculiar mixture of pride and sorrow that comes with fighting in our modern wars, and the difficult work of reintegration into civilian life. But more than simply a war story, *End of Active Service* is a powerful and affecting portrait of the challenges of life and fatherhood, with characters you come to care for deeply." —**Phil Klay, National Book Award–winning author of *Redeployment***

"Young writes with howling musicality, bounding between Iraq and Indiana with the dexterity of a pro and the mania of truth. The effect is irresistible, hilarious, and poignant when least expected. At once a raw portrait of trauma and a takedown of macho brouhaha, *End of Active Service* delivers shock and awe on every page." —**Jakob Guanzon, National Book Award–longlisted author of *Abundance***

"Warning: this is not a war story. It's the story after the war, the story of rebuilding, painful and raw, brutal in its bald honesty, beautiful, too, and startlingly funny. So intimate you'll feel it in your body like a gut punch, with a voice both taunting and tender. As we're told in the novel's incredible opening, this is a love story, though you won't find it all that familiar. A brilliant, necessary debut novel that surprised me again and again. I didn't want it to end." —**Katie Flynn, author of *Island Rule***

"A blistering account of America's forever war with itself. *End of Active Service* begins where our mythology leaves off, and in remarkable, machine gun–fire prose reveals the deep wounds we all carry. An important book for our time." —**Maxim Loskutoff, author of *Old King***

"Life after war is just another kind of war for the narrator of Matt Young's extraordinary, compelling, and brutally insightful debut novel, *End of Active Service*. Written in spare, poetic prose, Young's unflinching immersion in the life of his traumatized protagonist makes the war novel new again." —**Laura Sims, author of *How Can I Help You***

End of Active Service

Eat the Apple: A Memoir

End of Active Service

Matt Young

BLOOMSBURY PUBLISHING

NEW YORK · LONDON · OXFORD · NEW DELHI · SYDNEY

BLOOMSBURY PUBLISHING
Bloomsbury Publishing Inc.
1385 Broadway, New York, NY 10018, USA

BLOOMSBURY, BLOOMSBURY PUBLISHING, and the Diana logo
are trademarks of Bloomsbury Publishing Plc

First published in the United States 2024

Excerpts from this book have been previously published as individual stories
in slightly different form: "Allt Detta Kan Vara Vårt" (*The Cincinnati Review*)
and "Combat Glide" (*Monkeybicycle*).

This is a work of fiction. Names, characters, places, and incidents are either a product
of the author's imagination or are used fictitiously. Any resemblance to actual persons living
or dead, business establishments, events, or locales is entirely coincidental.

ISBN: HB: 978-1-63973-279-1; EBOOK: 978-1-63973-280-7

LIBRARY OF CONGRESS CATALOGING-IN-PUBLICATION DATA IS AVAILABLE

2 4 6 8 10 9 7 5 3 1

Typeset by Westchester Publishing Services
Printed and bound in the U.S.A.

To find out more about our authors and books visit www.bloomsbury.com and
sign up for our newsletters.

Bloomsbury books may be purchased for business or promotional use. For information
on bulk purchases please contact Macmillan Corporate and Premium Sales Department at
specialmarkets@macmillan.com.

For Jenna and Maeve

I'M GOING TO tell you a story—a love story. Might have to tell you about the war, too. But this isn't a war story. Really, though, when you get down to it, most everything is a war story, right? Like, tell me about taking your dog to the park and war's in there somewhere—retired bomb-sniffing dogs getting to live out their final days with their handlers, or hearts-and-minds propaganda about soldiers adopting strays and bringing them to the U.S., or some idiot Marine punting a puppy off a cliff in Hawaii. Talk about how you read some news article on microdosing mushrooms to mitigate traumatic experiences? Veterans with post-traumatic stress were the original test subjects paving the way toward legalization. Share some pictures from a road trip with your family? Gasoline, oil, Halliburton, Iraq. All roads lead home. And if every road leads home, then who cares which one you take? Makes it all easy to ignore. Had an officer who liked to say, America's not at war. *We're* at war. America's at the mall. Max would roll her eyes hard if she heard it, but there was a time I would've lapped that shit up. Asked for seconds. Anyway, I'm a civilian now. Don't have to listen to officers, so I get to decide what kind of story this is, and I say it's a love story.

I met Max at the Speed Rail, this dive in downtown Richfield, Indiana, two months after I left the Marine Corps and joined the First Civ Div. It was mid-November. My hair hadn't grown back. I was still shaving my face every morning like I expected someone to give a shit. I missed the clean, cutting cold of the Southern California night desert: cloudless skies that sucked warmth from rocks and Humvees and bone and spit it into the darkness as we all slept in formation.

Indiana winter sat heavier, dirtier. Choking leaf smoke rolled in from unincorporated suburbs like storm fronts; tarry black walnut clogged street gutters; crusty rock salt dulled the life from the entire city.

I was trying to feel alive. It was my twenty-third birthday. I hated my birthday. But Courtney Johns and I were going to celebrate. Court was my best friend. Had been since first grade when he asked me if I was poor when he found out where I lived and I shoved him down on the playground. We got close after that and stuck together. Normal kid stuff. Fucked around in the woods behind his house, went fishing, hunted morels, played war with paintball and BB guns. Once he shot me in the head with a BB gun. Accident, he said. Thing stayed under my skin for years until our platoon corpsman cut it out during my first deployment for no other good reason than boredom.

Court dealt a little bit, but didn't need to—came from money. Family was a farming dynasty that went way back. His great-grandfather had been a two-term mayor in the nineteen-twenties. We'd learned about him in high school.

Court didn't want to farm. He wanted to ride dirt bikes. Motocross. He was good, too. Could've gone pro—X Games shit—but during a race at the end of our junior year he cased a landing ramp and snapped both clavicles.

Left one healed all fucked-up. Bulged under Court's T-shirts. There was this kid we never liked. No reason. He was a little rat-looking cheesedick whose sister—I can't remember either of their names now—was a grade below us, and she was good-looking. Court used to lock eyes with the kid, the brother, in the hall and talk to that lump under his shirt and call it by the kid's sister's name and lick it.

We got a kick out of stuff like that back then. Couple of shitty little bullies.

Court eventually got a bone graft, but after his surgeries and recovery and rehab, he couldn't race anymore. Most people hung around him because his family had money and toys—the dirt bikes and four-wheelers, shit like that. His parents sold off all the toys, and people disappeared. I stuck around.

During senior year, Court threw parties with kegs and all kinds of liquor because his parents didn't care if we drank as long as we did it on their property and didn't leave. There was weed and pills and mushrooms, too. I don't know if they knew about the drugs. Fucking amazing to me what parents decide they don't want to know. Anyway, people showed back up for the parties. Girls liked him because he was tall and tan and blond—closest most of their Podunk, midwestern asses would ever get to anything like an ocean. Guys liked him because he was all good times and What-can-I-get-you? and no worries, and he made you feel like that, too. Like you were the only one in the room, yours was the only problem that mattered. And, like, he was the one who had all the answers. Charming is what I mean.

And so the minute we pulled up to the Speed Rail, Court was already chatting up the smokers shivering outside about the weather and slinging a little trash, and by the time we were walking into the place, he was getting into it over his new sound system with some bird-kneed giant baby with spiky, bleached hair who kept wagging his finger and saying, There's no way it bumps, man. No way! while his jowls swayed with his shaking head.

I'm telling you, it'll melt your face, said Court.

You need two subs at least, said the guy.

I stood next to the door, trying not to look cold.

Come on, man! said Court. I'll show you.

Fucking freezing, I said.

I should've said, Fuck that guy. Let's go in and have some shots, but I didn't. So many things I didn't say back then.

Jamo shots, man! he said. Order them up. I'll be right there, just got to show this fucking guy what a good box and an equalizer can do.

Like I said, everyone's buddy. So I was on my own.

The bar air was thick with moldy furnace heat, and all the people in the bar looked fat. Not something I would think now—or if I thought it, I'd at least think, *Damn that's kind of a fucked-up thing to think*. But back then I was still belt-fed. Fat-bodies, my drill instructors and sergeants called people like that. My head rang with their wood chipper voices: Double-time, fat-body! Your buddies are fucking dying while you drag ass at the back of my formation, fat-body!

When I was in, I never felt bad for those guys taking the heat—slobby skin pickers whose recruiters fudged a few numbers trying to get their quotas. Then boom! Some unsat, fat-body piece of shit who'd spent his entire life shoving his face full of Doritos and jerking it to anime was the guy on your right or left in the middle of the shit and he could barely pick his own fat ass out of the dirt let alone mine if I had a sucking chest wound and fifty pounds of gear draped over my shoulders.

Had every single swinging dick in that bar pegged like that: a bunch of weak civilians. Shitbirds. Sheep. Back on my first deployment, Ruiz had asked me, he'd said: You lamb chops? I didn't have an answer for him then, but the rest of that's a good story—one of those stories you can tell funny or sad, depending on who's listening to it.

★

So on my first deployment, we bought this sheep off a shepherd while we were on patrol somewhere along the Euphrates south of Fallujah, and my squad leader, Sergeant Moss, tied paracord around the thing's neck and handed the other end to me.

This is your sheep, PFC Pusey, he said—Sergeant Moss wasn't one of those guys who gave me shit or mispronounced my name. You know, never called me Pussy or whatever.

Don't let anything happen to it, he said.

Yes, Sergeant, I said.

I took it serious, you know. Once, back in the States before we'd deployed, Sergeant Moss made Ruiz carry a ten-pound rock everywhere he went for a week because he didn't show up to formation with a shave and fresh haircut on Monday morning—no shit. Guy was a hard-ass. So I figured maybe the sheep was punishment for something I'd done, and my brain flipped and twisted like a gymnast trying to figure it out. I knew better than to ask.

Let's go, sheep, I said.

When we got back to the patrol base, which was a house we'd comman-deered and reinforced with sandbags and HESCO barriers—these big-ass collapsible wire containers lined with heavy fabric engineers filled with earthmovers—Sergeant Moss said, Find a place for your sheep. Keep it out of sight. And, you fuckers, he said to the rest of the squad, not a fucking word to anyone about Pusey's sheep.

It'd come from on high that we couldn't keep local animals because they distracted the explosive-sniffing dogs, these dumb, happy-as-shit black Labradors that slept ninety-nine percent of the time. And get this, no kidding, I watched one walk right past an explosives cache without so much as pissing on it, let alone alerting anybody.

Local animals were diseased, too—fleas and mange that made their skin look like raw hamburger—and the higher-ups said the health of the entire Marine Corps was equal to the health of the individual Marine. A way to justify mass punishment: If one of y'all's fucked-up, so are the rest, they figured. So I was looking to get the sheep out of sight. Quick.

No one would've said anything. Squad was tight. No blue falcons—buddy fuckers. Corporal Israel Ruiz, Corporal Andy Nguyen, and Lance Corporal Abel Baptiste had been in for a little over two years by then, had all deployed before. They knew how the sausage got made, knew how to keep higher command's nose out of our ass and they made sure we did, too. Logan Cobb, Austin Crowe, and me—we'd all gotten to the battalion a few months before the deployment. Cobb looked good—big, strong motherfucker—but was kind of a dummy. Crowe and I argued about damn near everything. We were like a family. Most squads were like that.

Want to smoke a cigarette? said Ruiz. It'd been Ruiz who walked the three of us around the battalion to get our onboarding paperwork done, our gear issued. He didn't give a shit about customs and courtesies—like, didn't use rank with us, called me Dean. Blocked all the bullshit he could by taking the heat on his own. He was our mama bird.

Not right now, I said waving off the smoke.

Can't believe he's making you babysit a fucking goat, said Ruiz.

Sheep, I said. You want to help me build a hutch?

Ruiz took off his Kevlar helmet. I heard someone's got that JLo sex tape, he said. He undid the Velcro on his flak jacket and headed off toward the entrance to the house.

I found a spot behind the PB that was out of sight, but where the sun would hit in the morning, and built a hutch out of leftover broken HESCOs. I was pissed at first that Ruiz dipped out, and the sheep just stood there and watched me while I sweated, pathetic as hell—scrawny, wool clumped and matted with shit-stink river mud, eyes crusted, nose bubbling mucus whenever it breathed.

I kicked at it a couple times but felt bad when it kept coming back. Keep it safe, Sergeant Moss had said. The way it stood there like it was frozen calmed me down. I bent and stroked the thing's face, tried to clear the goop from its eyes. It was shivering.

The sun will warm you up in the morning, I told it.

For real, it was hard to leave. The thing needed me. Nothing much needed me then, not really. We were all young and strong—mostly too scared to ask anyone for anything, to expose ourselves like that. I stayed there after I was done. Talked to the sheep like I might've talked to a dog. Watched the sun set below the HESCO wall we'd built around the compound.

Every day I fed the sheep from whatever MRE I had—lemon poppy-seed pound cake and peanut butter and crackers. Not the best shit, but not the worst, either. During foot patrols I stuffed grass in my day pack. Fucker got fat. Eyes cleared. Nose quit bubbling mucus whenever it breathed.

Damn, man, you spend a lot of time with that sheep, said Ruiz once while I was feeding it before morning patrol. You two fuck yet or what?

Baptiste and Nguyen were with him, prepping their gear.

We found some guy cornholing a donkey on the last deployment, said Baptiste.

I don't believe that for a second, said Nguyen.

Filho da puta, I swear, said Baptiste.

You'd have to be eight feet tall to fuck a donkey, said Nguyen.

Sergeant Moss told me to keep it safe, I said. I'm not gonna mess it up.

We're supposed to be fucking warriors, dog, said Ruiz. What a bunch of baby bullshit. He kicked the hutch and left.

After a month, I thought maybe Sergeant Moss had forgotten about the sheep. Then, during a personal protective equipment check before patrol, he said, Good job with the sheep, Pusey. We'll slaughter it tomorrow.

Just like that—like he was giving me the weather. Right then I wanted to cry, you know? Or I wanted to send the buttstock of my rifle into Sergeant Moss's teeth and then run and release the sheep to freedom. Instead, I just said, Yes, Sergeant. Because what else was I supposed to do? I was a boot PFC.

Hear that, First Squad? said Sergeant Moss. Barbecue tomorrow.

The squad cheered and I hated every single one of them.

Yo, thanks, dog. Much love, said Ruiz. He patted my shoulder as we stepped off.

That night, I woke Ruiz and begged him to help set the sheep free.

He's going to kill it, I said.

No shit, he said. It's a sheep. What'd you think was gonna happen?

I didn't know what to say to that. I felt like a kid. So I just stayed crouched there next to Ruiz's cot.

Fuck, he said finally.

We slunk around the back of the main house to the hutch. Ruiz kept watch while I looped a lead around the sheep's neck. We snuck the sheep out of the compound, slipped the lead from its neck, and shooed it into the darkness.

Vaya con Dios, pinche puta, said Ruiz.

The next morning—after we made our rifles ready to condition one and passed by the windshield-sized plywood sign propped on dusty sandbags at the concertina wire gate of the PB that read, in messy black spray paint, COMPLACENCY KILLS, and stepped off on our foot patrol—we found a pack of stray dogs tearing apart the sheep.

Sergeant Moss didn't yell or anything; he dug a coffeepot-sized hunk of rock from the field where we stood and handed it to me. This is your rock, PFC Pusey, he said. Keep it safe.

Yes, Sergeant, I said.

I put the rock in my day pack and then slung the pack onto my shoulders and fell into the staggered formation as it set off in the direction where we'd last seen the shepherd.

All that shit about the sheep came flying back at me when I walked into the bar and saw those fat-ass, baaing civilians. I was jealous of them—all the couples and drunks groping each other against the pool tables and bar shelves in dark corners.

I wanted to be fat and happy just like them.

It would've made forgetting the last four years easier, which is exactly what I'd decided to do two months before when I'd flung my sweat-stiff jungle boots onto the telephone wire strung across Cristianitos Road on my way out of Camp San Mateo.

The guards yelled at me to cease and desist from their phone booth–sized post a hundred yards away. Jealous motherfuckers. I laughed, gave them the finger, but for a second, one of them looked like Ruiz and my nuts jumped up into my body; I hopped in my truck and floored it over the hills, let the brine wind blow that shadow away, told myself ghosts weren't real. I was trying to leave it behind. *Eat the apple, fuck the Corps.* Ruiz would have said some shit like that, would've hunched his shoulders and flexed his biceps like Macho Man Randy Savage, acted tough, then laughed at how dramatic and stupid it was.

I didn't want to think about Ruiz; I was pissed at Court. We were supposed to celebrate my birthday—get shitfaced, speed on backroads, maybe shoot at road signs. Not like we were going to rob a bank or any dumbass thing like that. But we had planned to cut loose a bit. I took it out on the assholes between me and the bar. Turned my body into something that could cut, forced those mouth-breathing civilians to move around me.

Some guy—big redneck-looking guy, cowboy hat and everything—didn't move, made me slide by, like, *Fuck me, right?* So I made like I lost my balance and knocked his beer out of his hands all over the group of assholes he was with and then disappeared into the crowd to the sounds of him swearing at me and telling me he was going to beat my ass. Felt pretty fucking proud of myself.

Yeah, it was an asshole move, but I'd only been out two months and I was edgy and I wanted to start some shit. Maybe wanted to feel big. That I've-got-my-finger-on-the-trigger-of-a-condition-one-rifle kind of big. Spent four years building me up like that, then just turned me loose on the world.

That's how I thought then. I was still blaming the Corps. But I missed it. The Marines was simple, like a knife is simple. People told me what to do, I did it. That's what I was waiting for: someone to tell me what to do. Point me toward the enemy. Give me some orders.

When I found a seat, I took off my coat and signaled the bartender—this thick-cut older dude, arms covered in tribal tats, a giant green rat with veiny bulging eyes inked on his flushed neck just below his jaw.

While I waited, I thought about Court and the BB and ran my fingers over the right side of my head where Doc's incision had scarred. Fat hadn't filled in the space from the BB and it left this little indentation beneath my hair, which was still scrubby.

I hated it. My hair. Felt homeless or something. I'd shaved my head with a razor during my entire enlistment because it didn't look bad and because it saved me fifteen bucks a week. You got to get a haircut every week or someone—some bullshit staff sergeant who thinks he's God's gift to the Corps—is going to give you shit. They call it good order and discipline. Health of the individual Marine. Whatever. Just a holdover from before people could shower every goddamned day and everyone had lice.

When I got home, Court told me I looked like a skinhead. Heil Pusey, he'd said to me while he did a little Hitler goose step. So I'd been letting it grow, but where Doc had cut me was a pale dime-sized patch where no hair would sprout. It looked like some barber had fucked my shit up. I rubbed the spot. Ruiz had said he would've broken a dude's jaw for some shit like that.

I couldn't stop thinking about Ruiz and the sheep, the war—kept trying to turn the page or close the book or any of that other stuff the transition assistance program manager had talked about during the weeklong required TAP class we all had to take before we landed back in the civilian world.

Bartender was taking his goddamned time and I started to get pissed, but I was trying to act like how I thought I was supposed to.

Thought about how the TAP instructor during that weeklong course had told us all to do breathing exercises when we got angry so we didn't break our wives' or girlfriends' noses or whatever.

You're going to be angry, the guy had said. You can't keep it in, but you also can't just let it out willy-nilly. It'll eat the world alive, that anger.

You don't need to go dropping the weight of it all on your spouse or significant other. They've lived through enough. And if you meet someone on the outside, they won't understand any of it. Instead, just close your eyes and breathe. Let the anger out in tiny little breaths.

He showed us. He said, Watch me. He drew his hands to his chest on the inhale and his elbows damn near rested on his gut, but when he did that I saw there was a faded-blue eagle, globe, and anchor tattoo on his forearm almost in the same spot as mine. He'd been a Marine. Desert Storm, I figured, maybe Bosnia or Mogadishu. Not old enough for Nam or Grenada or Beirut. Then he let out his breath, slapped his arms to his jeans, and smiled through his patchy beard.

Fat and fucking happy.

I waited at the bar for the bartender while my brain turned to steaming scrambled eggs and my insides turned to writhing, hot snakes like I was about to shit my pants and scream and puke, and so I closed my eyes and breathed in.

I was trying, making an effort. To do what? I don't know—just be. Be a civilian. Be me. I didn't know what that meant. I was twenty-three and the biggest thing I'd done was be a Marine. So there I was, breathing, pulling my shit together, trying to keep from going medieval on the fucking bartender, but then all these people from high school whose names I didn't remember started to recognize me and they were dapping my knuckles and clapping me on the shoulders and slurring stale beer spit in my face and saying shit like Oh, man! I thought that was you, and Welcome home, and I bet it was fucking hot over there, and I would've joined but my knees are all messed up, and Thanks for your service—no, I mean it. I really mean it, and Fuckin-A, I hope you fucked up a load of those camel jockeys let me buy you a drink.

Looking for war porn. Same as any bar the minute someone finds out you've been in the shit. Tough talk. Want to nod along and try to match the thousand-yard stare or tell you how disgusting it all is. It was all the same.

Tried getting the bartender's attention again, but the guy kept ignoring me. I tried to flash my arm—the one with the tattoo on it—sometimes it got a free drink here and there. No luck, though.

Hey! I said, loud enough for everyone around me to shut up a second.

Bartender looked up, scrunched his face, put his hand to his ear, shook his head, and then, get this: walked to the other end of the bar and started a conversation with this leather-handbag-looking tanning-bed addict with a faded tiger tattoo on her right tit peeking up through a deep V-neck.

I imagined popping up behind Tiger Tits, palming the bartender's sweaty head, and slamming his face into the epoxy-shined wood, the crunching explosion of cartilage and teeth. *Fuck it*, I thought, and I stood up to put on my coat and go find Court.

Then someone said: What are you drinking?

It was a woman. She was on the stool next to me, face all edges and angles in the overhead lighting. I didn't know her, but she seemed familiar. She had this bony nose and a cleft chin, thin lips, and her top front teeth folded inward a bit at the center seam, like a half-opened book. If I did know her, I couldn't place her, and pissed as I was at Court and the fat-body civvy shitheads and now this chucklefuck behind the bar who wouldn't do his job, I wasn't trying to get my dick wet, so I tried to blow her off.

Nothing, I said.

Come on, what do you want? she said.

You own the place? I said.

No. But Brick'll serve me before you, she said. He's a horny asshole.

She didn't wait for my order, shot her arm over the bar like she was hailing a cab, and I watched Brick the bartender paw at Tiger Tits's hands in parting. Then he backed away in a kind of cock strut while pointing and making assurances that he'd be back, until he spilled his middle-aged, raw-chicken skin over the bar in front of the woman, trilled his lips, and said, Hey beautiful. What's *your* pleasure?

It made me laugh: the old man shooting his shot with the max effective range of a dollar store water gun, and I turned away to scan the bar for Court, but the fucker had dipped. For good, maybe.

When we had our beers, I downed half mine in a gulp. Thanks, I said.

Max introduced herself. Maxine, she said. I go by Max.

From here? I said.

Michigan, she said.

I thought of Sergeant Moss—the only other person I knew from Michigan. Saginaw—he'd called it the Sag Nasty, the words coming from the back of his throat, getting caught on his tangled, lakeweed fangs: the Sag Nasty.

Everyone I know from Michigan has shit teeth, I said.

Are you saying I have shit teeth? she said.

That came out wrong, I said. I'm sorry.

She shrugged and said, I bet they're all from Saginaw.

I laughed hard at that and downed the rest of my beer.

What? she said, and took a drink.

I had a sergeant in the Marines who said the same thing, I said.

Marines, huh? she said.

I nodded and figured I had it in the bag then—I'd managed to slide the service in there, smooth like. It was usually a panty-dropper in a place like that.

You one of those guys who went overseas and came back thinking he's the one and only dick walking around?

She was serious. I cleared my throat, took a sip from the glass. She had me off-kilter.

I'm not that guy, I said. It was a lie.

Good, she said.

She smiled, took another drink, smiled, and then awkwardly covered her mouth while trying to turn her face to burp. I acted like I didn't notice.

My head swam a little from the beer I'd guzzled. The way Max held her glass, with her fingers perched on the rim reminded me of Ruiz. He drank vodka on the rocks and always brought the glass to his face like he was taking water from a ladle in, like, the nineteenth century or some shit. I pulled at the soppy corners of my napkin, and it came apart like cheap toilet paper.

Ruiz was dead, tango uniform—tits up. Worm food. He'd done it to himself. I didn't want to keep thinking on it. Was sick of him, you know? Especially when there was Max, gorgeous and funny and alive, and talking to her was the first time since being home I hadn't felt like some kind of bizarre animal on display.

I breathed through my teeth, sucked my tongue, and bitter beer spit oozed against the roof of my mouth. Max didn't know anything about me; I had this realization that I could be anyone. I didn't have to be a Marine—not in the way I had been.

Light reflected off the shelves of bottles behind the bar, and Max's fine copper hair reminded me of mushroom gills. It was the kind of thought I'd never had, or couldn't remember having; it was the kind of thought that the new, imagined me might have, and before I could stop myself, I said, Your hair is beautiful like mushrooms.

Like some fucking stroke patient.

She laughed, tilted her head back, and under the deep, fuzzy light the peaks of her face cast shadow into the draws. A hot white ball of fury collapsed in my chest and sent a shock wave of heat to my fingertips, and I thought for a moment I could kill her—her, Brick the bartender, Tiger Tits, Court, every fat-body in that goddamned bar. Lay waste to it like a five-hundred-pounder dropping hate and discontent on a tiny mud hut full of muj. On the outside, though, I was all good order and discipline aside from a couple of sweaty palms. I balled up what was left of the napkin, clenched it in my fist. I breathed. I could be anyone.

That's your line? said Max, and wiped a tear from the corner of her eye.

It was a compliment, I said.

It's a weird thing to say out of the blue: *Your hair is beautiful like mushrooms.* She imitated my voice and laughed again, hard enough to make herself snort, which turned into a hiccup-cough kind of thing that was ugly to watch.

That was a horrible impression, I said.

Better than your pickup line, she said.

You're kind of mean, I said.

What do I owe *you*? she said. You're a stranger.

Stranger danger, I said.

I felt good then, like I was back shooting the shit during a hurry-up-and-wait in the Marines, like the next thing we might do was go outside and find some rocks and try to toss them into a hole—which was the official Marine Corps pastime right alongside watching porn and bar fighting.

Max leaned toward me, hovered over her barstool, thighs flexing under her tight jeans. Let's play a game, she said.

I wondered if she was reading my mind.

What game? I said.

Truth, she said.

Fuck that, I didn't say.

No goddamned way, I didn't say.

I wouldn't know where to start, I didn't say.

What I said: How do you play?

You ask a question, she said. I tell the truth. Then you tell the truth. Then I ask a different question.

I'm going to need another drink, I said.

Max smiled, lifted her hand again, and Brick showed up with more beers. All around us people laughed and drank and ignored them all. Finally felt like maybe I was home. You know, in the big sense of the word. The where-you-belong idea of it.

How do you win? I said.

It's not that kind of game, she said. You ask first.

I'd played games you couldn't win before. Ruiz had had plenty.

What's your favorite color? I said.

Look, I was trying to say. *I'm easy, simple. What you see is what you get.* I figured she'd scoff and roll her eyes, make a show of my dumbass question. It's what I would have done. But she closed her eyes and turned up her face, jutted her chin and no-shit thought about it.

Lilac, she said after a minute.

Swear to God, it was the first time I hadn't thought anything about the war since being home. It all floated the fuck away and I felt light. Empty. I hoped Court would stay out in the parking lot for the rest of the night, slinging smoke and candy and whatever else, talking subwoofers with alcoholic boomers hiding from their families and drunk rednecks out for road sodas and tweakers looking to score.

In that moment I imagined the future, and we, Max and I, lived in one of the downtown apartments outside the bar—one of the expensive lofts built at the top of the weathered limestone office buildings and redbrick storefronts that sprouted from the empty sidewalks lined with classy, cane-shaped streetlamps to pull people back to the heart of the dying city. They were all nearly abandoned—so pricey no one could afford them. We'd build a new life together: wake up each morning smiling like idiots, drink coffee across a butcher-block table from one another, talking about our plans for the day—work or house projects, or debate what we'd have for dinner—then we'd screw each other silly in the shower. I'd kiss her goodbye and go off to a job that wasn't UPS where I wouldn't have to wear heavy work boots and stack other people's shit for eight hours at a time in a reeking semi-trailer. At night we'd stand naked under a blanket in front of our bedroom windows holding hands and looking out at the sprawling city lights and I wouldn't say a single word about how it reminded me of stars in the desert. We'd be happy.

Your turn, she said.

I tried to think of my favorite color and I ended up back on the Marine Corps bullshit. Some cadence I sang during battalion runs:

Back in seventeen seventy-five, my Marine Corps came alive. First there came the color gold, to show the world that we are bold. It was like a sickness; I couldn't stop: *Then there came the color blue, to show the world that we are true. Then there came the color red, to show the world the blood we shed. Then there came the color white, to show the world that we can fight.* None of it even made sense. *Then there came the color green, to show the world that we are mean.* The Marine Corps had real estate everywhere.

I was wearing a skivvy shirt underneath my flannel like some fresh-out-of-boot-camp shower shoe new guy, and when I looked down, there it was, showing below the hem, and I thought, *OD green. Olive drab.* And so I said, Olive.

I knew if time travel were real, in about ten seconds a future version of myself would show up and kick me right in the dick for such a stupid fucking answer. I took a drink, trying to keep from looking in her eyes, like if I didn't look at her, she wouldn't be able to tell how embarrassed I was.

They go together, she said.

What? I said.

They're contrasting colors, she said. They go together. Purple and green. Lilac and olive. It's color theory.

I wouldn't know about all that, I said.

She shrugged.

I was out of my depth, lost in the sauce. This new me didn't know a thing—I didn't even know what I didn't know. It was like how I was before I went in. Waiting for some woman to trip and just stumble on my dick or something. A sheep, goddamned lamb chops. I didn't know what was wrong with me.

All right, my turn, she said. She smiled, brought her hand to her face, and tapped her chin like she didn't already know what she was going to ask me. I could at least tell that. That she had a question on her mind.

Ask away, I said.

Do you love your mother? she said.

What a cockblock, I didn't say.

Which mother? I didn't say.

I thought we were going to keep this light? I didn't say.

What I said: Yeah, of course.

That was fast, she said. Maybe too fast.

What can I say? I said. Mama's boy.

Oh, that's a red flag for sure, she said.

Your turn, I said.

She and my dad live in Florida, she said.

That's not an answer, I said.

She took a drink and said, I mean of course I do. Love her. We don't talk much.

Back in California, I'd ditch a woman at a bar who was so up in her feelings, move on to the next one down the line. But I didn't mind with Max. I got the idea she needed someone to talk to and this new me was five-by-five with that. I thought that maybe leaving the Marines behind, forgetting Ruiz, might be as easy as just doing the opposite of everything I would've done when I was in. Take a breath instead of throw a fist. Shut my suck instead of run my mouth.

Max talked about her mom and I listened, but I was thinking about my answer. It made me restless, like she could see I'd lied—which I hadn't, not really, but I hadn't gone full Honest Abe—and that made me want to move around, fidget, crack my neck, pop off my stool and scream. But I held it in and listened and thought about my mom, how she wasn't really my mom, not in the biological sense of the word—hadn't birthed me. There was some other woman out there I didn't know, who didn't know me, who I didn't know anything about, who—like me in that moment— could've been anyone.

I'd always wondered if there was something wrong with me when I was born that made her want to give me up. My forehead started to sweat. The Marines had chased that nagging bitch of a thought out of my brain housing group when I'd joined. The Marine Corps was my family. It told me what I needed: three hots and a cot, some bad motherfuckers to my left and right. I didn't have to think about a damned thing. I was always thinking about it, though. How could I not? Every once in a while I'd get online and try to find her. But I didn't know where to fucking start. And it was my birthday, right? So of course I was thinking about it already.

Someone's popular, said Max. She pointed at my phone.

On the bar, it buzzed and lit up. Court.

Where u at fucker????

Iz ur bday bich!

Freezing my ballz off

???

Get the fuck out here

This shit broke let's head

I'll fuckin leave ur ass

Girlfriend? said Max.

He wishes, I said.

Chill. Be there in a min, I texted.

My friend's waiting, I said.

I thought this was a sure thing, she said, and laughed.

I don't have any cash on me or I'd pay you back for the beer, I said.

You can owe me, she said.

So I'll see you again, then? I said.

Are you going to ask for my number? she said.

And then I just stood there, staring at her like some night animal trapped in oncoming headlights, about to become a bloody smear on a bumfuck back road. When I didn't move or say anything, she took my phone from my hand and typed her number into my contacts.

Text me, she said, and tossed me my phone then turned back to the bar and started talking with a couple other women on her right.

It was a pretty good move. I had to piss and on the way to the head I couldn't stop smiling about it.

★

Fat and happy—it felt like it could happen, you know? Even the bleach and clogged toilet stink muscling up on the pumping heat in the shitter didn't get me down. My dick was a little hard from thinking about Max and my bladder full of beer and for a moment I forgot to breathe as the blood rushed to my head and the pressure in my belly let go—it was like a tiny high.

In the middle of all that feeling good, the door opened and I heard two guys with redneck country accents talking about spilled drinks and one said, There he is, and then my head smashed into the grimy tile wall above the urinal and my eyebrow burst like an overcooked sausage; warm piss soaked my shirt and the crotch of my pants. I put up my hands to protect my face and kept my elbows tight at my sides, curled into a ball—muscle memory. Tried to get my bearings. The floor stank and tugged at my skin while the two stomped any soft part they could find and yelled in tongues.

Comeintoourfuckingbaractingtoughspillingshitonmygirlourfuckingbarspillingshitacttoughnowmotherfuckeryoumotherfucker.

Could barely make out what they were saying.

Then one kicked me in the split of my ass so hard it made me spit up the beer left in my gut and I choked, waved my hands in front of my face, thought I might die, and then the other one caught me square in the left ribs with a steel toe and I yelped like a pig, cleared my throat, and maybe scared them into stopping and they were gone.

I WOKE UP on a futon mattress in my old bedroom. My mom had turned it into what she called her sewing room after I'd gone off to boot camp. To this day I've never seen her sew a thing. Whatever. She wasn't a bad mom or anything—had her own shit to worry about when I was growing up. Wasn't around much. It's not like she'd planned on all that. Lots of vets like to say civilians won't understand war if they've never been. But I don't buy it. War's the easiest thing to understand. Like, even my mom figured out that no plan survives contact.

Mom and my stepdad, Rick, hadn't left for work. I could hear their kitchen sounds: pan clang, coffeepot sputter, microwave beep.

He's asleep, Gale, came Rick's voice muffled through the bedroom door, and I knew she was standing on the other side, listening to see if I was up.

She had more time to worry now that she'd married Rick and quit her other two part-time jobs she'd had at Pizza Hut and Kroger—went all in on the family doctor's office after her coworker retired and a full-time slot opened up. She made appointments and kept patient files in order. Mom was organized like that.

She married Rick while I was on my second deployment—she hadn't told me or my older sister, Penny. That's what I mean about her having her own shit. Why would you need to know something like that? she'd asked when Penny threw a fit. You're both grown.

Penny was at Purdue, working through her PhD in English, and when she talked about it, it felt like I didn't know the fucking language at all. She had an entire life I'd only seen through Instagram: her dog in a heap on the couch, POV shots of her cat bedded down on stacks of student essays, baking attempts, farmer's market vegetables, graffiti she'd spotted while running around West Lafayette, a protest, a person at a podium reading a book, a concert, pint glasses of beer caught mid-cheers, the sky framed by an airplane window, stacks of books, a hike somewhere in southern Indiana, duck-faced selfies with friends.

We'd been close growing up—had to be, because our parents' relationship was a mess. Like, she'd made me breakfast in the mornings after our parents split back when I was five and she was ten. Our dad disappeared back to the Northwest, where we were from, and Mom had to work more and took early shifts, so Penny was in charge. Later she let me hang out in her room while she studied and listened to music and, like, this one time, when I was maybe eleven and she was sixteen, our mom went out of town somewhere and Penny threw a party and let me hang out with her friends and drink a beer. I loved Penny, though I hadn't seen her since I'd been home. She'd be in town for Christmas. It'd be our first holiday with Rick.

Mom had met Rick at church—the same barren, broken-down, redbrick-and-painted-white-wood Methodist building we'd all gone to before I turned eight and Penny turned thirteen and Mom gave up trying to get us through the door. She acted disappointed but she must have been relieved to get some space from us.

I didn't want to like Rick—he wore his graying hair in a ponytail and owned a hardware store and Mom called him godly. He joked and laughed a lot—something my dad had never done—and he listened to talk radio instead of music. That show with the two brothers who work callers through car troubles. He called himself a pacifist, hated guns. Didn't have a problem telling me he'd dodged the draft for Nam, said shit like War destroys the soul. I didn't think civilians knew shit back then, so I kept thinking: *How the fuck would he know?* The thing about all that was, it made me kind of like him; he had a code—didn't bend easy. I respected that.

My first week back home he had asked me to come to church. I said no and then every week for the next two months he asked. He talked to me about pitching in rent, about a man's purpose, about getting my own place. I tried catching Mom's eye when he said shit like that, pass her telepathic messages like *Not very godly of him* and things like that, but she played deaf and dumb and blind.

I didn't want a goddamned thing to do with church.

The Marines were all God and country on the outside because it was good for PR but on the inside it was all rape, pillage, and burn. The draft had been gone a long time and we were all there by choice—officers wanted to build clout to get into politics; enlisted dirtbags told everyone they wanted money for school but mostly just wanted to get paid to do some goddamned violence.

When the chaplain stood at the front of our battalion for memorials and whatnot and said, Let us pray, we all bowed our heads, went through the motions. But if we saw Chaps walking around, trying to talk to other Marines about God or whatever, we about-the-fuck-faced and headed the opposite direction. Dude was too nice—hands on your shoulders, nodding at every word you said, smile on his face, close-talking like he wanted to tongue-fuck your ear canal—he had to be a creep. We joked about what a pedo he must've been. Avoided him like the clap.

As far as I was concerned, they were all the same—religions, I mean: a bunch of turn-the-other-cheek bullshit. Spoken like someone who's never been fucking slapped.

As for getting my own place, I was working on it. Had some deployment money left, but not much. Made something like fifteen grand on each deployment, which seemed like a lot when there wasn't anyplace to spend it except the post exchange and the Iraqi shops that sold cheap tchotchke bullshit and pirated DVDs on the bigger bases like TQ and the MEK. I blew most of it at bars and titty clubs when we got home.

Two weeks after I got out, I landed a job loading semi-trailers at UPS during the twilight sort from four in the afternoon to ten at night. It was a bunch of young guys fresh out of high school in cutoff shirts and cargo shorts and work boots slinging cardboard from semi-trailers onto conveyor belts that led to other semi-trailers. It was loud and hot and everyone talked shit to everyone else. Reminded me of the Marines. Guys I worked with in my loading area, the Chicago Area Consolidation Hub—CACH— called me Old Man, even my supervisor. And I liked that. It made me feel like I'd been somewhere, seen something—like I was King Shit.

I'd slept in my clothes from the bar, smelled like insides and Simple Green, which made me think of boot camp. The thick, meaty knot on my forehead pulsed, seeped plasma onto my eyebrow, and I winced, trying to blink away sleep. Wished I had some of that Motrin eight hundred Doc gave out if we were really feeling it. You had to be damn near falling apart to get love from Doc or any other corpsman. If we came to him feeling lousy or whatever, he'd tell us to drink water and change our socks.

That was some on-high shit. Command wanted us strung out on hate and discontent.

Anyway, my eye wasn't worse than when I'd take an elbow rolling in the pit after PT. I was a bleeder. Ruiz always said that. Dog, you a bleeder, he'd say, and shrug his bowling ball shoulders. Like, nobody's perfect or something.

So I wasn't pissed at the guys in the bar shitter. Not really. Like Rick, they had a code. I would have done the same. *Respect* was the word that came to mind—sheepdogs among the sheep. When I thought of that, I thought of Ruiz asking, You lamb chops? Complacent. I'd been compla- cent. Complacency kills. I should've known better—going to war without a battle buddy.

Back with the sheep, I'd done pretty much the same thing.

After the dogs ate the sheep and after our patrol, in the atrium of the PB, I ditched that heavy-ass pack and sucker-punched Sergeant Moss while he was dropping his gear. Sergeant Moss took me down, mounted me from behind, wrapped his legs around my trunk, sank his heels into the gutters of my crotch, wrapped oak arms around my neck. My adrenaline was all I had left after hauling the rock on patrol and it burned through me quick. I flopped to my side, tried to tuck my chin into the crook of Sergeant Moss's elbow.

Tap, he said.

But I didn't tap. And Sergeant Moss flexed steady pressure against my carotid until I blacked out to yells and laughter from the rest of the squad and platoon who'd gathered to watch the show.

By the time Doc coaxed me back to the land of the living, everyone had cleared out except Ruiz.

Man, that was some funny shit, he said.

I coughed, felt like I had fish bones stuck in my throat.

Doc touched my neck. Tell me if you feel pain where I press, he said.

I shook my head, hawked thick, clingy spit between my knees, sucked breath through my nose.

They gonna NJP that ass, said Ruiz.

Tap next time, said Doc, and left, dapping knuckles with Ruiz on the way out.

Old boy fucked you up, dog, said Ruiz. What was that about?

I don't know, I said. I sat for a minute. The sheep, I guess.

You two really was fucking, he said.

It made me laugh. Then I got worried about the non-judicial punishment. Think they'll NJP me for real? I said.

Ruiz sucked his teeth, rubbed the patchy stubble on his chin. Who gives a fuck? he said. Ain't a real grunt without one.

Ruiz was on his second pump. Dude was a real grunt. John Wayne shit. Clint Eastwood shit. Locked, cocked, ready to rock. Knew his goddamned job. Had an NJP from his first deployment for disobeying a direct order. Corporal Nguyen knew the story but wouldn't tell it. We heard rumors about firefights and grenades—real hero shit. No one could get the straight dope from Ruiz.

We were quiet for a minute, tossed pebbles at a crack in the wall. Ruiz lit a cigarette. Chatter and laughter rose and fell throughout the PB. I heard Crowe talking shit to someone—probably Cobb, who was too stupid to do anything but smile. I laid back down on the frigid concrete, closed my eyes. It was December. I'd been deployed for three months. There were still five months to go. Sergeant Moss could make my life hell for five months.

Fuck, I said.

Problem ain't that you did it, said Ruiz. It's how you did it. Try to floor a dude without a plan and when he ain't looking? Bitch move. Got what you deserved.

Shouldn't have done it, I said.

Listen, he said. That sheep got fucked up by them dogs because it was a fucking sheep. That's what sheep are for. Lamb chops. You lamb chops?

Looks like it, I said.

Fuck, man, he said. Pussy shit. We fucking Marines. Motherfucking sheepdogs. Like, you got bulk, you just don't know how to use it for shit.

Way to kick me when I'm down, I said.

Ain't like that, he said. It's good. I mean, I could show you if you want.

I didn't want to be a goddamned sheep. Didn't want to end up with my guts torn out by wild dogs, bleeding into the fucking dirt. I didn't want to be a dog, either—sheepdog or otherwise, it didn't seem much better than a sheep—and maybe I was a sheep and there wasn't a damned thing I could do about it. In that moment, though, with Ruiz, in the atrium of the Iraqi mansion turned PB, another five months of deployment in front of us, I figured, what the hell?

In my room, I stood from the bed and the sharp pain turned to that deep, dull throb like when you rip out the root of an ingrown toenail. Entire body freezes for a minute at the peak of that tiny pain—you don't breathe, heart even seems to stop—and then as soon as the deed's done there's a rush for everything to catch up; you can feel your blood pumping in rhythm from all over your body to that one place.

I loved that feeling.

It's why I liked fighting—rolling with other Marines in sandpits, blood choking and air choking and cross-facing.

In that moment, it was like I wasn't there, like I didn't exist and never had. Or maybe I was somewhere in between traveling through time, like time sped up. Time traveler. I could only think about the next punch or the next kick or the next target.

I couldn't explain that to my mom or Rick. Couldn't see a way forward then. Couldn't imagine what might happen if I walked out there and said,

Hey, Mom, do you know how good bone-on-bone contact feels? Hey, Mom, do you know what it's like to see someone else's blood on your shirt? What would she do? Smile? Tell me to be careful, like she had when she watched me get in the duty van that took me down to Indianapolis early one morning to catch a plane to California? Nah, she and Rick would call the white coats to come collect me. Or maybe she would just kick me out. All I could think then was that they'd leave me. Cut and run. Maybe because that's what I would've done.

This new Mom, the one with the free time and all the worry and an ear against my door, who was maybe trying to make up for not being around enough when I was growing up? Maybe she would be calm and say, I might not have given birth to you, but I am your mother. Double down on how much she had hoped for another baby and couldn't have one no matter how long she and my dad had tried and blah blah blah.

I wasn't trying to hear anything like that.

Mom never talked about my adoption aside from telling me how much she wanted to have another kid and couldn't, never anything real, never anything about my birth mom, so I'd quit asking a long time ago. It was never a dirty secret or anything. Can't remember not knowing I was adopted, but, damn, when I was little, if I was curious and I'd ask a question, no matter what it was—Mom, what do you think my birth mom is like? Mom, why did you want to adopt me? Mom, why do you think my birth mom didn't want me?—she said the same thing: I might not have given birth to you, but I am your mother. Then I'd wander away and forget about it like anyone forgets about anything. Until I remembered and the whole cycle started again.

Like, once, in second grade we had show-and-tell, and I was a weird kid—like all kids are weird—so I decided to bring *myself* in. I got up in front of the class, right after some kid who'd brought in a guinea pig—I remember the thing wouldn't stop making that noise they make, the one that sounds like a cheek pop—and the next kid up had a wooden bow and arrow he'd got from the Johnny Appleseed Festival over the summer.

I stood there with my hands behind my back like some Poindexter professor, and when the teacher asked what I'd brought to share, I said,

Myself. I am adopted. That means I have another mom and another dad, but I've never met them.

It got quiet and kids were picking noses and whispering and then my teacher said, Dean, if you forgot it was your day for show-and-tell, it's not okay to lie.

Believe that?

Okay, I said, and sat down and listened to the last kid talk about his chintzy, fake bow and arrow.

Then at recess some other kid, maybe the one with the guinea pig, I don't remember, said my mom was probably a prostitute. I didn't know what the word meant so I ran away and started crying and I cried for so long and hard that it freaked out the teacher, who seemed young even to me, and she called my mom to come and get me.

What happened? My mom said.

He lied to the class and told them he was adopted, and another boy made fun of him, said the teacher.

Uh-huh, said my mom.

That's it. Fucking *uh-huh.*

Then in the car she said that shit she always did: I might not have given birth to you, but I am your mother.

Part of me started to think the whole thing was a running family joke—no one talked about it because it wasn't true and they were just waiting for me to get the punch line. Another part of me started to feel guilty for wondering where I belonged when my mom thought I only belonged one place. That got to me, so I stopped asking. Like I said, though, I never quit thinking about it for very long.

Eventually, I figured she must've been scared. Like, maybe if she talked about it, I'd get the itch to go find my real mom and she'd end up nothing but a placeholder while I fucked off into outer space or wherever my birth mom was.

Maybe I would have.

But then I found the Marines and that itchy feeling of not belonging took a shit because *that's* where I belonged. Everyone in boot camp was at square one: according to every single drill instructor, each recruit should have been an abortion; according to every sergeant in the fleet, each new join was nothing but meat for the grinder. Should have never been born. Waiting to die. Some more moto, death dealer, hard-ass nonsense Ruiz would've laughed at.

I put my head against the door to try and hear whether my mom and Rick had left. My gut didn't feel right. I thought probably the guy with the steel toes had cracked a rib. I had to shit and I wasn't looking forward to it.

Sunlight shone through the chest-high windows—same ones I'd snuck out of to smoke weed with Court and finger girls at parties after Penny went off to college. I probably hadn't even needed to sneak out after she left. Like I said, Mom had her own shit, right? I get it now. Couldn't see it then because I was wrapped up in my own. Selfish, maybe. Definitely.

I hated it then—where I was, who I'd been, what I was, keeping it all to myself, letting it out in tiny little breaths. I thought for a minute I'd go out and tell them that. I'd tell them who I was—even if I didn't really know. I'd tell them I didn't have a fucking clue about anything. That I'd needed to get out of that room, that town, away from myself. I'd tell them about war and I'd tell them about slugging Sergeant Moss and every fucking terrible moment from both deployments and the bar fights I couldn't remember and how funny it was to watch a person turn into a loose sack of skin when you connected fist to jaw just right. I'd tell them that once, in San Clemente, during a bar fight Nguyen had teed up this civilian's face like a fucking football and I kicked the guy so hard that when I saw him again in town, his jaw was wired shut. I'd tell them how I wasn't drunk for that one.

Cried then, and the tears mixed with the gooey plasma from the cut above my eye and I couldn't even really wipe it away because it hurt too much to touch. I didn't open the door. Stood frozen. Felt like I was getting sucked into some kind of emptiness.

Forced myself to move, kept myself going, pushed through, improvised, adapted, overcame. Laid back down on the mattress, breathed in and out, got my phone and texted Court.

Yo. WTF?

Court didn't ask me shit about the Marines. When I was with him it didn't matter who I'd been or what I could be. I just fucking was. Like, Court didn't care about all that, but I wanted him to ask about it all. I wished he had been there.

While I waited for him to reply I found Max's contact info and opened Insta. My feed was a mess of landscape sunsets and saturated filters and perfectly angled selfies and toddlers posing with newborn babies from my high school friends who had gotten pregnant right after graduation and were on their second or third kid and witty motivational quotes about finding your worth and ads for protein supplements and workout gear and my still-enlisted Marine friends' photos from their last deployments—Thailand and what was maybe Afghanistan but definitely couldn't have been Iraq—and my veteran friends' photos of their framed DD-two-fourteen paperwork and PR weight-lifting videos and everyday carry images of the knives and knuckle-dusters and fancy tactical flashlights and pistols they fit into their pockets and photos of guns and videos of shooting ranges and their newly grown beards and the beard oil they used and their veteran-owned mustache comb company and images of new tattoos and on and on and on.

I hadn't posted a photo since before I got out. My profile pic was a four-year-old, grainy, disposable-camera scanned photo of me at eighteen in a desert, twenty pounds lighter, sunburnt, dressed in an untucked skivvy shirt and desert digital pattern cammie trousers. There was a rifle slung around my body, a cigarette in my smiling mouth, and I was throwing the camera the bird while the sun went down behind some date palms. Most of the pictures on my profile looked like that: me in a desert with a gun.

I was scared if I replaced those pictures, pushed the grid down and out, because the Marines was all I'd ever done, that I might disappear, too. Couldn't have formed the thought in that moment back then, but it was like I was a skipping record or something, hitting the same notes over and over, not sure where I'd end up if I moved the needle.

Max's profile was public, so I scrolled through the images: a basket of neon lemons at the grocery store, a dock at a lake being taken apart, a perspective shot of her tanned legs on a beach captioned *Hotdogs or legs???*, a series of photos of breakfast food, she and her friends—one I thought I recognized from the bar—drinking from a single milkshake with three separate straws, sparklers on the Fourth of July, book covers, morning cups of coffee, a burned dinner attempt, a bachelorette party, her twenty-first birthday, bar graffiti, her posing in the empty living room of an apartment.

I could've scrolled for hours. There were hundreds—little frames of Max in rank-and-file formation. A life—all these contrasting pieces shoved into a space to make them fit together.

I tried to imagine my life like that, but whenever I brought the pieces together, instead of sticking, they smashed into one another and broke apart like waves on sand and then I was choking on the piss and bleach soaked into my clothes and the smell started to shift to something like the plastic and ammonia shit-stink of burning trash and gas-bloated WAG bags and tires and kerosene and hot dirt, and when I opened my eyes, all I could see was thick snot like spiderwebs coated in morning dew covering the upper-lip peach fuzz of this Iraqi teenager we'd detained after we found him in the vicinity of an IED blast.

The kid was naked and bent over, spreading his ass cheeks so Doc could perform an intake evaluation of his physical health. It reminded me of the military entrance and processing station in Indianapolis where you go to sign on the dotted line and for a moment it was like I knew the kid, like we might've gotten along fine playing *Halo* and talking about *Maxim*'s Woman of the Month while eating pizza rolls and drinking Mountain Dew in some air-conditioned basement in the middle of a soupy Indiana summer.

Qum, Doc, said to the kid and the kid straightened his body so I could see a funnel chest so deep the kid's heart must've been a goddamned donut curved around his sternum.

Meestah, said the kid.

All the kids called us mister like that.

Meestah, me zien. Amreeka zien. Ali Baba mu zien.

Yeah, yeah, motherfucker, said Ruiz. If America's so fucking good, why'd you try to blow us the fuck up? Ruiz stood perpendicular to the kid, rifle at the low ready, itching to waste him, flicking the fire selector back and forth from safe to fire—*click, click, click, click*—and the noise made the kid cry and stare at the dust-covered freezing floor repeating over and over: Amreeka zien, Meestah. Meestah, me zien.

★

It was a tiny moment, but it looped in my head, made my legs restless, my face hot, and I turned to the wall of my bedroom and closed my eyes, went internal, shut down, heard the creaking floor outside my door under my mom's light feet, and my brain got loud with it all: *Qum. Click, click, click, click. Knock, knock, knock, knock.* Dean? *Your hair is beautiful. You lamb chops? Our bar. Meestah, me zien.* Dean? *Your friends are fucking dying, fat-body! Move your ass! Double-time!* Dean? *Act tough, motherfucker. Lilac. Meestah. Iz ur bday bich!*

And then my mom's hand was on my forearm, her palm papery and cool, and she rubbed my shoulder, and I wanted to turn and hug her but pretended to be asleep.

Dean? she said.

Rick's voice came from the hallway, telling her to let me sleep, and the evil in my guts churned and burbled and I thought I might shit my pants.

We're heading to work, she said. Breakfast is in the microwave. Dean?

Gale? said Rick. Let's go, hon.

She hesitated, and I hoped she couldn't see my tenderized face.

After they'd gone and I heard the door latch snap into the strike plate, I checked my phone.

Bro, you got fucked UP by them dudes, Court texted.

No shit, I texted.

We'll get em, he texted.

Fuck it, I texted.

Party tonite, he texted.

Yeah, I texted.

I undressed, stood naked in front of the mirror, inventoried the damage. The bruise on my ribs was the size of a softball, pus-colored at the center, spiraling out to firework blasts of purple and blue. I held my arms above my head. No reason for the hospital. What a waste of time anyway. Wouldn't let myself be some weak malingerer. I did a squat and the pain in my ass didn't change much, so I figured it was probably just bruised, but the squat got things moving and I had to sprint to the toilet. Barely made it. Beer and adrenaline and stomach acid came fiery and searing from me and I sweated and cursed and felt dizzy from my own stench, which usually I didn't mind so much.

Afterward, I chugged water and pulled on PT gear and ran speed intervals around the neighborhood for close to an hour until bile burned the back of my throat and then I did bodyweight circuits. The swelling in my head went down and my ass and ribs held a steady beat that kept in time with my resting heart rate. I ate soggy toast and cold, runny eggs from the microwave and showered away the waxy rind of bar and blood and beer I'd simmered in. I felt better.

None of it seemed wrong then—the bar fight, avoiding my mom, keeping the Marines to myself. Part of me wishes I could go back in time, shake myself. If I did though, my past self would beat me fucking senseless.

There were a few hours before I had to be at work, so I pulled on some skivvies and went to the closet where I kept the Colt AR-fifteen carbine I'd bought the week I got home.

The rifle calmed me down. Like, if driving a forearm into some drunk's face in a bar made me a time traveler, holding the gun put me everywhere all at once. A god. Ruiz would've called that blasphemy, then made fun of me for being all Sparta, warrior, ooh-rah bullshit about it.

The next closest thing to that feeling was maybe busting a sweaty, well-earned nut.

I kept the rifle locked in a thick plastic case. Mom and Rick didn't know about it. They'd have flipped—just like Rick, Mom hated guns, didn't even like seeing pictures of me holding them. Rick had told me more than a few times that the very idea of a gun scared him. Mostly after some mass shooting. Tears in his eyes whenever he said it. Always felt embarrassed for him.

Anyway, the AR was more like the M-four I'd used in Iraq than the M-sixteen I qualled with on the range, but that was okay.

I hadn't shot a real gun until I got to the Marines. Paintball guns and BB guns, but never a real one. Court hunted with his dad every year, but they never invited me, and, really, I was glad. I didn't want to shoot a deer.

★

The primary marksmanship instructors got us pumped to shoot. They taught us everything there was to know about the M-sixteen-A-two lightweight, magazine-fed, gas-operated, air-cooled, shoulder-fired weapon system.

We learned weapons safety rules: Treat every weapon as if it were loaded, never point a weapon at anything you do not intend to shoot, keep your finger straight and off the trigger until you're ready to fire, keep your weapon on safe until you intend to fire, know your target and what lies beyond.

We learned to fire at three distances—two hundred, three hundred, and five hundred yards—using three types of targets: Able, B-Modified, and Dog—which didn't look like dogs but the head and shoulders silhouette of a man—from four different firing positions: prone, sitting, kneeling, and standing.

They did it all in three weeks. Talked at us, drilled knowledge into our brains while we sat, left hands on our left knees and right hands on our right knees on ass-numbing aluminum bleachers they called the School House in the Southern California early summer, ocean salt and baking earth stuck in our noses. I remember feeling motherfucking elec-trified. What we'd all joined up for, you know?

At the end of each day, we performed weapons maintenance and relayed all the statistics we'd learned at the School House.

Platoon, length of an M-sixteen-A-two service rifle, the platoon guide would call out—the guide was a recruit who wasn't a complete idiot that the DIs could trust and picked to be in charge of the platoon and act as a go-between for us and them.

Length of an M-sixteen-A-two service rifle, thirty-nine point six two five inches, Guide, the platoon would answer.

Platoon, weight of an M-sixteen-A-two service rifle when fully loaded.

Weight of an M-sixteen-A-two service rifle when fully loaded, seven point seven six pounds, Guide.

Platoon, maximum range of an M-sixteen-A-two service rifle.

Maximum range of an M-sixteen-A-two service rifle, two thousand six hundred fifty-three meters, Guide.

Platoon, maximum effective range of the M-sixteen-A-two service rifle.

Maximum effective range of the M-sixteen-A-two service rifle, four hundred sixty meters, Guide.

On and on and on.

We called it all in perfect unison; chanted like monks. I dreamed those numbers.

I didn't love my rifle or want to screw it or anything. That kind of whack job shit you see in movies. Psycho baby killers getting the thousand-yard stare while they lube their rifle or whatever. Some guys—gash hounds and lifers—named them after women: Darla and Mary Sue and Francine and Vera. Always old-timey names like that. Never learned that *This is my rifle* thing—our DIs and PMIs called it a *Full Metal Jacket* bullshit waste of time. They didn't care about that. They cared about shooting.

After the School House we circled around fifty-gallon oil barrels painted with Able, B-Modified, and Dog targets like they might look from the two-hundred-, three-hundred-, and five-hundred-yard firing lines and practiced muscle memory with the different firing positions—got comfortable being uncomfortable in the itchy, dying straw grass and sand.

The primary marksmanship instructors weren't DIs. DIs weren't allowed in the practice pits or the bleachers and kept their distance at the range until shooting was over. It was the one place they didn't want to stress us out. The only other place they weren't allowed was church services on Sundays because, Jesus Christ, what kind of PR would it be for a DI to tell a recruit to pick up their doggone Bible with their dick skinners and open their cock holsters loud and proud and sing "Amazing Grace"? But I never went to church anyway—stayed back at the barracks and cleaned and wrote letters to Penny.

Anyway, our PMI was a linebacker-thick sergeant; when he held a rifle, it looked like it'd sprouted from his arm. He walked the circle we made with our bodies and moved us into different positions.

Try this, Marine, he said.

He stooped next to me and moved my body like one of those tiny wood artist's mannequins. Then he put a hand on my lower back and told me to sight in on the Dog target painted on the practice barrel.

How does that feel? he said.

Good, sir, I said.

Before our final qual he gathered our platoon and critiqued the work of mass shooters.

Y'all, knowing what y'all know now, could kill more, he said. It's all about the basic tenets of marksmanship: high, firm pistol grip; shoulder pocket; chipmunk cheek; sight alignment; sight picture; breathe, breathe, breathe; squeeze, squeeze, squeeze. Remember: let the shot surprise you.

After I cleaned the Colt, I dug in the closet, threw on my salt-faded fatigues and combat boots—DIs called them moon boots, maybe because they were supposed to be for the desert. All that dirt and hardpan in the suck ended up compacted by Humvees and tanks and AAVs and MRAPs and all kinds of other vehicles that it turned into fine powder—moon dust. To this day, whenever I get those rose-colored glasses about my time in or if I start to feel too much like a civilian, I go rummaging through the hard black plastic footlocker where I keep all my old gear, and I still find that moon dust in little drift piles in the corners.

Anyway, I always wore my jungle boots in country because they had side vents that kept me from standing in an inch of foot sweat. Part of me wished I hadn't tossed the jungles on the wire over Cristianitos Road. I loved those fucking boots, but they were coming apart at the seams.

I slung my rifle and moved through the house like I was in a raid.

Clearing a house is like solving a puzzle: How do you move through a place you've never been as fast as possible, as efficiently as possible, exposing the least amount of your body as possible?

We moved through houses like water. The thing I liked about clearing was that no one was in charge—or who was in charge changed based on who made the call first and loudest. Rank went out the window. You might be an LT or a gunny, but if you shit the bed during a raid, you were no one.

Mom's house was an L-shaped, three-bedroom, two-bath ranch—I pied windows and buttonhooked into rooms and checked my overhead. I made myself a small target behind the Colt and moved my body heel, toe, heel, toe, heel, toe—what Sergeant Moss called the combat glide. Like the "Cupid Shuffle" or something.

We practiced for hours, first on the flat, sunbaked parade deck and then for even more hours in the uneven scrub on the undeveloped land we called the Backyard just beyond. Sergeant Moss put quarters on our front sight posts, and when the quarters dropped, so did we. Follow it! he'd shout and we'd do push-ups with our rifles laying across the tops of our hands to keep them off the concrete or out of the dust while Sergeant Moss berated us about our dedication to the Corps, our loyalty to the platoon.

It's not that you're going to get yourselves killed, Sergeant Moss said. It's that you're going to get *me* killed. So fuck you for getting me killed. Fucking push, boot bitches.

While I moved through the house, I thought of Sergeant Moss, what he'd taught me: Surprise, violence of action, speed. I thought of Corporal Nguyen: Slow is smooth; smooth is fast. I thought of Lance Corporal Baptiste calling targets in Portuguese. I called out my movements to my imaginary fire team, to Ruiz.

Open door left! I said.

Closed door right! I said.

Moving! I said.

I combat glided down the center of the hallway, a step away from the encroaching walls. People think the wall is safe if they're in a gunfight. Bunch of slinky spy motherfuckers riding their shoulders along the walls, guns pointed to the ceiling. Bullshit. Ricocheting projectiles from targets blind-firing out of a doorway down a hallway hug walls. New guys always make that mistake. The wall seems safe, they want to feel something sturdy, so they flatten themselves against it, but then here comes a bullet ricochet-skipping across a wall like a stone on a lake and boom: they're dead because they needed a crutch like a blanket or a thumb like some whiny baby.

Dead fucking baby.

It was a good time, clearing the house; I changed scenarios, closed doors, moved furniture—the possibilities were endless. And it felt like I was doing something. Preparing myself. Staying sharp. Really, that's bullshit. I know now I was trying to feel big. Important. Powerful.

Trouble started when I went outside. Some neighbor called the cops. I didn't know he called the cops. I waved at the guy—old man across the street sprinkling salt on his sidewalk—and he didn't wave back, which in Indiana is basically a giant fuck you, and then I watched him shuffle away. Figured he needed to take his Metamucil or change his Depends. But the guy must've called the cops.

Like I said, I didn't know that. I put it together afterward.

So I set an imaginary outer cordon because you can't clear a building if you don't have a defense and a way to catch squirters—loose shits trying to make a break for it—then I stacked on the house and simulated breaching from the outside.

Like, it was my house. Not *my* house. My mom's house, right? But I'd grown up there. Anyway, I was moving through the house and running scenarios and taking imaginary contact and fucking shit up, wild and high, replaying the beating I'd taken at the bar, imagining the hate and discontent Ruiz and I would've rained down on those two rednecks when there was this knock at the door.

Not just a knock, but like a *knock* you know. Like, *BAMBAMBAM*. Like I owed a motherfucker money. That kind of knock. So I answered it.

Two cops.

I stepped out the door and had time to say, What the fuck?

Gun! said Officer One and grabbed my wrist, yanked me off balance. I bit it off the stoop, twisted an ankle down the stairs, fell onto the walkway mouth first—chunks of tooth gritted against my gums and ragged teeth cut my tongue. I lost air.

Officer two, perpendicular to me, gun drawn, flicked her safety off—*click*—I heard it plain as day and I was the Iraqi kid, naked and snotty and crying. She checked in with the cop whose knee was buried in my spine and then stepped into the house, announcing her presence, called for anyone else to show themselves. I knew the exact route she'd take through the rooms.

When they realized their mistake, before they told me to keep my gun inside and then fucked off back to the donut shop, the dude with his knee in my back kept asking, What the fuck, kid? You want to fucking die or what? You want to fucking die?

Fucking cops. Think they'd never seen a gun before.

BIG FUCKING CHIP on my shoulder back then. Me against the whole world. That was life, right? Survival of the fittest. Shit like those fucking idiot cops kept proving to me that it was pointless to ask anyone for help. People were more likely to stick a knee in your back and keep you on the ground than anything else. Maybe why I liked working at UPS so much. One place where I kind of had to rely on people and they had to rely on me. And the work was simple, physical, repetitive. Semi-trailers smelled like burnt-onion body odor and the floors spat box dust and it was always hot like the trailer was alive, like I was standing in the guts of some gigantic animal. Everything moved fast—conveyors, rollers, boxes, me, time.

Loading a trailer is like laying bricks: got to be methodical, rely on your load partner to pick up the slack, build their half of each wall so it meets your half in the middle and then goes up layer by layer evenly, so it's sturdy.

My new load partner was a peak-season temp—Christmas traffic had picked up since it was November; there was barely time to rebuild a wall, make it sturdy, sound, let alone get to know someone. The entire game at that point was shoving as many boxes as possible into a trailer as fast as you could to keep the rollers from backing up onto the main conveyor.

Supposed to be able to rely on your partner. When I'd first started working back in September, my load partner had been shit-hot. Like we shared a brain. Then he got transferred to another area and I got stuck with my new partner.

I called my new load partner Turtle. He was slower than old people fucking. And just a temp—seemed pointless to learn his real name. He was the kind of guy someone like Crowe would've just let loose on, ridden until the dude broke and not bothered to put him back together. Good riddance.

Never tried to break the guy. Maybe I shouldered him out of the way in the trailer when I was rushing or tipped his wall when it was shoddy; I just wanted him to go faster. Work better. Pull his weight. Figured: pain retains.

Let's go, pick up the fucking pace, Turtle, I'd say. Guy didn't move well. Shrugged and slumped his shoulders, paused to clean his Coke-bottle glasses—DIs called them birth control goggles.

Worst was, he took time to pick and choose which box he wanted, never took the next in line.

I clocked in and headed to the trailer I loaded that went to CACH. One or two of the belts in other parts of the warehouse were already running.

Sometimes if the load was heavy you had to come in early, which wasn't so bad. Overtime was time-and-a-half. They started us out at ten bucks an hour and upped it by a buck after ninety days.

I was a month away from eleven an hour. After a year I'd get another fifty-cent raise along with bennies and union membership. Monthly, it was half what I'd made in the Marines by the time I'd gotten out, but, anyway, Indiana was cheaper than Cali and better than a PB in the middle of Nowhere, Iraq.

Thuds echoed off the polished concrete and sheet metal from each box tossed onto the aluminum rollers that sang as they carried the cardboard to the conveyors. I could tell by the noise it was all something heavy. Ingram books, maybe. None of the sorters were on the line yet—probably smoking meth out of a lightbulb in the parking lot—just a supervisor with a jam pole pushing cardboard down the conveyor toward a barrier that drove all the packages from one trailer into another—a truck-to-truck transfer.

When I made it to CACH, I found my scanner and signed in and gathered with the other five guys who worked in my area for the pre-shift meeting with our supervisor, Tyler. He was short, spiked his black hair shiny with gel, and wore too-tight polo shirts that made him look younger than he was. Up close, deep lines in his heavy brow and nicotine teeth gave him away.

I grabbed a wrist scanner and signed in with my employee barcode at the supe station near all the overweight freight that sat below the catwalk, right in the middle of the eight trailer bays.

Tyler gave his pre-sort speech: Big one tonight. Eight trucks. Remember: safety is priority number one. No standing on the rollers. I don't want to see any Nancy Kerrigan bullshit—especially in the drop trailers. Rollers are for packages. Step stools need to be in the trailers, and you need to use them. Bob's going to do random inspections all through peak because the temps are going through training. Don't get my ass chewed. I know you hate the stools. I know they take up room in the trailer. Jesus, they take two seconds at most to use. Just do it, all right? Team lift the overweight freight. Don't be a tough guy. And save it for the end. Let me catch one of you out here trying to grab overweight while the belt's backed up. Check your zip codes. Work together. Help each other out. I don't want any misloads. Find a misload? Set it outside the trailer mouth and I'll take care of it. The only way we get out of here is when everything is unloaded and reloaded. Don't ask me if you can go home early. We're all in the same boat here. This is peak.

Spiel was pretty much the same every night. Harped on teamwork, the buddy system. Made me think of our company gunnery sergeant, Gunny Bat—his real name was Batungbakal, but no one could pronounce it so we called him Gunny Bat—and how he gave the same safety brief each Friday afternoon when we weren't deployed or training to deploy:

Now none of you go be dumbasses this weekend, good to go? Don't show up on Monday with a fresh haircut? I'll punch you right in your goddamned mouth. No barracks cuts—I'm looking at you, Martinez, you nasty motherfucker. We are professionals, gentlemen, you best fucking look like it. I get a call from the doggone motherfucking Oceanside PD you're in fucking jail? I'm gonna let that ass rot until Monday morning and pick you up after you been passed around like Susie Rottencrotch by every diseased motherfucker up in that bitch. Use good goddamned common sense and the buddy system. Just because we home don't mean we not at war. Good to go? We always at war. Now listen up: if you're under twenty-one, don't drink. If you drink, don't drive. If you drive, make sure the car's good to go. If you're married, only fuck your wife. Don't fuck other men's wives. Wrap it before you tap it. Make sure she's eighteen, consenting, and not a dude. Don't fuck dudes. If you do fuck dudes, don't get caught and don't fucking talk about it. Don't buy a car at twenty-six percent APR at Oceanside Military Motors. If you get in a fight, you win that motherfucker and haul ass from the scene of the crime. Now drop on your fucking faces and give me twenty before we get the fuck out of here. Kill?

Gunny Bat would've given me shit for getting my ass beat, but he would've reamed Court for not being there. You were in charge of your buddy; your buddy was in charge of you. That was the shit of it—responsibility or whatever, you know? Each person holds up the other; you fail if your buddy fails.

Turtle and I were in the first bay.

Come on, I said.

Decided then that Turtle was my battle buddy. We were in it together. Tyler had said so. Made it my mission to bring a little Corps into the civilian world.

House stood on the catwalk above us. He picked for CACH. Our trailer was western states only—OR, WY, MT, UT, NV, AK, ID, WA, CA—with specific zips. Basically everything that routed through Chicago. It was House's job to roll through the thousands of boxes on our conveyor and send the right shit to the right chute and fix whatever the first line of sorters screwed up because they were too stupid or moving too fast or were too high.

Turtle and I took the stairs to the trailer bay catwalk and scanned the barcode hanging outside the trailer so whoever the hell kept track of our misloads could tell Bob the manager to chew Tyler's ass and Tyler could chew our asses. Shit always flowed downhill. No different than the Marines.

We stood at the threshold, waiting for the buzzer to sound the start of the sort. It was a drop trailer.

Let me tell you, drop trailers are the fucking worst. The backs are level but then after ten feet or so there's a three-foot drop-off—it's like loading a double-decker trailer. Mostly we tossed smalls in the belly of the thing and then let the trapdoors lining the side of the trailer down so we could build on top of them. They took forever to fill. Have built-in rollers right down the middle, so while you're building walls you're constantly tripping and sliding on the damn things. Plus, you've got to bend over to pick up the boxes, and then when you're in the belly, you've got to hunch to build under the rollers. And because Turtle was so slow, I was the one who ended up down there, building out both sides of the belly so we could close the trap doors at the same time to keep the main wall even.

After a couple drop trailers, my back would feel like a water balloon getting squeezed at one end and my right leg was always numb.

My ribs and ass ached from the fight in the bathroom; pressure drummed in my forehead and the flickering fluorescents in the warehouse and dim of the trailer fucked with my eyes. I might've had a concussion. I hadn't thought to check my pupils.

The trailer was murky—air thick and dark. It was snowing out, flurries, but I could hear them landing soft on the trailer's skin and the belly was damp with condensation—stank like wet cardboard, which reminded me of wet dog, which reminded me of Play-Doh, which reminded me of the thick, sweet smell of rot. It stuck in my throat, gagged me. Smelled like the sheep had smelled when it stood next to me while I'd built its hutch—dirty and sick.

I expected to turn around and see the thing in the shadows of the belly under the rollers, gutted and bloody, dogs playing tug of war with its insides. I couldn't make myself turn to see, wanted to haul ass out of there. It was like when I'd thought I'd seen Ruiz at the guard post after I'd tossed my boots on the wire at the Cristianitos gate. Shadows. Ghosts.

Breathing didn't work; every time I breathed too deep, it sent a twinge up to my left temple.

Before the fat and happy TAP instructor had talked about letting everything out in tiny little breaths, Ruiz had taught me to stay calm—how to push through pain and panic when someone had you wrapped up, squeezing and pulling and tweaking delicate parts.

Wasn't any real trick. Just muscle memory, repetition. Eventually I learned the limits of my body, could tell discomfort from pain, and even then, with enough repetition, I learned to lean into the pain, love it.

★

After I sucker-punched Sergeant Moss, he didn't have me NJP'd but he made me police the burn pit and stir WAG bags for two hours a day for two weeks. Called it extra military instruction. After every patrol I dumped kerosene on the pit and stood shins-deep in melting plastic and the platoon's stinking insides, stirring it all up with a charred shovel handle so it burned evenly. Crowe and Baptiste spent a pretty good amount of time laughing at me.

Then Ruiz started teaching me how to roll.

He'd wrestled in high school. Won a state championship, even. Said it didn't mean anything because his dumb ass had still ended up in the suck.

Everyone thinks Marines are in-shape, cut brick shithouses, but in country, if you're a grunt, you're always exhausted and all you're eating are T-rats and MREs, so your fitness goes to hell. You end up lanky if you're foot mobile and fat as fuck if you're stuck in a Humvee.

So we worked on conditioning first: ran through sets of push-ups and bicycle crunches and squats and lunges and burpees; then we'd grapple— arms tangled, legs woven, breath heaving in each other's faces.

Gonna be tired in a scrap anyway, said Ruiz. Got to train how you fight.

Rolling with Ruiz sped up the clock. First time I got that time travel feeling.

Soon we were four months in with four left. Sergeant Moss and I were good to go. I'd served my sentence. He put me up for a meritorious promotion to lance corporal and found some other shitbag in our platoon to ride.

When we rolled mobile in the Humvees, all the dismounts piled in a high-back—a glorified pickup bed with bench seats covered in muddy Kevlar pads from old flak jackets. Our LT made us ride low because of snipers, so the six of us back there hunkered down with not a thing to look at except each other and the cold, gray sky. People always think Iraq's hot—Bet it was hot over there, they all fucking say—but the desert in the winter? Cold as a witch's tit.

Sometimes, while the trucks patrolled at ten miles per hour for four or five hours at a time, I'd sit across from Ruiz and work him over in my head. Find his weak spots. Imagine ways to make him tap.

Sometimes we played games to pass the time—Rock, Paper, Scissors; I Spy. Corporal Nguyen got us into Twenty Questions and the movie game and the alphabet game. But he only wanted to play those because he always fucking won.

Once, when we'd been halted for what must've been three hours waiting for EOD to show up and detonate a dead cow that might've been stuffed with explosives, Ruiz introduced Nervous.

Fuck is that? said Corporal Nguyen.

Shit, man, said Ruiz. Never played Nervous? Some kind of boot? Been in the Corps less than five minutes or what?

We all laughed at Corporal Nguyen even though we didn't know the game, either. The wind picked up and drizzle that carried gritty sand in its droplets pelted our heads and flaks.

This is bullshit, said Nguyen. No muj would be out in this shit.

Fucking A, said Crowe.

Cobb snored and Corporal Nguyen and Ruiz and Baptiste eyed me and Crowe, like, *Come get ya boy,* and so Crowe took off his Kevlar and turtle-fucked him awake, startled him so bad he gave this little scream that didn't sound right coming out of his giant body.

Goddamn, said Cobb.

You're about as useful as a fucking football bat, Cobb, said Crowe.

Give him one! said Baptiste.

Corporal Nguyen and Ruiz looked at each other, shook their heads.

Nervous? I said.

Right, said Ruiz. So I'm gonna put my hand on my man's knee here, yeah?

He put his hand on my knee.

Then I just move my hand real slow, said Ruiz. Slow like this motherfucking truck moves slow, feel me? And I ask if old boy's getting nervous while I move my hand up his leg. I'm going to keep asking, and if he say he nervous, he loses.

No one asked if there was a way to win.

I hadn't been touched in months—not like the way Ruiz touched my leg in the back of that truck. I wasn't being cross-faced. I hadn't been injured—no one was applying a pressure dressing or stabilizing a cervical spine after an IED blast. No angry protesters were grabbing my cammies or rifle or skin. I wasn't embraced in a stinking mess of tears after someone got hit.

This was different.

You nervous? said Ruiz.

No, I said.

Nervous? he said. His palm pressed into my quad and his fingertips continued toward the meat of my inner thigh.

No, I said. I'm not.

While I waited in the trailer for the sort to begin, instead of pushing through the pain like Ruiz taught me, I ended up thinking of his palm on my thigh, and then I thought of Max at the bar the night before. Same feeling, maybe. It calmed me down. It had been easy. Talking to Max. Being around her. Telling the truth, whatever that was.

Figured that must be the way all the sheep civilians must've felt all the time, like life just fell into place. Fat and happy.

Even Turtle must've felt like that. Maybe that's why he was never in a hurry. Maybe that's why this job didn't seem to mean a ghost's turd to him. He raked his face with a scraggly fingernail and leaned against the trailer wall.

House picked the first box for our trailer and sent it down the chute to our rollers and I warmed up to Turtle for the first time. Maybe it was Tyler's work-together pitch or maybe I was that new me from the bar again—I could be anyone. I let Turtle have that first package—it was a good one, decent size for a base box, wide and sturdy. On the label was a big, bold *CA*.

I lived in California for a while, I said pointing at the label.

Turtle fumbled the box in his cottage cheese arms trying to scan the barcode. It didn't even piss me off watching him juggle the thing like a clown. Almost made me laugh. Like watching a kid try to imitate a parent and completely bungle it.

House sent down the next box and five more followed. They wouldn't stop until the union-mandated ten-minute break we got around six in the evening. Box was headed to Washington. I scanned it and made my way to the rear of the trailer to place it on the floor.

That's a good base box, I said.

Turtle didn't say anything; he walked back to the rollers and grabbed another box.

Hauling other people's shit around felt like extra military instruction that night—so I was slow, fucked off while the rollers and chute filled up and imagined what it would be like if Turtle and I were friends. Like Ruiz and I were friends. Like Court and I were. Like the kind of friends who knew the deep, dark shit about each other. Like I knew when Court was in middle school that his barber used to reach down his pants and feel him up if no one else was in the shop and Court knew I'd jerked it once or twice thinking about Penny. All he did was shrug and say, She's not really your sister.

I'm from Washington, I would say to Turtle. It's where my family adopted me and we lived there until I was three. I don't remember it. I used to dream about it.

And then Turtle would stop working, and boxes would be piling up in the chute and we wouldn't give a damn because we were such good friends that he would want to listen and because the new me would want to talk.

I'd tell him how, in those dreams, moss and lichen and dripping hemlocks burst from the soft places beneath my fingernails, and clear mountain rivers seeped from my pores. I'd tell him how after Ruiz cashed out I dreamed I was in the desert, surrounded by burning sagebrush and wild fennel, and I tried to get away but my feet turned to roots growing into that fine desert moon dust sand and the fire burned closer and closer, eating up all the scrub and wind scorpions, choking me. I was cooking, my skin boiling until it burst, spilling an entire river of icy snowmelt and smooth rock and trout scales over the inferno.

Fuck would a friend say to something like that?

Turtle had piled smaller and smaller boxes on top of the first base box he'd set down. He was making a leaning column. Wasn't sturdy. Wasn't right.

Smalls should have gone in the belly or in bags at the very top of the wall.

I was almost to the ceiling of the trailer on my second wall, but there was nothing to support my side and he wasn't catching up. I breathed in and out even if it hurt, leaned into the pain. Calm as hell.

I was going to show Turtle the right way to build. Teach him how to build the way Ruiz had taught me how to fight.

I rearranged the janky tower he'd built into a decent platform and when he came back, I waited for him to say something—thank you or whatever—and when he didn't, I said, Here, let me show you. And tried to take the package from his hands.

The guy flinched, dropped the package, and headed back to grab another. Boxes piled up in the chute. House yelled for us to hurry it up from the pick stand outside the bay.

Let me help you, I said.

I wasn't helping, not really. Should've seen it.

Don't touch me, he said.

I'm not touching you, I said.

My arm was wedged between the box and his body, squeegeed warm sweat from his chest.

You're harassing me, he said.

You're doing it wrong, I said.

I jerked the box again. He pulled away and slipped on the rollers, fell backward onto his ass; the box flew, then slid into the belly with a thud. House hollered for us to get our asses moving; he didn't want to shut down the belt. Boxes spilled off the rollers into the belly of the trailer. It was a three-foot drop and some broke open. A package of fluorescent light tubes fell, imploded. Turtle was beet-faced and heaving, bowed up like he was ready for a brawl, and I was just trying to help.

Not supposed to step on the rollers, I said.

You assaulted me, he said.

He said it like that: *assaulted*. Like, what the actual fuck? There I was, trying to help the guy out, and he was throwing me under the goddamned bus.

What's going on in here? It was Tyler from the mouth of the trailer.

Nothing, I said.

We were going to work it out, you know? Like Sergeant Moss and I had worked it out, like Court and I had worked it out when we were kids. I thought maybe Turtle and I could be like that.

We'd work this out, I'd apologize for being a dick, invite him to Court's party. We'd get hammered and I'd tell him about my dreams, about Washington, about the war, about Ruiz, about Max. He'd lay down some sage, guru speech if I gave him a chance, and whatever he said would fix everything—make me forget all about Cali and fires and Washington and fir trees and whenever a box came down the chute with a *CA* or *WA*, I'd get a funny feeling like I must've known someone from there once, and Turtle would say something about always wanting to visit the West Coast, and I'd say, Not me. I fucking love it here. We'd be friends, you know?

He assaulted me, said Turtle. I want to file a complaint.

You tripped, I said.

House! Kill the belt! Tyler said over his shoulder.

The belt motor cut and not three seconds later angry echoes from the sort line started up: What the fuck? yelled someone. Break the jam and let's fucking go! yelled someone else.

Is that what happened, Bill? said Tyler. Did you trip?

Bill? I said.

Yeah, *Bill*, said Tyler. He pointed at Turtle.

I didn't trip, said Turtle. He grabbed me.

It's dark in here, said Tyler.

He grabbed me, said Turtle.

All right, said Tyler. He sighed. Bill, I need you to go to Bob's office to write out a statement.

I was trying to help, I said. You shouldn't stand on the rollers. But Turtle was already on the catwalk heading for the stairs.

Tyler dropped to a crouch just inside the trailer. Did you grab him? he said.

More calls from the sort: What the fuck, Tyler? yelled someone. House, just start the fucking belt! yelled someone else. You're backing up all the belts! yelled someone else. Some asshole whooped like a peacock over and over. The entire line slapped the belt, chanted, Fuck CACH! Fuck CACH! Fuck CACH!

Dean? said Tyler.

I mean, not on purpose, I said. I was reaching for a box, and, shit, man, he was standing on the rollers.

I jumped into the belly and pulled from the mess of boxes.

I'm going to need a roll of packing tape, I said.

I'll get some guys in here, said Tyler.

I could use the help, I said.

No, I mean, some guys to take over for you, he said. Until this is sorted, you can't be here.

The guy doesn't know what he's doing, I said. I was trying to help.

Protocol, he said. Someone from Bob's office will call you to take your statement probably tomorrow.

And, like, I understood standard operating procedure, right? But it all just seemed like something that we could have solved right then and there.

I can give you my statement now, I said.

Protocol, he said. Come on. I've got to walk you out.

My finger hurt from how hard I punched my employee code into the keypad. I turned to tell Tyler what a joke it all was, but he was already power walking back to CACH.

BEFORE I LEFT for the Marines, the roads out to Court's were all cracked and elevated—most without a centerline—cutting through nothing but miles and miles of soybeans and corn outside the city limits.

In the summer it was a giant ocean of green. Like, so much green that it had a fucking sound, a smell.

In the winter the harvested corn looked like a field of punji sticks and the soybean fields were just frozen, shit-smelling dirt.

Court's place was a fifteen-hundred-square-foot limestone ranch with a walkout basement on a hill overlooking a cornfield in the sticks south of the city a couple miles from his parents' house. It used to belong to his grandma—she'd moved to Florida year-round a few years back and gave the place to Court. Before that she was a snowbird.

In high school, when the weather turned and bonfires weren't enough heat and his grandma headed south for the winter, we partied there. Court never let anyone upstairs back then, but the basement was finished, and with a couple space heaters it got the job done. I don't think his grandma ever knew, but, damn, you could've gotten a contact high just from standing at the top of the basement stairs.

The fallow, snow-covered fields made the entire stretch feel like a tomb and that made the parties we had rage that much harder—no one wanted to leave the warmth. And there weren't suburbs anywhere, no soft lights spilling out of windows—a few manufactured double-wides scattered here and there, all farmers, most related to Court some way—so it felt like if you left you were just walking out into nothing, like how I imagined the bottom of the quarry Mom used to take us to swim in in the summer or maybe how I imagined dying to be before I knew better.

The quarry scared me. One minute you were up to your chest, the next minute there was four hundred feet of nothing below you. Deep, icy blackness pulling at me just beyond where my feet were planted in the sand.

Now, out by the quarry, there were subdivisions I didn't know, with names like Plantation of Richfield and Richfield Homesteads and Richfield Grove. Farmland had been filled and paved over with concrete. Mansion monstrosities sat on two or three acres each and butted up to man-made ponds with fountains in the middle that kept them from freezing over. They'd dumped in that blue dye shit by the ton to keep the weeds from growing and if there hadn't been an inch of crusty snow cover, guarantee the grass would've been that fake-looking, perfect emerald flattop mowed to the length of a lifer's high and tight.

Richfield proper was pretty small—maybe seventy thousand people—but it sprawled because the city kept annexing land, and when they did, everyone got worried about having to pay for municipal utilities or where their idiot kids would go to school or licenses for extra garages and sheds and whatnot or what color their new neighbors might be. Shit I heard constantly growing up. To everyone in the burbs, the city was an infected spider bite—putrid at the center—and they were trying to outrun the rot.

I passed the entrance to the quarry and a chill ran through my body—something about the dark. Shadows and ghosts. It kept coming up. I wish I could've seen the signs then, but I was too mixed-up to see much of anything.

Low winter sun hit my rearview and blinded me as I pulled into Court's driveway. It was early still.

I stayed with Court sometimes a couple days at a time, came and went as I pleased, had started that at his parents' house in high school after

Penny'd moved away to college. I'd thought about asking him if I could move in, but I knew Court. He'd be cool with it for a couple weeks, we'd chill—barbecue, get drunk, watch Animal Planet—but he'd get restless.

Like, not just like the guy didn't want to keep a girl because she'd weigh him down kind of restless, you know? But pulling the motor out of a Civic at three in the morning and taking the motherfucker apart just to put it back together kind of restless. And the dude was paranoid about his stash, even with me.

Fiends were wild for pills, heavier shit. Different than a little puff, a toot or two. Every once in a while, he'd pass me an Ativan when I couldn't sleep just like Doc used to.

I shot Court a text that I was early.

Out back dropping clays, came the reply.

Turned down the radio and heard dull shotgun blasts. It was just about break time at work. Wondered who they got to fill the trailer. Wondered if Turtle had gone back to loading after he'd given his statement. No missed calls from Bob's office.

I got hot again. Assault. Jesus-fucking-shit-covered-Christ. Thought about what I'd like to do to Turtle. Thought about Sergeant Moss choking me out in the atrium of the PB. The sheep. My mom touching my shoulder, *Meestah, meestah, me zien, click click click click, BAMBAMBAM, You lamb chops? What's your favorite color? Did you sleep at all? You want to fucking die? You nervous? Tiny little breaths. Tiny little breaths.*

I opened Insta to distract myself. A new post from Penny loaded at the top of my feed—a picture of her kissing a woman on the mouth with the caption, *Love is love*—and all I could fucking think was *Don't ask, don't tell,* even though she'd told us all a long time ago.

My mom had been surprised by it—probably felt guilty that she was surprised by it. She'd been in survival mode since our dad went AWOL six years before and we'd both grown up during that time. She'd missed it. Penny was a junior in high school; I was in seventh grade. Mom kept saying that it was okay, that she would love her no matter what, that it was okay she was gay. And then Penny said she wasn't gay, that she was queer, and my mom said, That's what I said, and Penny got mad, and none of us ever talked about it again.

Sat in Court's driveway thinking about Ruiz and Nervous and the sheep, how that shit was eating me up and how I wanted to tell Court about all of it, but he had his own shit going on. Everyone had shit, right? And it all felt so typical—some vet running his suck about Iraq that and Marine Corps this and Oh I'm having such a hard time, boo fucking hoo—that it was embarrassing. Never occurred to me they might *want* to hear it.

Could've told Max, maybe. Part of me regretted gaming her game the night before, and I wanted to spill my guts in front of her and root around in that mess like a hog. But the Marines always said not to air dirty skivvies, and, anyway, who was I? What was really so bad about anything I'd done? Gone through? What did I even have to spill my guts about? I was no one. And when you're no one, you can be anyone, yeah? Possibilities of that started to fuck me up.

Like once during training, we were all—all the new joins, the boots—sitting crisscross applesauce in a school circle under cammie netting in the Mojave before running a range, learning about the platoon's standard operating procedures. We wanted to make sure we did the right thing, reacted the right way in each and every situation, because the salts running the range threw some weird scenarios at us, trying to mess us up, so we started asking Sergeant Moss what if? What if this happens, Sergeant? But what if that happens, Sergeant?

Sergeant Moss got a bug up his ass, not just for the interruption, but like he didn't understand the question. Then he said, What if grasshoppers had machine guns?

Each of us looked at one another. Laughed. No one answered because we all figured it was a trap or whatever.

Finally he said, We'd all be fucked.

Meaning that it was impossible to plan for everything, so shut up. Improvise, adapt, overcome.

What if? What if? What if? That's where I was. What if this new me did this? What if this new me did that? Fucking infinite possibilities. How was I supposed to make a choice?

In country the commander on the ground with the situational awareness was never wrong—you didn't have to worry about getting done by higher unless you were murdering noncombatants. Even then, most guys got off.

Anyway, I was rolling into a kinetic environment without ass, without rules of engagement or even SOP. Lost in the fucking sauce. Too many choices.

What if I went home, got my rifle, and paid Turtle a visit at work? What if I went home right now and went to sleep? What if I went to the nearest recruiting station and joined back up? What if I texted Max? What if I drove my car into the quarry and let it sink to the bottom? What if grasshoppers had machine guns?

I'd text Max. I'd invite her to Court's or meet her at a bar. Re-create the night before—the part before I'd got my shit pushed in by those good old boys. I'd tell her the truth—all of it, lay it out on the table, pile it up like cordwood in front of her, ask her to be the match.

Hey, it's Dean. From the bar last night, I texted.

Then I texted for her to come to the party at Court's. Gave her the address.

Didn't wait for the reply, tried not to think about whether I should've texted her or not or what I wrote or what if? What if? What if? and headed to the backyard to drop some clays with Court.

Pull, said Court, and I pressed the remote button for the autothrower. He brought the over-under to his face from the low ready in a way I admired—practiced and deliberate—like the shotty was an extension of him. Like my old PMI when he held a rifle. The neon orange clay disintegrated over the punji sticks of harvested corn popping through the snow, rained down with the flurries.

Hit, I said.

Court lit a cigarette, handed over the gun.

How you smoke menthols? I said. Taste like shit.

Nah, man, he said. Smooth.

I shook my head. You love that fake-ass gangster shit, I said.

I brought the gun to the low ready.

Pull, I said.

The clay burst.

Hit, motherfucker! he said.

It felt good putting rounds downrange. I forgot about Turtle and the bar hicks. The world smoothed out. God with a gun, right?

What we into tonight? said Court.

Your party, I said.

Yeah, dog, he said. Not until later. It's payday.

You get a job? I said.

Hell no, he said. But motherfuckers going to be looking to spend. Bring all them freaks out and shit. Hit the club, hit the titty bar, hit the supply. You know this, man.

Popped the breach and reloaded the shotgun, handed it back.

You get your nut since you been home? he said.

That was his way to ask me if I was all right, if I was firing on all eight, if I had that PTSD shit everyone always talked about. If my dick was working, I was probably five by five.

First week back, I said. That night at Broad Street? Don't remember it. Had a fucking kid, though. Woke up in her bed and there he was, five or six, standing in his Underoos, mean mugging me.

Shit, man, he said. They all got kids. Dangerous game these days. Everyone cuffs up last year of high school but no one ever puts a ring on it. Next thing you know, you're sitting down for motherfucking pancakes and coffee, and there's some crotch goblin on the couch watching cartoons. Then bitch got to run out for some shit.

He did a bad imitation of a woman's voice.

Can you watch him? It'll be right quick. Promise. By the time they get back you might as well go to the park with them, right? Grab some lunch, stay for dinner, another night—and they treat you good that night, too—then you're moving in your shit, trying to find space under the sink next to the Vagisil and tampons for the glass jar with your nuts in it. Pull.

Hit, I said.

Shit's a trap, dog, he said.

He handed the gun back and I thought what he'd said didn't sound bad—pancakes and parks and dinner. Fat and happy.

You don't want that? I said.

Crying brats? Someone nagging me about putting the seat down? he said.

You watch too much TV, I said.

I do love Animal Planet, he said.

It was getting dark. I popped the breech again and went to load up but Court stopped me.

Check it, he said. Send two. Pull.

When I loosed the clays he drew a pistol from inside the waist of his pants and sent six shots into the air after the clays.

Miss, miss, motherfucker, I laughed.

Shit, he said. Still getting the hang of it.

You're doing it wrong, I said.

What? he said.

No accuracy one-handed, I said. Looks tough, yeah, but accurate? Fuck no. Like this: Watch.

I put my feet a bit wider than my shoulders with my toes forward, held my fists out in front of my chest, pretended to grip a pistol, made sure my grip hand thumb overlapped my support hand thumb, and pointed forward.

Isosceles stance, I said. Arms and chest make a triangle out, legs and ground make a triangle up. Sturdy.

Court imitated me.

Pull, he said.

I launched it.

He tracked it for a second, then squeezed the trigger and blew it out of the sky.

Hell yeah, he said.

How'd that feel? I said.

Good, dog, he said. Come on, let's get warm.

In the kitchen, Court grabbed beers from the fridge and we headed downstairs. His place was clean, minimal but not bare. All the furniture was black and gray. Looked serious, modern. Expensive and unlived-in. He'd put in dark hardwood laminate, re-carpeted the bedrooms, painted the walls. There was a nice big TV upstairs, overstuffed sofa, a table in the kitchen, food in the pantry.

I had a hard time imagining him going to the grocery store—figured his mom probably dropped shit off for him once a week or something.

Court spent most of his time in the basement. He'd put a pool table down there, a second TV bigger than the one upstairs, a gun safe and a reloading press in the laundry room. He dropped the shotty off in the safe and came back.

You rack 'em, I crack 'em, he said.

I racked the table for eight ball while he turned on the TV. Polar bears crossed ice in the Arctic and some British guy narrated. Court broke, sunk stripes, had a run until a mis-aimed bank shot.

What's up? You here early, he said.

Work bullshit, I said.

Why you want to bust your ass with that nonsense? he said.

What else am I going to do? I said.

I couldn't sink a thing. Scratched. Court stayed silent, but I knew he meant I could sling for him. He was middle management—had a couple guys in the north and east who pushed for him. He pointed at the TV with his cue.

Earlier there was some shit about this Arctic shark, he said. Asshole-ugly, but the motherfucker was four hundred years old. Imagine all the shit you'd get to see if you lived that long, he said.

I feel four hundred, I said. Living that long sounded terrible to me.

We've got a couple hours to kill, he said. You want to bounce to the Rail, find them dudes, throw some bows?

He shadowboxed a couple of punches.

No point, I said.

I checked my phone. No text from Max; no call from UPS. Standing by to standby. Court sank his last stripe. Tried to ride the rail to the eight ball, banked out.

Damn, he said. How you going to let that shit go?

Live and let live, I said.

It's what I figured a civilian would say. I didn't have an angle, sunk the cue ball behind the seven so Court would have to take a long shot up the table.

On the TV a dolphin with a fucked-up spine swam with sperm whales, and the British guy talked about how the whales had adopted the dolphin after it was abandoned by its pod for being unable to contribute to the group. They weren't sure why the whales had adopted the dolphin, and it was likely the situation was only temporary.

My head ached and rang and my stomach burbled and Max asked me if I loved my mother and my mom asked if I was okay and Tyler asked me if I pushed Turtle and Court missed his shot again. Table scratch.

Teach you that in the Marines? he said.

If you hadn't been fucking AWOL, wouldn't be a thing, I said.

I wasn't mad at Court, not really, shouldn't have dumped on him, but I was overripe—like I might split open at any minute—and I couldn't stop myself. Or didn't want to.

Supposed to have my back, man, I said. That's what we call being a blue falcon. A buddy fucker. Get you fragged downrange.

I lined up a shot and missed. Ruiz's Macho Man face and his laugh filled my brain housing group.

Meant sinking the cue behind your mess, he said. Tactical business right there.

I took a breath and held it. Checked my phone. Nothing. Exhaled.

I fucked up man, I said. It's not on you.

It's good, he said.

He had a clean shot, called it, and sank it.

Let's get some food, he said. El Dorado's got a buffet.

The titty bar? I said.

Wings are fire, dog, he said.

El Dorado's parking lot was chunked-up asphalt and oil slick-topped potholes filled with snowmelt, a couple semis in the back, and a handful of cars. There was a ten-dollar cover Court didn't have to pay because he got the dancers coke and the bouncers knew him. I still had to shell out.

Do my man a solid, he said. Just got back from Iraq.

The bouncer—big pock-faced, sweaty ogre in a leather jacket blocking the door—shook his head. Court shrugged at me. I paid.

Inside it was all black lights and aluminum chairs and matted red carpet, same as any strip club. Place had three stages but it was dead, so only one was going—white girl in a leopard G-string and platforms backed into the pole, bent over, and shook fake tits at what must have been the semi drivers, who catcalled and hollered and drank cans of beer. It was the kind of place that served beer in cans, kept their liquor below the counter.

Court greeted the dancers on break and the waitresses hanging at the bar and the bartender by name. One of the truckers held up a twenty-dollar bill to the dancer onstage, who squatted over the money and took it with her ass cheeks. The dancers on break whooped and when the song ended a few seconds later the stage girl took the big spender to the back for a private dance.

The buffet was a folding table with four aluminum trays—two filled with hot wings, the third with soggy french fries heated by Sterno cans, and the fourth with chopped, browning salad greens. We plated up and sat at the bar.

A group of six guys came in, rowdy and loud even though it was only eight. Now there were two stages going.

Court dapped knuckles with the bartender, a paper-white, stoop-shouldered guy with center-parted hair who could've been twenty-five or fifty and was so tall he would've needed a height waiver to enlist.

What's good, Harley? said Court.

Same shit, different day, said the bartender.

Harley worked a piece of flaking lip skin with his teeth, picked his nails.

This my boy, Dean, said Court. Just got back from Iraq and shit. Hook him up.

Harley nodded at me, popped the top on a tallboy, slid it my way.

Cousin was over there with the Army, said Harley. Told me all about it. Hope you bombed them fuckers to dust.

He was waiting for me to ask about his cousin so he could tell me the story. Like I said, same shit everywhere. Tough talk never bothered me much. Like, I didn't care that he wanted a war story. It was the ownership. I didn't give a shit about that dude's cousin or what he saw. In fact, I hated him for spouting war stories to his meth-head, beanpole, Lurch-looking motherfucking cousin. Dudes were guilty or jealous or ashamed they didn't have their own story, so they figured if they picked one up from their second cousin twice fucking removed, they could shoot it off in a bar some-where and maybe get some play. Or if they were somewhere no one knew them, and they thought they could get away with it, the story became about them instead of someone they knew. Stolen valor. That was something I cared about then. I wanted to be the hardest dude in the room.

Lily working tonight? said Court.

In the back, said Harley.

One of the dancers at the end of the bar called Harley over; he dapped Court's knuckles again and lumbered her way.

Goddamn, Court laughed. Got to civilize you, boy.

What? I said.

Iced the fuck out of that dude, he said. Hate coming off you like stink on shit.

Didn't think it was that obvious, I said.

Evil-ass motherfucker, he said.

Court ate a drumstick and we sat in silence. I wanted to explain all that shit to him about the Marines. About war stories. About the TAP instructor and Ruiz and the sheep and wanting to be fat and happy, but I didn't. I thought about that deformed dolphin and the sperm whales.

Wings is right, yeah? he said.

My phone lit up on the bar, an incoming call from UPS.

Be right back, I said.

I speed-walked outside, jammed a finger in my ear, and answered.

A woman's voice spoke back: May I speak to Mister Dean Pusey, please?

This is, I said.

Mister Pusey, please hold for Bob, said the voice.

I didn't know Bob's last name. He called people by their first names—the kind of thing where he must have thought it made him a real man of the people, but to everyone sweating blood in the trailers it came off superior as a diamond-crusted shit.

Ruiz would've laughed at that. I wondered if Bob *had* a last name.

I'd left my coat inside. Flurries picked back up, reflected hot-pink neon from the sign on top of the building. Two guys and a girl got out of a car and walked past me laughing loud about tucking bucks and motorboating tits and I wanted to tell them to shut the fuck up. I went over everything in my head: I hadn't touched the guy, had only tried to help. I never harassed the guy. I motivated him.

Dean? said Bob.

Yes, sir, I said.

It was more a force of habit than any kind of customs and courtesies bullshit and I hated myself a little for it. Bob laughed a short, forced-air laugh.

No need for *sir* or anything like that, Dean, he said.

Sure, okay, I said.

I just want to thank you for your service as a soldier, Dean, and I'm confident we can figure out this incident to the satisfaction of all parties involved.

I want to be as helpful as I can, I said.

Good, Dean, he said. Good. We think the best thing for you and for the hub is a lateral transfer to the night sort—eventually the preload—Dean. We need good people there, Dean, and your numbers and attention to detail are strong.

Should I give my statement? I said. I mean, I wasn't harassing the guy. I was trying to help.

I hear you, Dean, and I appreciate your commitment to the job, he said.

You don't want my statement? I said.

I think we have everything we need, Dean, he said.

Can I ask if this is punishment? I said. Because, like I said, I was trying to help. He slipped on the fu—he slipped on the rollers, sir.

Oh, no, Dean, he said. Not at all. I simply saw your numbers and thought, if you're amenable to the night sort, Dean, that you would be a great fit. If you are, Dean, I'll let Tyler know and we'll inform Grant, who would be your new shift supervisor, so he can get you lined up for the transfer.

What the fuck does amenable mean, Bob? I didn't say.

Hey, Bob! Fuck you, Bob! I didn't say.

So much for my service, I guess, Bob, I didn't say.

I'll be waiting for you, Bob, in the parking lot, Bob, with a Colt carbine, Bob, I didn't say.

What I said: That sounds great, Bob.

Fantastic, Dean, he said. That's wonderful. I think you're going to flourish in the night sort, Dean. We'll start you out Monday. Remember, you'll report to Grant. You can call Monday for the start time. Have a great weekend, Dean. Buh-bye.

The line went dead before I could say anything else. Snow fell in big, wet, fluffy flakes; my hair was soaked and I shivered. I tried to get back inside, but the bouncer-ogre wanted another ten dollars.

I was just in there, I said. I walked out to take a call.

I don't remember you, he said.

What the fuck? I said.

Got a handstamp? he said.

I flashed my cold, purple hands under the ogre's nose. I wanted him to hit me, wanted time to speed up so I didn't have to be there in the decaying parking lot of a dumpy strip club.

He shrugged. Ten dollars, he said.

I paid.

Court had pulled another Houdini—nowhere in sight when I got back in the club. My entire body throbbed like a toothache and I got Harley's attention by knocking on the bar hard enough to bruise my knuckles and ordered a shot and a beer.

There was a good crowd by then and all three stages were running, so Harley didn't have time to stand around jawing bullshit, which was good. I sat alone and drank hard, trying not to think about Turtle, Max, the look Rick would give me when I explained about my hours, my mom's hand on my shoulder, the woman in Washington who could be anyone. I couldn't be anyone I decided. I was someone. I wondered who.

I ordered another shot and a beer back and sat at the bar and opened Instagram and searched *dolphin whale adoption*. I scrolled the shadowy, dark blue grid that popped up—mostly the same image of the dolphin, its spine behind the dorsal fin zigzagged like an accordion, swimming through the massive shapes of the sperm whales.

I searched *adoption*.

The top result was this generic-as-fuck website called adoption dot com. The name made me laugh. Just so obvious, you know? It was fucking embarrassing.

I scrolled images on their page: black-and-white photos of reunited birth families and adoption stories. Everyone looked so goddamned happy.

I ordered more to drink and searched *adoption Washington state* in Google and back came a flood of websites for adoptees' and adoptive parents' rights, Washington State government child and family services, independent adoption agencies, adoption lawyers, private investigators.

It was all so much, it made my ass twitch, and I couldn't stand to sit on the fucking stool for another second. I got down in the pit, start tossing cash—rounding the bar, tucking bucks, shelling out for private dances.

Court filled in the rest later.

I'd gotten up onstage, started barking in a mock DI voice, performing the Marine Corps Daily Seven—calisthenics—and then tried to slug the pock-faced bouncer-ogre whose name was Guy, which I guess confused me because Court said I kept asking, What's your fucking name, guy? And then he said, Guy. And we went like that round and round until I cried into his cowhide shoulder about how sorry I was that I'd tried to slug him and he lifted me offstage like I was a baby.

Next thing I remember we were back in Court's basement. Music was loud. People everywhere. I inhaled a line of coke off the coffee table in front of the giant television where a shark swam in black water.

Court slapped my shoulder. Yo, that's it! he said. That's the fucking shark I was talking about.

When I leaned back the couch swallowed me up.

Court said to the group of people crowded around the coffee table, She was a snowbird and then she moved and left me the place.

I liked the sound of the word: *snowbird*. I struggled out of the couch, took another line, tasted medicine in my throat, and tried it out: Snowbird, I said. I recognized one of the girls in the group from the club and then I thought I recognized her again from high school and I couldn't remember her name but I remembered during a pep rally she'd won a Chubby Bunny competition—how many marshmallows you can fit in your mouth at once. I locked eyes with her and chanted, Chubby Bunny Chubby Bunny Chubby Bunny. She rubbed her nose and stared at me. Stomping came from overhead and I knew who owned each footstep. Someone knocked on the sliding walkout door and Court turned and said over the music, Don't let that fucker in! and gave the guy the finger and I laughed and everyone laughed and we snorted more lines and my phone blazed in my pocket and it was Max and I leaned back and let the couch swallow me up again and texted her: *It's a party. Come. It'll be fun.* And my body folded in half in the couch and in half again and I was like that bent, deformed dolphin or maybe that old-ass shark down in the heavy dark and all the breath forced out of me and I felt like drowning like dying until I jumped up and took a great big gasping breath and chanted, Chubby Bunny Chubby Bunny Chubby Bunny, and the girl took a great big rail of snow into her nose and outside it was still snowing and the guy was still knocking on the glass and Court shouted, Fuck! Off! and the guy was gone and then he wasn't, then he was coming down the stairs saying, Please, man. Please. Come on. I'm good for it. Please. Please please please please. And then Court stood with the pistol in his hand and my eyes dilated and I heard my veins open and Court moved in slow motion like a car wreck moved slow smooth fast toward the guy and I ground my teeth and my asshole puckered and I flew like a snowbird glided like a shark got behind Court became the two-man in the stack during a raid the one who always makes the kill and I bumped Court who wasn't Court but Ruiz out of the way and smelled fear sweat and the guy stepped in front of a light became a silhouette a target and I grabbed him around the neck and tackled and mounted and choked and laughed and baa'd and woofed into his ear over and over again baabaabaa woofwoof WOOF. You lamb chops, motherfucker?

MAX AND HER friends found me running down the road by Plantation of Richfield or maybe Richfield Grove. I was headed to the quarry. I'd swim to the pontoon where the older kids sunned themselves in the summer. I was going to find Penny. On my way I scouted the barren fields for the sheep—kept an eye out for stringy, diseased canines like a good sheepdog, imagined all that dark nothing below me in the water. That's where I belonged, with all the toothy, slimy monsters down in the blackness.

Ruiz knew who I was. He ran next to me, keeping pace.

We fucking warriors, dog, he said. *You a killer. Motherfucking dealer of death. Oohrah, Marine Corps*—he clapped his hands twice: clap clap—*KILL!* He galloped and whooped and sang running cadence and laughed. *Moto bullshit*, he said. *But for real, dog. You a monster.*

Max pulled up next to me, rolled down her window, and asked what I was doing, asked about my face.

I like running, I said, and Max laughed like she had in the bar. It didn't make me angry. I felt good and looked to Ruiz to see if he was laughing, too, but he was gone.

Do you want to run with me? I said.

The wind cut and I did a few side-straddle hops to move my blood.

Maybe you should get in, she said.

Later I didn't know which was a bigger red flag: the coked-up asshole running down a road in a snowstorm in Bumfuck, Indiana, at two in the morning or the woman willing to let the coked-up asshole into her car.

She and her friends—Brooke and Rose, they said, when I collapsed into the back seat—had been at a bachelorette party for a work friend.

This is Dean? said Brooke in the front seat.

Max, said Rose in the back seat. She looked at me like I had a dick growing out of my forehead and scooted toward her door. I tried to smile at her.

What? said Max. He's a good guy. Really.

Maybe he's got some more of whatever the fuck he's on? said Brooke.

My smile felt too big and my heart couldn't pump fast enough or it was pumping too fast, and I tried to catch my breath but it got caught in my throat, which was closing up from the blasting car heat, and my nose started dripping, so I sat there clearing my throat and sniffling, trying not to do either, trying not to move because everything sounded too loud in my ears like a rifle shot in a small room, and my skin was glowing and I was small inside my clothes and itched all over and I wanted to get out and run more, wanted to turn back the clock, ditch Court at El Dorado or at his house, mind my business in the trailer at work, chuck the Colt's upper receiver into the foul St. Joseph River, which ran through the center of town, turn to my mom and let her hold my battered face and tell me where I belonged, but I couldn't talk.

My mouth was so dry, it was moon dust, and I cleared my throat and snorted snot and managed to ask if anyone had any water but no one answered and I wasn't sure whether I'd asked at all so I just shut the fuck up and stared out the window.

So we're not going to this party? said Brooke.

If we're not, can we stop somewhere? said Rose. I want some fucking French fries in my mouth right now.

You always want something in your mouth, said Brooke. Such a slut.

That's just *fucking* rude, said Rose.

All three of them laughed and I didn't exist. Out the window the moonlight hit a mound of snow in the dark field and it looked like the sheep on its side dying, already dead. I closed my eyes, put my head against cold glass, and thought of Ruiz in his rack at the PB, annoyed I didn't know what the hell Sergeant Moss was going to do to the sheep.

I wanted to tell Max, Brooke, and Rose that story. I wasn't even in it to get laid at that point. Just wanted to make them laugh, laugh with them, but I'd gone apathetic. It was a word Sergeant Moss had taught all us boots during the relief in place, after we were in country but before we'd taken over the area of operations from the unit heading home.

★

Battle buddies aren't just for keeping you from fucking ladyboys in Thailand, Sergeant Moss said.

He stood in front of our section in a plywood-and-pine-board, engineer-made command-and-operations center. Whenever we had downtime, Sergeant Moss made sure to give us some hip pocket knowledge.

Get out your doggone notebooks and write this down. I don't know why I still have to tell you motherfuckers that shit. Go on. Get them out.

Aye, aye, Sergeant, we said.

There are four mindsets: red, orange, white, and black, he said. Good to go?

Yes, Sergeant, we said.

All us here downrange? he said. We're mindset orange. We're on alert, assessing threats. Good to go?

Yes, Sergeant, we said.

Those nasty civilians stateside? he said. Your moms and pops? Your Susies? Mindset white. Lost in the sauce. Unaware and unprepared. Complacent. What the fuck does complacency do, PFC Pusey?

Complacency kills, Sergeant.

Give him one, he said.

The other boots around me responded, Kill!

Sergeant Moss was pacing now.

Now, when we throw down, said Sergeant Moss, go kinetic, engage the enemy? We flip our trigger to mindset red. No more assessing. Your training takes over. Muscle memory. We're in the shit, engaging targets, killing bodies.

Oohrah! We all said, motivated to pop our combat cherries.

Stow that shit, he said.

Aye, aye, Sergeant.

Most times after kinetic action we drop right back into orange and go about our fucking day, he said. Sometimes, though, we might get stuck in red. Can't sustain red. Adrenaline'll burn you up or the hypervigilance'll break you. That's how civilians get fucking dead. Itchy trigger fingers. We are not here to kill civilians, good to go?

Yes, Sergeant.

He stopped pacing and faced us.

We are fucking professionals, he said, and we will have a plan to kill every motherfucker we meet, but up until the point someone gives us good doggone reason, we will treat them with courtesy and respect, good to go?

Yes, Sergeant.

Sometimes after we've spent time in red, if we don't ease ourselves out, the very goddamned earth drops out from beneath us. He paused, then pointed to Cobb and said, Like your Susie's ass blossom after Jody's done pushing her shit in, Cobb.

We laughed.

That's mindset black, gentlemen, said Sergeant Moss. Panic. Breakdown. Apathy.

What's apathy, Sergeant? said Baptiste.

It means not giving a fuck, dummy, said Sergeant Moss. Marines do stupid shit in mindset black—end up suck-starting their M-sixteens. We don't need weakness downrange. Look around at all the Marines in this room. They are your responsibility. You are theirs. You see a Marine you think is fucked-up, you say something. You don't, and shit goes bad, you got to live with that. We police our own and higher stays out of our shit. Good to go?

Yes, Sergeant, we said.

I was coming down hard. Sergeant Moss would've told me to clean my rifle or PM the high-back or PT to get myself right. What did civilians do to get right? I didn't have a fucking clue.

Are you going to Florida for Thanksgiving? said Brooke.

My parents didn't ask me to come, said Max.

Sad baby orphan, said Brooke.

She leaned over the center console, stuck out a fat lower lip, and patted Max's hair. *Like mushrooms*, I thought, and hated myself.

Just show up—they're your parents, said Rose.

Brooke looked at Max, put her hand on Max's thigh, and I thought, *Nervous?* And then Max cleared her throat but didn't say anything and then Brooke said, Anyway, it's probably going to be, like, eighty degrees there and I bet no one even goes to the beach because they think it's too cold. That's how it is in Arizona whenever I visit my grandparents—no one's in a pool unless it's a hundred degrees.

I'm just going to stay here, said Max. Maybe get a jump on some work. I'll see them at Christmas and take all the guilt they throw my way for not going to church then and use it as an excuse not to see them for another year.

Rose blew a raspberry, gave a thumbs-down. That is the most boring, adult thing I've ever heard, she said.

Oh, well, it's just two days! said Max.

I could tell she was a little defensive. Felt like I knew her already. Loft apartment visions danced in my head.

We should do Friendsgiving! said Brooke. Just the three of us.

What about Cooper? said Max.

Fuck him, said Brooke. He hasn't texted back all night.

I think he might be kind of an ass, said Max.

Don't say that! said Brooke.

Why not? said Max.

If you hate on him like that and we stay together, it'll be weird, said Brooke.

I'm taking Hudson to my family's big dinner in Indy, said Rose.

That's huge, girl! said Max.

Bitch, you're not invited, said Brooke. I meant me, Max, and Dean.

Brooke! said Max, but she and Rose laughed.

I mean, if he's still alive back there, said Brooke. Are you alive back there, Running Man?

My dad loves that movie, said Rose.

They talked about movies they'd just seen and then music and then Max turned up the radio and Brooke sang along in the front seat and held her phone into the back seat like a microphone for Rose to sing the chorus into.

Snow and moonlight and shadows became a flipbook cartoon out the window and I watched those goddamned dogs chase down the sheep over and over and over and tear into its neck and gut, turn it inside out across the dark snow that reminded me of the bottom of the quarry—empty nothing full of monsters—and when the dogs looked up at me through that darkness there was my reflection, my face on their bodies, and they howled and their howls turned into something like a moan and a grunt and a sigh and a sucking breath all at once and through the dark my hand grazed Turtle's elbow and my mom touched my shoulder and the bar hick palmed the back of my head and Ruiz reached across the high-back Humvee and grasped my thigh, said, You nervous?

I was fucking done with it all—wanted to scream, beat my head against the glass, open the door and drop onto the road, roll under the rear tire of Max's car or reach forward and grab the wheel, send the entire vehicle into a death spin on the icy road, flip into the embankment, crash into a telephone pole, burst into flames.

If you come to Friendsgiving, Dean, you have to sing! said Brooke.

I bet he's got plans with his parents, said Max. He *loves* his mother.

She looked in the rearview and winked.

And the color olive, she said.

The last part of the word passed from her mouth and she licked spittle from her lower lip and a switch flicked inside me and I had to shift in my seat to keep my dick from pressing into my zipper.

Does the mama's boy talk? said Brooke.

Dean, are you okay? said Max.

I might have just killed someone, I didn't say.

I wish I was fucking dead, I didn't say.

No, I didn't say.

What I said: *The Running Man* is a good movie.

It lives, said Brooke.

Max's apartment was in the type of complex where the buildings were made to look like houses—wood-plank siding and internal stairwells and false gables. Inspection ready from a distance—balconies and play-grounds, basketball and volleyball court—but close up it was a movie set. Fake. Two-dimensional. The kind of place where kids came to visit their lonely, well-off, middle-aged dads every other weekend and slept on shoddy, twin-sized IKEA beds in rooms that never stopped smelling like fresh paint. I'd had friends who lived like that in high school and it made me glad my dad had just fucked off. Anyway, you could tell the place wasn't cheap and I wondered how she afforded it.

While we shuffled to Max's apartment through the couple inches of snow covering the parking lot to the wet, salt-crusted walk, I realized I didn't really know shit about her aside from her favorite color and that she didn't get along with her mom and that her parents lived in Florida.

I felt like a complacent, shitbird civilian lost in the sauce without any situational awareness and then I remembered Max asking me if I was okay in the car, her eyes in the rearview, the way she'd winked and said *olive* and I gulped air and whistled it through my teeth in little spurts that puffed breath like a steam engine into the insulated night until my head swam over and over with the phrase *fat and happy.*

We'd stopped at a diner drive-thru and Rose stumbled, occupied by her bag of food, and wolfed down shoelace French fries while Brooke rained hate and discontent over the phone onto her boyfriend, Cooper, who had finally called her back.

I walked next to Max, wanted to take her hand or drape an arm around her shoulder, pull out my phone, snap a handful of pictures of the two of us. I wanted to fuck her and stay the night and wake up and have breakfast and coffee and take pictures of our plates full of food and go to the store to pick up groceries for lunch and dinner and snap pictures of heaping goddamned avocados and shiny bell peppers and I wanted to go to the movies and catch a photo of our feet up on the backs of the chairs in front of us and then I'd stay the night again, let myself get fat and happy and post every single one of the pictures to Insta, push down the guns and deserts and Humvees and sunburn, crush them under the weight of a new life.

When Max unlocked her door, Brooke stayed outside, bawling out Cooper. Rose pushed her way inside the apartment, which opened into a living room with two love seats surrounding a coffee table. She dropped onto the nearest couch, dumped her food onto the coffee table, and turned on the TV in the near right corner.

I followed Max to the kitchen, which I could see partially because of a pass-through that looked into the living room to make the place feel bigger. I waited outside the kitchen in the small space set aside for a circular breakfast table and stood looking around at the walls, her photos and art—one, near the entry, was a great big picture of a woman sleeping in the desert while a lion watched her.

Do you want some water? she said.

I owe *you* a drink, I said.

Got money on you this time? she said.

I'd given my last cash to Coco or Persia or Lyric or some shit.

No, I said. Guess you still got me on the hook.

I could almost hear her goddamned eye roll.

You sound like Brick, she said.

Ha ha, I said.

My palms were chalky, and I couldn't stop snorting from the coke, like there was a chunk of cement stuck in my nose and I had this fucking twinge up inside near my eyes that was making them water, making me squint even in the soft apartment light. Brain was ringing, pulsing against my skull.

Rose was passed out on the couch and I stood in the dining space while Max clinked glasses in a cabinet and ran the tap, and all of a sudden I wondered what the fuck to do with my hands.

Just standing there next to the table, my hands felt unnatural hanging at my sides, dumbbells crashing against my thighs. They were too big for the pockets of my jeans—swollen from the booze and coke and cold and heat. And the fight.

Guy went limp in the choke I'd had him in, and I didn't let go because he hadn't tapped, and then I was running through the field.

I rubbed my hands together, ogling them like they were my first pair of tits, and when I crossed my arms to shove them up into my pits, pain shot through me and I bit my tongue and my head pounded.

Hungover, and I hadn't even slept.

A gun would've felt good in my hands then. I tried to distract myself with how I'd clear the apartment in a raid: the kitchen pass-through made

Max's entryway even more of a fatal funnel—some fucking muj would post up right behind the thing and spray and pray until someone in the stack chucked a grenade over the bar counter.

To my right was a short hallway, two doors across from one another—a bathroom and bedroom, I guessed—it would've been best with four men, two men in two stacks on opposite sides of the hall—

What were you even doing out there? said Max. She set full water glasses down on the table, sat. I followed. Forgot all about doors down the short hallway.

Truth again? I said.

Always, she said.

I was going to kill myself, I didn't say.

Talking to my dead friend, I didn't say.

Looking for my birth mom, I didn't say.

Hunting packs of wild dogs to avenge an Iraqi sheep, I didn't say.

What I said: I was running.

That's what you said, she said.

She saw through me then—all the bullshit I was on. She knew it. I cupped the water glass in both hands, imagined crushing it, the glass splintering into my palms. Wasn't mad or anything—it was the kind of moment where you're walking down the street and all of a sudden you see yourself tripping and face-planting into a curb or getting mowed down by a bus and every little detail is in slow motion, zoomed-in, HD. You can almost feel it—organ burst, bone crack, skin tear, blood spurt. The images grinding teeth, nails on a fucking chalkboard.

Like, Court and I used to get high in the loft of his family's barn and we'd dangle our feet over the edge and I couldn't help but picture my body slipping from that height, arms and legs cartwheeling, landing on my head, skull caving in, teeth severing my tongue, eyes exploding from their fucking sockets. Shit used to make me wince, gag, damn near hyperventilate.

When I asked Court if he ever thought about shit like that, he said no, and it all felt like a sign. Like he'd die in his sleep at a hundred and I'd be mangled to death in some horrible accident before I was twenty-five. Call it fate.

And your face? she said, and pointed to the space above her eyebrow like the damage had been done to her.

That's two questions, I said.

You got me, she said, and took a sip of water.

Felt like I had control, then, like I knew shit about the world, how it worked, and Max didn't know a goddamned thing. There she was, condition white: unaware and unprepared, thinking I was some little bird with a broken wing, like she was going to fix me, and I'd gone to condition orange: alert and assessing.

I didn't feel envy, like in the bar. Instead, I hated her a little. All the choices she'd made in her life had to be balanced in the universe somehow, and I imagined I was on the other side of the fucking ledger. She'd made me who I was whether she knew it or not. Maybe people like Max were keeping me from being anything but what I was.

So? I said.

So what? she said.

So why were *you* out there? I said.

I like you, she said.

I like you, too, I said.

It was what she wanted to hear; I'd sighted in on that much. Wanted to use her up, get my nut, afterward laugh in her face, tell her to fuck off, tell her how she didn't know a fucking thing about me, and then leave her there, wrecked in her bedroom, ghost her fucking texts and calls, disappear into the early morning with a new story for Ruiz. Or not Ruiz because he was nothing but dust. Moon dust. Court. I'd tell Court.

But then I meant it, too, right? I liked her—that dream life in the downtown loft, the breakfasts and grocery stores, the fucking movie theater. It wasn't nonsense. I wanted those things—needed them.

Give me your right hand, she said.

I let go of the water glass and set my hand palm down on the table between us. She ran her fingertips from my wrist to the tip of my middle finger and when she did that, no shit, my tongue got thick and my eyes welled up.

It was like how Ruiz had said once after a brutal-ass company hike, he'd said, Yo, güey, ain't nothing like dropping your fucking pack.

That shit came to stand for anything that felt good—like if a dude was short-timing, about to get out, you'd see him and you knew, could tell by the look on his face, he didn't give a shit about nothing. He'd dropped his fucking pack. It was relief. Freedom.

I'm going to read your palm, said Max.

You believe in that shit? I said it so my tears wouldn't spill over.

She slapped my hand. Surprised me.

Don't be rude, she said.

She was serious, face got hard and dark, and she stared at me for a minute. I cleared my throat.

Sorry, I said.

She softened.

Okay, she said. Ready?

I nodded.

Long, oval fingernails mean you're good at keeping secrets, she said.

Got nervous then. Cleared my throat. Asked how she knew how to do it, read palms.

My mom—she hates stuff like this, she said. Calls it witchcraft.

Do it to piss her off, then? I said.

When I was thirteen, she said, my best friend had a birthday party and we were into stuff like that—tarot, astrology; we'd get the Ouija board out every time we had a sleepover—so we were going to go to a fortune-teller, but my mom wouldn't let me go. So I bought books from a local used bookstore and learned how to do it myself.

She smiled and pet my hand, massaged it. I imagined her hand around my prick, fingernails dancing along its length; chills shot from my crotch up into my flip-flopping stomach, breath catching in my throat.

I coughed, shifted, and said, I thought you were going to read my palm.

Rose snored on the couch.

Max flipped over my hand, ironed my thick, hot palm with her cool, dry palm, traced lines on the meat near my thumb and then through the center.

It's not easy for you to focus on any one thing; you've got a lot of energy, she said. You like being outside. You don't take enough time for yourself.

Her finger tracked a curved line from my ring finger to just below my pinky.

Loyalty is significant to you in work and relationships, she said. Communication is important to you. You've been in love.

She tapped two small lines above where she'd ended on the outside of my hand, then she got quiet and stared in my eyes and I no shit thought that maybe if I didn't move she wouldn't see me, like I was prey. And any control I thought I had took a shit, and all I could do was watch while she brought my hand to her lips and kissed my fingers.

I was at the bottom of the quarry, floating. I was a god with a gun. Nothing and everything and nowhere and everywhere and no one and anyone.

After Nervous, after EOD exploded the cow, back at the PB, the platoon racked out—aside from the guards on the roof assigned overwatch for the next two hours and whatever NCO pretended to be awake as guard commander. In one of the empty rooms on the second of the three floors, Ruiz got me off with his mouth.

I'd had a couple girlfriends in high school. The last one broke up with me before I left for boot camp. She wrote me letters sometimes—all sorts of stuff about how she prayed for me and how it was okay to kill someone for God. Only let me put it in her ass. Sex out of wedlock is a sin, she said. One of those saddleback Catholic girls. I wondered what it might feel like for Ruiz to fuck me—weight against my back, arm around my trunk, hand gripping my shoulder, pulling me to him.

I got a girlfriend, I said. I didn't know why I said it—I know why now, I guess.

I got a girl, too, he said. Not here, though, is she? Sometimes you just got to get your nut, dog.

Ruiz swished some water around in his mouth, spit in a corner.

Guys need it more, he said. Why bitches can't be grunts.

I don't know about all that, I said.

My hand shook while I buttoned my trousers and I was grateful there wasn't a moon shining through the iron-barred, glassless window so Ruiz couldn't see. There was a wardrobe full of clothing in the room and sleeping mats piled against a wall left behind by the family our section leader had paid a hundred dollars US. They'd been given fifteen minutes to clear out.

What you want to get another sheep? he said. Fuck that instead?

That what you tell your girl? I said. *Gotta get my nut.* I imitated him.

Shit's racist, man, he said. That vato voice you use.

That's what you sound like, I said.

Don't matter if that's what I sound like, he said. Pfft. Pinche wedo.

He lit a cigarette and offered me one.

I don't want it, I said.

Yes you do, he said. His voice was thick with cheap, stale tobacco— Miami or Gauloises, eastern European.

I took the cigarette and he lit it and we sat in the dark, cherries flaring.

Do you believe in God? I said. I expected him to laugh at me, but he didn't, barely even paused.

I do, he said.

My ex used to only let me fuck her in the ass because she thought God would send her to hell otherwise, I said.

Silence for a minute, and then Ruiz laughed and then I laughed and then we fell into that feedback loop laughing—the kind of thing where you're not even laughing at what got said but the other person's laugh. That box of a room might as well have been the entire universe.

Our laugher died down to cackling tremors and coughs and deep breaths and I said, Jesus, there's something fucking wrong with me.

Nah, said Ruiz. He took a drag, exhaled. You good, dog.

SPENT THE NEXT couple weeks fucking like bunnies, Max and me. Every night before work, seemed like. Had this routine where I'd text her, show up to her apartment, we'd talk some about her work and my work, watch TV, maybe, and then I'd lean over and kiss her neck or she'd put her hand on my thigh, kiss my lips. She said what she wanted. Wasn't shy about it. Taught me a thing or two about that. Kept me coming back. Got so I dodged Court whenever he texted. He called me cunt-struck. And in the moment I was, like, Fuck you, man.

But he was right.

Max was all I could think about, flashes in my head all day long: wet mouth, bent knees, ass curve.

Tried to run the flashes out of my head, sweat them out with body-weight circuits, the gym, miles of running. Tried to keep myself from becoming complacent.

Slick skin, hair tickle, hot breath.

Nothing worked. Thing was, I didn't care.

Thick tongue, gooseflesh, arched back.

Had nothing to hide when we were together like that. Never spent the night, either, because of work, so it stayed casual.

Wanted more than that, though—wanted that downtown flat and the movie dates and the grocery store trips, and I said that to Max. One night before I left for work, while I was putting on my pants, I said, Let's go on a date.

And she asked me if I wanted to go to a flea market an hour north in Amish country; she wanted to look for some lamps.

I said yes even though I didn't know what the fuck a flea market was.

Text me your address, she said. I'll pick you up Saturday morning.

It was cold—that crack your skin, freeze your nose hairs kind of cold. Roads were wet and salted, and an inch of fresh snow shined like a wet coat of paint while it warmed up on the fields we drove past. Blinding in the early morning sun. I had to squint. Wished I would've brought my sunglasses. I expected someone—Sergeant Moss, maybe—to get on my ass about not having my personal protective equipment squared away.

Max played a radio show I'd never heard—*This American Life*—hosted by a nasally guy who couldn't pronounce the letter *L*. Like *cold* sounded like *code*.

Have you really never heard this before? she said.

I thought of Rick—the car guys he listened to—and told Max I listened to that.

Oh, yeah, she said. *Car Talk.* I can see that.

And I guess that made me feel kind of good, you know. Godly, maybe. Like Rick. Like this new me. Maybe I'd grow a goddamned ponytail and wear carpenter jeans and get hard-ons over levels and hammers and plumb bobs or whatever. Start going to church.

Max went back to listening. Got into it, laughed at things I didn't know were supposed to be funny, looked over at me to see my reactions, if I was having a good time, if I was getting it. And I wasn't fucking getting it at all. But the new me tried his best, got a taste of what fat and happy was like.

Then we ran up behind a horse and buggy on the road ten minutes out and slowed to a crawl and the show ended and it was quiet and we stared at the ass end of the black buggy bumping along on the patched, salty asphalt and my palms started to sweat.

Flexed thighs, body weight, soft moan.

I'd never been alone with a woman like that. Sober. In a car. Going to a flea market.

It's perfect this morning, said Max.

Everything looks dead, I didn't say.

. *Lay on your fucking horn and get this goddamned horse out of the way*, I didn't say.

What the fuck is a flea market? I didn't say.

What I said: Yeah, it is.

The heater was on blast. My face flushed. I wanted to turn it down.

I miss the sun in the winter, she said, and closed her eyes while the car crawled forward and my breath caught in my throat seeing her like that: gold winter sun on her pale skin, softening her, turning her hair amber. Wanted to tell her she looked beautiful, but I didn't.

That's not safe, I said. Tried to make it sound like a joke.

She laughed, opened her eyes. I wonder if they're cold, she said, and pointed at the buggy.

I tried to figure out that laugh: Was it a You're-funny-and-I-want-you-to-keep-being-funny laugh? Was it a You're-a-silly-fucking-idiot laugh? Was it an I-can't-believe-I-asked-this-fucking-guy-to-come-with-me laugh? I wanted to know so I could keep doing it, or fix it, and I was mad at myself for caring so much about what she thought.

Fresh horse shit dropped to the road between the wheels.

We lived near them where I grew up in Michigan, she said. The Amish.

I used to see them—like the men—at McDonald's in the morning on my way to school, getting carted to and from construction sites, I said.

I'd ride my bike by their houses and I was always kind of jealous of them, you know? she said. Big families outside together, doing work.

They scared me a little, I said. Always looked so angry.

Max laughed again and nodded.

And that laugh made me smile and then I couldn't stop smiling, grinning like a fucking fluffy white lamb chop civilian, and there was a part of me that thought, that kept saying, *You don't deserve this.* But it was small and weak around Max, so I rolled it easy and kept on thinking, *Fat and happy, fat and happy, fat and happy.* Turned it into a goddamned war cry in my head while we dropped into questions—Truth again. Not quite the real shit, but right on the edge of the real shit. I asked, What's your favorite movie? She asked, What's your least favorite sound? I asked, When's your birthday? She asked, Are you happy? I asked, What makes you angry? She asked, What's the hardest thing you've ever done? I asked, Who do you think would come to your funeral if you died tomorrow? She asked, Are you a dog person?

I lied and said yes about the dogs.

Our PB got overrun by stray dogs on that first deployment. A pack of them, couple dozen strong. Maybe word got out about the sheep. They were smart—made it through the concertina wire and HESCO barriers into the compound. Started scrounging the trash pit for MRE discards. Then they figured out how to get into the makeshift chow call. Ate all the Otis Spunkmeyer muffins and diarrheaed everywhere. Drove Command fucking crazy. Funny at first, right? No one liked those fucking muffins anyway.

Then we had to pick up their shit. Few guys had run-ins with them—got menaced or barked at—chunk a rock and they'd scatter. But then Hernandez, one of our Humvee drivers, got ambushed on the way to the piss tubes in the middle of the night. Dogs almost dragged him off. Would have if Letoa hadn't shown up and blasted one and scared the others. Hernandez lost a couple fingers, had to get evacuated. Someone told me later he got medically separated and moved back to Honduras.

First time anyone in our section had used their rifle aside from zeroing that deployment. War was all IEDs and weapons caches and hearts and minds by then. Couple guys in another section had wasted some fools digging a hole at night on the side of the road; snipers had blasted a dude they said was spotting for a mortar team while a platoon in another company was taking indirect fire. It wasn't like we were assaulting Fallujah or Ramadi. We were occupiers. Bored most of the time.

Anyway, after Hernandez got evaced, we all wanted to hear Letoa tell the story and we crowded him in the chow hall, which was really just a small outbuilding, and poked him until he gave it up.

Like, I wake up and have to piss, right? And so I grab my rifle and it's condition four, but I dunno, man. I have this feeling—

Scared of the dark, Letoa? Crowe said.

Fuck you! said Letoa. Ain't scared of the dark. Had a feeling, like I said.

Fucking dumb is all I'm saying, said Crowe.

Let him tell it, Crowe! someone said from the crowd, and then more calls followed and Crowe started arguing and yelling back until Ruiz told everyone to shut the fuck up and let Letoa talk.

Yeah, said Letoa. So I have this feeling and I grab a magazine and pop it in, condition three, and head to the piss tubes and it's fucking pretty dark, just stars, but I know the way and light discipline and all, so I don't use my SureFire or anything, but then I hear just like a bunch of growling and I stop and I'm thinking, *Fuck. Is that bomb dogs?* And it freaks me out a bit and then I hear Spanish and recognize Hernandez's voice so I call out to him, like, Hey fucker I almost wasted you, and I take another couple steps and there's a bunch of rustling and commotion and then screaming and so I pop on my SureFire and there's Hernandez on the ground maybe fifteen meters away and I can't see him except a leg because there're like ten dogs jumping all over him, yipping and barking and growling, trying to pull his pant legs and shit, and I don't even think, just rack my rifle to condition one and drop the first dog I sight on. Rest bounced quick.

After Hernandez, Command had us set out food full of rat poison around the PB, and guys got touchy about that. Yeah, we were in a war, killing people for digging holes on the side of the road, and yeah, the dogs had fucked up Hernandez, but they're just dogs, they said; and We aren't here to kill dogs, we're here to kill the enemy; and There's no honor in killing dogs, especially with poison; and This is a bullshit waste of taxpayer money; and Isn't there a real mission we need to execute, and, anyway, isn't this just like Command to make a problem in the first place, and then we're the ones who suffer the consequences and have to fix it?; and Dogs are man's best friend; and I don't want to go back home and tell people all I did was kill dogs. I'd rather kill people.

It went on and on.

I was fucking happy for it. Fuck those mutts, right? Was thinking of the sheep.

Anyway, the dogs were too smart to take it, the poison, and then we got overrun by flies from all the rotting food.

Command put Sergeant Moss in charge of a solution. He took us out to the trash pit for a recon.

Could make a hunting blind, Sergeant, said Crowe.

No, PFC Crowe, we won't be doing that, said Sergeant Moss.

You'd get one, maybe two before they scattered, said Nguyen.

PFC Cobb, Lance Corporal Pusey, any ideas? said Sergeant Moss.

Knew he already had a plan mapped out, that this was a test.

I like dogs, Sergeant, said Cobb.

These ain't dogs, güey, said Ruiz.

We're not fucking dogcatchers, man, said Baptiste.

L-shaped ambush, I said, but no one heard me.

Didn't say we were dogcatchers, said Ruiz. I said *these ain't dogs*. Who gives a shit about these mangy fucks? You want to adopt one? Take it home? Get on, like, fucking *Good Morning America* or whatever?

Cala a boca, said Baptiste.

Both of you shut your fucking sucks, said Sergeant Moss. Pusey?

L-shaped ambush, Sergeant, I said.

Give him one, said Sergeant Moss.

Kill, they all said.

Corporal Ruiz, you and I will set your fire team in the defilade position. Corporal Nguyen, your fire team will take the enfilade position. Lance Corporal Baptiste, we'll see about getting you a SAW for the night. I'll take the first shot. When I do, the rest of you open up. Aim for the center of the pack. Go clean weapons, eat chow. Rally back here at nineteen hundred.

Took three days to burn the bodies.

When we got to the flea market, the gravel lot out front was packed. But Max didn't care. She was looking for a bargain—the kind of person who didn't toss things. Held on to them, tried to figure out how to clean them up, spit and polish. Make them better, new. Like, all her furniture came from thrift stores, Goodwill or whatever. She fixed and refinished it all. Patched it up. Held on to her clothes. Sewed them. Knew how to sew. She was an old soul like that.

She'd been on her own for a long time, taking care of herself—college on her own, job on her own, apartment on her own. So, yeah, compared to that stuck-in-the-past, repeating high school reunion at the Speed Rail? She was goddamned ancient.

The market looked like a giant red barn—two stories trimmed in white; must've spanned what would've been an entire city block.

Inside, at the wings, there were rooms full of antiques that looked high-end and expensive but in the middle were market stalls—crafts, wood-work, airbrushed T-shirts, knitted fucking dog collars, used clothes and furniture, homemade salsa and sauerkraut, local honey, all kinds of shit. The ceiling at the center was vaulted and the noise of people talking rolled over whatever easy-listening-radio bullshit they were pumping through the sound system. People wrapped in winter jackets moved from booth to booth, smiling and talking, sipping coffee from paper cups, holding hands. It was the kind of place that set my teeth and sent my shoulders to my ears.

Oh! said Max. This honey is the best. You've got to try it.

Great, I said. I love honey.

She led me through the crowd to a table covered in mason jars full of honey where another couple maybe in their early thirties were chatting up the older woman behind the table, who was bundled in enough snivel gear for a goddamned Arctic expedition.

Barb, the guy said to the older woman, this is unbelievable—the color, the bouquet—

The younger woman interrupted, Oh, the bouquet—

The guy interrupted back, The *mouthfeel.*

Babe, said the woman. Yes, Barb. We just love it so much.

I'm so glad, said Barb. Bless you.

So, so much, said the guy.

The guy and the woman stepped to the side and positioned the jar of honey they'd bought and started taking high- and low-angle pictures. Watching them do that while Barb looked on, while other people walked around them, glanced in their direction, maybe talked about them, made fun of them, made me embarrassed.

Barb turned toward us, said hello, asked if we wanted to sample anything.

Can I try the blackberry? And the wildflower? Oh, and the alfalfa? said Max.

Barb prepared three small paper sample cups, each with a tiny wooden spoon, and placed them in front of Max. I shifted on my feet, looked around, checked my six. The guy and the woman were talking excitedly and laughing and I wondered if that's the kind of thing Max wanted, if it was the kind of thing I wanted. Did the new me want to be an Insta-boyfriend? Was I going to be someone who said *mouthfeel* without expecting to get socked in the fucking face? Was I going to be the kind of guy who knew what *mouthfeel* was?

Dean, you've got to try this, said Max. The wildflower. So good.

Get a jar of it, I said, and took out my wallet. I had cash this time, had made sure of it.

Just try it first, she said, holding the miniature spoon up to my mouth, the cup underneath catching a slow drizzle of honey.

I opened my mouth and let her put in the spoon.

So? she said.

Wow, I said. That mouthfeel. I shook my head.

That made her laugh and we bought a jar of the wildflower honey and thanked Barb, who told us to have a blessed day, which got under my skin because who the fuck was Barb the honey seller to bless me? And then we walked around the stalls, and when we passed one full of cruci-fixes and needlepointed pillows with biblical quotes, I asked Max if she believed in God.

I think so, she said.

I nodded.

Then she said, No.

I laughed and thought about Ruiz in the PB. How sure he'd been. I wasn't so sure. I was happy Max wasn't, either.

Yes and no? she said. I'm a recovering Catholic, I guess. I go to church sometimes when I'm lonely. I don't think there's, like, some old man in the sky, but I get feelings sometimes.

Feelings? I said.

Yeah, she said. Like in a place like this. Places with lots of people all close together. I get feelings. I guess you could call it God.

And just like that, we quit dancing around the real shit and dove right in—God, family, the deep dark. Then she asked about the Marines, because of course she was going to ask about it. I told her I didn't want it to be the only thing that made me. Which was true.

We walked the entire place talking, and it was like that kind of shit you see in movies: the talk came easy. Max found a chair she wanted to buy but it wouldn't fit in her car and I acted like the guy from the honey stall and called her babe and made her pose with the chair like I was taking fancy photos for Instagram and she laughed more and then I said maybe we could come up again except we'd take my truck so we could haul something bigger and she said, Yeah. Definitely next time. And then we went back to the car with our jar of honey and drove home listening to another podcast.

The entire time I kept thinking, *What the fuck does she see in me? What is going on? How did I fall into this thing? What does she want from me?* And so when she dropped me off at my Mom's house I said, What is happening here?

I'm dropping you off, she said.

No, I said, and motioned between us back and forth.

I like you, she said. You're a good guy. You make me laugh.

Same things she'd said in the car and at her apartment when she found me running down the road.

And you think about things. And you're a little dark and twisty. And you're nice. And I want to see you again. Keep seeing you.

Yeah, I said. Me too.

WEEK BEFORE CHRISTMAS, I posted that picture of Max posing with the chair to my Instagram page. I liked that it was just Max. Nothing of me. She was sharp. Her eyes reminded me of sage bushes from the Backyard on Camp San Mateo but then I decided that was wrong; they looked like the black walnut leaves on the trees that lined the neighborhood where I'd grown up.

Posting the picture against all the guns and middle fingers and sand felt good. Like I'd drawn a goddamned line in that sand, and on one side was the war and Ruiz and the sheep and all the fucking high school, civilian shitheads who kept asking me if I'd killed anyone and on the other was me and Max and the newness I was making for myself.

That same night, Penny texted that she'd seen the picture and that she'd bring her girlfriend to Christmas if I brought mine.

Not my gf, I texted.

Whatevs. You're like an Insta-boyf, she texted.

I regretted posting the picture—felt like a hangover. Like I'd done something wrong, a kid who'd snuck sweets and had chocolate smeared all over his face. Couldn't catch my breath.

I'll be in town tomorrow. Beer and catch up? Can't wait to see youuuuuuu brooooooo!!! she texted.

What about your gf? I texted.

Iris is doing early Xmas with her fam in Chi, she texted.

Ok, I texted.

Chicago, she texted.

[thumbs up emoji] I texted.

She'll be there Xmas eve, she texted.

Sounds good. At work. Got to go, I texted.

It's midnight what are you doing at work??? she texted.

The conveyor in front of me powered up and I shoved my phone in my back pocket.

On the night sort I loaded package cars, not semis. I was in charge of three cars each night and morning; it was still peak, so the night sort combined with the preload and ran from midnight to six or seven in the morning. Once peak ended the shifts would separate—night sort from eleven at night to three in the morning and preload from four in the morning until eight in the morning. Some guys called it sunrise, got all bent out of shape when you called it the preload. I guess *preload* didn't make them feel special. Either one was bullshit. It was the graveyard shift.

It was killing me.

Most of the guys on graveyard were older—thirties and forties—and aside from the belt motors and spinning rollers, the warehouse was quiet: no one talked shit about fucking anyone's sister or mom, no peacock calls, no one screamed to break jams. Dudes drifted through the motions of the shift like ghosts, chatted on break about their kids and wives and weekend plans, went home.

The shit of it was I couldn't figure out my sleep schedule: the pattern and rhythm of it was all screwy so that I'd go a couple days at a time without sleep. It fucked me up. I'd get this ringing—not in-my-ears kind of ringing, but at-the-base-of-my-skull ringing, like something-was-drilling-into-my-brain kind of ringing. And then my eyeball—the one the bar hicks had busted against the wall, which I couldn't close the eyelid all the way over anymore—would start twitching and I'd imagine the bone seam of my grape splitting open like a busted zipper, my brain swelling and pulsing and pushing on my eyeball from the inside.

The overhead fluorescent lights were even worse at night—made the shadows deeper so everything was washed-out white or pitch-black—and I started catching these little flutters out of my busted eye in the deep, dark, nothing shadows, and I fucking *knew* it was Ruiz or the sheep or maybe those wilds dogs—that they'd followed me home from those fallow fields out by Court's the first night I'd gone home with Max.

I'd get distracted staring into those shadows, trying to make them step into the blinding white, and I'd end up letting a few boxes go by I should've loaded. My new shift supervisor, Grant, a weekend warrior Army Reserve captain, got on me about it. But not like Tyler or Sergeant Moss.

Are you all right, Dean? he said.

No, I didn't say.

There are ghosts here, I didn't say.

Yes, I didn't say.

What I said: not a goddamned thing. Just went back to work. Guy reminded me of Chaps—that soft smile, close talking, *I care* bullshit. He kept on.

You know, transitioning to civilian life is hard for a lot of people. Sometimes it helps to talk. Just know that I'm here if you ever want to.

Want to what? I said.

Talk, he said.

Grant was tall and lean, somehow tan in the middle of winter, wore an expensive puffer coat, stood with his hands on his hips like some fucking superhero; stood like that was the only way to stand.

I thought about the fat and happy TAP instructor. *It'll eat the world alive.* What did Grant know about it? Fuck all. Guy was a goddamned accountant or some shit. Anyway, no one could get their fucking story straight: Keep it in. Don't air the dirty laundry. Let it out in tiny breaths. Talk. Let it all out.

For a split second I wanted to drop-kick the box in my hands right into Grant's face and spear him off the catwalk and go to work on him, juice his cheeks with my knuckles, let the wet-flesh slap of punches echo in the warehouse in place of all the grinding machinery, ease the ringing in my skull.

But whatever was inside me, flaring, swelling, pushing to get out, all of a sudden deflated. Like I was just too goddamned tired of it all. I shuffled into the truck like a floppy cock and loaded the box where it was supposed to go and out of the corner of my eye, I swear, I saw Grant hovering, but when I went to tell him I was fucking fine, there was nothing there.

★

Three months left of our first deployment, during a mounted patrol, an IED went off next to our second truck. Buried too deep and too far away from the road to do damage. No one hurt. Sergeant Moss had us check our fives and twenty-fives, then push out for overwatch. That's when we spotted the bird-chested teenager with the snot in his peach fuzz mustache running from the scene and rolled him up.

After we got him back to the PB and Doc finished the intake, the human intelligence exploitation team got down to business—put the kid in the high kneeling. Rough, unfinished concrete bit into his knees, and when he tried to rearrange himself, redistribute his weight, one of the HET guys, a brown dude who might've been Middle Eastern, screamed Arabic at him and boxed his ears or slapped him across the face with a rolled-up newspaper while the other guy, white guy, smiled and asked him calm questions. Good cop, bad cop. It wasn't the first time I'd watched them do it.

Fifteen minutes later the HET guys told us that the kid might've been up to some shit, but there wasn't enough evidence to keep him detained. Explosive residue tests are unreliable, the brown guy said, and the white guy just kept on shrugging and sighing and finally said to take the kid back to where we grabbed him.

Ruiz was pissed.

Dog, if this was last deployment? he said. We would've just popped two in the motherfucker's grape when we saw him running and said he showed hostile intent.

Nguyen nodded and said, Hearts and minds. People back home don't have the stomach for what needs to get done, so we're just cops now. Keeping the peace.

Nah, dog, said Ruiz. Cops fucking shoot people.

I'm going to be a cop when I get out, said Cobb.

Shut the fuck up, boot, said Ruiz.

Ruiz wasn't usually like that. Cobb sank into his gear like a turtle.

The high-back jostled and bumped down the road on the way back to where we'd found the kid. We'd flex-cuffed his hands behind his back again and his head lolled like he might be sleeping.

Do you guys think that JLo tape is even real? said Baptiste, who was next to Ruiz.

Mujahadeen, said Ruiz, and reached across the truck and slapped the kid above his ear, but the kid didn't look up, which pissed Ruiz off even more.

Ali Baba, he said, and kicked the kid's shins; the kid still didn't look up.

Ruiz pulled the M-nine from the pistol holster he'd rigged to his chest and put it in the kid's face. None of us said shit while the kid squirmed and cried and spoke in broken English. Nguyen and Cobb on either side of the kid leaned away.

Part of me wanted Ruiz to pull the trigger, thought about his rough finger pressed against the metal as it had pressed into my thigh while he asked if I was nervous, or into the space behind my balls right before I'd come, and then the kid pissed himself, a dark spot spreading across his crotch, and Nguyen shot up from the soaked bench seat.

Nasty motherfucker! said Nguyen. Goddamn!

Cobb escaped the piss and we all laughed at Nguyen. Ruiz put his M-nine back in the holster.

When we got to the village where we'd snatched up the kid, before we could cut his flex-cuffs and kick him out and send him on his way, a woman appeared, came screaming toward our convoy, and we all, all the dismounts, drew down on her until AJ, the terp we'd taken with us, popped out of the command truck and told us she was thanking us for bringing home her son.

We let the kid go and the minute his feet hit the dirt the woman turned to a flurry of slaps and yelling while the kid was trying to talk and defend himself but she hit hard.

We all laughed and watched, egged her on until she ran out of breath and the kid managed to run away into the house. Speaking Arabic, the woman gestured to us and pointed toward the two-story building where the kid had run.

She would like to know, said AJ, if you would be wanting some chai and some samoon.

The woman led us to the two-story house. Four kids chased one another in the courtyard and ran away when the woman shouted and waved at them. Inside, Sergeant Moss and AJ followed the woman to the family room and talked to her while the rest of us from the high-back cleared the house.

When we made it to the sleeping roof, Ruiz let Sergeant Moss know over the Motorola radio on his flak we'd taken an overwatch position, then he lit cigarettes for us and we stood quiet, looking south into the desert.

The sky was lead, still and gray, and faded into sand that reminded me of the old, decaying deer bones Court and I would find in the forest behind his house, so that everything in the distance bled together.

Just beyond the village was a local cemetery—a mix of vaults and headstones—and to the east of that cemetery an unobstructed view of the supply route intersection where our patrol had been hit that morning.

Ruiz radioed to Sergeant Moss about the view, crossed himself, took a drag from his cigarette, and held it.

Reminds me of home, I said.

The fuck, dog? said Ruiz. Ain't you live in the fucking woods or whatever?

I mean the cemetery, I said. Tons of old cemeteries near, like, main roads and highways and shit. We'd get drunk and play Ghost in the Graveyard in them.

White nonsense, he said.

We laughed.

Then I thought I heard someone scream—high and shrill, kind of like a kid, a baby. It was distant. An echo. All around me. Creeped me out. The graveyard and all.

Fuck was that? I said.

Ruiz shook his head. I don't fuck with cemeteries, he said.

Ghosts aren't real, I said.

Last deployment? he said. This dude fucking wanders up to the entry control point we were manning just outside the city. Dude's out past curfew but he stops when Nguyen tells him to. La tataharak, Nguyen says, all hard and shit to the dude—you know Nguyen, moto as fuck, he can't just tell dude to stop. Anyway, the dude, he stops on a fucking dime. Arfae yudik, Nguyen says, and dude's hands shoot to the sky. We're coming up on him then and dude looks fucked-up—fucking gash on the right side of his face dumping blood, man dress all fucking torn and shit.

So I call over the radio for a corpsman and we're about to flex-cuff this motherfucker and get HET on him because we're thinking either he's muj or muj just fucked him up over some shit when he starts talking perfect fucking English, but like English that don't make sense. Like, his words sound good or whatever, but they don't fucking mean nothing and he keeps repeating it over and over.

What was it? I said.

Fucking just, like, gibberish or whatever, he said. Shit like Spit bowl sizzle broken hole dead blast spit sizzle, and, like, it all runs together, but I look at Nguyen and I'm, like, Did you hear this motherfucker just say blast and dead? And he's all Fuck yeah, I did. And so he radios the SOG again and lets him know and then the corpsman shows up with a couple other bodies to take dude away and we're about to put him in flex-cuffs and he fucking looks at us and goes stiff as a board.

I mean fucking statue, dog, he said. Like, this motherfucker froze.

Then he moved his head real slow over his right shoulder, like this, he said. Yeah, that fucking slow, and looks out into the dark and starts screaming, top of his fucking lungs, screaming. No words or nothing. Just screaming. And then he drops.

What the fuck does that have to do with cemeteries? I said.

Shut the fuck up, all right? he said. Couple days later, dude finally comes to, can't speak a fucking word of English now, but tells the HET guys in Arabic he's a gravedigger. Says he was finishing his work and this little girl wandered up to him, told him she was lost, and scared, asked for his hand. What are you doing lost in a graveyard? I said to her, dude says. And the little girl told him, I'm here with my mother. Can you help me find her? I think she went toward the center of the cemetery. That's where my father is buried.

It was getting dark and almost curfew and dude knows we got itchy trigger fingers in the dark but he's a good guy, he says. And just wants to help the girl, so he takes her hand and walks her toward the center of the cemetery.

We knew the place. It was pretty big, surrounded by these date fields. Anyway, they've been walking and calling for the girl's mother and dude says he must've lost track of time because the sun's down now and he doesn't remember it setting.

Then he notices that the hand in his hand isn't little anymore.

It's big. Like, fucking huge, wrapped around his, fingers all long and bony, and when he turns to look at the little girl it's not the little girl, it's this too-tall, thin, old woman with no face dressed all in black. I woke up here, dude says. I can feel her still in me. And then he just starts crying, scratching and scraping at his arms and face, drawing blood and shit, until some corpsman sedated him.

You're just trying to freak me out, I said.

Shit in this world we don't know, all I'm saying, he said.

In the UPS warehouse, shadows had me thinking about all that shit in the world we don't know. After a few days of graveyard and avoiding Grant, I'd either pass out from exhaustion in the middle of the day while falling down an internet hole of Max's Insta page or adoption websites or sometimes reading Ruiz's obituary or I'd text Court to hook me up with a few Ativan.

Was still tired after the Ativan. Kind of tired that tightens you, wrings you out like a soggy towel. It'd never done that to me when Doc stuffed us full of them on the Freedom Bird headed back stateside, but my brain wasn't as cloudy afterward with what Court was giving me at least, so I said fuck it and took them when I needed to.

Sometimes even when I didn't just to make sure.

Didn't feel like explaining any of that to Penny or about why I was at work at midnight in the first place. She'd already texted me a handful of times since even before I got home, talking like:

Is there a VA in Richfield?

Where's the nearest one??

You should see what kind of services they offer!

There are some vets in my grad program, can I give them your number???

Fuck that. Wasn't a goddamned malingerer, some shitbird trying to get a couple hundred a month for back pain or tinnitus or whatever. Didn't want any more of their fucking money. Fuck did Penny know about anything? Not really your sister, Court had said.

When I asked Court what had happened to the guy I'd choked out at the party, he said someone took him to the hospital, but he didn't know anything else, just kept saying that the guy was into him for a couple yards, so who fucking cared?

I'd been keeping Court at one-arm's distance. Was convinced he was like the Marine Corps: something I had to leave behind to move forward. Anytime he texted about the Speed Rail or El Dorado or shooting clays or a party, I'd think about that ancient, ugly-ass, fucking shark gliding through the cold, dark ocean he loved so much and the deformed adopted dolphin flicking and bucking its way along with the sperm whales, trying to keep up.

I'd text, *Got to work*, and he'd shoot back a bunch of eye-rolling or angry emoji.

It was true. Did have to work. Made time for Max, though.

Max didn't give a shit about Animal Planet or big TVs or guns. She watched these snappy shows full of bright light and women who talked so fast I never knew what the fuck they said. And she was like that, too—quick and funny. Impatient. Didn't give a shit that I couldn't keep up or didn't get the pop culture references.

She'd gone to a community college in Michigan and was saving up to transfer for her bachelor's at Indiana University—didn't like the idea of owing anyone anything—and had taken a job at an insurance company in Richfield as an underwriter because of the money.

She had only asked a little about the Marines, kind of timid questions. Usually she was probing and prodding hard. Forcing a conversation. Wasn't like her—the caution—or wasn't like how she acted otherwise. How long had I been in? Where had I deployed? Did I miss it? So I answered, sure I did. Kept it simple: that I'd just gotten out, that I'd been to Iraq, that I didn't want it to be the only thing I'd done with my life. But nothing about the sheep or the dogs or Ruiz or the teenager or IEDs.

She didn't know I had new hours at work, that I'd been transferred, or anything about Turtle. I was looking for a new place to start over, and the night of Court's party felt like *it*.

Less I told her about everything before that moment, the more it all faded, the more I believed I could leave it all behind me. I was so young. Seemed so simple back then: turn the page. Leave the past behind. Max made me feel like that, and because of it I wanted to be with her every goddamned second. Like, in-country guys had good luck charms or pre-patrol rituals or whatever to keep their number from popping. That was Max for me. But the minute I walked out of her apartment, I was back in the suck.

I rotated a box on the conveyor, looking for the load designation sticker that told me if it was for my truck. It was. I hefted the box and was about to walk it into the dingy package car and place it on the shelf where the load designation sticker told me to place it when Rithipol, this wiry Cambodian who went by Rith and worked the three trucks across the conveyor from me, said, Not yours, Marine Corps.

He hadn't spoken to me since I'd started working across from him. Grant had told me his name, that he was Cambodian, a Navy vet, corpsman, blue side—not green side with the Marines. It was hard to guess his age.

I looked at the box again, and he was right: the code wasn't what I'd thought. Not even close. I squinted my eyes trying to figure out how I'd seen the number wrong. Tried to remember how long it had been since I'd slept.

While I stood on the catwalk, mean mugging the bold black alphanumeric code like some lobotomy patient, Rith shoved four boxes that were mine to my side and reached across the conveyor for the one in my hands.

Come on, he said. It's not a box of crayons. Can't eat it, Marine Corps.

I gave it over and went to grab the boxes I'd let pass, and as I walked past the other package cars, something in the shadows flittered and skipped along with me.

The next night I got to the Speed Rail before Penny. It was five o'clock and dead inside. Some guys at the bar watched golf on ESPN Classic and a couple drank beer and whisper-fought in a dark corner. I wished I'd chosen a place drenched in light, but it was too late to text Penny and change up the location, so I took a booth with a buzzing overhead lamp.

Part of me had hoped the bar hicks would be there, which is why I'd chosen the place. I was relieved, too, I guess. All those nerves Ruiz and I had deadened in body-hardening sessions were finally growing back.

I stood for a moment in the fatal funnel to shed my coat and didn't check the corners of the bar and didn't think one goddamned time about what complacency got you. I was soft. My hair had finally grown over the patch of scalp and my old skivvy shirts were tight around my chest and waist; I'd quit wearing them. I had beard stubble; it tickled Max, made her laugh when we kissed, and I liked that—when her face flexed into a smile, lips stretching against mine, our teeth clicking. Bone on bone.

When a waitress came around, I ordered a pitcher and two glasses and wished I was more excited to see Penny. Knew how she would look at me—like she wanted to say, *I told you so*, like I was some ugly goddamned pound dog that would never get adopted.

And she *had* told me. After I told her and my mom I'd signed up during Christmas break my senior year.

Just tell me why, Penny had said. Give me a reason.

It's just something I feel like I have to do, I said.

Dean, she said, and took a deep breath. That's such bullshit.

She was right. It was bullshit. I joined up because I thought I wanted out of Indiana and hadn't taken the SAT and felt stupid asking how the fuck else I was supposed to get to college, get out of Richfield. Didn't even really know why I wanted out of Richfield.

Didn't know what I didn't know. Motherfuckers would rather die than ask for help. Ruiz had probably said that shit to me once.

Penny and me and my mom, we were in the kitchen when she'd asked me. Penny stood with her hands on her hips. My mom ran a mixer at the counter, making cookies. She had a couple days off and was trying to do mom things. I leaned against the fridge and texted Court about a party at his grandma's place.

Mom, tell him that's bullshit, said Penny.

Language, said my mom.

Mom, said Penny.

He's eighteen, said my mom.

My mom didn't turn around when she said that—just shrugged her shoulders, rubber spatula flinging cookie dough through the air, and went back to work. Maybe she didn't really think I'd go through with it if she didn't make a big deal of it. I knew it bothered her. Maybe she didn't feel like she had a say because Penny was the one who'd been around—made my lunches, got me ready for school, washed my sheets and clothes. But Penny had been away for five years. She liked to think she still knew me, but she didn't. Families are like that, right? Little fucking time capsules. Never see you as anything but what you were.

You and Dad protested Vietnam, said Penny.

That was your father, my mom said. I never cared for politics.

You really want to die for someone else's oil? said Penny.

No, I said. I really want to go to Court's.

The rest of the visit she lectured me on Middle East foreign policy and the zero-sum game of war and being on the right side of history. She showed me videos of Rumsfeld addressing Congress, Iraq War protests staged by vets, documentaries about the realities of the military-industrial complex. She gave me books about masculinity and violence.

I'd shrugged my shoulders to all of it. I didn't give a shit about WMD or illegal wars or freedom or anything. I'd looked at the people around me—teachers, parents, friends—and I didn't want their fucking lives. I hated them and myself and everyone and the entire goddamned world and I wanted to burn it all down.

I wanted to hurt people, be hurt. I didn't know why—my adoption, my dad leaving, fucking puberty. I didn't give a shit.

A few weeks before Christmas break, a recruiter in the cafeteria at lunch had showed a group of us YouTube videos of Marines leveling Fallujah. I wrote my name and number down on his list. Simple as that.

The new me had told Max I'd joined for the GI Bill benefits—that I was going back to school, that I was waiting for my UPS bennies to kick in after a year so I could double-dip. Wondered if I could sell that to Penny, if she'd buy it, if she'd leave it alone.

Sweat broke out in my cracks and crevices thinking about all the questions Penny, who wasn't even in the bar yet, hadn't even asked, and my tiny little breaths caught in my lungs thinking about all the things I'd have to talk about if she asked those questions—the sheep, the dogs, Ruiz, the Iraqi teenager, Sergeant Moss, bar fights, bar women, bodies, blood, Max.

The list got longer and longer and a tightness near my heart pulled me in toward my beer and I thought of the Iraqi kid's funnel chest, how his entire body seemed to curve around the bowl in his torso while he stood there crying, begging us for his life he didn't know we weren't going to take. *Hostile intent. Two in his grape. You good, dog. Not really your sister. Ain't nothing like dropping your fucking pack. La tataharak. Dead blast spit sizzle. Dean, are you okay? Are you all right, Dean? Tiny little breaths. You're good at keeping secrets. Let it all out. You a monster, dog.*

All of a sudden I was tired—kind of tired where you have to tell your body to do things it normally does automatically. Squirt of piss left the tip of my prick and I had to focus to keep my bladder from letting go, to keep my heart pumping, my eyelids open.

When I looked up, there was Penny standing next to the booth, and for a moment I was scared: it was like she'd stepped out of the shadows, like she'd been in all those dark spots with Ruiz and the sheep and the dogs the entire time. Some kind of ghost. *Things in this world we don't understand.*

God, you look like shit, she said.

Are you a ghost? I didn't say.

You're not really my sister, I didn't say.

I'm going to take an Ativan and go to sleep, I didn't say.

What I said: It's a cold. Not used to this shitty weather. I'm a California boy now.

Get up and give me a hug, she said. Do Marines give hugs?

I stood and let her wrap her arms around me. Her head came to my chest and she rested her cheek there and I felt delicate face muscles tensing as she clenched her eyes and tears soaked through my shirt; my heart dropped into a regular rhythm without me willing it to double-time and my breathing steadied.

I missed you, she said.

People are starting to stare, I said.

She laughed and sniffed and pulled away and wiped her eyes. Then cleared her throat and sat, poured herself a beer, and took a big drink.

So, she said.

I took a drink. Could've asked her about classes or Iris or teaching or her pets or anything, really, but part of me—the part that had hoped the bar hicks would be there—wanted to make it hard on her, you know? So I didn't say anything, just sat there all good order and discipline, waiting for her to speak.

Oh! I meant to text you, she said. I saw this writer read some essays from a memoir last month? And she was a veteran who'd been to Iraq.

Yeah? I said.

It was so *real* and the writing was breathtaking and during the Q and A she talked about how writing helped her, she said.

How do you know? I said.

What? she said.

How do you know how real it was? I said.

Penny took a drink.

Probably some officer fobbit trying to talk up a couple bullshit mortar attacks, I said.

I think you would've liked it is all, she said.

Tapped my phone screen to see if there was a message from Max. Knew Penny hated it when people looked at their phones during a conversation.

How does it feel to be home? she said.

All right, I guess, I said.

I'm sorry I wasn't here when you got back, she said.

It's okay, I said.

How's work? she said.

It's money, I said.

Have you looked at colleges yet? she said. There are some great schools on the West Coast. I go on the job market this spring. You could live with me and save on rent.

Jesus, I said.

What? she said. You've been home for a couple months. It's going to feel harder and harder to apply and most applications are due soon. I don't go back until February. I'll go to whatever campuses with you to check them out if you want. We could take a week and just go.

Where was that five years ago? I said.

What's that mean? she said.

Nothing, I said. You're worse than Mom.

What about a therapist? she said. You've been through significant trauma. The vets in my program said that's really important—to talk it out. I could give you their numbers. They said it was okay.

I laughed. Wasn't anything wrong with me; it was that everyone— Penny, my mom, Grant, whoever the fuck—expected there to be something wrong with me.

Max was the only person who didn't make me feel broken. Maybe because I hadn't told her who I really was. Maybe if she knew, she'd feel the same as all the others. Maybe it was only a matter of time.

Started thinking that it wasn't even the Marines or the war: that it was *me*, something radiating out of me—some kind of fucking sickness. Maybe my birth mom knew I was fucked-up from the get-go.

I'm trying to help, she said.

I thought of Turtle in the trailer.

I don't need help, I said.

We got quiet and drank our beers and I could tell I'd hurt her, that she was thinking about making a break for it, and the hard-ass in me softened.

I'm just waiting until I've got a year at UPS, I said. They pay for school. I can double-dip between that and the GI Bill along with the housing allowance and bank some savings.

That's a plan, I guess, she said.

I knew Penny thought that if I didn't make a move soon, I'd be stuck in Richfield. For her, that was a maximum-security life sentence.

During whatever break from school, when we were stuck in the house with nothing to do, before she'd left for college, she'd dog on Richfield— flat jokes, corn jokes, hick jokes, boring jokes. Penny wasn't really joking; she was pissed at our parents for moving and that anger had leveled up to some true hate and discontent toward Indiana, but she was funny about it—I'd laugh so that my jaw ached and it got hard to breathe—and I remember thinking during every single one of those moments that I wanted to swallow her up, fit her inside of me so she'd be with me forever, so she couldn't run away.

Tried to remember what that felt like.

Eventually, during those long, boring days, she'd end up telling stories about Washington—our old house, the apartment before me, haystack rocks on the coast, Mom teaching her how to ski in the mountains. Always got a kick out of that. Mom skiing. Couldn't even picture it. Hard to see your parents as real people.

Anyway, after grad school Penny planned to move back to the Northwest. Had always talked about it as if it would be both of us. Like life would be different there. Like that was where we belonged. She talked a big game, but she had a life—her own life. And that would come first.

Like, the summer I was eleven, Penny, Mom, and I, we went to the quarry to swim. Because Mom hated getting wet—it took her an hour to finally wade in past her knees—she made Penny take me in, which I didn't mind because we were close like that, but I was probably getting old for it. Anyway, the quarry dropped out quick, like I said before.

I wasn't a bad swimmer or anything, but it freaked me out, thinking about what might be down there, and Penny always wanted to swim out past the buoys that marked the drop-off to the pontoon where all the high schoolers sunned themselves and played King of the Mountain and grab-ass and whatever. Usually I won her over and we stayed shallow and played Marco Polo and then hit the snack shack for ice cream, but that day she'd had it.

Come *on*, she said treading water on the far side of the buoys.

I don't want to, I said.

I'm going, she said.

Mom said we're supposed to stay together, I said.

God, you're a fucking baby, she said, and pulled toward the pontoon.

So I followed her. She pulled away fast. It got cold after the drop-off and I panicked. Thought about all that dark nothing below me. Things that lived down there. Things with eyes and teeth and tentacles. Swore weeds reached up from the deep, grabbed at my legs, curled around my ankles, were trying to pull me down. With all the shallow little breaths, I couldn't keep my body afloat and I slipped under, clawed my way back to the surface, spit water, tried to yell for help but swallowed more water, didn't see Penny anywhere, slipped under again. Sank faster that time, pressure hit my ears and the cold shocked me, and I shot to the surface and reached out farther than I thought I could with my eyes still closed and felt the rough rope connecting the drop-off marker buoys in my palm.

When I got back to the beach, Mom asked me where Penny was.

Snack shack, I said.

Spent the rest of the day baking in the sun. Never told anyone what happened.

I was being unfair, holding a grudge, making an excuse. But, really, life didn't seem different to me anywhere. It was all the same: Washington was Indiana was California was fucking Al Anbar. Plus I didn't remember Washington, and the thought of being in the same state where my birth mom most likely lived and not knowing who she was made me want to rip off my skin.

Every woman I passed who looked middle-aged, I'd wonder, *What if that's her? What if that's her? What if that's her? What if she's dead? What if she moved? What if she had other kids?* What if? What if? What if? What if grasshoppers had motherfucking machine guns? It was too much, you know?

Whatever. The fat, happy fuck was right. What's the point in dredging up the past? That seemed to be all Penny wanted to do: not just an afteraction; she wanted to quarterback everything—get me to talk about the war, get me back to the Northwest, move my clock backward, keep me locked up where she thought I belonged.

There isn't a point to any of that. It's the kind of shit that drops guys into mindset black: Should I have done this? Should I have done that? I've seen it happen, just like Sergeant Moss said.

Anyway, sitting across from Penny, I wished the bar hicks would walk in. I wanted to speed up time right then.

Dean, said Penny. There's just not a lot of opportunity here.

The way she said my name reminded me of Bob and I knew then that she wasn't really listening, that she wasn't interested in taking my statement. That's what I thought then.

I love you, I didn't say.

I need you, I didn't say.

I don't want your life, I didn't say.

What I said: I'm excited to meet Iris. Who's watching the dog and cat?

Then I picked up my phone, snapped an aerial shot of the half-empty pitcher and our glasses on the table, and posted the pic to Insta with the caption: *Beers with seester. Good to be home!*

IF PENNY HAD an idea of who she wanted me to be, my potential, Mom had an idea of who she thought I was. Treated me like a kid. And, yeah, I was her kid, but it was like when she looked at me she saw that kid sitting on the beach, afraid to go in the water. So there I was, crushed between a memory and a fantasy, the weight of them like an overloaded ruck breaking my back. Kind of how I'd felt after I'd first gotten to the fleet—constant need to prove myself. Had to be bigger, stronger, faster. Really, I should've told Max my family had died in a plane crash or that they were a part of a suicide cult. Maybe something more believable like a car accident when I was a kid. That I was an orphan raised by the state with no real home to speak of. You feel like home, I could've told her.

At the Speed Rail a month and a half before, when she asked me if I loved my mother, I should've looked her right in the eye and spun some goddamned yarn, then burned that fucking bridge. Scratch that: wired it with det cord and blasting caps and C-four gotten some standoff distance with a timed fuse, plunged the igniter, blown the thing to fucking kingdom come, and walked away from the blast like a bad action movie hero. The should haves were just as bad as the what-ifs, though. It was all useless quarterbacking. Grasshoppers and machine guns.

The new part of me, the anyone part, wanted Max at the house for Christmas, and that new me was getting stronger; the edges were sharpening up; everything seemed brighter. Light cutting through early morning fog.

New me figured if I got Max around my family, it would show them that I wasn't this landed fish flopping around for breath. Like, See? Look at her. Can you see me like she does? *That* is who I am. *That* is who I've always been.

I wanted them all to stop looking at me like how I imagined my birth mom must've looked at fetus me on the ultrasound machine. Like I was a defective, some kind of monster. Or like how Sergeant Moss looked at me when he handed me the rock that morning in the fallow field. Like I should have been a goddamned abortion. Or like how the people at Court's had looked at me the night of the party, like I was going to lose my shit, start blowing people away, then blame it all on a goddamned dog—or maybe a sheep.

Thought about the Colt in my closet, my PMI from boot camp, Sergeant Moss, Court. *Don't anticipate the shot. Got to civilize you, boy. You all could've killed more. Slow is smooth; smooth is fast. Give him one! Kill.*

The Marine in me was still a door kicker looking for the next fight, and the line I'd drawn in the sand between the new me and the old me was just a line. Wasn't anything stopping the old me from stepping over— didn't know if there ever would be.

Anyway, that part of me was still in mindset orange, you know? On patrol in the shit, alert, watching an alternate supply route intersection from the roof of a mud hut next to a goddamned cemetery, ready to Mozambique—that's two in the chest, one in the head, otherwise known as a failure drill—some muj motherfucker trying to fill a hole with a one-five-five round or surface-lay an EFP.

That part of me didn't want Max anywhere near my family; it ground its teeth thinking about the embarrassing stories Penny and Mom would tell— like how when I was five or six I'd wear my mom's pantyhose and pretend to be a dancer or how I'd forgotten my lines in the school play in fourth grade and stood onstage and cried, ruined the whole thing. And I got hot about concerned looks Rick would give, how he would tiptoe around every little thing. How he would say my mom's name whenever she doted or lingered just a bit too long. *Gale*, he'd say. *Gale*.

Weakness, that's all they'd see: just some weak baby lost in the sauce; no impact, no idea. Max was the soft point in my defense.

It was all my fault anyway—the picture I'd uploaded to Insta of Max. First a bunch of Marines posted comments on it: *Jody gonna get ya girl. Yo dawg she blind?* That was shit I could stomach. I could give and get with those fucking jarheads. But then Penny had followed Max minutes after I'd posted the photo and dm'd her that she was excited to meet her at the party on Christmas Eve. She hadn't mentioned anything about it when we were at the bar, but Max showed me the next day, smiling. She said Penny seemed sweet. *She's not really my sister,* I wanted to say, but instead just said, Yeah, she's great. After that, I deleted the post. An old picture of the desert moved back onto the grid.

Anyway, Max was flying out Christmas Day to visit her parents through New Year, and like a fucking idiot, I'd told her I had a family, so I had to invite her to the party Christmas Eve or I'd seem like an even bigger asshole than she probably already thought I was for not inviting her before my sister had and also deleting a picture of her I'd posted—she'd asked if I was embarrassed of her and kind of sounded like she was joking, but like that serious kind of joking, and so I told her I was going to repost it, but just wanted to crop it and put a filter on it.

But, really, I hadn't wanted her there until I'd met Iris.

Iris and Rick were alone in the living room. He liked her; her dad was a carpenter, designed chairs and tables, owned a woodshop Rick had heard of and followed on Facebook. He'd scrolled through the feed, blabbing about joinery and finish techniques and whatever the fuck else, shoving picture after picture in front of my face. He was falling all over himself asking Iris questions like she knew any goddamned thing about woodworking.

Maybe she did. I liked Iris, too. She didn't thank me for my service and didn't bring up her cousin who'd been a Marine. It was Penny who'd brought him up the night before at the bar. He was in Baghdad, she'd said. He got injured, she'd said. Who gives a fuck? I'd wanted to say. Like Iris and I were supposed to be best buddies because her cousin got his bell rung? Who the fuck hadn't?

But, yeah, I liked Iris. She was short—shorter than Penny, who wasn't taller than five and a half feet—and thick in the middle and thighs. Hair was long and loose and so black it was like it pulled in everything around it. A black hole. She didn't smile much, and her eyes seemed serious. When she talked, she had this Southern twang that reminded me of the Marines I knew from Texas even though she was from South Carolina and her parents were from Oaxaca.

Was jealous of her. The way Penny looked at her. The way she put her hand on Penny's knee. The way Rick fawned over her. I thought of Penny swimming out to the raft at the quarry, leaving me floundering.

Max was late. I'd told her four in the afternoon—my family didn't eat a real meal on Christmas Eve; Mom just put out heaps of snacks and we all grazed until it ran out—and it was almost five. I tried not to care, but the Marine part of me was twitchy. Fifteen minutes prior to fifteen minutes prior—that hurry-up-and-wait nonsense. Good order and discipline.

Court texted: *Moms wants to know when ur coming tonite*

I wished I hadn't invited Max. I wished I didn't know her, hadn't met her. Wished I was at Court's, having Christmas Eve cocktails like they had every year and telling war stories when they eventually asked about what Iraq had been like.

We're just so glad you're home safe sweetie, his mom would say.

Yes, ma'am, I would say.

Just nuke the entire goddamned country. Turn it to glass, his dad would say.

Yes, sir, I would say.

Black-and-white. Simple.

Can't. Max coming over. Tell ur rents I said merry xmas, I texted.

Cold, bro, he texted.

For a gash??? he texted.

So much for family I guess, he texted.

I didn't text back. That was just Court. Dramatic. No big deal.

I went to the kitchen to grab a beer and my mom started giving me a hard time and that doubly pissed me off.

What's her name again? she said. Macy?

Max, Mom, I said. Her name is Max. Short for Maxine.

And she told you she was coming? she said. You talked to her?

She'll be here, I said.

I cracked the beer and stepped into the cold from the fridge, let it tighten my skin, hold me together. The wine mulling on the stove coated the kitchen in thick sweetness that made it hard to swallow. One of Rick's vinyls, an old Christmas album, played on the turntable.

Don't leave the door open! she said.

I shut it and tipped the beer to my lips.

You deserve a nice girl is all, she said.

I think Mom's asking if you have an imaginary girlfriend, said Penny, coming into the kitchen. Do we have any vodka, Mom? Iris likes vodka.

It's just weird I haven't met her is all, said Mom.

Maybe you're being catfished? said Penny. She'd found the vodka and started mixing a drink for Iris.

What's catfishing? said my mom. Is that like a kink? A *sex* kink?

Mom, I said.

Penny laughed. Please stop saying *kink*. I'm not nearly drunk enough for this conversation.

I saw it on *Dr. Phil*, said Mom, then turned to Penny and said, *Kinks.* We all laughed.

It's not a big deal, said Mom. You know Rick has a kink—

Penny interrupted her, My God, Mom. Stop.

Mom shook her head and took another drink and stirred the pot on the stove. I'm just saying it's perfectly natural is all, she said.

Catfishing is when a person pretends to be someone else online, said Penny.

I'm not being catfished—you've seen a picture of her, I said. Jesus Christ.

Don't say that, said my Mom.

Jesus Christ, I said. Jesus Christ. Jesus Christ. Jesucristo. I thought of Ruiz. *Vaya con Dios pinche puta.*

It's Christmas Eve, said Mom.

Why'd you delete it? said Penny. The picture. Anyway, it's, like, super easy to fake an identity online these days. More than a third of social media accounts are fake.

You know I saw that on *Dateline*, said my mom.

We went to a flea market together, I said. I've been to her apartment a ton.

Dateline doesn't lie, said Penny. She took a sip of the drink she'd made for Iris and walked out.

I texted Max, *ETA???*

In response three dots blinked and blinked and then disappeared, but no text showed up. I downed my beer and got another. My head hurt. I'd started getting these headaches deep behind the eye that didn't close all the way, like under the front of my brain. Ativan helped. Court had offered k-pin. He was thoughtful like that. I felt bad for ditching him and his family. Wanted to be a better friend.

In my room I swallowed an Ativan from the bottle I'd gotten from Court and downed the rest of my second beer. I sat in the dark on the futon that had been stripped and folded into a couch because we had company and pulled out my phone.

Max still hadn't texted back. I opened Insta and found Iris's profile. It was private. I didn't send a request. Who the fuck was she? Like she was so goddamned important. What'd she have to hide? I decided I didn't like her after all—the serious eyes and the unsmiling face. *Would it kill you to fucking smile?* I thought.

I scrolled my feed, glazing over pictures of people with their families and Merry Christmas wishes and stopped on Cobb's post. He'd uploaded a picture of our squad from after the high-back got hit by an IED. Wasn't serious. Bomb had been buried too deep to do much but jostle us around in the back, get our heads ringing. Mine had never really stopped. Tinnitus or whatever. Who didn't have tinnitus? Wasn't a big deal.

Sergeant Moss and our driver, Corporal Fox, got the worst of it. IED went off under the cab. They both had class three concussions, but Fox busted his jaw on the steering wheel and had to get evacuated to Balad. He eventually went to Germany and then stateside. When we got home a few months later he met us at the parade deck, his jaw still wired shut, and tossed us beers over the armory fence while we waited to turn in our weapons. He drank from a straw in his can.

Anyway, the picture was all of us: me, Ruiz, Cobb, Nguyen, Crowe, and Baptiste all standing in front of TQ surgical after the doctors had cleared us, smoking and looking like the walking dead while we waited for Sergeant Moss to be released. I don't know who took that picture. One of the gunners from the other Humvees—maybe Shepard or Letoa.

Cobb had turned the picture into a meme with white block letters over the top that read GODBLESS and then beneath us all in the dirt THE MARINE CORP. Fucking Cobb. I didn't know whether he hadn't had room for the *S*, if his brain really had been scrambled by that IED, or if he was that goddamned stupid he didn't know how to spell the name of his own branch of service.

Cobb had been made for the Marines, should've been on recruiting posters. He was a specimen, but he was a real goddamned knuckle-dragger. All the Army and Navy jokes about Marines eating crayons were because of guys like him. He just never really got it.

I flicked my thumb over the screen and took in his page—full of misspelled memes about liberal tears and snowflakes and 'Merica and Marine Corps moto sayings like *Pain is Weakness Leaving the Body* and dumb jokes about women making sandwiches but then a few rows down it was just picture after picture of the desert.

At first, I thought it might be the same picture posted over and over again, or that the Ativan and the beer was fucking with me, had slowed me down to where I hadn't caught up to what was really there. I shut my nonfiring eye and let the light of the phone into my other, sighted in, and realized all the pictures were different.

The shots were washed-out, almost flat, looked like orange paint sample cards in a home improvement store. They'd been taken by a disposable, probably, and then Cobb had snapped pictures of the pictures with his phone. But then in one, when I held the phone at an arm's distance, I could make out buildings in the background. Hard to tell at first because of all the orange, which I took for a sandstorm. Finally, I saw the images were all different angles of the intersection we'd watched from the Iraqi teen's house.

At the widow's house, when our relief—Cobb and Baptiste—showed up to the roof an hour or so after Ruiz had told me the story about the gravedigger, it was dark. We headed downstairs to get some chow and maybe pop off a workout before we racked out. Sergeant Moss had decided to take the house for a night to keep watch on the intersection. The rest of the platoon had gone back to the PB along with Corporal Fox and the high-back. It was just our squad and AJ the terp. The plan was to push out in the morning to a rally point north of the cemetery where the rest of the platoon would pick us up.

Sergeant Moss kept calling it an ambush operation to get us motivated, make us feel like Secret Squirrel special ops or something, but it mostly just felt like more bullshit watch duty.

The stairwell was dark and Ruiz's story, as much as I didn't want to admit it, had freaked me out, so when I heard this sound from one of the rooms below—like a moan-groan-grunt kind of a thing, some kind of animal almost—my asshole puckered and my hackles went up. Brought my rifle to the high ready.

Damn, dog, said Ruiz. Motherfucking jumpy as hell. Think this was your first day and shit.

What was that? I said.

Who cares? he said. Fucking hungry.

Ruiz pushed past me on the stairs and disappeared around the corner and I strained to hear him greet the others but couldn't.

The moan came again. My spit was thick and caught in my throat so that I couldn't stop swallowing. Chem lights that the squad had cracked and dropped around the house glowed from the floor like Halloween. Kept imagining turning the corner and seeing some giant black thing devouring Ruiz, its enormous mouth stretching over his shoulders, teeth tearing into him. *I can feel her still in me*, the gravedigger had told them.

I hoped it would be fast. That it wouldn't hurt. Dying. I was spiraling.

Hadn't known anyone who had died then. Closest I'd gotten was during the relief in place when we were taking over the AO from the other battalion; saw an Iraqi Army jundi take shrapnel in the femoral from a victim-actuated improvised claymore—not much more than a pipe buried in the ground at an angle stuffed with black powder, wadding, screws, whatever other scrap metal.

We took the IA out with us sometimes on short-range patrols to teach them how to do the job, but, like Cobb, most of them just never seemed to get it.

There was a lot of blood. It was brighter than I expected. Jundi didn't do much but stare at the sky and sigh over and over like a guy waiting for a late bus or something. He was probably in shock.

Sergeant Moss caught me staring and told me to push out security and pay the fuck attention. Then they evaced the jundi and I never found out if he lived or died. Asked a couple guys from the other battalion and some corpsmen. No one knew.

Part of me wanted to know so I could tell people back home that I'd seen a man die and I was disappointed then that I wouldn't have an end to the story. Figured I'd probably just tell people he'd died. Most likely he had. I'd forgotten about him until that moment on the stairs.

I buttonhooked around the corner, safety off, ready to plug a nonstandard response into the chest of whatever fucked-up thing was there.

Lance Corporal Pusey, came Sergeant Moss's voice. Flag me again with a loaded weapon and I'll skullfuck your entire family.

I lowered my rifle and tried to put it back on safe quietly.

Sergeant Moss sat cross-legged against the wall of a large room with Ruiz, Nguyen, Crowe, and AJ. Cushions had been placed on the floor and pillows lined the wall on top of the cushions. Two large metal trays of food had been set on the ground in front of them.

AJ pointed at the platters and said, Dolma, biryani, khubz, baba ghanoush, chai. A feast. He scooped something onto a piece of flatbread and stuffed it into his mouth and made sounds like he was fucking.

Don't eat any of that, said Sergeant Moss. It'll give you the shits.

Sergeant, this is rude, said AJ. Very rude. This woman gives us her home. She supports the Americans.

I gave her the quartering funds, said Sergeant Moss.

For her to see your empty plates will invite famine to her home, said AJ.

Sergeant Moss sighed, said, Have some bread. And the tea.

I don't want none of that, said Crowe. He had his rifle broken down shotgun-style, scrubbing dirt from the visible parts of the bolt with a toothbrush. Damn hajji food. Probably poison.

Ignorance is unbecoming of Marines, Lance Corporal Crowe, said Sergeant Moss.

I saw AJ roll his eyes and give a look like Do you hear yourself?

What's that mean, Sergeant? said Crowe.

A hajji is a person who's completed the haj—a religious pilgrimage to Mecca, said Sergeant Moss.

What's a pilgrimage? I said.

I didn't know shit. I was nineteen.

A long trip, Lance Corporal Pusey, said Sergeant Moss. Usually to a place of worship.

Got two fucking mosques on every block here. Why they need to take a trip? said Crowe.

We laughed. AJ shook his head.

Another moan came from the adjacent room, along with a sound like rattling chains, and I whipped my head to the open door to my left.

Ruiz nudged Nguyen. Yo, I told him about the gravedigger from last deployment and got him all freaked the fuck out. Look at his fucking face.

Oh, damn! said Nguyen. That was creepy as *hell,* though, for real. That scream? He shivered a bit and ate from his MRE. What do you think happened to that guy? he said. I almost dropped his ass.

It's just her kids, said Sergeant Moss.

Sergeant? I said.

Sergeant Moss shrugged, then lay across the cushions and closed his eyes. See for yourself, he said. Then eat some chow and rack out. AJ and I talked to the woman. She and all her kids—even our little troublemaker—haven't left since we got here. They're in until we leave tomorrow. Hear this: they are not detainees. This is their house. We are guests. We will leave no fucking trace here. Understood?

We rogered up with *Oorah*s and *Kill*s.

As for us, said Sergeant Moss, two on the roof, two on watch down here—Nguyen and Crowe first—two asleep. All night long.

I wanted Ruiz to come with me, but he and Nguyen had forgotten about giving me shit, had gotten lost in their first deployment in a way I wouldn't understand until I'd done more than one pump.

When I saw the kids, I wasn't sure what to think. Entire family slept in the room on a heap of carpets and mats and blankets. I counted five small lumps; her oldest son—the one we'd detained and then returned—was number six and slept in a corner on a mat away from the younger kids.

The woman wasn't asleep but rubbing the back of a seventh, who lay across her lap. A rope harness wound around the kid's chest and a chain trailed from the top of the harness to an iron ring in the center of the floor. Seventh kid wore a long shirt, and when the woman rubbed the kid's back, the shirt rode up and I could see small, malformed legs, a partial foot. The woman saw me, stopped her work, smiled, looked at me like she was asking if I needed anything, made like she was about to stand, then the kid moaned, and the woman went back to rubbing its back.

The child has many problems, said AJ who scooped food onto some bread and into his mouth.

I took off my gear and sat on the ground. It's chained up, I said.

She, said AJ. The child is a girl.

Whatever, I said. It's fucked-up.

Americans always must have something to say, said AJ. He tsked and shook his head.

Snap! said Ruiz. Old boy calling you out, dog.

The woman must work because her husband was killed at an American checkpoint when a bomb went off, said AJ. There is no one else to tend the child while she sleeps. What should she do? You have this answer?

She's chained up like an animal, I said.

AJ shrugged his shoulders, ate more food.

Only at night, said AJ. The girl has many problems. She cannot walk, but she crawls. The woman is afraid the girl might wake in the night and wander from home. Become lost.

Fucking backwater, said Nguyen.

Once, said AJ, we had very good hospitals and social services. He stared at Nguyen until Nguyen looked away and went back to his MRE.

Should've just dumped her in a garbage heap, said Crowe. Spartans had it right, man. Toss the fucking retards off a cliff. Drain on society.

Cállate, pendejo, said Ruiz. You're gonna tell me your white trash family ain't on fucking food stamps? Drain on society. Fuck outta here, dog.

Just saying, said Crowe.

And we all saw that dumbass movie, motherfucker, said Ruiz. Come in here trying to act smart and shit. Boot-ass bitch. Come get ya boy, Winny.

Nguyen held his hands up like Crowe wasn't his problem and AJ poured himself a cup of chai.

Someone else could take care of her, I said. That woman's got to know it's fucking wrong.

You think she does not know? said AJ. It is not the girl who is hurt by this, I think. Besides, the girl already has lost a father. Better she stay with her mother, yes? To lose one's family is a kind of death, don't you think?

Got the feeling he was talking straight to me.

Fucking parents, said Nguyen. My dad used to make me kneel on uncooked rice when I fucked up.

Belt, said Crowe, raising his hand without looking up from cleaning his rifle.

Pops had this big-ass class ring he won in a poker game from some white boy, used to turn that shit around and go to town on me, said Ruiz.

I thought about my birth mom, how she'd given me up, and how the woman in the next room hadn't given up any of her children. Wondered what was so goddamned wrong with me. Decided then I'd never have a kid. Said it out loud to make it real.

I'll never have a fucking kid, I said.

And then, to keep myself from crying, I shoved bread in my mouth.

All of you: shut your fucking sucks, said Sergeant Moss, his eyes still closed.

Cobb woke us for downstairs post two hours later. Nguyen and Crowe were on the roof. AJ snored.

I got to wake up Sergeant Moss, said Cobb.

Your funeral, dog, said Ruiz, who stretched and tied his boots, which he'd slept in.

Monte de merda, said Baptiste storming into the room, looking at Cobb's back.

Corporal Nguyen said I had to, said Cobb.

His giant body crouched next to Sergeant Moss.

Sergeant Moss, he said.

I'd never heard Cobb so quiet.

What's up, B? I said.

Sleepy motherfucker, said Baptiste.

For real? said Ruiz.

Sergeant Moss opened his eyes, took a deep breath through his nose.

Sergeant Moss, said Cobb again.

What shithead? said Sergeant Moss.

You could tell by the dull jab Sergeant Moss was tired.

Sergeant, said Cobb. I fell asleep on post. Corporal Nguyen said I should tell you.

That's fucking no good, dog, said Ruiz.

Baptiste kept swearing in Portuguese.

I don't think it was for very long, said Cobb.

Dog, that's such bad fucking juju, said Ruiz. No fucking bueno. Yo, that's how them fucking Ricky Recon bubbas got smoked a couple years ago, right? Right, Sergeant? An entire section—

Corporal Ruiz, shut the fuck up, said Sergeant Moss. Go walk the house. Make sure we're buttoned the fuck up.

Roger, said Ruiz.

I don't think it was for very long, Cobb said again.

Fucking malingerer, said Baptiste still standing. No discipline in that giant-ass body. Waste of space.

That's right, Lance Corporal Baptiste, said Sergeant Moss, who hadn't even sat up. Lance Corporal Cobb is lacking in discipline.

Fucking A, Sergeant, said Baptiste.

And you, Lance Corporal Baptiste, are a salty senior lance corporal of Marines who's seen some shit, yes? You are locked, cocked, and ready to rock at all times.

Yes, Sergeant, said Baptiste.

I could tell from Sergeant Moss's tone things were about to take a turn for Baptiste, remembered the rock I'd carried on patrol for a month not so long ago, but Baptiste didn't seem to notice.

You were on watch with Lance Corporal Cobb, correct, Lance Corporal Baptiste? said Sergeant Moss.

Yes, Sergeant, said Baptiste.

Because Lance Corporal Cobb is your battle buddy, correct, Lance Corporal Baptiste? said Sergeant Moss.

Yes, Sergeant, said Baptiste.

Because *you* are a salty motherfucking senior lance corporal of Marines with the experience of a deployment, who has seen some shit, and is always locked, cocked, and ready to rock, correct, Lance Corporal Baptiste? said Sergeant Moss.

Yes, Sergeant, said Baptiste.

Then why the fuck did Corporal Nguyen have to wake up your battle buddy? Why didn't you do your job as a salty senior lance corporal of Marines who has the experience to fucking know better, Lance Corporal Baptiste? said Sergeant Moss.

Baptiste didn't say a thing.

Ruiz came back. Five by five, Sergeant. All good, he said.

No one had moved. AJ continued to snore. It was like a goddamned painting.

What do you want to do, Sergeant? said Ruiz.

Get LT on the wire, said Sergeant Moss. Ambush is compromised. We'll ride out the night here. Stand to.

Ruiz relayed what Sergeant Moss had said over platoon TAC. I heard whoever was on radio watch over the handset roger up and then I heard LT's voice break in, Ummm, interrogative . . .

I lost whatever was being said as Ruiz held the handset toward Sergeant Moss, who took the PRC-one-seventeen toward the stairs to listen to the LT's question. He didn't give up Baptiste and Cobb, made up some bullshit about some local national spotting us when they went outside to take a piss.

In the morning the woman served us breakfast. More khubz, yogurt, something that looked like stewed tomatoes, and chai. We didn't eat any of it and I wanted to apologize, but we'd never been taught the word for *sorry* in Arabic. We egressed. I picked up the rear. When I turned, the woman was waving. I waved back and watched the girl crawl from the doorway behind the woman, chasing after her siblings, who ran toward the cemetery.

We met the platoon two klicks north of the cemetery and loaded up the high-back with Corporal Fox driving. AJ got in the LT's Humvee. LT wanted to patrol through the intersection as a show of force and then head south to one of our sister companies' forward operating bases. That's when the IED detonated.

Afterward, when the area was secured and EOD had been called and we'd all been evaced, EOD did a crater analysis and told the LT, who later told us, that the culvert running under the road near the intersection had been packed with a couple one-five-five rounds and propane for accelerant but that it'd been too deep to do much damage and the openings in either end of the culvert had acted like relief valves. EOD said it was detonated by a command wire they'd traced a few hundred meters over a berm to the east. A berm in direct sight line of the corner of the house where Cobb had stood his post.

A clusterfuck. LT went nuts running damage control, trying to keep the heat off his ass. Tried to burn Sergeant Moss—who never confessed to knowing about Cobb and Baptiste. Rest of us kept our mouths shut, too.

It was Cobb who broke down and told the LT what happened, that he'd fallen asleep. And then Baptiste covered Sergeant Moss's ass and told LT he'd lied about being spotted by a local national.

Both Cobb and Baptiste got busted to private, lost their pay for a month, and Baptiste got shipped off to guard duty—a shitbird detail—for the rest of the deployment, and that was after Sergeant Moss went to bat for him.

We saw Baptiste whenever we were back at the MEK for hot chow or an R and R PX run for cigarettes and dip and pirated movies or whatever. Mostly we stopped waving at him. Kind of like face blindness or something. We weren't around him, had no way to stay in contact, so he faded away. Sergeant Moss always checked in, though. Would get out of the high-back, tell us he'd meet back up with us at the PX. When we rolled away, I'd see him shaking hands or patting shoulders. Once I even saw him go in for a hug. It always reminded me of the woman rubbing her kid's back, and a part of me wished I was Baptiste.

Cobb should've gone to guard with Baptiste, but he went home instead.

After the blast, he started crying and then he didn't stop—not in like a he'd-get-sad-and-guilty-every-once-in-a-while-and-let-it-out kind of way, but like nonstop, shoulder-shrug, snot-bubble sobbing.

Cried so much, it ended up being just how his body *was*. He blubbered and stuffed Otis Spunkmeyer muffins into his perfect goddamned mouth in our tiny makeshift chow hall at the PB while we tried to ignore him. He wailed and filled sandbags. Like, I'd be trying to crank one out in the shitter and Cobb would be one over, dropping the kids off at the pool, crying his eyes out.

Whole thing made people nervous. The weirdness of it all. At first, senior Marines yelled at him, gave him a hard time, but the crying outlasted it all. Seemed like Cobb had fucking lost it. People talk about cracked. That's what cracked looks like. Sergeant Moss said it was mindset black. That we should stay away from him.

Shit breeds like a goddamned yeast infection, said Sergeant Moss.

Doc told him to stay hydrated and get some sleep but Cobb cried in his sleep. Doc gave him Ativan and Flexeril and he still cried. Finally, they berthed him in a storage room near the command and operations center at the PB and kept a suicide watch posted outside his door and escorted him to and from chow and the shitters.

One day we woke up and he was gone.

Good fucking riddance, said Crowe.

When we got home, he was with Corporal Fox—more standing next to him than anything—tossing us beers over the fence, not a tear in his eyes. None of us talked to him much.

I was in my room at my mom's, wondering when Cobb had taken those photos of the desert. I tried to remember what it was like after the blast; it came in fits and starts. Less images, more sounds and feelings. Crowe's laugh after everyone rogered up they were five by five, Baptiste telling Crowe to be a goddamned professional; Ruiz's hands on my face and neck, checking me over; Nguyen banging on the roof of the cab, calling for Sergeant Moss and Corporal Fox; Cobb crying and apologizing.

My room—my mom's sewing room—dim with weak winter dusk when I'd sat down, was dark. My phone read seventeen thirty. I'd lost close to an hour. It made me laugh at first—like in that way getting high when you're a teenager makes you laugh. Like you can't believe something can make your body feel that way. That it can forget reality like that.

Didn't know if I'd slept or zoned out staring at the desert on my screen, but it felt good as hell. Couldn't even feel the futon under me. It was like part of me was up and out of my body, floating in the desert, looking at myself from the intersection. Fucking time travel. It made me think of Cobb sleeping on post. *I don't think it was for too long.*

A text notification from Max popped up over Cobb's desert pics, knocking me into the present. *On my way!* it read.

Had a hard time standing, and when I finally managed it, ended up with a head rush that turned my vision to white noise and thought I was going down, but when I reached out through the dark I got hold of the door-knob and righted myself. Moonlight through the window cast everything in a shade of blue and I wondered what the color was called. If maybe Max knew. And then Max was kissing my fingers, hands running the length of my forearm, my skin turning to gooseflesh, and her fingers were Penny's grasping the back of my shirt while she pressed her face into my chest and cried, and her fingers were my mom's brushing my arm the morning after the bar fight, asking me if I was okay, and her fingers were my birth mom's fingers as I imagined them reaching down to the space between her legs where my head was emerging, feeling my warm, bloody hair, and her fingers were the Iraqi woman's fingers running over her daughter's back, making circle after circle on crinkled nightshirt fabric, and the fabric was the color of the desert from the pictures Cobb had taken, *I don't think it was for very long. Meestah me zien. I'm trying to help. Click click click click. Dean, are you okay? I'm trying to help. I can feel her still in me. I don't think it was for very long. I'm trying to help.*

This is some bad juju, dog, said Ruiz from the shadows on the futon, the sheep in his lap. He looked at me and smiled and I dropped to the floor.

Are you all right? said Iris. She stood over me. She'd turned on the light.

I blinked, rubbed my eyes. My phone vibrated on the floor. Max calling. Ruiz and the sheep were gone.

I was in the bathroom and I heard a noise, said Iris.

I'm scared, I didn't say.

I hate you, I didn't say.

Penny is mine, I didn't say.

What I said: Just walk into people's bedrooms?

I sat up.

Sorry, she said. It was the noise. It was loud.

She motioned to the bathroom and we locked eyes and I could tell she wanted to say something to me. Imagined it was about her cousin, and right then I hoped she *would* say something. Like there was part of me begging for it. *Just say something, goddammit,* I thought. *Tell me about how he got hurt. Tell me about how when he finally got home and got out of the Marines he was angry at fucking everything. Tell me about how he got too drunk at his homecoming party about how he slammed you into the wall and pried his car keys from your fingers. Tell me how he got pulled over for a DUI about how he got fired from his job when he had to keep calling in to make the alcohol class appointments and probation meetings about how his fiancée left him about how he eventually violated his probation and went to jail for ninety days. Tell me about how he came over one day and patched the drywall—the divot made by the back of your head. Tell me about how he went back to school and got a degree in social work and became a high school counselor. Tell me about his AA meetings and how he goes to church and his new girlfriend who has two young kids by a guy who skipped town after she told him she was pregnant. Tell me about how he looks when they call him Dad in front of people.*

But Iris didn't tell me any of that. Maybe because she was a withholding ball-breaker. Maybe because it wasn't real. Maybe because I didn't ask her. Instead, she turned and left, and I got up off the floor and thought again about the Colt in my closet while I backed out of the room looking at the futon.

I was angry—at Max for being late, at myself for fainting like some fucking weak bitch, at Court for giving me the Ativan, at my mom's passive aggression, at Penny's college-educated-holier-than-thou-anti-war-liberal bullshit, at Rick's interest in Iris, at Iris. Everything about Iris. I decided right then to hate her. I texted Max: *Just come in.*

Rick answered the door and Penny took Max's jacket, an olive peacoat, and I forgot about how much I hated them all because it was right then that I knew I loved Max. Was in love with her.

How do I describe something like that? Scared the shit out of me.

Then my mom said, Dean are you all right? Your face is flushed.

And I shot Iris a look like Don't you fucking say a goddamned thing.

My mom reached for my forehead with the back of her hand and I ducked around it and Rick said, *Gale,* in that way he had that made me want to peel off my skin.

Penny made introductions and I didn't want to deal with her trying to make jokes, so I stepped into the kitchen and got myself a beer and downed it, let a burp rise and release from my mouth yeasty and hot and silent, grabbed another and one for Max and met her in the living room, where everyone was still standing.

I'm still your mother, you know, said Mom. I'm allowed to worry.

When did you start worrying about us? said Penny, she looked at me, overblown, dramatic confusion on her face.

Technically you're not my mother, I didn't say.

Is that how you support the troops? I didn't say.

Hold me, Mommy, I didn't say.

What I said: It's a new development.

Penny and I were allies again. I handed Max the beer and she smiled at me and stepped through the circle, kissed me on the cheek whispered that we needed to talk, but I couldn't answer; it was like her words hit a wall in my brain: heat shot out from the point of her kiss's impact to the rest of my face and neck down to my chest and nestled into my guts, and, no shit, I thought I'd been burned, that my skin might be scarred red forever. *First there came the color red, to show the world the blood we shed*—it was Ruiz's voice in my head.

Silence settled over us and my skin was radioactive, set the room on fire. Oniony sweat stink from my armpits wafted to my nose. I crossed the room and cracked a window. My mom looked like she wanted to say something but didn't. Rick fiddled with the turntable until Jim Nabors's baritone thundered "Go Tell It on the Mountain" from the speakers.

Penny talked to Max, who kept looking to me, trying to get my attention, but I was reeling from the kiss or the Ativan and the beer or my worlds colliding or the ghosts in my bedroom—any number of things. Finally, Iris said something about how this was awkward and then when we all laughed, I decided not to hate her, and she suggested we play charades because there wasn't a better way to get to know people.

I know a better game, I said, and I was thinking of Truth in the bar with Max, but what I said came out prickish and it made Iris blush and Penny stare and Rick clear his throat and so I smiled and looked at Max then I said, Never mind. Charades sounds great. Really.

And I wondered what was wrong. *We need to talk. Fuck fuck fuck fuck. This is some bad juju, dog.* Ruiz. Always Ruiz. There was no getting away from him. She'd realized how fucked up I was. That I was defective. But we were playing charades and I bet she wouldn't break up with me in front of my family. Not on Christmas Eve.

We all wrote five things or people on slips of paper, folded them up, and tossed them into a bowl. I hadn't played since before my parents divorced. We played couples. Laughed at Rick's intense eye contact, my mom's unintentional sound effects that Penny kept censoring, Iris's spot-on imitation of a cuckoo clock. We got fresh drinks.

Max fit in. Laughed easy. Snorted when she really got going.

It was her turn to act. She grabbed a paper from the bowl, nodded at Penny to flip the hourglass timer we'd swiped from another game, and made a movie camera sign.

Movie, I said.

She nodded and held up one finger.

One word, I said.

She nodded and put her arms over her head like she was holding a huge ball.

Big, I said.

She shook her head and kept making the giant ball-holding motion and walked around.

Iris giggled.

Balloon, I said.

That's not a movie, said Penny.

Max shook her head, tried again, emphasized the imaginary ball she was holding. Puffed out her cheeks.

Up, said Rick.

It's not your turn! said Mom.

Max shook her head, looked at the timer, jumped up and down, and shook her hands, wiping the slate clean. Held her hand to her ear.

Sounds like, I said.

She made giant stomping motions across the room.

Giant, I said.

Also not a movie, said Penny.

She shook her head, swiped her hands through the air again. Put one hand up to shield her eyes and pointed with the other, jumped up and down, put her hands to her cheeks, and silently screamed.

Scream, I said.

She shook her head and did the motion again, this time she added bumping into the coffee table.

No props! said Penny.

Shut up, I said.

Max did it again, this time without the table. Time was almost up.

Cars, I said.

She shook her head.

Oh, I know it! said Mom.

Twister, I said.

Max shook her head and did the motion one more time, then walked forward and held her arms out like wings and closed her eyes.

Titanic! I said.

Yes! she said. God, I should've done that in the first place.

Oh, I was going to say *Crash,* said Mom.

That was good! said Iris.

Who wrote *Titanic?* said Max. I want to know who my nemesis is.

Rick raised his hand and smiled.

Okay, Rick, said Max.

She sat next to me, exhaled, put her hand on my knee. I tried not to think about Ruiz or the sheep on the futon in the dark or Cobb or Corporal Fox's ruined face or the legless little girl or the goddamned crippled dolphin or the very serious something Max wanted to talk about that was probably her breaking up with me or that I loved her or what seemed to happen to anyone I loved, which is that they ended up gone disappeared unauthorized absence absent without leave and I was abandoned deserted. Tried not to think about how I might have been losing my fucking mind because everyone was smiling for once; everything was working out.

Later, after my mom and Rick had gone to bed and Penny and I cleaned up the kitchen, I ran out of excuses not to be alone with Max.

You're being cagey, said Penny.

I don't know what that means, I said. I was trying to be difficult.

How's this? she said. I want space to make out with my girlfriend and watch Christmas movies. Go away.

I showed Max my room. I was embarrassed by it—living at home, sleeping on a futon—after spending so much time at her place the last month, seeing how she'd made it on her own, and I couldn't figure out what the hell she saw in me.

It's all—attraction, love, relationships, whatever—it's all weird like that, right? Like, hard to pin down, the tiny things that keep you coming back to a person. Sure, there's the They make me laugh, or I feel safe around them, or They're my best friend—but that doesn't really get at the heart of it, right? Those are the easy answers—one-arm's-distance answers. Like, how can you fucking know why you love someone when people change so goddamned much? It's just a constant choice. Like, every single day those people who've been married for forty, fifty years wake up and say, This is it for me. I'm going to make this fucking thing work. Somehow, with all those infinite what-ifs and should haves, they keep walking forward.

In my room, I couldn't stop talking for once, or maybe it was that I didn't want to let her say what she wanted to say—I'd realized I loved her, wanted to keep making that choice, and I didn't want her to say any different. So I went on and on about Rithipol at work and how much he looked up to me and how well I was doing and how the shift manager wanted me to become a supervisor because of how well I'd taken to the job and about how Grant asked me for advice about his soldiers who were about to transition because it seemed like I had a really good head on my shoulders and about how I was planning on applying to college and how Penny was going to visit colleges with me as soon as I narrowed it down to five because right now I was thinking about seven or so between Illinois, Indiana, and Ohio and in the meantime I might just knock out my pre-reqs at the local community college so I could keep costs down, move out, get my own place, that even Court was thinking about college and moving closer to the city and he and I were thinking about getting a place together, being roommates, because that was one of the things I missed about the Marines, the camaraderie, that esprit de corps, having a battle buddy looking out for me, and how, yeah, Court needed that, I think because he was kind of lost and I thought I could help him and if I had that back I don't think there's a whole lot that could stand in my way.

All of it a load of bullshit, of course—some truth stretched; some outright lies. It didn't seem to matter then. I just wanted to keep her from breaking it off and figured maybe if I impressed her a bit, showed her I was moving forward, that it might convince her to stick around. People move fast in the Midwest—marriage, kids, house, whatever—something in the water, maybe. Most of the people I grew up with were married by twenty-two and usually had two or three kids in as many years, and once you hit twenty-five, pickings got slim. Hard to find someone who didn't come with a full load of fucked-up baggage.

I'm pregnant, Max said. Just like that. *I'm pregnant.*

I didn't hit the floor. My vision stayed sharp. The room was bright.

How? I didn't say.

Are you sure it's mine? I didn't say.

You can't keep it, I didn't say.

I didn't say any of that—not because I didn't want to, but because she didn't give me a chance.

I'm going to keep it, she said.

Her hair was piled on top of her head; it lengthened her face, made her seem—shit, even now I don't even know the right word. Deliberate, maybe? Confident? Established? All of those. It made me feel small. Like a boy. Not even a boy. A little baby. Shit-covered, screaming baby.

Say something, she said.

I think I love you, I said.

Can you believe that? That's what I said to her. Like it meant anything then.

I want to keep talking about this, she said. She looked at her phone.

Okay, I said.

But I'm going to miss my flight, she said.

Okay, I said.

Look. I like you but I don't know you. Not really. Not yet. If you want to be a part of this, like, a parent part, I want you to be. Whatever that looks like. Like I said, I'm going to keep it. The baby.

It was like every time she said it—*I'm going to keep it*—she grew a bit in front of me, or I shrunk. Like saying the thing was giving her some kind of power, filling her up. *I'm going to keep it. I'm going to keep it. I'm going to keep it.* Some kind of spell. I thought of her reading my palm again, my fingers in her mouth. Then she was walking out of the room and down the hall and to the front door and I was following her. On TV, Jimmy Stewart was about to kill himself and I thought, *Just do it, you fucking pussy.*

I had a good time, she said. Your family is great. You're fun around them.

I didn't say anything.

I'll be in Florida until the fourth, she said. We've got some things to think about. Text me.

Then she was gone.

In the kitchen I took shots of vodka and then made myself a strong drink and went and sat on the ottoman in front of the chair where Penny was sitting. Iris snored on the couch. The movie flickered white and blue over the room; deep shadows bled into the outer dark. Hair prickled on my neck like something was circling in that blackness. Thought about the Iraqi dogs, the crippled dolphin pumping and jerking its way through the dark ocean, the adoption dot com Instagram page, my birth mom.

Max left in a hurry, said Penny. What'd you do?

I snorted and drank and shook my head, looked at Iris, said, Are you just getting your nut, or what? I was drunk.

Don't be fucking gross, said Penny. She hit me with a pillow.

After a minute she said, I like her—Iris, I mean.

Mom thinks I'm fucked-up, I said.

We're worried about you, she said.

You think I'm fucked-up too, I said.

I didn't say that, she said.

My birth mom knew it, I said. That I'm fucked-up or whatever. Defective. Should've been a goddamned abortion.

That's pretty dramatic, she said.

No matter what she says about being my mom, I'll never really be part of this family, I said.

This is exhausting, she said. You're exhausting sometimes.

Maybe I *am* fucked-up, I said.

Look, she said. We keep trying to talk to you, but it's, like, never good enough. You're right, we don't know anything about what it was like for you, because you won't tell us. What are we supposed to do with that?

We keep trying and you keep pushing away. There's not much more we can do. People learn.

Fuck does that mean? I said.

It means you teach people how to treat you, she said. Keep pushing and people will stop coming back.

I woke early on Christmas, packed my things, took the Colt from the closet along with my cleaning kit, and went to the dining room at the end of the hall. I flicked the switch to the chandelier over the dark-stained, circular dining room table that still had the leaves inserted to fit all the food from last night. I sat and broke down the rifle, laid out the pieces, and went to work cleaning every millimeter. Lost myself a bit—enough that I didn't notice Mom, Rick, Penny, and Iris standing around me.

Dean, said my mom.

What the fuck? said Penny.

Dean, said my mom.

Not in my house, Gale, said Rick. I've given him all the grace I can, but I won't abide this. I will not have a gun in my house.

You're being such a macho asshole right now, said Penny.

Do you hear me, Dean? It was Rick; he stood over me. Dean? Did you hear what I just said? This is unacceptable behavior. You are a member of this family, and I understand that you grew up here, but it is your mother and I who pay the mortgage—

I slid the rear retaining pin home and stood with the rifle at port arms and started reciting the Rifleman's Creed—what I remembered from *Full Metal Jacket*, at least: This is my rifle . . .

I'm going, said Iris.

—and we have had more than enough patience with you, Rick continued. We've tried. We've gone more than halfway, but you're not meeting—

I hit him in the gut with the buttstock of the rifle and he crumpled.

Screams.

Det cord. Blasting caps. C-four. Fuse. Igniter. Boom. Just like that.

THREE WEEKS LATER Court and I were downing shitty beers in the detached garage at his parents' house where he'd worked on his dirt bikes when he was racing. Garage was still outfitted for it—looked like a professional autobody shop. Engine crane, pneumatic lift, all kinds of electronic testing equipment and tools. There were a couple couches, a decent set of speakers Court played old rap over, and a beer fridge in the back corner near the residential door. Walls were covered with photos of him racing—midair between doubles, jostling at the starting line, hoisting trophies over his head.

Texted me last night she's bleeding, I said to Court. Don't know what it means. Got our first doctor's appointment to go to later today. Supposed to have an ultrasound, too, I guess.

Might be good in the long run, said Court.

What do you mean? I said.

Maybe she'll lose it, he said.

She didn't think it was that big a deal, I said.

Hadn't given any thought that Max might lose the pregnancy—not something I figured just happened, you know? Like, I figured that could only happen if she fell down the stairs or something. Didn't know anything about it aside from my mom talking about not being able to get pregnant and whatever else I hadn't slept through in health class.

Even sure it's yours? he said.

Who else's? I said.

Court stopped whatever he was doing under the hood of his Honda Civic and looked at me like I'd just tried to convince him the sky was polka-dotted fucking pink and green, took a pull of his beer, and went back to the engine compartment.

I could tell he was getting sick of me staying with him—short with me, you know? Might've been that I wouldn't shut up about Max. Court's whole thing—his philosophy, he called it—was that relationships weren't natural. Wasn't how anyone functioned. The same person every single day till death do you part? he'd ask. Fucking unnatural. Never mind his parents, who seemed pretty goddamned happy with each other after, like, thirty years or whatever, but I guess you never really know what's happening in a marriage.

Mostly I figured it was a line. Court had been saying shit like that since high school and lots of girls had taken it as a challenge, like they were going to change his mind. No joy.

Anyway, when I showed up Christmas Day, he hadn't given me shit about ditching him the night before and he didn't ask me why I was there. Opened the door, told me I could stay as long as I needed. He kept me bundled up in Ativan and I kept the house field-day clean and helped him out with his car and taught him more about pistol shooting. Kind of like how I imagined it might've been if I'd never gone into the Marines. But, yeah, I could tell he was getting sick of it.

Probably I was, too, though I don't think I saw it then. Didn't feel like I could be sick of him because I had to be grateful for the room. Wanted him to ask about why I was there, and like I said, I wanted him to ask about the Marines. All that want—kept waiting for him to offer up a crumb of anything. Followed him around like a puppy. Must've drove him nuts, now that I'm telling it.

You remember Cole Harris? he said without looking up from what he was messing around with in the engine compartment.

I nodded, remembered Cole—big, moon-faced kid. Looked like a farm boy, but he'd never seen a day of hard work in his life. Nice as hell, though. Dad owned a couple car dealerships in town. Cole was set to work at one after he graduated.

Dated Faith Sutton all through school, said Court. Their families vacationed together. All Cole could fucking talk about whenever he was over here after he had a couple beers was getting married, starting a family, buying a house—white picket fence, dog, American fucking Dream. Whole nine yards. And then Faith got pregnant right after senior year and they rushed to plan the wedding—even asked me if my parents would let them get married out by the pond, under that big cottonwood? Invited us. You were gone by then. Sure, I said. And then, get this, motherfucking week before the whole thing was set to go off, Faith tells him she doesn't think the kid's his. That it's maybe Drew Allen's.

Weren't he and Drew friends? I said.

Best fucking friends, man, he said. Tight. Never saw the two fucking separate. Like, Drew must've fucked Faith in the same room as Cole without Cole knowing, those dudes hung out so much.

Court could tell a story. Could've listened to him all day. He went back to the car.

He ever find out if it was his kid? I said.

Yeah, he said.

His face strained and he clenched his teeth, was trying to push his hand deeper into the guts of the car, but couldn't.

Come here, he said.

Put my beer down next to the other empties and made my way over. Court knew I didn't give a damn about cars, but when he needed my help, he was patient about it. Patient like Ruiz had been patient teaching me how to roll. Court never talked down to me because I didn't know what a head gasket was or where to find the alternator. Didn't coddle me, either. In another life he could've been a teacher. Good teacher. Knew how to change my oil and replace my spark plugs and brake pads because of him.

Here, he said.

He kept one hand in the engine compartment and beckoned me with the other.

Feel down here where my hand is, he said.

I reached my hand in, followed his toward the front inside of the compartment.

You feel that hard plastic bracket? he said.

Yeah, I said.

Can you get your hand under it? he said.

Yeah, I said.

He pulled his hand out.

Okay, he said. For the intake pipe to fit, that bracket's got to come out. Should be a nut right in the center underneath. Try to unscrew it.

Got leverage, pushed my hand deeper, and nodded to him.

I liked that he needed me. It's why I'd started to come around to Grant at work. Guy made me feel like they couldn't run sunrise without me and that made me give a shit, you know? And it was hard to give a shit when I was standing by to stand by, waiting for a mission. Hard to give a shit after the Corps, after Iraq. After what I'd done Christmas Day to Rick and the rest of my family. It was, like, what's the fucking point of anything? You see how people treat each other, learn all kinds of terrible shit about yourself—how easy it is to be cold and turn away, how easy it is to look at someone and see a target silhouette instead of a person. But there was something calming about it, maybe. Like I knew what I was capable of on one hand. Made the other hand seem a lot farther away, though—fucking pinprick in the darkness. Being with Max made that light seem a little closer; same with Court right then, too.

So whose kid was it? I said.

Court went to the beer fridge, got two beers, popped one, and drank.

Well, they didn't get a test or anything while she was pregnant, he said. I don't know if you can even do that.

He looked at me like he expected confirmation or denial, and when I shrugged, he went on: Cole came over one night, got hammered—I mean blackout. Guy was crying on everyone's shoulders and telling us how much he loved her. How he didn't believe she'd do a thing like that. How he knew the kid was his. How he forgave her and Drew. Called them both up, drunk as a skunk, and forgave them over the phone. And life went on, right? Like, dude's going to doctor's appointments, the wedding's back on, they move in together, and then the kid's born.

Yeah? I said. The nut came off in my palm and the bracket shifted, trapping my hand, so I pulled it out with the other. Looked at it—nothing but dull, hard formed plastic. Held it out to Court, who waved it aside. I put it on the ground next to the car.

Kid was Black, man, he said.

So it was Drew's? I said.

Nope, said Court. Drew asked for a paternity test. And guess what? *You* are *not* the father!

Said it all like Maury Povich, made himself laugh, finished his beer, crushed the can in his hands, and shot it into the trash by the fridge. Picked up the intake pipe he was going to install and walked back over to the car.

Cold air intake, he said. Pulls air from outside the engine compartment. Cold air's denser—lets the engine breathe better.

Wait, I said. Then whose was it?

Some guy who went to Parkside, he said.

Parkside was the high school north of us. Rivals.

Fucking idiot married her, he said.

Who? I said. The Parkside guy?

Cole, he said.

No shit? I said.

He finished with whatever he was doing to secure the pipe inside the engine compartment, looked up at me.

Been married two years now, he said. Fucking ceremony was by the pond under the cottonwood like they'd wanted. Beer?

No, I said. Got that appointment in a couple hours.

Court shrugged.

Love's crazy, I guess. I was thinking about Max when I said it. I loved her. I did. That was crazy to me, but I loved her.

Fuck you know about it? he said, walked to the fridge, and threw a beer at me even though I'd said no. I opened it. You hear what I'm saying?

Yeah, I heard you, I said.

Telling you, man, he said. Shit's a trap. You know how I feel about it all.

I nodded and drank while he got the creeper, a socket wrench, and a cone filter and slid under the front end to secure the intake and attach the filter. Looked around the garage, all those pictures of Court racing. Place was a memorial. Worse. Some kind of crypt. Cemetery. Cemetery full of shadows, ghosts waiting to eat me alive from the inside out. Couldn't swallow the beer in my mouth. Like I was too full. Like everything I hadn't said, everything about Christmas, about Penny, about Max, about

Ruiz, and Sergeant Moss, and the sheep, like they were all crowding my throat, choking me. *Tap. You nervous? Good at keeping secrets. Tiny little breaths. Not in my house. Tap. Bad juju, dog. Let it all out. Just not a lot of opportunity here. Give him one! Tap.*

I ran to the garbage and spit out my beer, did a silent dry heave. Decided then I was going to unload it all to Court. Every last bit of it. I don't know if it was a good idea. Probably wasn't ready. Or Court wasn't. But he was there and I felt like in that moment if I kept it in for another minute it would kill me. Or I'd kill myself.

I know about it, I said.

What? he said from beneath the car. His hands grasped the bumper and he came sliding out, sat up, wiped his hands on a rag, looked at me.

Love, I said. I know about it. I love Penny. You're my friend. I love you.

Sisters and friends ain't what I'm talking about, said Court.

And my voice shook and my heart pounded hard enough to break my sternum but I kept talking, sped up until I lost my breath and I told Court about the sheep and Sergeant Moss and the teenager and Nervous and the PB and Ruiz and it was the first time I'd said *love* and *Ruiz* at the same time but it felt right.

I loved him, I said.

Don't know what I expected from Court, what I wanted. Maybe just for him to tell me I'd be all right or maybe I wanted him to ask for my help again. Shit, maybe I just wanted a goddamned hug. Instead, he said, This ain't the Marines, man. No one's got your back in the real world. Got to be a lone wolf.

He laid back down and slid under the car.

When our battalion got back from that first deployment, California was burning. Air quality forced a safety stand-down. Training ceased. There was talk we might be called in to help dig firebreaks. We bitched about the possibility. Grunts in garrison bitch about everything—uniform inspections, having to march in formation, extra duty, chow hall food, the idiots who serve it, the weather, anything that wasn't porn or the gym or alcohol. Even then we could find something to bitch about: taking too long for the money shot. Not enough goddamned dumbbells. Only eighty proof?

We did weapons maintenance at the armory, cleaned every inch of the barracks, sat through hip-pocket classes on customs and courtesies from staff NCOs and officers. But when the weapons and barracks were clean and no one could stand another goddamned lecture on the precise angles at which the garrison cap could be worn, or whatever other bullshit, we crowded into barracks rooms and watched porn and talked shit and scoured the internet for that fucking JLo sex tape.

When our blood boiled from the fucking and the insults, or even just the boredom of it all, we rolled in the smoke pit—nothing more than a ten-by-ten sandbox.

In skivvy shirts and camouflage trousers we grappled on our knees, shot on one another's waists, strained against each other. We blood choked and air choked and arm barred and cross faced and laughed and cheered and sweated into one another's eyes.

I got amped up watching it all and it felt for a minute like we were back in the suck, speeding up time. It was the first time I realized I'd rather be there than anywhere. Kind of like a little gut punch—knowing something like that about yourself. Felt proud of it, maybe—like I'd figured out where I belonged—but it was like the whole situation, Iraq and the Marines, was so fucked that it made it hard to move sometimes, like everything was slow motion.

Next to me Ruiz said, Me and you next.

My palms went sweaty. Since getting stateside, shit felt off between us. I didn't say anything about it, but it was like when you're a kid and you try to push two magnets together and one keeps moving the other across a table. I crossed my arms, went rigid. Nah, I said.

'Sup, güey? he said. Don't want to fuck up that pretty face or what?

He reached out and ran a finger down the side of my face and I slapped him away. Marines did that kind of homoerotic shit all the time. But there was a part of me that worried someone might think Ruiz was serious. It felt serious to me—felt like his finger had opened me up, unzipped me.

What? he said. You nervous, dog? He smiled.

I wanted to send hammer fist after hammer fist into his cheeks and nose and eye sockets, turn him inside out. I wanted his body against mine—chapped lips on my belly button, chin stubble raking my neck. It must've been all over my face, playing there like the porno we'd all crowded around laptops to watch and critique.

Fuck off, I said.

Then, in the pit, a Marine broke another Marine's nose; there was a tidal wave of blood, and Doc called an end to the rolling. Marines broke off, went their separate ways, and without the crowd I eased up.

Fuck it, dog, he said. Let's hit the Backyard.

We ran from the barracks quad into what everyone on the camp called the Backyard—an unofficial training ground full of verbena, sagebrush, button celery, wild fennel, AAV husks, and tarantula holes. We used it to practice patrols, ambushes, contact drills, any and all SOP.

Grit from the wildfire turned the sky queasy shades of yellow and green. Rustling scrub and dirt-muffled footfalls became our soundtrack.

Ruiz led along a skinny goat path. My quads and calves warmed. The Backyard was all ocean salt and wildfire smoke and hot dirt, and over my shoulder I saw how small and perfectly rectangular the barracks had become. I saw Marines, like ants, caught up in a bump-and-shove on the basketball court. I imagined my body—the downward thrust of my legs, the planting of my feet—moving the earth beneath me. I was alive. In that moment I wanted to stay in the Corps forever, would've reenlisted right then and there.

At the top of the goat path was a firebreak the width of a four-lane highway and the two of us stood, hands on hips, chests heaving, looking to the east at the billows of smoke.

I feel like God up here, I said.

That's fucking blasphemy, dog, said Ruiz. Now we *got* to fucking fight.

He took a basic stance—strong foot back, legs bent, back straight, arms up, guarding his face—jabbed at my shoulder.

I waved him off, walked in a circle with my fingers laced on top of my head. Tried to catch my breath.

You think about the deployment at all? I said.

I think about the next deployment, and the next one, and the next one, he said.

That's not what I mean, I said. Wanted to get us straight—if I could figure our shit out, I could figure my shit out. That's what I was thinking.

Keep thinking now that I should've just asked him. If I'd only asked him, maybe it'd be different. What if? What if? What if?

What else is there? he said.

You're going to reenlist? I said.

Ruiz shrugged. If they'll let me.

You think they won't? I said.

War ain't ever gonna end, he said. I've only got one NJP and they need bodies.

Ain't a real grunt without one, I said mimicking his voice.

Racist-ass shit, dog, he said.

We laughed at that.

For real, though, he said. Ain't shit back in AZ but rednecks and saguaros. Not going back. He picked up a rock and chucked it over the edge of the firebreak. Besides, he said, I like Cali. The fucking ocean.

Yeah, I said. Not so bad.

Ruiz nodded. Tossed another rock and the Santa Anas dried our sweat, coated us in dirt and ash.

All right, let's go, I said, and shoved his bowling ball shoulder.

We dropped to our knees onto the chunky, overturned firebreak dirt clods, hands up, protecting ourselves. I knew I could take him but decided I'd let him win just to feel his body weight across my back or chest. Wanted to say I would follow him, that I would reenlist and deploy again and again and again, grate my soul raw, just to feel that weight. Instead, we shuffled on our knees in silence, waited for the other to make a move, while miles away thousands of acres of chaparral went up in flames.

The waiting room at the doctor's office was full of other couples. Place was too warm, smelled like baby wipes. Made my stomach flip. Max was already there and sheet white when I walked in, and that set me on edge—she hadn't seemed nervous or anything over texts the night before.

I'm bleeding a little bit, she'd texted.

What does that mean? I'd texted.

Not sure, she'd texted.

K, I'd texted.

That was it. We'd been texting constantly while she was gone, back and forth the entire time she'd been in Florida with her parents, which made me think I had a sense of her. So the things she'd sent made me feel like *Oh, yeah, that's not a big deal, then.* But seeing her look so out of it—frizzy-haired and puffed-up like she'd been crying—had me nervous, set me thinking about what Court had said earlier in the garage about it maybe being a good thing, the bleeding. Didn't seem like a good thing in my head. Was the first time I'd thought about it, really. First time I'd realized the thing inside of her would be a baby at some point. Our baby. About as far as I could get. Heart sped up and I moved quick across the room and sat next to her.

Hi, I said. Didn't know what to say.

Hi, she said.

Waiting room was quiet except for the sound of whispering, happy-looking couples and pages over the intercom. Shifted in my seat, felt out of place, kept my hands in my lap, tried to look like I had it together. Max picked up a magazine; it was called *Parents.* Happy family on the cover: dad one, dad two, kid one, kid two. Dad one held a dog. Dad two held kid two like luggage. They all grinned from ear to fucking ear—even the goddamned dog. Max flipped through it; her face was pinched.

I couldn't stop thinking about Ruiz and the Backyard—how our future had seemed pretty written in stone then: We'd re-up and re-up and re-up. Keep fighting until they told us to stop. And they'd never tell us to stop. If it wasn't one place, it'd be another. Had seemed easy even if the war was hard. A bit of black and white standing out in the gray. That's what we were supposed to do, hand we'd been dealt. All we'd had to do was be together, get each other's backs. Court didn't get that—didn't want to. Had always been okay on his own or had had a family looking out for him. Max was like me, like Ruiz. She was looking for family. We could be that for each other in a way Ruiz and I hadn't gotten a chance to be.

I'm scared, she said. What if something's wrong?

It'll be okay, I said.

That's not helpful, she said.

Kind of put me on my ass, you know? Her response. Got pissed, like I wanted to explain to her what I meant. Like I wanted to say, No, not that this will be okay. This might not be okay, but it'll eventually be okay because we've got each other. But then the door to the exam rooms opened up and a nurse called Max's name, and Max was up out of her seat marching toward the door and the nurse while I hustled after her, avoided eye contact with the other couples who all looked fucking in it together. Battle buddies.

We stopped in the hallway and the nurse weighed Max, then took her blood pressure and asked her some questions about the blood: how much, frequency, color. Then in the exam room she handed us both clipboards, told Max to get undressed and put on a gown, then she left.

Turn around, said Max.

Didn't fucking get it, like pretty sure we'd seen each other naked. But I followed orders. On all the walls were posters—calming beaches and forests full of fir trees and then every other poster next to those was of newborns swaddled in crocheted pastel blankets with giant bows on their heads or put in bowls of fruit or whatever that all had text in curling script reading something about how motherhood was a gift and how moms made families.

Took a lungful of air, let it out in tiny little breaths. Exam paper crackled as Max got herself positioned on the chair that stood in the center of the room next to the ultrasound machine that together looked like some kind of fucked-up throne.

Okay, she said.

I took a seat, looked at the form on the clipboard. Family medical history. Didn't know how to fill it out. I always used to just say no to everything. History of heart disease? No. History of cancer? No. History of diabetes? No. History of mental illness? No. Never a big deal, right? It was only ever me impacted by those nos, and shit like eczema or Alzheimer's felt so far away when I was sitting at the battalion aid station, filling out a pre-deployment health assessment.

More than that, it was a weakness. Not knowing. You don't know what you don't know. Ignorance is unbecoming. Unaware and unprepared. Lost in the sauce. Worst part of that was there were answers. I just didn't know how to get to them.

Felt the weight of all the shit I didn't know then and thought it'd probably be better for Max if I just fucked off. The newborns snuggled in all their crocheted blankets stared at me from their bowls of gourds and grapes and what-the-fuck-ever-else, daring me to say something, to fill the silence of the buzzing overhead lights the ringing in my head.

Maybe it's a good thing if you lose it, I didn't say.

Wish we were battle buddies, I didn't say.

I'm not cut out for this, I didn't say.

What I said: I don't know how to fill this out.

Max was about to say something, but another nurse knocked and came in. She was a middle-aged woman, no-nonsense. Could tell what she was about just by looking at her, same way you look at a hammer and know what it's for.

Hi, Mom, she said to Max and then asked her some questions about her bleeding and Max answered them.

Well, the nurse said. Spotting during all stages of pregnancy can be fairly normal. We'll know more after the ultrasound.

The nurse turned to me. Are you Dad? she said.

Moms and dads and babies and families—all of it crushed me.

He is, said Max.

Do you have any questions before I get the doctor? said the nurse.

I don't know how to fill this out, I said, and held up the clipboard.

She wants to know if you have questions about the baby, said Max.

This *is* about the baby, I said.

That's about *you*, said Max. You're making this about *you*. No one cares about that right now.

I just don't know how to answer any of the questions, I said. I want to answer them right.

They're simple questions, said Max.

We were a couple of scared kids bickering past each other. Nurse saw that; she'd probably seen worse.

Can I ask what you're finding difficult about the form? said the nurse.

Max stared at me, annoyed as hell, and I felt like that awkward, flailing dolphin trying to swim, but the nurse reminded me of a corpsman—that hammer look to her, right? Got me steady.

I'm adopted, I said. I don't know anything about my family medical history.

Oh, said the nurse. That's an easy fix. I'll just make a note of it in your file.

She left to get the doctor.

Max and I sat in silence.

Shouldn't have asked you to come, she said.

I just wanted to do it right, I said.

What a fucking mistake, she said, and started crying.

So they had the right information, I said.

I'm scared out of my fucking mind, she said, and all you can think about is yourself. Could you be a more typical guy? You didn't even try to hold my hand in the waiting room. Just said hi.

You barely looked at me, I said.

And I don't know what's going on, she said, and I didn't think I would give a shit if something like this happened, because, honestly, up until I started spotting last night, I was still thinking about getting an abortion, but when I saw that blood, some fucking part of me felt like it grew claws, like now I want to tear anything apart that gets close to me, and I didn't even know you were adopted—which, how fucking embarrassing for me to not know. You're really adopted?

Yeah, I said.

And, she said, we've only known each other for two months and you don't even know my middle name—

Mine's Anthony, I said. Dean Anthony Pusey.

Olivia, she said. Maxine Olivia Foster. But we don't know anything about each other, and when I told my mom and dad over Christmas, all they said was that it was a sin and then refused to talk about it the rest of the time I was there. And now we're in this fucking room and my ass is sweating and sticking to this tissue paper bullshit and I can't catch my breath and the pictures of these fucking babies are driving me fucking crazy and I don't know what I'm doing. What am I doing? What are we doing?

Hugged her. Was the only thing I could think of to do. That was how the nurse and the doctor found us.

MAX LEANED INTO me hard, and I leaned back. Looking at it now, I think she was trying to save me. If she could distract herself that way, then she could ignore her own shit. Little bird with a broken wing is what she saw. Maybe what I showed her. Easier to let someone save you than do it yourself. I knew how to take orders. It's what I'd been waiting for. And there was Max, telling me how to be in the world. It was ugly of me, letting her do the work. Saying it out loud feels like everyone in the world's staring. Palm sweat, thick tongue, face flush. Shame. It's shame. Laying all my shit at her feet and letting it sit there until she sorted it out. In moments where I can be generous, it was more than just me, though; it was our relationship. That was her real mission. Kept saying shit like If we're going to do this . . . Like If we're going to do this, you've got to tell me stuff, like that you're adopted. And If we're going to do this, you've got to come to all the checkups and appointments. It was like she was psyching herself up for a fight.

I was at her place before work one night and we got into it. It was March. I'd been out of the Marines for five months and, since leaving Court's at the end of January, I had been living in my truck—this white, beat-to-shit Dodge with a bed cap that my dad had left behind when he split. I insulated the bed with Reflectix from Home Depot, covered the bottom with blankets, a layer of sleeping pads, and on top of that more blankets. It was warm enough and dark enough for racking out during the day. I could've gotten an apartment. I had money. Instead, I got a PO box and bought a camp stove and boiled ramen and mac and cheese, ate peanut butter and jelly sandwiches and cans of tuna fish.

Didn't tell Max. I felt light.

I'd had the same feeling in Iraq or in the field, even—in the Mojave, freezing under a blanket of stars. It was good, so I didn't fuck with it. Baggage—people, things, memories—had filled me up. They were heavy and loud. Sleeping in the truck quieted everything. Dampened it like a fresh layer of snow.

Anyway, it was warming up. Almost springtime.

Winter was over. The ground cover had thawed and refrozen so many times, it'd turned to ice pellets, retreated from the bases of trees. Snow-melt ran in the gutters, sending the entire salt-scuffed city down the drain. Grass showed in front yards. Trees hadn't budded and the sky was a slate sheet and damp cold got into your bones, but the worst of it was over.

After work I lifted weights at a twenty-four-hour gym where I had a membership and showered in the locker room. Then I ate and took an Ativan and passed out in the blacked-out truck bed until Max was off work.

I was convinced I'd kicked it—the war—that I was getting my fresh start. I passed a community college to and from work every day and I started to think about enrolling—that downtown apartment, the brick one with the big windows and the whole nine yards, kept flashing through my head.

Anyway, that was another part of the reason I didn't get a place of my own: figured Max and I might move in together and I was waiting for her to ask about it. That seemed like the kind of guy she wanted, or maybe the type of guy I wanted her to think I was, or, shit, maybe the kind of guy I wanted to be—patient, even, kind, something like that.

We were dating. I guess you could call it that. How much can you date a woman you got pregnant by accident?

Us getting together—it all felt backwards. She was already pregnant and we didn't leave her apartment much. Sometimes, before my shift at UPS, we'd go to the movies or out to dinner. Mostly we stayed in and watched TV like an old married couple. She was sick all the time.

Everything made her puke. She'd tell me about driving to work in the morning while spewing in her travel mug.

Shit like that made us closer, I think. I'd never known someone's body like that—seen all the parts people usually hide.

So that night, when we fought, we were at her apartment. I'd made dinner—nothing special, a couple steaks and a bag of salad I'd bought from Kroger. It seemed like the kind of thing I was supposed to do, and I felt big doing it. The cashier had been a guy I knew from high school. He'd recognized me, said he'd heard I'd joined the Marines.

Of course you did, he said when I told him yeah, that was right, and he snorted and shook his head like *Of course you did, you big dumb fuck,* and then he told me he was in the Air Guard, that he'd deployed, that he'd been stationed at Al Asad Air Base, that he'd taken incoming mortars, that he'd seen someone get injured.

I mean, I got the guy's entire fucking life story in the time it took to scan three fucking things and shove them in a bag. I just kept nodding and backing up because I knew he wanted to trade stories like baseball cards, but I wasn't about it.

I carried that shit back to Max's with me and started to get the feeling like maybe I should've told the guy about the sheep or the widow's house and the little girl. The IED. Ruiz. The dogs. Anything else because he'd at least been there. Might understand in the way Court couldn't. Or didn't want to.

Max and I, we were at her apartment after dinner watching some old nineties show about lawyers that she had seen probably five times through and that I couldn't follow. The ringing in my head was bad—kept replaying that conversation with the grocery store cashier. Ruiz's voice was all, *Bad juju, dog. No fucking bueno. Vaya con Dios, pinche puta. I don't fuck with cemeteries. You good, dog. You a monster, dog. You nervous? You lamb chops?*

It's the size of a banana, said Max.

There's no way, I said.

Really, a banana, she said. An apple last week. Remember?

I still hadn't tuned in to what she was saying.

Why do they all use the same bathroom? I said.

What are you talking about? she said.

The show, I said. They all use the same bathroom.

It's supposed to be progressive, she said.

It would never work, said Ruiz.

It would never work, I said.

You can't pee in front of a woman? she said.

They'd just be asking for problems is all, I said.

What does that mean: *asking for problems*? She imitated my voice.

It had become a habit with her to imitate my voice. I didn't love it. I mean, it didn't make me laugh like it had that first night in the bar. Just reminded me of how fucking stupid I'd felt when I'd said the thing about her hair looking like mushroom gills. It made me feel like we knew each other, though. Like, I didn't get worked up over it or anything.

I'm not saying anyone's asking for it, I said. I didn't say that. I said there would be problems, that's all. Men and women are different.

We're *different*? she said. My God. How did you figure it out?

Dog, said Ruiz's voice in my head. *This bitch*.

You know what I mean, I said.

Please enlighten me, she said.

I said it before, güey, said Ruiz. *Women can't be grunts*.

Just different is all, I said.

Like, boys have a penis and girls have a vagina kind of different? she said. Are you scared of the vag, Dean? Does it give you stage fright?

She was smiling, but there was a kind of shadow there. I couldn't shut up. Ruiz in my head, coming out of my mouth.

There's a reason men and women have boot camp separately, I said. Why there are different standards. Why women aren't combat arms. It would add a dynamic, I said.

A dynamic, she said.

Yeah, I said.

I moved around on the couch, cleared my throat. Thought of Ruiz and the dark room at the PB, our laughter echoing off the polished concrete. *You good, dog*, he said in my head.

Well? said Max.

I knew I wasn't making much sense to her, that nothing was coming out right, that I was jumping around, digging a hole. Like I said: I couldn't stop.

Imagine this twig puta tryna drag some casualty to cover, said Ruiz. *Tryna fireman carry a dude just had his leg blown off.*

So, like, you, right? I said.

Me, she said.

Imagine you're a Marine, I said.

Okay, she said, and closed her eyes and pressed her lips together.

I'm a big asshole who doesn't understand evolution, she said.

She'd never really talked about the Marines like that before, and it stung, I'll admit that, but I ignored her. I could do that by then. Those months together, just us mostly. Just me and Max together. It was like the Corps. Put a couple guys together in the shit for a week and they'll be ready to tear their own guts out for each other even if in the next minute they tell each other to fuck off and pound sand.

Can't believe you let her run her fucking suck like that, said Ruiz.

Now, I said, imagine if we were deployed to Iraq together and in the same fire team and we got into a gunfight. I would try to protect you instead of try to complete the mission. Or maybe I'd still be on the mission, but I'd also be worrying about you, and that would be distracting.

My logic was ridiculous; hard to even tell the story.

Your training wasn't very good, then, she said.

What? I said.

You know, she said, if you can be distracted by one helpless lady.

It's biological, I said.

Pheromones, dog, said Ruiz. *Why I never shower after the gym. Gets females horned up.*

Isn't that what every single war movie is about? she said. Some guy gets hurt or captured or something and some other guys disobey orders to save him. Then they die, or get medals, or die and get medals.

It's not really like that, I said.

What's it like? she said.

What? I said.

War, she said. She shut off the TV.

She'd never asked before; it threw me. After Court, I'd decided I was done with war stories, but when she asked, I started thinking of the doctor's office, how close I'd felt to her then, telling her about my adoption. Shit, even just my middle name. And I thought about the cashier at Kroger and before I could stop myself said, We shot dogs.

Dogs? she said.

Yeah, I said, and laughed. All these fucking dogs, I said. They were getting into the wire, eating all these muffins—they gave us Otis Spunkmeyer muffins all the time, who the fuck knows why—and they were getting into our base, eating all these muffins, and just shitting everywhere. Entire place smelled like apple cinnamon dogshit. And so we set a trap for them one night, an ambush, and just . . .

I was telling it funny, like I'd tell it to a bunch of Marines, but when I looked over at Max, she wasn't laughing.

There's your difference, she said.

What? I said.

Men and women, she said. You just want to destroy everything. You don't know how to nurture.

You asked to hear it, I said.

And I do want to hear it, but that doesn't mean I have to like it, she said.

I was goddamned mad about the entire thing—fucking sand-chafing-my-nuts-on-a-twenty-klick-hike pissed. The kind of pissed where you're nothing but the feeling—skin flayed away, bones powder, just one giant pulsing nerve. And it was like I was in a crowded bar and everyone was trying to dap my knuckles and slap my back and Mom and Penny were asking me if I was okay and Rick was telling Mom not to worry and Max was just trying to understand it all while I threw lie after lie at her and there was Ruiz telling me, *Put this bitch in her place, güey,* and Grant was telling me to let it all out and the fat and happy TAP instructor was telling me, *Tiny little breaths. Tiny little breaths.*

My entire life was laid out in front of me then and I knew this was how I'd feel for the rest of it if we stayed together. I decided never to tell her another goddamned thing about the Marines. I wanted to slam my fist into her guts and turn the little pollywog inside her into a bloody smear on the seat of her sweatpants, then go suck start the Colt in my truck. And Ruiz was in my head all *Get some, get some, get some!*

Everything was telling me to cut my losses, ditch Max, the baby, get the fuck out, reenlist, run back to California. Run.

I wondered if that was what my birth mom had thought over and over while I grew inside her. *RUNRUNRUNRUNRUN*, I thought. Like prey. Like a sheep. Lamb chops.

I stood to leave.

You're leaving? she said.

You don't want me here, I said.

What are you going to do when we move in together? she said.

So I didn't run, right? Of course I didn't. Instead, after she said that thing about moving in together, I breathed. Tiny little breaths.

You want me to move in? I said.

You're already over here most of the time, she said.

It'll still be different, right? I said.

Yeah, she said. You won't be able get away from me as easily.

All that heat blew out of me. Ruiz went with it. I got shaky on my feet, dropped onto the other love seat, leaned my head back, and thought about the stupid shit I'd just said, the terrible shit I'd just thought.

What the fuck do you even see in me, I said. For real.

You don't know by now? she said.

I guess I'm just a big asshole who doesn't understand evolution, I said. She juked the dig.

Dinner, she said, and waved her hands at the food.

Looked at her and shook my head like *What the fuck?*

Steak and salad? she said.

Okay, I said.

You're predictable, she said. What you see is what you get.

I clenched my jaw so I didn't laugh in her face and my palms started to sweat. The quiet of the apartment made me want to tap my foot, drum my knees, run screaming out the fucking door, but I forced myself to stay still.

I need that, she said.

Someone who follows orders, I said.

Someone I can count on, she said. I can't count on my parents—not even Rose and Brooke, really. So it's just me, and I've got to be perfect. And that's been fine so far. But I don't think I can do that anymore.

We sat for a minute looking at each other.

And the last couple months have been good, she said.

Even after this? I said. I meant the fight.

Couples fight, she said. I'm not going to cut and run.

What's that mean? I said.

You know, she said. Not everyone's going to leave you.

Cleared my throat. Shook my head. Couldn't find my tongue.

I'm not going to leave you is what I mean, she said.

My ears were hot and my skin itched and I got the time travel feeling like when I'd fight or hold a gun. Like I didn't exist.

But it was different then.

Like, it wasn't that I didn't exist. It was like my past present and future were all one thing then. Like I was whole. And before I could say anything or even think to say anything, Max said, We should move in together.

Truth? I said.

Always, she said.

★

It was Nguyen's twenty-second birthday, and we were about to get kicked out of a fucking Dave and Buster's in Carlsbad.

Nguyen lived in Carlsbad with his wife, Amber, and their newborn son, Raven. They called him Ray. There wasn't shit to do in Carlsbad but Legoland, so before Ray was born we had used their place as a home base to pregame before we hit SD—Pacific Beach, Ocean Beach, the Gaslamp—fucking tourist traps or whatever—lots of civilians looking for a good time. We didn't think it would be any different that night, but of course it was.

We never made it down to San Diego.

First thing that went wrong was by the time Ruiz, Crowe, Baptiste, and I got to Nguyen and Amber's apartment, they were waiting for us in their SUV. But both of them were asleep. Ruiz knocked on the car door and Nguyen startled awake and rolled down the window.

Jesus Christ, said Ruiz, smells like fucking Bengay and Fixodent up in this bitch.

Fucking bobbing for cock in there or what? said Crowe.

Bobbing for cock was DI speak for nodding off.

Give him one! I said.

Wasn't that we were really making fun of each other, we just didn't know how to say something like You matter to me, or How are you doing? or whatever, so shit came out like Fuck you, you white trash piece of shit, and Your mom should've swallowed, and You're so fucking ugly, it looks like your face was on fire and someone tried to put it out with a pitchfork. All these years later I still have to fight the urge to talk to people like that.

Most sleep I've had since Iraq, said Nguyen.

He stretched and let us in. Amber stayed asleep.

I was excited to see Amber that night. Hadn't seen her, really, since before the deployment when she'd come out to bars with us and talk us up to other women. She was short and thick, legs like tree trunks. Brown, curly hair. Smoked a lot of weed. Called herself basic. She was familiar—felt safe, you know?

We weren't around women a lot. Some guys were married, but they kept their wives separate from the Corps, and, like, we got laid a lot, but those women didn't know us. They were one-night stands; we gave them fake names. Targets more than anything. Hurts to say that now. It does. But it's the truth.

Once, we had a group of woman Marines embedded with us during a training exercise, a program called the Lionesses. They were like infantry without being called infantry because the Marine Corps didn't let women in combat arms roles back then. Needed them because there were all kinds of problems with men searching women in Iraqi culture, so the Marine Corps improvised. Improvise, adapt, overcome. Oorah. Kill. Semper Gumby, Ruiz would've said. We didn't get close to them—the Lionesses—because Gunny Bat said if he caught us talking to them, he'd fuck us up good, and Gunny Bat didn't screw around.

Anyway, we didn't have much contact with women. Maybe if we'd gone to boot camp on the East Coast where they had the female training battalion, it would've seemed more normal to us. But on the West Coast, the Corps kept us so separate that whenever I saw a Marine who wasn't a dude somewhere around Camp Pendleton, I did a double-take. Like a fucking unicorn sighting or whatever.

So having Amber around felt like some kind of gift. If she was out with us, I'd rather talk to her—be near her—than down shots and try to get laid. Liked people thinking maybe we were together.

Nguyen pulled into the Dave and Buster's parking lot.

That was the next thing that went wrong.

Fuck we doing here? said Ruiz.

We're not up for the Gaslamp, man, said Nguyen, and he pointed at Amber. Her mouth was open and she was snoring quietly.

Besides, said Nguyen, it's the first time we've left Ray with Amber's mom. Don't want to be too far away.

Fucking video games? said Baptiste. Wanted to get my dance on, man.

Daddy's gone fucking limp noodle, I said.

Man, all I want to do is have a couple beers, play some video games, and catch up with you all, said Nguyen.

Love, he said—that's what he called Amber: love—Love, we're here. He put his hand on her arm to wake her up.

Nguyen was the guy who'd taught me the most painful way to perp-walk a detainee, who had a Bronze Star for clearing out a machine-gun nest on his first deployment, who ran the fastest three-mile in our company even after he'd taken grenade shrapnel in his left leg. This guy who—I'd seen his power, right? Seen him command a fire team—speed, surprise, violence. He seemed so different to me then. Thin somehow, gentle. I regretted what I'd said. He adored her, his family. We didn't exist for him in that moment. I envied him and thought maybe I wanted to be someone like that, thought that I was supposed to be someone like that.

Inside Dave and Buster's, people yelled to be heard and laughed too loud. Axe body spray and fried onions gagged me. Neon buzzed on the walls, and huge flat-screens played sports highlights on a loop. We sat in the middle of everything at a high-top table and it put us all on edge. Had only been back a few weeks and we were all still checking over our shoulders and shooting our heads in the direction of loud noises. We were soft targets. No armor, no weapons. Fucking mindset white. Unaware and unprepared.

Drinks helped us care less. When the server came around, Ruiz ordered vodka rocks like he did. Amber a club soda with lime. The rest of us got beers. When the server asked, even though I was under twenty-one,

I gave her my military ID, she looked at it, looked at me, shrugged, and brought me a beer. Went like that most places.

Damn, I think she likes me, said Crowe.

Didn't even look at you, said Baptiste.

I think she's into Dean, said Amber. You should get her number! She looks nice.

Not my type, I said, trying not to look at Ruiz.

Yeah, said Baptiste. Dean fucks goats.

How many times did LT walk in on you fucking a rubber glove wedged inside your rolled-up sleeping mat? I said.

Cala a boca, said Baptiste. He waved his hand in front of his face and took a drink.

And it was a sheep, I said. Not a goat.

I took a drink.

And you know I never fucked the thing, I said.

Shouldn't have bitten, but I did, and then Baptiste and Crowe were on me about the goddamned sheep, making jokes and kissy noises and all kinds of other dumb bullshit.

Ruiz wasn't paying attention; he raised his glass, interrupting the ribbing. Well, he said, Happy birthday, Winny.

We followed him and said happy birthday and then sat in silence, looking around us. There were a couple other groups of Marines—could tell by their haircuts and too-tight T-shirts—but the families were clearing out because it was getting late.

We drank our first round quick and ordered another.

Some party, said Crowe.

Just feels good to get out of the house, said Nguyen.

For real, said Amber. It's so good to see you guys! I've been telling Vinh we should have you all over, but there hasn't been a good time.

It didn't sound like Amber—or it did, but like Amber trying to sound like Amber.

Vinh? said Crowe.

That's my name, said Nguyen. Vinh Andrew Trung Nguyen.

We're trying to use Vinh's Vietnamese name more so Ray understands his culture, said Amber. She was smiling and nodding and talking loud so we could hear.

That's white nonsense, said Ruiz. He snagged the server and ordered another drink and we laughed. Probably because none of us had any say in who we were, and that seemed okay to us back then. Crazy that you'd get bent out of shape about something like that. Black, white, brown—didn't matter. Most of the time we didn't feel like anything but Marines. We were all fucking green. Pointless to see anything else.

Take it easy, bro, said Nguyen.

Would it kill you to not be an asshole for one second, Israel? said Amber. Right then she looked ten feet tall and bulletproof. All that Amber-trying-to-sound-like-what-she-thought-she-sounded-like shit was gone.

Babe, she said to Nguyen, I'll be so fucking happy when you don't have to deal with all the macho bullshit anymore.

Love, said Nguyen, not now.

What? she said. It's true.

Shit, man! said Crowe. You getting out? Congratulations.

Not getting out, said Nguyen.

Ruiz stared down Nguyen and I felt like I was eight again and my parents were fighting.

You know you can buy out your contract? said Crowe.

Man, that shit ain't true, said Baptiste.

It is! said Crowe. Heard about this guy who done it from One-Five after he won the fucking lotto. Imagine showing up to formation the next day and just sitting down and posting up the double bird when Gunny tells you to get to the position of attention.

Baptiste was nodding along now.

Where you going? I said to Nguyen. I figured he'd go teach something somewhere for a couple years—division schools for machine gunners or maybe he'd be a MOUT instructor or something—before he came back to the battalion. I had more than two years left, but I was already thinking about reenlisting. Ruiz was going to reenlist. Always spitting shit about how even the worst day in the Corps was the best goddamned day because he was still a Marine. He was always only half joking. We all gave him shit, but he sold it hard. The way he talked, it was like twenty years was cake, like it'd be over in a blink, and we'd all stay together and nothing would ever change.

No orders yet, he said. But drill field, maybe. SOI instructor or something?

You want to be a DI? said Crowe. Man, fuck them dudes. Made my life a living hell.

Goddamn Crowe, I said.

What? said Crowe.

I rolled my eyes and drank.

Still infantry after that, said Ruiz.

Babe, said Amber. Just tell them.

Server came around and asked how everything was and we all muttered good and ordered more drinks.

Hey, Crowe said. He reached out to the server, tapped her elbow. When do you get off?

One a.m., said the server.

She didn't see the setup. Was maybe too busy gathering our empties.

Do not, said Amber to Crowe.

Crowe smiled, nodded his chin, and raised his eyebrows at the server, said, Can I watch?

Oh my God, said Amber, and then to the server: I'm so sorry.

The server looked at Amber like she didn't understand why Amber was sorry and left.

Damn! said Crowe. I mean, damn.

See? said Amber to Nguyen. See?

I've been thinking about the air wing, said Nguyen. Maybe going officer.

The fucking dark side? I said.

Too smart to be an officer, dog, said Ruiz. Need a couple more concussions.

We all got a kick out of that. Fucking officers.

You guys can't really think you'll be able to do this job forever, right? said Amber. Can you imagine life at thirty? Forty? Vinh's got chronic pain and he's only twenty-two. You guys wreck yourselves. For what? Fuck that. Fuck them.

Twenty-five seemed ancient to me then. Couldn't think about thirty. Figured I'd be dead by then, really. Amber didn't understand shit, but she'd never talked like that before, had never been so typical. Made me angry. Like finding out your friends put a KICK ME sign on your back or something.

Fuck does that mean? said Crowe. *Chronic pain.*

Means he's a broke-dick, said Ruiz. He drank his drink, shook his head, and crossed his arms.

Sick-bay commando! I said, and pounded my beer.

Shit, Winny, I think you'd make a good LT, said Baptiste.

Like I said, no orders yet, said Nguyen.

The TVs switched from sports highlights to a commercial for *Real Housewives of Orange County*, where everyone looked like plastic and pointed and yelled and flipped tables.

So we're not going anywhere else? said Crowe.

Gonna go play some games, dog, said Ruiz. It's a fucking party.

Ruiz sounded like he'd sounded on deployment whenever he was talking about fucking shit up—like we were calling for air to drop a MOAB on a building or getting ready to clear a house in a raid.

Got to piss anyway, said Crowe.

Me too, said Baptiste. We'll find you after.

They got up and left.

Amber, Nguyen, and I trailed Ruiz, who walked through the game floor like he was on a mission. Amber tried to talk to me. She had a good memory—asked about Penny, and my mom. Gave her short, quick answers. Kind of shit I usually reserved for officers or the chaplain or whatever if I got cornered. I got sick of it and finally asked them about Ray.

We're trying to get him to use a bottle right now because I have to go back to work, said Amber.

Six weeks isn't enough time, said Nguyen.

So unfair, said Amber.

And he's got some kind of allergy, said Nguyen.

But we're not sure really what it is, said Amber.

So many pictures of dirty diapers on my phone, said Nguyen.

Doctors can't figure it out, said Amber.

It's so frustrating, said Nguyen.

I'm only breastfeeding, said Amber.

So it's something she's eating, said Nguyen.

I've cut, like, everything except boiled chicken and potatoes out of my diet, said Amber.

It's been really hard, said Nguyen.

Like, there's a reason all the baby stuff you buy has warnings not to shake your baby, said Amber.

She and Nguyen laughed.

But seriously, said Amber, it was so hard to leave him tonight.

So hard, said Nguyen.

Even with my mom, said Amber.

I had a three-beer buzz going and was working on my fourth, half listening, wishing we were drunk in a too-loud club in the Gaslamp, spitting lines at civilians, when I walked right into Ruiz.

Goddamn, said Ruiz. You pinche putas done talking shit or what?

He'd stopped in front of a Boxer punching bag arcade game—kind of thing that measured how hard you could hit. Couple of middle-aged guys were finishing up their round. We stood back and watched them. Both hit in the seven hundreds—thing went to a thousand—and walked away laughing and shaking their heads.

Ruiz stepped up.

Really? said Nguyen to Ruiz.

You're just proving my point, Iz, said Amber.

Ruiz smiled and scanned his card and the bag dropped. He took a fighting stance, strong leg back, hands up, struck snake-fast, the bag slammed up into the cradle, and my guts felt like they were free-floating around inside me as the digital readout sprinted up into the nine hundreds, stopped at nine hundred forty-one.

You know those don't mean shit, said Nguyen.

The machine reset.

Ruiz shrugged. Dean, hit that shit, dog, he said.

A couple people had stopped to watch.

Highest score gets a hundred bucks? said Ruiz.

It's not even a real punch, said Nguyen. You've got to, like, match the angle to the upward swing of the arm. No one hits like that.

Love, said Amber, can we just play something else?

I thought of Nguyen in the car, how an hour ago I'd wanted to be someone like him, gentle and calm—how I'd envied him. Admired him. Felt embarrassed by it then. He was deserting us. Right or wrong, that's how I saw it: black-and-white.

Let's do it, I said.

Ruiz flexed up his shoulders, that Macho Man Randy Savage shit he did, slapped my back and chest. Get some! he said. Get some, dog!

Knew then where I belonged. I stepped up and smashed the bag as hard as I could. The score readout clicked to eight hundred ninety-three.

Damn, I said.

Not bad, not bad, said Ruiz. He squeezed my shoulder, and I took a spot next to him. So close I felt the heat coming off him. Swear I could hear his heart keeping perfect running cadence.

The machine reset for the last time.

Ruiz grinned a big shit-eating grin at Nguyen and then went to the position of attention and saluted. Last hit's yours, sir, he said loud like he was reporting during a formation or something. People standing around laughed even if they didn't know why they were laughing. I finished my fourth beer and was a little drunk then and the whole thing made me laugh, too. It felt good, being on Ruiz's side. We were in the fucking thing together, we'd keep grinding ourselves away, we'd break together, and fuck anyone else who was going to jump ship.

Babe, let's just go, and play, like, Skee-Ball or something, said Amber.

No, it's okay, said Nguyen.

He took a step to the side of the machine, paused for a second, and then kind of gave the bag this mix of a straight punch and a hook, like a reverse uppercut or something, sent the bag home so hard it rattled the entire machine, and the numbers, ruby red and blinking, ticked up into the nine hundreds, shot past nine hundred forty-one, and stopped at nine hundred eighty-four.

The little crowd cheered.

Nguyen faced Ruiz, gave him a return salute, and quick as lightning Ruiz popped him on the chin and Amber screamed and I was trying to pull them apart while they fell to the ground and rolled, swearing at each other, and Nguyen kept saying, I'm going home, I'm going home, and then a couple beefy security guards were escorting us out of the building.

Outside it'd gotten cold. Amber huddled with Nguyen. He wiped her face and said, Everything's okay, love. Everything's okay. Amber went to get the SUV. Baptiste and Crowe were still inside.

Ruiz, Nguyen, and I stood catching our breath on the sidewalk, eye-fucking each other, waiting to see who would jump first, maybe. And then Ruiz started laughing. I'm going home! I'm going home! he said, making fun of Nguyen. And then the three of us were laughing. Tears-in-our-eyes laughing.

Crowe and Baptiste, drunk as skunks, came out asking where the hell we'd gone and what the fuck happened just as Amber pulled up.

Y'all know you can get a yard of beer here? said Crowe, stumbling to the car.

On the drive to base Baptiste and Crowe slept, Ruiz rode shotgun, and I drove, stayed quiet.

What? said Ruiz. You want to dip, too?

Can't believe Nguyen's bitching out, I said.

Yeah? said Ruiz. Fuck you know about it?

Earlier, when we were heading south while the sun fell into the Pacific on our right while we rolled past the surfers at Trestles and the San Onofre nuclear power plant and the endless miles of coastal scrub and beach, I'd watched Ruiz from the back seat. Imagined him pinning my corporal chevrons on my collar when I earned them, thought of the next deployment, my eventual reenlistment, our redeployment home. And when I thought of home, I thought of California. Not Washington or Indiana. California. Something that was mine. Ours.

I know I'm sticking around, I said.

A WEEK AFTER that dumb fight with Max, she and I found a place—a ground floor two-bedroom in her complex with the same layout but with an extra bedroom and bathroom to the left of the entrance. Max invited Rose and Brooke and their boyfriends, Hudson—*Call me Hud*—and Cooper—*I go by Coop*—to help us move. We promised them food. Max didn't like Cooper or Hudson, but she didn't know how to tell Brooke or Rose. She'd brought it up probably three times that week.

Why don't you like them? I said.

They just bother me, she said.

Then why invite them? I said.

We need help, she said. They're just . . . boys.

They were older than me—twenty-five? Twenty-six?—and both worked in a law office downtown. Junior associates. Never shut the fuck up about it, so, like, that made me feel good, what she said. If they were just boys, then I wasn't, right? I stopped sorting dishes and hugged her and told her it wouldn't be a big deal. We'd work fast.

I didn't mind Cooper and Hudson. The six of us had gone bowling together back in February. They talked about the gym a lot, ball-tapped each other like they were still in high school. Reminded me of officers in the Corps—beefy frat boys who droned on about golf and football. Loyal though. Got that feeling from them, and that was familiar to me. Like, I hadn't liked Crowe at all, but dude was loyal. Loyalty was important.

I thought about inviting Rithipol from work—he would've brought persimmons and we could've traded Marine Corps–Navy shit-talking—but I didn't know his number and anyway I figured asking the dude to throw boxes around on his day off would be shitty. I thumbed a text to Court and my palms got sweaty and my face burned imagining what he might think about the entire situation—Cooper and Hudson and their pretty haircuts and polo shirts. Imagined how he'd look at me like I was this totally different person.

I didn't want to be embarrassed about the life I was making. Kept telling myself I wasn't. Kept telling myself I *wasn't* a different person, that I'd always been *this* person, that there was no fucking point getting worked up about it because if this was who I'd always been, then Court had never even fucking met me and we didn't have business. I sent the text but didn't wait for a reply.

It wasn't for-real winter anymore, but the wind had picked up and clouds rolled low and fast in the sky; the sun was on and off and the world was damp. Rose and Brooke helped Max pack up the last of her stuff while Cooper, Hudson, and I carried boxes from the old apartment to the new place.

Every time I walked through the door, I couldn't help but think what a fucking nightmare the thing would've been to clear: the fatal funnel with the kitchen see-through, the two wings with bathrooms and closets and all kinds of other hidey-holes for whatever muj to lie in wait ready to merc you in the back for a tiny slipup.

It made me feel good though because I wasn't clearing it, right? Now it was my defensive position. It was my home. *Good luck, motherfuckers,* I thought.

I marked egress points and fallback positions while I dropped boxes labeled KITCHEN and LIVING ROOM and BEDROOM.

I hadn't thought like that in three months—since Christmas, really—and the shit bounced around in my brain, loose change in a dryer. The new me didn't know what to do with it; it was driving me fucking bonkers. *It'll eat the world alive. Tiny little breaths. Tiny little breaths.* I inhaled carpet cleaner and fresh paint and held my breath and clenched my jaw until my vision went fuzzy, then let it out a puff at a time. I wanted to scream. It was like there was no getting away from any of it. No matter how hard I tried to drop my goddamned pack and sprint away from it, somehow the fucking thing was always there.

Cooper and Hudson were in the living room, shooting the shit.

I think we've got a few more boxes and then just the furniture, I said.

Hudson leaned against the wall, texting on his phone, and Cooper sat on a box marked KITCHEN that he'd dropped in the living room. I made for the door.

Watched this shit on the History Channel last night about Flujah, said Cooper.

Fallujah, I said.

You were there, right? said Cooper.

Not during Phantom Fury, no, I said.

Too bad, Cooper said. Looked fucking tight.

That's what he said: *tight.* He stood, bent his knees, and pulled his arms up to mimic a rifle.

Pew, pew, he said, and fake-sighted in on an imaginary target, then moved around the living room.

Hudson looked up from his phone. We got to get to the range soon, man! he said.

I would've fucked shit up for sure if I'd been there, said Cooper. He moved like he was trying to be some high-speed door kicker. Headshot, headshot, headshot, he said. Should've joined up.

Combat glide's legit, dog, said Ruiz.

I almost signed up, said Hudson, but I blew out my knee in a lacrosse match in high school.

Cooper stood to his full height. Bro, same, but football, he said. No one in the stands can really see it but the field's a war zone, you know?

You should come blast with us, too, Dean, said Hudson.

Yeah, maybe, I said. Been a while since I put rounds downrange. I thought of Court. The rifle locked in the bed of my truck.

You're a good dude, Dean, said Cooper. Like, Marine Corps. Badass. Thanks for your service, man. I don't think I've said that. Have I said that?

We should go grab some more boxes, I said.

No rush, man, they're taking their time packing that stuff up, said Cooper.

Hey, how's it going with you and Brooke? said Hudson.

It's all right, I guess, said Cooper. He looked at me and smiled. Can you keep a secret, Dean?

Sure, I said, and shrugged.

Incoming, said Ruiz.

I mean, you might get this more than Hudson, but Brooke can be a fucking handful sometimes, said Cooper.

What's that mean? said Hudson.

Dude, said Cooper. Come on.

What? said Hudson.

You know, said Cooper. Rose is just . . .

What? said Hudson.

Nice, said Cooper. That's all. She's nice. And she's good-looking, don't get me wrong, bro. But you can tell she's grateful.

Whatever, man, said Hudson. He shook his head, dropped his head and kept his eyes glued to his feet like the goddamned secret of life was etched into his kicks, and I saw red creep up his neck.

Cooper turned back to me. But you know what I mean, right, Dean?

I liked Brooke. More than I liked Cooper. She was a little sharp, yeah, but funny and kind and had good taste in movies. Something about Cooper felt like talking to a Marine, though. Almost like Ruiz. Like, the guy was quick, with it. Charming, I guess. And they'd invited me to go shooting with them. I figured they probably imagined Marines a certain way and so I was trying to act like that. Part of me—as much as I didn't think much of them—wanted them to like me, too.

She can be a cunt for sure, I said.

Jesus, said Hudson, looking up at me.

Cooper burst out laughing.

He stepped forward and clapped me on the shoulder.

You're not fucking wrong, though, he said. She still brings up that night *last year in November* when I didn't answer the phone. Doesn't believe I forgot to plug it in.

Did you? said Hudson.

Fuck no, said Cooper. I closed down a strip club.

Hudson shook his head. You're a dog, bro, he said.

They slapped hands.

What club? I said.

Belle Exotic, said Cooper.

I nodded. Had never been—it was the kind of place that didn't have a buffet. My mouth filled with brown, limp, ranch-soaked lettuce chunks and soggy crinkle-cut fries, and thick, spicy chicken meat and I was thinking I might blow fucking chunks all over Cooper and Hudson's perfect fucking everything and Court was laughing, saying, We got to civilize you, boy, while he clapped me on the shoulder and then Guy the bouncer was squeezing my shoulder, carrying me offstage while I cried into his leather jacket and his hand was Mom's on my shoulder was Ruiz's hand moving up my thigh and that hand was my hand in Max's wet, warm mouth and Max's mouth was Penny's was Ruiz's was my birth mom's was the sheep's. A ricocheting bullet flying down a hallway hugging the wall heading right fucking at me.

You get it, though, right, Dean? said Cooper. I mean, you're moving in with Max.

He smiled at me, perfect teeth.

Bro, come on, now, said Hudson.

No, said Cooper. No disrespect, bro. She's great. And, like, props. But, Jesus. Sometimes if she could just shut her fucking mouth, you know?

He smiled and talked at the same time, like those fucking guys who make the dummies talk without moving their mouths.

And where are they? said Cooper. How come they're not hauling heavy-ass boxes across an apartment complex, you know?

Some people just want it all handed to them, said Hudson. Like, Rose? You think she's nice or whatever, but she keeps complaining about how she should've gotten this manager position at work but they hired an outside guy instead.

Shit, man, said Cooper. Like, men and women are just *different*. That guy's probably got a ton of experience or education or whatever, but because he's a *guy*, people just automatically assume he got the job *because* he's a guy.

I couldn't get a word in. Didn't really want to. Kept thinking, *We're not the same*. But really—and this is the shit of it—I knew we were. It made me hate myself for what I'd said to Max about men and women being different, to Cooper about Brooke, to Penny about Iris, all the women in bars in SoCal, fucking JLo. I owed JLo a fucking apology.

You seem like a good guy, Dean, said Cooper. Marines. That's some shit. Not SEALs or anything. But still—you read that book? You know the one. Leading and winning or whatever.

He snapped his fingers trying to remember the title.

That's what they need to teach in school, said Hudson.

I mean, Iraq? said Cooper. Afghanistan? It all looks kind of tame. Not like Nam or anything. SEALs, though. I can get behind that.

There isn't still fighting over there, right? said Hudson.

After we finished, I begged off help and drove around for a good thirty minutes to keep them all from asking why all my shit was already in my truck. I pulled into a McDonald's where I'd parked during the day a couple times and opened Insta, went to Brooke's page, clicked a picture of her and Cooper together, and followed the tag to Cooper's profile. His page was public; the bio read: *Libertarian, lawyer, Christ follower, sportsman.*

I scrolled through professional-looking images of handguns and rifles and short videos of Cooper on an outdoor range practicing tactical shooting and memes sporting that ΜΟΛΩΝ ΛΑΒΕ bullshit under Spartan helmets splattered with blood or the yellow of the Gadsden flag and pictures of what I figured was Cooper's left hand laid out with the various expensive-looking knives and military watches and carbon-fiber card carriers with hidden razor edges and miniature surefire flashlights he was carrying in his pockets that day. Beneath the posts were quotes about tyranny and inalienable rights and a fuckton of hashtags: hashtag two-a hashtag comeandtakethem hashtag thisissparta hashtag constitution hashtag America hashtag murica hashtag merica hashtag usmc hashtag usarmy hashtag usn hashtag usaf hashtag everydaycarry hashtag edc hashtag tacticool hashtag liberty hashtag freedom hashtag socialismsucks hashtag fuckyourfeelings hashtag patriot hashtag guns hashtag pewpew hashtag selfdefense hashtag rangeday hashtag concealedcarry hashtag firstlineofdefense hashtag righttobeararms hashtag highcapacity hashtag gunstagram hashtag gunlife hashtag handgun hashtag longgun hashtag donttreadonme.

Each image had thousands of likes and comments.

I wanted to roll with Cooper. Fuck him up. Coop. He was big, but he moved slow from what I saw in the videos—like how I'd moved before Ruiz had taught me: *You got bulk, you just don't know how to use it for shit.* That's what I'd tell him, and then I'd show him. I could take him easily, bend and squeeze and flex, make him tap. I thought of Sergeant Moss wrenching my neck, of Ruiz's hand on my thigh, on my stomach, in my hair.

When I got back, I brought in a garbage bag of clothes, a few pairs of shoes, and the rifle in its case. Everyone was standing around in the new place. Max was putting dishes in a cabinet; the front door was open. Max lived in one long hot flash and wore short sleeves, her skin pale and awkwardly out of place in the last stretch of cool weather.

Girl, aren't you cold? said Rose.

I don't remember what being cold is like, said Max.

Seemed like one of those hard-ass things Ruiz would've said, then made fun of, and I loved her for it and wished I hadn't brought in the gun, but then they all looked at me.

And Court was there.

You didn't say Court was coming, said Max.

They hadn't met, really, but Max had heard stories—the bar the first night we'd met when Court had ditched me, the party when she'd found me running. She had opinions.

Looks like I missed all the work, said Court.

I was happy to see him now that he was there. It was like I wasn't a completely new person, like I had some foundation under me or something.

What's that? Max said. She appeared in the kitchen pass-through, pointed at the rifle case.

Bro, said Cooper. Is that what I think it is?

I opened the case and showed them the Colt. Rose asked if I got it in the Marines and I laughed at that. It was cute. Like the Marine Corps had given me a going-away present or something. Fucking gold watch or whatever.

I bought it after I got out, I said.

I don't think it will fit in any of the closets, said Max. She stood with her arms crossed above the swell of her belly.

Talk about home security, said Court.

Hudson and Cooper laughed. I hated that they laughed.

Complacency kills, I said.

This isn't the Marine Corps, Max said.

Typical, said Cooper. You just don't know how to use it.

She held her index finger in front of his face and mimed squeezing a trigger and said something about monkeys and I thought about Sergeant Moss calling us monkeys when we did something stupid.

It's not hard, he'd say. This is the goddamned Marine Corps, not fucking Harvard. You're a bunch of fucking monkeys. Just do what you see me do. Monkey see, monkey do. Got it, monkeys?

I could teach you, I said.

I was serious. I loved her and I loved the rifle. It made sense to me. But Max made a face like I'd dropped my pants, squatted, and shit in the middle of the living room.

Taught me how to shoot this bad boy, said Court. He took his pistol from the holster inside his waistband held it pointed to the ceiling, finger straight and off the trigger, which made me smile. *Keep your finger straight and off the trigger until you are ready to fire*, said my PMI in my head.

Jesus Christ, said Max.

Oh, man, said Cooper, that's pretty. Can I see?

Court removed the magazine, cleared the breech, and handed the pistol to Cooper, who started examining it, Hudson looking over his shoulder.

It's no big deal, Max, said Brooke. I carry one in my purse. She pointed to her oversized shoulder bag on the table behind us.

I wanted to apologize to her for what I said to Cooper then. I wanted to ask her what it was—the make and model, the caliber, the load, the recoil. I wanted to hold the gun in my hands, break it down, reassemble it. I wanted her to describe what she felt when the firing pin struck a chambered round, what the burnt carbon reminded her of.

B, that's kind of badass, said Rose.

Max shot Rose a look.

She had a quick switch. Could tell she was getting heated.

I mean, I don't think I would ever buy one or whatever, said Rose.

We can get you a gun, babe, said Hudson.

Court was talking to Cooper, who was aiming the pistol at the wall. He had a good Weaver stance.

I cannot fucking believe this, said Max.

What? said Brooke. My dad gave it to me. Coop taught me how to shoot.

Max went back to slamming dishes into cupboards.

Cooper handed the pistol to Court and slung his heavy arm over Brooke's shoulder, his bomber jacket strained against his biceps.

I was scared at first, said Brooke, but it's pretty fun.

You're a great shot, babe, said Cooper. They kissed.

I wanted what they had.

There was that shooting last week, said Rose. The mall in Seattle?

Saw that, said Court.

Oh my God, said Brooke. I read that a girl in one of the shops dumped the guy like a day before he did it.

Did she die? said Cooper.

Babe, said Brooke. That's a fucked-up question.

I don't think so, said Rose. But he killed *six people*.

Six isn't very many in a shopping mall, I didn't say.

If he'd controlled his breathing and used proper sight picture and alignment, he would've killed more, I didn't say.

He should've made a bigger target—blocked the exit and corralled them like cattle with the fire alarm, I didn't say.

I would've killed more, I didn't say.

I kept my mouth shut.

Six doesn't seem like very many, said Court.

I was thinking the same thing! said Cooper.

How bad do you think she feels? said Hudson.

A dish shattered in the kitchen. Don't know if Max dropped it by accident or on purpose. She was mad though—red-faced and sweaty. I watched her close her eyes and take a breath.

Max, are you okay? said Rose.

I'm fine, said Max. She came out of the kitchen into the living room.

It was one of the shoppers that shot the fuck, said Court.

See? said Cooper.

Everyone needs to learn to defend themselves, said Hudson.

People *need* to eat and drink water and fucking sleep, said Max.

She balled her fists so hard, her neck flexed and her jaw set. Part of me wanted her to send a right hook into Cooper's face. *Do it*, I thought. *Fucking do it.* We'd beat him together. But she turned to me instead.

Why do you need it, Dean? she said.

I don't *need* it, I said.

Better to have it and not need it, right? said Brooke.

That's right, babe, said Cooper.

I'm sorry I brought it up at all, said Rose.

Then why do you want it? said Max.

It was us then, just us, having the conversation. The other five of them dropped away like the goddamned floor had opened up and swallowed them. She wasn't fighting; this wasn't like the men-and-women thing. She was reaching out a hand. She was trying to get it, trying to understand. But Court was there. And Cooper and Hudson—as much as I wanted to curb-stomp both of them—they made me want to be tough or whatever. Aggro King Shit. I didn't want to back down.

I could have then, right? Realized Max was right, that the rifle wasn't me, it was the Marine Corps, it was the past. It was an anchor. I can see it now of course. This big fucking anchor keeping part of me in the past, in the goddamned desert, on a rooftop next to Ruiz, in the bed of the highback with his hand on my thigh, in the dark room of the PB, in a goddamned shitty forever war. I could've ended it right there, maybe. Who knows?

You're right, I didn't say.

I'll sell you the rifle right now, Coop, I didn't say.

I love you, Max. Marry me, I didn't say.

What I said: I like it. I like shooting. I don't need a reason.

It doesn't matter if people need them or not, said Court. This is America.

I don't know what that means, said Max.

She knew what it meant. That was how Max argued. If she didn't like something, she'd act like she didn't understand it so the other person would have to explain it to her and that made them sound stupid as fuck most of the time. And it was like, okay, we're adults here having a conversation adults have. I felt good about that: being in our apartment—*our* apartment—right? With my best friend and the woman I loved, and we were having a conversation. Didn't matter if it was an argument or not; didn't matter if it was more yelling than anything else. Something comforting about it. Reminded me of Mom and Penny, maybe.

It's the media, said Court. Twisting everyone up.

You think so? I said.

Sheeple, said Cooper.

While they all went back and forth and back and forth, I said, I'm going to get the burgers ready. But no one heard me or no one cared.

You lamb chops, dog? said Ruiz.

The only thing that stops a bad guy with a gun is a good guy with a gun.

I don't know who said it—Hudson or Cooper, I think. I decided I hated them after all. Something like that would have been rich coming from Court. Anyway, it was bullshit. I didn't think I was some fucking hero or anything. All that fly-where-eagles-dare, America-the-Beautiful bullshit. I never bought it. Like I said, I joined to fuck shit up and hurt people. All Ruiz's sheep and sheepdog and wolf talk—when it comes down to it, wolves and dogs are both hunters. Sometimes it's hard to know the difference.

I was zoning out, knuckles deep in ground chuck, when shouting came out of the living room.

You're fucking wrong, said Max.

You don't know what you're saying, said Court.

You know what? said Max. Get out!

You need to calm down, said Court.

I think we all need to calm down, said Rose.

Need to handle your woman, said Court.

What? I said.

Max shoved him in the chest and surprised everyone and Brooke laughed that nervous laugh people do when they're not sure if something's real or fake and Court cocked his arm like he was going to hit Max and Cooper got in the way and Rose screamed and Brooke and Hudson stood around wide-eyed.

Get out! Get out! Get out! said Max over and over.

Court looked at me, and I knew he was waiting for me to tell Max to shove it up her ass. That he was family. But I didn't.

Fuck this shit, said Court. He left through the still-open door.

My clenched fists were covered in egg and onions and meat and Max was red-faced furious and Cooper whispered to Brooke and Hudson comforted Rose and it was the first time I can remember being embarrassed of Court, and part of me felt good because of that, like it meant I was growing up and part of me felt like a total shit. Big fucking blue falcon.

In the end, the external storage closet was a compromise: it had a knob lock and a dead bolt and technically wasn't in the apartment. Eventually, I thought about the rifle less and less—the rigid pistol grip stretching the meat between my thumb and index finger, the butt pressing into the hollow of my shoulder, the stock pulling at my cheek—and life moved on. Everything was good. Until it wasn't.

WITHOUT COURT, IT was easy to fall into what Max and I were making. After the shit with the rifle, I wanted it—the birthing classes and doctor's appointments, that life. I liked showing up with her at the ob-gyn, nurses fawning over what a good guy I seemed. I read the books she gave me and looked for others at the library. Cleaned the apartment Marine Corps clean when Max couldn't bend over anymore. Followed orders. Gave her the What-you-see-is-what-you-get version of me she thought I was. Liked that she needed me, that we were each other's family. Except the more I kept pounding the Corps down with every little change, the harder it fought back.

One weekend we went to IKEA in Indianapolis. It was terrifying. Striking and bright, people juking and bumping. Sharp, hard edges. Intersecting geometric shapes. Endless rooms of just-so low-set furniture, retro colors. I wished I had a shell. Fucking Kevlar shell—vest, helmet. Rifle. Goddammit, I wanted the Colt. It was the first time I'd really thought about it in two months.

I wish I had my rifle, I didn't say.

Can you imagine clearing this? I didn't say.

Speed, surprise, violence of action, I didn't say.

What I said: Jeez, this place is big.

The new me said shit like *jeez.*

Really, I *did* say everything—just to Ruiz. Since moving in with Max, Ruiz had come in from the shadows, had been squatting in that ringing at the base of my skull. Popped out every now and then and we'd shoot the shit like when we were back in country at the PB. That didn't seem weird to me then. It was like *Yeah, where else would he be?* I had myself fooled I was the big swinging dick in charge. Like I was managing to keep it all separate—the war and Max—and I figured if I knew where Ruiz was, I didn't have to look over my shoulder in the dark. Complacency kills.

I took a wide-set stance, held an imaginary rifle at the high ready, and combat glided a few steps along the path marked with light-projected arrows from the exposed guts of the ceiling. Heel, toe, heel, toe, heel, toe.

Slow is smooth; smooth is fast, dog, said Ruiz.

A couple stared.

Don't be weird, said Max.

It had been good between us. Because she was nesting she liked safety, routine. That was five by five with me—the new me who said *jeez* and talked to Rith at work during break about what it was like being a dad. The new me who didn't want to jam his thumbs into Grant's eyeballs every time the guy smiled his perfect fucking smile, who had started sending Max GIFs and memes of those fast-talking TV shows during the day when she'd text to complain about coworkers. The new me who had himself fooled he was in charge.

Fatal funnels everywhere, güey, said Ruiz. *Watch your six.*

I pretended to be tail-end Charlie, turned one-eighty, cleared the rear, turned forward, continued my patrol. I dared whatever bad guys to show themselves. *Fuck around and find out.* It was gung ho, lifer nonsense.

Oorah! Ruiz flexed his shoulders. *Get some, killer!*

We definitely need this, said Max, snapping a picture of a high chair's price tag—ANTILOP printed across the top—with her phone.

Put it in the cart, I said. I'd never been to IKEA before, but I knew the jokes: cheap shit, hard to put together, couples fighting, blah blah blah blah blah.

The tag tells the warehouse location, said Max.

Like a grid coordinate, I said.

This isn't Iraq, okay? she said.

Grid coordinates are on all maps, I said, but Max was already in the next room, seven months pregnant and on a mission to prepare for the baby. The fetus. She didn't like me calling it that, but I didn't know what else to call it. Scared me to think of it as a baby. Like, if it was a baby, I was already a dad, and that freaked me the fuck out in a way I couldn't really talk about.

I turned the corner and walked into a guy's ass while he was bent over, taking a picture of a tag that read SÅNGLÄRKA. I didn't say I was sorry and hurried to catch Max.

Lost in the sauce, boot motherfucker, said Ruiz. *Complacency kills, you fucking new guy.*

What he meant was that I was a fucking fetus, too—out of the Corps eight months, working part-time loading package cars at UPS, pregnant twenty-something girlfriend teaching me how to be a human, diddy bopping around IKEA like I knew what the fuck a SÅNGLÄRKA did. So maybe I felt closer to the thing in Max's belly than I wanted to admit then. Neither of us had asked for any of this.

Max waddled from room to room, measured furniture with an IKEA paper measuring tape, took pictures of tags; I followed, pushed the cart. Cooper would've called me a beta or a cuck or something, probably. My face got hot and I tried not to think about that, tried not to think about my arm around his neck, cutting blood flow, about Sergeant Moss's arm around my neck in the atrium of the PB, about my arm around the party guy's neck while I baaed and woofed into his ear. About Ruiz. About the sheep and the dogs who had my face—teeth chomping torn open guts, blood-smeared skin.

Max tossed a KRAMA, a LENAST, a KLÄMMIG into the cart. I whispered the Swedish nonsense words and their thick weight held me down, anchored me to the soft fabrics and plush pillows and throws, and Ruiz and all the other shit faded back into the constant drone at the base of my grape.

While Max shuffled and took pictures, I sat on a POÄNG in a living room and then the fetus was in my arms. Not a fetus anymore: a baby. I was in the future. The baby's eyelids drooped. I bounced in the chair while the TV projected an old, muted sitcom blue and white over the

LIDHULT and the LACK and the walls covered in KNOPPÄNGS and SKAT-TEBYS and HOVSTAS.

At a GERTON piled with textbooks and papers I wore glasses and typed on a computer under buttery light from a VIDJA while the baby played on a STADSDEL with a LILLABO.

I made egg scramble in an OUMBÄRLIG while the baby—a toddler now—stood on a BEKVÄM, watching. Max played music from an ENEBY and danced with our dog through the kitchen, making the toddler laugh.

I stood at the threshold of a room. There was a NORDAAL against the far wall. Two tiny chests rose and fell under the LATTJOS. Two.

I walked into another bedroom and there I was. Sleeping on a SULTAN FLOKENES next to Max. Fat and happy.

Overhead, dog, said Ruiz. *Check your goddamned overhead.*

When I looked up, I was back in IKEA. The present. I pointed my imaginary RIFLE into the wiring and girders, the SPOTLIGHT blinded me like an explosive flash, and then I was upside down in the bed of the HIGH-BACK. It was February and the kind of cold that gets caught high up in your nose and makes you sneeze. My EARS rang and my FACE hurt and Ruiz was still alive and asking me if I was good, and we could hear Corporal Fox moaning from the cab and I always figured after an IED there would be something—RPGS, a FIREFIGHT, HELICOPTERS, yelling. Like the world would freeze and make space for *something.* JUSTICE. REVENGE. But there was nothing. Nothing but QUIET and MRES and GEAR from the HIGH-BACK spilled across the broken asphalt and icy winter rain from a lead sky and calm chatter over the radio while our LT called for a MEDEVAC and there was that goddamned RINGING that wouldn't go away.

BESTÅS and RIFLES and STRANDMONS and HUMVEES and GRUNDSJÖS and DESERT and GURLIS and BODIES piled everywhere, Max in the middle of it all, resting on a gray KIVIK that reminded me of that Iraq winter sky. On Max's left sat Ruiz. Deader than dogshit.

I wasn't nervous or anything like that. I wondered what the Swedish word for *happy* was, and then I thought that was a pretty fucking cheesy thing to think and my entire head felt like it might split open at the seams from the ringing but it didn't change anything. I was happy.

Look alive, motherfucker, I said to Ruiz.

That's cold, dog, he said.

Comfortable? I said.

My feet are killing me, said Max.

I'm happy, I said.

I was going to ask her to marry me right then, in the goddamned bedroom section of IKEA. Sweet, greasy Swedish meatball stink hanging in the air, brain pulsing against the inside of my skull, Ruiz's body, tangled and twisted and bloody, strewn over the cushions.

Are you? I said.

I'm gassy, she said. And I'm tired. And I feel like I want to vom, but I want to stuff about thirty meatballs in my mouth, and I want to yell at every single person in this place for wearing whatever perfume they're wearing.

I might've mumbled something about how we could stay here awhile. That it was nice. That we could pretend it was all ours. Maybe not—I don't know if I said it out loud to Max or in my head to Ruiz or to the fetus or not all.

What I said for sure to Max was Marry me, but at the same time a shopper appeared and called to another, Here's the couch we were looking for! The shopper collapsed onto the lounger attachment for the KIVIK on Max's right.

What? said Max.

No, said the sitting shopper raising and waving a hand. In here!

I don't think this will fit in our living room, said the second shopper, standing, hands on hips.

Measure it, said the sitter.

I thought you brought the measuring tape from home, said the stander.

Wait, what? said Max.

It's comfortable, said the sitter, looking from Max to the stander.

A thousand bucks? said the stander to the sitter. Then, to Max, The colors on these things. Can you believe?

The sitter and the stander laughed and Max laughed and I laughed and Ruiz laughed and I imagined the fetus laughing, too, Max's belly jumping. All of us pretending like we got the joke while at the same time, thousands of miles away, on a road with no name, standing in the cold rain, surrounded by Humvee wreckage, I waited for something to happen. Maybe I was still there. Maybe the blast had split time.

Then Max leaned over Ruiz, the swell of her belly pressed onto him, and my breath caught in my throat; she snapped a picture of the KIVIK's price tag.

I'm ready, she said. Let's go home.

Home. Hard to fit the goddamned word into my head. I was supposed to have gotten home eight months ago. Richfield was supposed to be home, right? It hadn't felt like that, of course—not Mom and Rick's, not Court's, not even really the truck bed.

Max felt like home.

I wanted to tell her that. I should have then, just like I should have at Christmas.

We don't got to go anywhere, I wanted to say.

I tried to think about the last time I'd felt like I had a home—a place I belonged, felt safe, looked forward to, or whatever. I shuffled through images of the PB, the high-back, any of the bivouac sites we'd bedded down at for more than a night. The barracks room I'd shared with Ruiz when we got back from that first pump was closest. That had felt like home.

Ruiz and I bought sheets from Target instead of using the issued sandpaper and wool bedding the supply sergeant had given us. Kept the place squared away, fridge stocked with beer. Picked up a blender and Ruiz, he made these smoothies with bananas and peanut butter and blueberries and protein powder and whatever else he could find before we hit the gym in the morning.

Does a body good, güey, he said. Get you big and strong like me.

Flex, flex, flex. Laugh, laugh, laugh. Like playing fucking house or whatever. He talked about me picking up corporal, about reenlisting, about us getting a place out in San Clemente together, about parties and the beach and surfing, living like real boys. That's what he said: *real boys.*

Mostly he talked shit about a housing allowance. Make bank, dog, he said. Like it was really about the money. Which I knew was bullshit. No one who was about the money would re-up as a goddamned grunt. But it didn't matter anyway because he went and fucked it all up.

Shot himself in the mouth with a Springfield XD-forty he kept in one of our room's wall lockers, maybe a month after the night at Dave and Buster's.

I was at Dental, getting a cavity filled so I'd be deployable. Combat effective. Can't be combat effective with a fucking cavity. Well. Can't be combat effective without a fucking face, either.

When I got back it was a big scene—MPs, rubber-necking Marines, the entire Corps, it felt like. It didn't take long to figure out what happened. Everyone was talking about it.

I faded into the crowd, didn't know what to think, lost in the sauce, no impact, no idea. It was like I'd been partly sliced away, scooped out or something, and I was wearing a Dean suit and the suit was still walking around, but I was rattling around inside, flipping ass over teakettle, falling into the dark. Apathy. Mindset black. *It means not giving a fuck, dummy,* came Sergeant Moss's voice in my head.

Nguyen spotted me.

Fuck, man, he said.

I nodded.

Fuck, man, he said.

He stood next to me on the basketball court below the barracks. Ever since Raven was born, he'd been talking all philosophical and shit about life. How it mattered—*really* mattered. I wasn't sure.

I turned and looked toward the Backyard, found the top of First Sergeant's Hill. Thought about how small I'd look from up there. How easy I'd be to fucking squash if I was that small. Thought about all the ways to die right then. I wished for a fucking meteor to impact or a fault line to give way and send a goddamned tsunami to wash over us, wipe the slate clean.

Crowe found us.

Baptiste was on duty, said Crowe. Heard the shot.

Fuck, man, said Nguyen.

There wasn't any love lost between Ruiz and Crowe.

Gave those walls a new coat of paint for sure, said Crowe.

Nguyen started crying and walked away.

Letoa was up in the company office, said Crowe. Seen Ruiz after his reenlistment got denied. Good fucking riddance, I guess.

I wanted to breathe fire into Crowe's face, but I didn't say shit. If I let loose on him, I might not stop. Anyway, I thought back then that offing yourself was a bitch move. So, yeah, I wanted to knock the little whiskey tango trailer park motherfucker's fetal alcohol nub teeth into the back of his throat, but I didn't want to sound like a coward.

And really my first thought wasn't even about that. It was about San Clemente—parties, surfing, our housing allowance. And I felt guilty for that, like put out that he'd shit the bed, fucked the plan. So maybe that was the thing that kept me from turning Crowe's face inside out. I was feeling a little good fucking riddance right then, too.

Six Marines from another battalion pushed and yelled and clapped and talked shit behind us in a half-court pickup game. I turned from Crowe, who was jawing, to watch them. A skinny brown kid with Dumbo ears charged the basket like Reggie Miller and let a layup roll off his finger-tips. The ball thunked the backboard, snagged in the net.

I wondered if they'd been playing the entire time. If they'd heard the shot. If Ruiz had heard them talking shit while they balled while he racked the pistol's slide, chambered a round, opened his mouth, angled the muzzle upward between his teeth so the front sight scraped his hard palate and his tongue cradled the underside of the slide, made his mouth water while he squeezed the trigger as he'd been trained: slow. Steady.

Stomach acid burned in my throat, nostrils. Made my eyes water. I was going to pop. And then my inside and outside slammed back together and I went from black to red.

Hey, I said to the players on the court.

No one said shit. Didn't even notice when I walked into the center of their game and said it again until one of them, the ball carrier, knocked into me. I grabbed the ball and punted it off the court and then all six of them bowed up to me. One of them was a staff sergeant who said, I'm a staff sergeant. I'm a staff sergeant. Over and over, like a couple extra ranks were supposed to mean something to me right then.

He must've just come from the drill field because he gave me the old four-finger point—the knife hand, DIs called it—and started chewing my ass. My nose was in his mouth. Peas from that night's chow hall chicken tetrazzini were stuck in his molars.

I hoped for a fight but we got stuck in schoolyard bullshit, toeing up to one another, talking smack, daring the other to throw down first. Maybe the ballers saw something on my face that freaked them out—like I wasn't just about the fight; like if it started, I wouldn't stop, and they'd have to put me down for real. Like a fucking dog. It was true. I wanted them to fuck me up—break my bones, split me open.

Then Sergeant Moss showed up and got in the middle of it all, pried me away, apologized to Staff Sergeant Knife Hand, got me out of the quad, away from the crowd.

We sat in his car and I waited for him to tear into me. The car was some sedan from the nineties—manual window cranks, cracking vinyl on the dash and steering wheel, fast-food wrappers on the floor. In the back there was a car seat.

I realized I didn't know shit about Sergeant Moss. It was like seeing one of your high school teachers at the grocery store. He rolled down the window, lit a cigarette, held it in his right hand, rubbed his face with his left, put his head back, and I saw then that he wasn't much older than me.

For a year after high school, before I joined up? he said. I cleaned carpets for Chem-Dry. It was a good job. When I get out, I'm going to buy me a franchise, turn the page, and never think about this shit ever again.

He didn't say anything else. Finished his cigarette and left me in the car.

A group of Marines walked by talking about Ruiz.

Fucking bitch, said one.

Malingerer, said another.

At least he used the wall as a backstop, said another. They all laughed at that.

I knew what he meant: Know your target and what lies beyond. I thought about that over and over. *Know your target and what lies beyond.* It felt like some kind of brainy shit a college professor would ask a class full of students: What lies beyond? I wondered if Ruiz had the answer—thought about the stubble of his chin, his hulking mass running First Sergeant's Hill the sheep the back of the high-back the dark room at the PB.

By the time I walked back to the barracks, the quad had cleared. My room was sealed off with caution tape. I wondered about my stuff, then felt like a shit. It was dusk. There were a couple guys I knew from the School of Infantry who had been dropped into another line company in the smoke pit and I raised my hand and wandered over to ask to bum one but the pit cleared out before I made it. Like dudes were worried I was carrying a fucking virus or something. They were looking for Ruiz's weakness, maybe, knew we were close, did the math—superstitious shit.

Right then I had this feeling like that must've been what it was like for the sheep when we shoved it into the dark on its own and my heart started pumping and my eyes fuzzed out. I thought about going unauthorized absence, heading back to Indiana, but knew I'd have to deal with Mom and Penny and I couldn't decide what was worse: being abandoned or being smothered.

Letoa called down from the second-deck duty hut: Pusey! Go to the company office to see Gunny Bat for room reassignment.

In the hallway of the company office, I waited for Gunny, who was in a meeting, so I could hand over my barracks room key and get a new one. While I waited outside Gunny's office, I hoped again for some kind of natural disaster, what Ruiz would've called an act of God, to drop the two-story box on my head. Tons of concrete—the entire Headquarters and Service company, the staff shops: manpower, intel, ops, logistics, comm, the sergeant major, the executive officer, and the battalion commander— would all crush me to jelly. Nothing but a little smear on some concrete. With any luck, they'd never even fucking find my body.

I heard people arguing in Gunny's office.

Been a while since someone joined the third-deck dive team, said one.

We were due, said another.

But now? said another. This is a fucking bag of dicks.

We should make an example, said another.

They give posthumous awards, said another. Why not posthumous punishment?

I knew they were in there seated around the conference table—Gunny, First Sergeant, LT, XO, Skipper—lips heaped with dip, thick bodies shoved into cheap office chairs.

This shit breeds like a fucking yeast infection, said one.

He won't be the last, said another.

Suicide awareness training isn't scheduled for another four months, said another.

The hallway of the company office was painted white and was filled with banners from war campaigns the company had been a part of all the way back to World War I, photos of former BCs, shadow boxes of awards and commendations, aerial shots showing how Camp Pendleton had changed from the nineteen forties on, swords, oars, rifles with fused insides so they couldn't be used, a wall of brass tags embossed with the names of the company's dead.

Ruiz's name would never be on that wall. Suicides didn't get a place at the table. Fuck an act of God. I stood there under the weight of it all. Crushed.

We'll have to modify the training schedule, said a voice.

Can we do that? said another.

For one Marine, said another.

This is a clusterfuck, said another.

New generation is weak, said another.

Goddamned internet, said another.

A few minutes later they all streamed out and I gave the proper greetings and received none in return and then Gunny's house mouse—a nerdly little new-join PFC who'd been dumb enough to raise his hand when Gunny asked who was good with computers during a safety brief a few weeks ago—rushed into Gunny's office.

Lance Corporal Pusey is here, Gunny.

Send him in, said Gunny.

PFC House Mouse popped his head out and said, Lance Corporal.

Almost singsonged my rank. Then smiled. Fucking genuine, no-shit smile. I made a note to make the kid's life miserable whenever I could.

Gunny Bat was behind his desk and I squared up at attention and gave him the greeting of the day.

At ease, he said.

Aye, Gunny, I said.

I tried to loosen up but couldn't figure out how. Like there was nothing holding me together; my backbone wouldn't stay straight.

Ruiz, said Gunny Bat. Doggone battle buddies, right?

Gunny Bat was a mountain of a man, squat and muscled. Had a head like a pyramid with a fuzzy high and tight on top.

Yes, Gunny, I said.

You were at Dental? he said.

Yes, Gunny, I said.

Know about the pistol? he said.

No, Gunny, I said.

But listen to me now: Fuck, yeah, I'd known about the pistol, and I knew ten other guys in the platoon who had them, too, but I wasn't stupid, and I wasn't a blue falcon, a motherfucking snitch. The shit always flowed downhill. If I knew about the pistol and Ruiz was my battle buddy, where the fuck had I been, right? That's what he was hoping for. No skin off Gunny Bat's dick to let a one-and-done lance corporal take the heat.

I'd decided in the hallway I wouldn't re-up. I guess he didn't know that, but he probably figured. Anyway, like, instead of the battalion's shitty oversight, it would be easy to say I'd let it happen. I'd known about the pistol and hadn't told anyone. I thought of Sergeant Moss and Baptiste and Cobb.

Notice anything unusual about him in the last few days? said Gunny Bat.

Lance Corporal Letoa said his reenlistment was denied, I said.

Doggone lance corporal underground, he said. Bunch of chatty Cathys. He sighed and rubbed his face and the entire mountain of him crumbled some.

Sergeant Moss put you up for a meritorious promotion, he said.

Aye, Gunny, I said.

Get pinned next month, he said. You thought about reenlistment?

No, Gunny, I said.

Corps needs good Marines, he said.

Yes, Gunny, I said.

He shuffled some papers on his desk. Found a room key. We traded.

This won't last forever, he said.

Roger that, Gunny, I said.

I didn't know what the fuck he meant—Ruiz, the war, life? I popped to attention. Gave the greeting, about-faced, stepped out.

A week later we had a suicide awareness stand-down. Command delegated the duty to this junior LT who had lost his rifle during a training op a couple weeks before Ruiz had punched his ticket.

We'd ended up in a six-hour police-call-by-the numbers after the training range. Meaning the entire company stood shoulder to shoulder, on line, across fucking acres of the range, while First Sergeant stood behind us giving the order to step every ten seconds and look around our feet. It would've gone on all night long, but some lance corporal snuck away in the dark from the fuck-fuck games and happened to light up in the same port-a-shitter where the lieutenant had left his rifle.

The LT pulled up a PowerPoint.

Fucking death by PowerPoint, said a Marine.

If we sit here by choice, is it suicide or murder, sir? said another.

The LT ignored the Marines, but dude was sweating bullets. He was more red than white by then.

Good morning, Marines. My name is—

Oorah, sir! said a Marine.

Marines laughed.

The LT coughed. Oorah, Marines, he said. My name is Lieutenant May. This morning we'll be discussing suicide awareness.

He cleared his throat.

Feelings of sorrow, despair, and inadequacy can contribute to an individual's negative mental state, said the LT. Now, if a Marine is found to be suicidal, or attempts suicide and fails, that Marine should be placed on suicide watch.

The entire thing bothered me—fucking suicide awareness or whatever. Feelings. Like, what the fuck, right? We'd signed up to do the goddamned job. It wasn't like we'd signed up for fucking butterflies and rainbows. It was war. The LT's whole spiel was a load of shit to me. I was fucking pissed at Ruiz. He'd known what the fuck we were doing. He wanted to keep doing it. So, what the fuck? Because they denied his reenlistment? Was that really it? And I was sick of guys I'd thought were my family treating me like the goddamned plague.

Is that where we watch them finish the job, sir? I said.

Marines laughed—the end of my quarantine.

Fuck, yeah, said Crowe, and slugged my shoulder. We could film it and put that shiz on rotten dot com.

Marines, said Lieutenant May.

I bet you fucking beat it to *Hostel*, don't you, Crowe? said Letoa. You're a sick fuck.

More laughter.

Marines, said Lieutenant May.

I knew Ruiz, said Corporal Shepard.

The laughter stopped. We got quiet for Corporal Shepard. He'd deployed three times and held weight.

He was my boot, said Corporal Shepard. And this shit's sad, but listen, I don't want some weak bitch to my left or right in a firefight.

Nodding heads bobbed in the dim room.

This is serious, Marines, said Lieutenant May.

Who the fuck am I to keep someone from doing what they want to do, sir? said Corporal Shepard. It's a free fucking country. I'm not the fucking wizard.

Wizard was the battalion psych. Navy doc. We avoided him more than Chaps.

More nods.

Marines, please, said Lieutenant May.

If someone wants to do it, we should let them, said Corporal Shepard. Weed out the weak. None of this shit is in my job description. I'm a motherfucking killer. We're all killers.

Crowe started chanting, Kill yourself. Kill yourself. Kill yourself.

We all joined in.

Ten minutes after we left IKEA to head home, Max got hungry and pulled off the highway—she got sick when I drove—and into an Applebee's parking lot. She was fucking panicked. Best way I can put it. Like, I kept asking if she was all right and it took me a couple asks to realize she was just excited about eating, which made me laugh when I said it, but she didn't see what was funny, which made it funnier to me.

Anyway, there we were at Applebee's—we had to sit at a table because Max's belly was too big for a booth—and it was a Saturday and we had money and a place to live and I wasn't thinking about the war and we hadn't been out together aside from places like IKEA and Target and

Walmart since what seemed like before Christmas and the overhead light behind Max caught those little flyaway hairs women get when they put their hair up and she was biting her lip and pinching up her face like she was trying to read fucking ancient Greek or something and I had this realization that I'd never seen her so still. Like, she wasn't someone who stayed still. And it felt good knowing that. Mostly because I'd learned something about her, observed something.

Observe, orient, decide, act. It was the OODA loop. Sergeant Moss had boiled every decision we made down to the OODA loop. All part of his Slow-is-smooth, smooth-is-fast routine.

Ruiz didn't agree. He'd called it repressive; he'd said, Dog, that's repressive. And after we all gave him shit about the twenty-five-cent word, Sergeant Moss had asked him to explain himself. Explain yourself, Corporal Ruiz, he'd said. Ruiz had said something about how if you were always trying to reorientate—that was the word he'd used: *reorientate*—then you'd end up stuck in observation and orientation and never make a goddamned decision.

I'd thought Sergeant Moss would chew his ass, but he didn't, and instead he agreed; he'd said, That's an excellent point, Corporal Ruiz. Marines, any decision, even a bad one, is better than no decision. Give him one. And we'd all responded, Kill!

The server brought water, took our orders, and I was thinking of the OODA loop through it all—bad decisions mostly, how you didn't know they were bad until you made them. I wanted to ask Ruiz why he had decided to do what he had done, wanted to ask my birth mom. And then I got mad at myself for such weepy goddamned thoughts and then I got jealous of the fetus—that it would grow up knowing Max, that Max would hold it and feed it from her body, wipe its ass, rock it to sleep. And so then on top of all that feeling guilty I got paranoid everyone there knew what I was thinking, and I fidgeted in my chair and looked over my shoulder and fiddled with a bit of straw wrapper.

What are you thinking about? said Max.

The Marine Corps, I didn't say.

My dead friend, I didn't say.

I wish you'd gotten an abortion, I didn't say.

What I said: IKEA.

Max looked at me a minute and that paranoid feeling—the one that made me twitch and hunch—I got it times ten, like she was in my head right then like she knew I was thinking some evil shit.

I think I've been farting since we walked into IKEA, she said.

I laughed.

No, seriously, she said, like I haven't stopped. It's just, like, a never-ending silent-but-deadly stream.

I hadn't noticed, I said.

I had noticed. You couldn't not notice. I'd smelled worse. None of that shit—farting, puking, tit-leaking—bothered me. It was more data or something, more knowing. I'd observed. And maybe, too, now that I'm thinking about it, there was probably something there about her not being able to have her guard up. She was exposed, right? All the cards were on the table: this is everything. And there I was. Still there.

I read that it's a good sign that I'm leaking already, she said. It's colostrum and it means I'll have good milk production.

I repeated the word *colostrum*.

You should come with me to the lactation class next week, she said. I think it would be good.

Yeah, I said. For sure.

How's your mom? she said.

Damn dog, said Ruiz. *Better check that overhead again.*

The outside world never seemed to make it into our bubble. I liked it that way. Now here Max was shoveling a big pile right between us.

She didn't give birth to me but she is my mother, I didn't say.

I haven't really talked to her since I buttstocked her fucking husband on Christmas Day, I didn't say.

I will gnaw my goddamned leg off to get out of this trap, I didn't say.

What I said: She's good.

I wish we saw her more, she said.

She works a lot, I said.

My mom and Penny had been texting me since I left the house on Christmas. It's not like I was giving them the silent treatment or anything, but I was trying to keep my life simple. Living-in-a-truck simple. Max and the fetus were enough to keep me in place. I saw when Penny liked and commented on my Insta posts. Sometimes she messaged me there.

I never read those and definitely ignored her and my mom's calls, but when they texted, I usually rogered up that I was alive so they wouldn't file a missing person report and went about my goddamned day. They knew I was living with Max. That she was pregnant.

When was the last time you saw her? said Max.

Couple weeks ago, probably, I said.

Dean, she said.

What? I said.

Look, we just don't have a great relationship, I said. You should understand that.

She looked at me, arms crossed and resting on her belly, unzipping me again.

It's not the same, she said.

She's not your mom, I said.

I've been talking to Penny, she said, about what happened at that first OB visit.

Here we go, I said.

She ignored me and leaned over the table as far as she could and said, Have you thought about trying to find your birth parents?

I thought of the dolphin flipping and bucking through the ocean with the sperm whales.

You think my mom and I don't have a great relationship now, I said, and laughed, but Max was straight-faced. Couldn't tell if it was hunger or sincerity, and I got angry then. Like, I was probably hungry, too. But what the fuck did Max know about my family? Nothing. She knew what I had told her and apparently what Penny had told her and that burned my ass, too. Really, I was probably angry at myself for keeping her at one arm's distance. Couldn't sort that in the moment, though.

I was about to tell her she didn't know a damn thing when the server brought our food and set it down and we quit talking and smiled at each other—that awkward-ass thing couples do when they're fighting but don't want the server to judge them. My guess is that servers know and just don't give a shit, like we probably could've been hissing and spitting at one another and the server wouldn't have fucking cared as long as he got a decent tip. And then he set down a beer in front of me.

He didn't order that, Max said.

It's from a patron at the bar, said the server.

You can take it back, said Max.

I hadn't had a drink since we'd moved in together, called it solidarity, but really it was survival. Just then, though, I was glad for the beer, its diversion of our conversation about my family, and I wanted it—wanted the sweating glass in my hand, wanted the bubbles to pop and explode down my throat, wanted the anchor of it in my stomach.

Well, wait a second, I said. That would be rude.

It's weird, said Max.

Why's it weird? I said.

I can come back, said the server.

We both ignored him and he left.

Who actually does that? said Max.

People used to buy me drinks all the time in California, I said.

It's weird, she said.

Some people respect sacrifice, I said—a solid jab.

And then a guy, maybe early forties, beer gut, patchy stubble on his face—*Fat-body fat-body fat-body*, Ruiz chanted—walked up to the table.

Just wanted to thank you for your service, sir, said the guy.

He called me sir. Guys like that called me sir. It was always fucking weird, Max was right, but it made me think of good times in California when people would buy me beers at bars or baseball games and Max and I, we were arguing, and so I leaned into it to piss her off and I smiled and thanked him and hammered it up a bit and expected him to shove off but then the guy kept up.

It's a real shame, he said.

I cleared my throat, looked at Max; she was a blade. All the pregnancy fat melted from her face and she was all angles and edges, fresh from the goddamned fire.

Damn shame, said the guy.

Maybe Max was resentful of the Marines or whatever, but I think the guy was in the wrong place at the wrong time is all. Collateral damage for whatever showdown we were in about my family. Anyway, if he'd just looked at Max, he might've been cut to fucking ribbons, but he didn't, and he wasn't going away.

What's that? I said.

The way you all get treated, he said. Second-class, like. You know, in the media. I don't ever hear anything about war, soldiers. Ain't right. We got to get behind you. Rally. No one's looking after you—media, damn government, no one—we got to get behind you. Would've joined up myself except I fucked my knee—excuse me—messed up my knee in high school. But I got a cousin in the Army. Ranger. Seen some real shit. Got medals. Don't talk about it. But I said, Clint—that's his name: Clint— people got to know what you done.

I nodded, looked around the guy, tried getting the server's attention, but he was leaning against a bar stanchion, staring at his phone.

We're going to eat now, said Max.

She was mindset red then, and the guy turned his head to her, and I saw from how his eyes had to catch up with the movement how drunk he was. Mindset white. Unaware and unprepared. He looked her up and down, turned back to me, kept talking.

Turned on the news the other day, he said, seen some report about a kitty cat come home to its owner after fifteen years—

Yo, dog. Stand the fuck up and knock this fool out, said Ruiz. *Look at you, peeking around this fat fuck like* Oh, please, someone come save me. *Shit.*

He's just drunk, I thought. *It's not a big deal.*

—not a thing about the war, and I been thinking about that, and then I seen your tat when you walked in—Marines! Hooah!—and I recognized it—

Please, said Max, we'd like to eat.

Drunk is un-fucking-predictable, dog, said Ruiz. *Unpredictable is a risk. Complacent-ass motherfucker. Nut up. What's complacent get you, Corporal Pusey?*

I didn't answer him.

—and said to myself, Stan—that's my name: Stan—you got to buy that old boy a drink—

You'd be doing everyone in this motherfucker a favor, said Ruiz.

That's not me anymore, I thought.

You think it works like that? said Ruiz. *Bro, I'm fucking dead and I'm still a Marine.*

You're just in my head, I thought.

Whatever you say, dog, said Ruiz.

—so I just wanted to thank you for your sacrifice and shake your hand. Thank you for protecting freedom.

He held out his hand and I shook it and he kept jawing away, repeating himself this time, and before I even knew it, Max stood from the table and jabbed the guy with a straight punch in the thick of his cheek, just below his eye. Her form was pretty goddamned good—didn't keep her hands up afterward—but her power come from down low and she'd followed through like she was trying to hit something behind the guy's head.

Jeez, I said.

Let your woman do it for you, said Ruiz. *Fucking shameful, dog. Ain't you going to even stand up? Do something. Finish the job. Double tap. Mozambique. Nonstandard response. Something. Anything. Make a decision. Even a bad decision is better than no decision. Stand the fuck up and—*

Bitch, the guy said, and then kept saying it over and over like Max had knocked all the other words out of him. He took his hand away and squinted up his eye and winced, testing the damage. There was a welt. The server was heading our way.

Come on, said Max.

No one stopped us. We left Stan by the table, muttering to himself.

We were back in the truck, making our way through the maze of parking lots at the shopping center where the restaurant was, and I started laughing while I replayed the whole goddamned thing in my head: pregnant woman punching a drunk in an Applebee's.

I'd go to war with you, I said.

Max slammed the brakes hard enough to make the tires screech and a second later the smell of burnt rubber flooded the cabin while we idled in the middle of the lot.

What, you want to go hit some more people? I said. So much for nurturing.

If you're in this, you're in this, she said.

I put my hands up like *Where the fuck do you think I am?*

Stop, she said.

What's that mean? I said.

It means you've got to deal with your shit, she said.

My family isn't me, I said.

That's childish, she said.

You just punched a guy, I said. In an Applebee's.

I felt like I was losing my fucking mind right then; like, all I kept saying in my head was *What about this thing you did? What about that that thing you did? What about you you you?* Her logic didn't add up to me. My ego. Didn't know that then. Didn't know the word. Didn't know how to slow myself down. Just knew it felt good to keep poking, poking, poking. Getting at a fraction of that time travel feeling. Quick zap to my brain housing group.

She closed her eyes and shook her head. You've got this family— she said.

And I jumped down her goddamned throat: You don't know shit about my family, I said.

She took a breath, put both hands on the wheel.

You know more than most that family isn't just blood, she said.

She was talking about all of it then—Penny, Mom, the Marines, my adoption—and I hated her for knowing me, for how easy it was for her to pin me down, to know my SOP: better to leave than be left. I cleared my throat and looked out the window, acted like I wasn't bothered by a damn thing.

I never had what you have, she said. I want it for us, and for that to happen, I need you to see what you're doing.

She started crying, rubbed her hands over her belly.

I put my hand on her leg, told her I was sorry. Told her I'd call Mom and Penny and make nice. Told her we could sit down and figure out adoption stuff together. Told her I wanted her to be a part of it.

But it was bullshit. I wasn't going to do any of it. OODA loop. I'd observed, oriented, decided, acted. Maybe it was a bad decision, but it was the only fucking decision I could think of to keep myself looking like who she thought I was. And there was something about her idea of my family that drove me apeshit, dug and burrowed under my skin, like she was looking at an entirely different thing than me, and not just that but that I was looking at it wrong. My own family. I couldn't get past it—felt like some kind of injustice—and the burnt-rubber smell was making my head pound, and she was probably just hormonal, I kept thinking, and wasn't she just a hypocrite? What about *her* family?

Wish I could've seen past myself. Maybe I would've heard what she was saying. Maybe it all would've been different. What if? What if? What if?

MAX WAS IN labor in late August when the sheep came out of the shadows in the windowless basement delivery room at the hospital. It looked the same as when I'd first seen it in that fallow wheat field outside Fallujah: scrawny, wool clumped and matted with Euphrates River mud, eyes crusted, nose burbling mucus. For a minute I thought: *Hey, bud, how'd you get out of your hutch?* And then I expected to get chewed out by some higher command for keeping a non-approved animal at the PB and I knew Sergeant Moss was going to ream my ass and then I realized I was losing it; I wasn't in Iraq. But then I worried instead that Sergeant Moss, an attending nurse, or the doctor would chew me out for bringing the filthy fucking thing into the delivery room, but no one else seemed to notice the sheep.

Max hadn't wanted meds but she eventually begged the nurses.

Don't think about it, I didn't say.

Go internal, I didn't say.

Pain is weakness leaving the body, I didn't say.

What I said: Can we get her the goddamned epidural?

But the anesthesiologist took an hour to show up, diddy bopping into the room, yukking it up with a nurse, and by that point Max was in transition and wouldn't have been able to sit still. One of the nurses offered fentanyl as consolation.

In between contractions Max's body went limp with the drugs and her eyes closed like she was asleep and then the baby started crowning and I lost the sheep in the long shadows of the room, its shit-stink stuck in the back of my throat.

When I watched the baby coming out of the space between Max's legs, I couldn't think of anything but dropping it.

Most of the baby's body was still inside Max, but its head was in the world—black, blood-slick hair; teardrop face a pinched, flattened piece of meat; boxer's nose chunky with fat, white gobs of cheesy vernix—I'd been expecting it from the books and birth classes; thick lips purple, peeled back from dark gums.

That's your face, Dad, said one of the nurses—they called us Mom and Dad so they wouldn't have to remember our names just like at the ob-gyn. She smiled at me, braced Max's naked thigh against the shoulder of her mint-green scrubs.

Bullshit, *my face*. Max and that kid were carbon fucking copies. Their eyes closed the same way. They couldn't have given a shit less about me right then. It was just the two of them.

Then Max woke, her face contorted in pain, and for a split second I thought the baby's face shifted, too. Max started moaning and crying. Oh, no. Oh, no, oh, no, ohnonono, she said over and over. Her eyes were still closed.

Grab just below the jaw, said the doctor. Mom's going to push; you're going to pull. Ready?

I nodded, and I could feel the doctor's eyes on me, and I wanted to punch the bitch right in the nose. Like, of fucking course I'm not ready, goddammit. Then the nurse patted my arm and I felt better.

Max was crying when she started pushing—gritting her teeth so fucking hard, I thought they might splinter and shoot from her mouth like the scrap metal from that improvised claymore that had taken out the IA jundi. And this noise was coming out of her—like a moan but deep, from her diaphragm. Some kind of animal. Predator. Cougar. Say that now and I think about Max being a cougar—like a hot older woman—and it makes me laugh, but all I could think of then was dropping the kid.

The nurse held Max's hand in a ball of white-knuckle flesh and sweat and I moved from where I'd been bracing Max's blood-spattered thigh and took the kid's squat head in my hands.

I knew the sheep was watching from the shadows like I knew the doctor was looking at me. Anyway, I could smell the fucker, its stink mixing with Max's blood and shit and hospital sanitizer. I thought about the baby's skinny body slipping from my hands, the smack it would make against the linoleum. And everything about my birth mom started up in my brain housing group. Quarterbacking shit. What-if shit. Mindset black shit. I was slipping over the edge.

Pull, said the doctor. Pull, pull, pull.

The baby squawked, and when I heard its voice, I pulled away thinking I'd done damage, broke its neck, and then the doctor hip-checked me out of the way.

Shoulders, she said. Then both her arms up to the goddamned elbows were inside Max, who didn't even fucking notice in her drug daze, and then instead of facing Max's left thigh the kid faced the right.

You're up, Dad, said the doctor, her hands and arms bloody. You still want this?

The question hung between us and I could feel the moment split itself in half and then split again and it kept on splitting into halves of halves forever until it eventually snapped back together. And then I was holding the kid whose arms were stretched like wings, bouncing and jerking at its sides like it was trying to take flight. It made me think of breakfalls Ruiz and I practiced when we rolled—practiced falling over and over, slapping our arms to the earth at the last minute to redistribute the impact of the ground on our bodies.

I saw it was a girl so I said, It's a girl, and gave her to Max.

I didn't drop her and I almost cried right then and I wondered if this was what it was like when I was born—like, did my birth mom have anyone to do that? What if she held me? What if she didn't want to? What if they just took me away and she never even saw me? What if? What if? What if? Then the sheep was behind me, stench of shit dirt and mushrooms in my throat, and I had time to think, *Beautiful like mushrooms*, and then the sheep rammed its nasty body against the backs of my legs and everything went black.

★

Ruiz had been dead six months. I was in Iraq again. A truck full of fucking Army Reserve doctors at Al Taqaddum had T-boned our Humvee a week prior and rung my bell. Doc checked me out and decided I didn't need to get to Medical, but I figured it was LT who didn't want to fill out the noncombat incident paperwork.

Anyway, I hadn't been able to sleep. I begged Doc for an Ativan. He kept all that shit in this giant ruck sack that must've weighed fifty pounds—pressure dressings, tourniquets, medical shears, latex gloves, burn gel, IV fluids, yeah, but also Motrin eight hundred and Norflex and Ativan and morphine.

I'd never convince the fucker to give me a syrette—the shit was inventoried—but I thought he might give up an Ativan. You had to give a corpsman a reach-around to get anything aside from Change your socks and drink water. Command wanted us angry. Shit, the *Corps* wanted us angry. Hate and discontent. Anyway, it was like all that shit was in Doc's bag to bait us. Ask for meds? Boom, you're a fucking broke-dick malingerer and everyone knows it.

The exception was probably morphine, because if Doc was giving you morphine, you were probably dying anyhow.

I didn't die when the seven-ton T-boned us, but I was pretty sure I had a concussion even if Doc said I didn't: my head pounded, everything gave off these pulsing auras, the ringing got worse. I guess, maybe, I was seeing things.

I'm dying, I said to Doc.

Jesus, I'm trying to take a shit, Pusey, he said.

I was pressed against the plywood door of the WAG bag shitter.

I just need some sleep, I said.

You're not dying, said Doc.

I'm seeing things, I think, I said.

You think, he said.

Doc, I said.

Then catch the Log Train to the aid station, he said.

He knew I'd never let anyone see me get on the logistics train unless I had a sucking chest wound.

That night I pulled opium-laced tobacco smoke from the metal-tipped, velvet-covered hose attached to a hookah in the interpreters' hooch at the entry control point we'd been stationed at just outside the city. I felt like a kid puffing breath clouds on a freezing morning, waiting at the bus stop, and then I breathed in hot sugar and chai and spicy body odor, stifled a cough. Heat pinpricked up my neck and the two interpreters sitting in a circle next to and across from me on the pillowed floor in the dim room laughed.

The smoke, it sticks in the mouth sometimes, said BJ.

Throat, said AJ.

Throat, said BJ.

AJ nodded.

We called the interpreters meaningless names—AJ, the same guy from my first deployment, and BJ a young new guy. The battalion before us called them something else. Didn't matter much. We called them terps. Terp up! we said, and, Get the fuck over here, terp! They must've hated it.

I'd never been opium-high before and I floated and sank and forgot to breathe and got dizzy and gulped for air. Sucked it deep into my gut and hiccupped. It was the best I'd felt in months.

You feel better, yes? said AJ, the older of the two. Dude was probably thirty. Could've been forty. Maybe fifty. I never asked him. Looked older. Desert does that to people. War, too.

Yes, I said.

Good, said AJ.

I like you, Corporal, said BJ, the youngest. You do not yell many of the time. Not like Lance Corporal Crowe.

Much, said AJ.

Much, said BJ.

We smoked a bit more.

Yes, we like you, Corporal, said AJ. You are fair with us.

I didn't think about the terps. Didn't see a use for them. Like, it didn't matter what the locals said to us when we went patrolling out in town. If they wanted a new well or needed food, we wrote it down, gave it to Command, but nothing ever got done, and we moved from district to district—no return presence, no relationships built. So what the fuck did it matter? We didn't have much to say to them that we couldn't say with a goddamned rifle and the shitty Arabic we'd been taught.

Crowe didn't trust them, the terps. There had been a third—CJ—and Crowe accused him of stealing from the T-rat chow hall after hours. Command fired him. Sent him out on foot. To the wolves. The wild dogs. Poor little sheep. I'd watched him go and didn't feel much about it.

Mostly, I just wasn't a direct asshole—didn't call them hajji or raghead or any of that shit—and I knew AJ from the first deployment. Asked him about his wife. His kid. After that, you'd think I'd gotten them tickets to see Katy Perry. Both of them fucking loved Katy Perry.

Tinny Arabic pop music sounded from a portable radio. I pulled from the hookah.

It help you sleep, said BJ.

No, he must not sleep here, said AJ.

He will not sleep here, said BJ.

Marines will ask where he is, said AJ. He cannot sleep here.

BJ threw up his arms. The two spoke Arabic loud and fast.

Where do you live in America, Corporal? said AJ.

California, I said. I didn't think they'd know Indiana.

Hollywood, said AJ.

There are much girls? said BJ.

Many, said AJ.

Many, said BJ.

I've never been to Hollywood, I said.

But you live in California, said AJ.

We like the movies from California, said BJ. He imitated a line from some movie that I recognized and tried to pull out of my memory, but my brain was syrup.

When I get my visa, I will live in California, said BJ.

You will not live in California, said AJ. You will live in Michigan or Illinois where all Iraqis go.

My family lives in Indiana, I said.

I will live where I want to live, said BJ. The two fell back into Arabic.

I closed my eyes and knew what they were saying even if I didn't.

When I opened my eyes, AJ and BJ had quit the bickering. They sat close, grasping hands, talking, smoking cigarettes. Heat spread above my collar again and my grape deflated, pinched together behind my forehead. I couldn't look at the two of them.

You do not do this in America, I think, said AJ. He lit a cigarette.

I coughed and pulled my legs to my chest and I tried to send my thoughts directly into AJ's brain, and then AJ held a thick, square-fingered hand out, and I took it, and we sat there, the three of us floating on the opium, holding hands.

I cried myself awake on an extra hospital cot in the postpartum room. I had the kind of headache where you can feel your brain touching the inside of your skull with every throb. The ringing was always a steady drone. The sheep was bedded at my feet.

Get the fuck out of here, I said to the sheep. But I didn't say it in my head like I'd been talking to Ruiz.

I'm sorry? said a nurse.

I hadn't seen her in the dim room. She was the same woman who had held Max's hand in the delivery room. She had been scribbling on the whiteboard hanging on the back of the room's door.

Nothing, I said. I was dreaming.

I kicked my feet under the covers at the sheep. It didn't move. Just stared at me.

They're sleeping, said the nurse. She pointed at Max in the main bed and the baby in the clear bassinet next to her.

I nodded at her. Gave her a thumbs-up, then felt like an asshole for giving her a thumbs-up.

You did great, said the nurse before slipping away.

But I knew that was bullshit and I started thinking maybe it'd just be best if I left. Got up right then, walked out the door, and fucking left.

I swung my legs to the linoleum. And then the baby fussed and woke and so did Max and she looked at me and said, I want to name her River.

So we named the baby River, and nurses came in and gave Max a sitz bath to take home because she'd torn, which they said was better than having to cut, though every time they said *tear* it puckered my asshole, and they showed us how to swaddle the kid and laughed when we got it wrong but didn't show us again, and we watched a video about why we shouldn't shake her. Our baby.

The entire time the sheep was on my heels. It didn't go away like Ruiz did. And I kept trying to find a good time to tell Max about it—the sheep, Ruiz. All of it, you know? But there's not a good time to tell the brand-new mother of your kid you're being followed around by a zombie sheep. Ghost sheep. Whatever the fuck.

It was all fucked-up. But I kept thinking it wasn't me, not my brain, it was something else—that thing in the cemetery that had gotten inside the gravedigger, maybe. I started to think I could feel it moving around under my skin.

It made sense to me. When had it gotten to me? What did its face look like? Probably my birth mom's. Maybe it got me that night in Iraq at the widow's house. Maybe it was in the dark room at the PB. Maybe on the basketball court after Ruiz had killed himself. Maybe that night after Court's party when I watched those dogs with my face chase down the sheep over and over and over on a loop. OODA loop. *Dog, that's repressive*, said Ruiz with his hand on my thigh and then his hand was AJ's holding mine, heavy hookah smoke escaping his lips turning to cigarette smoke hanging above the smoke pit outside the barracks to smoke snaking from Ruiz's torn, dead mouth to wildfire smoke settling thick over the top of First Sergeant's Hill to smoke coming out of me in tiny little breaths. *Dog, that's repressive. Any decision is better than a bad decision.* And the entire time I was cradling this baby in my arms, drinking hospital coffee and texting my mom and Penny pictures of her sleeping face.

And then when it was time to take her home, I kept asking the nurse if we could just leave.

Just like that? I said. With the kid?

The nurse looked at me a minute and said sure and slow, Yes.

It floored me. Like, there was more oversight for a Marine's rifle than a goddamned baby.

That first day home, all three of us tried to sleep in our bedroom together like some kind of family. I'd hit twilight sleep and start awake to Max whispering and grunting at me, but the white-noise machine and electric whirring of River's automatic rocker and the ringing in my head drowned her voice, and I put my hand up to my ear to show her I couldn't hear. She used more hand and arm signals and I figured out she had to go to the bathroom.

I helped her from the bed; pain radiated from her in the dark. A kind of heat. I wanted that pain to be mine. I was the one who deserved it.

The world I'd been dropped in felt like a patrol. Like war. When we got up and the bed frame popped like wood knots in a campfire, my head went on a swivel and I held my breath, my body, like I'd seen the hand signal to freeze on patrol. River didn't move, though. The rocking machine where she slept kept up. Max huffed morning breath into my face and pointed to the bathroom.

I waited outside the door to help her back to bed, and I didn't need to look down to know the sheep was there. I watched River sleep: her fat bottom lip stuck out, shiny with milk spit. I kept trying to catch any kind of movement and I had this feeling of complete terror.

I kept thinking she was dead. River was dead. That the sheep was the motherfucking angel of death. That angels were real and that this was my goddamned punishment. I couldn't move, didn't want to know what a dead baby felt like, so I just stared through the hot, dim room, held my breath until my lungs burned and finally River struggled against her swaddle, pursed her lips together, nursed an imaginary boob in her sleep. And this, I don't know, kind of panic-love-jealousy burrowed into my guts. I loved the kid. I knew that then. But I hated her, too, for making me feel like that. For making me afraid. Like I'd felt standing outside my barracks room after Ruiz had killed himself.

Then, from the crack in the bathroom door, Max called for me.

Blood spattered the toilet seat. Droplets raced each other into the bowl, turned the water rusty, stained the porcelain. A drip exploded on the linoleum between her feet like a sunburst.

I'm sorry, said Max. She leaned on the body-length counter between twin sinks, closed her eyes against the vanity lights.

I wiped the blood, tossed the double-ply into the water, and didn't flush because of River. Milk leaked through Max's oversized T-shirt.

Are the stitches okay? I said. Did they come out?

I don't think so, she said. Stretched.

I winced at that.

Can you help me with these? she said.

I stooped at Max's feet, arranged a pair of those mesh underwear on the floor, and she put a hot palm on my shoulder to brace herself and stepped into them. I helped her slide them up and when I stood, she grabbed me in this awkward, jerky hug that made me think of a dying spider, the way its legs curl, and I wanted to push her away, which made me feel like a shit, but I couldn't shake the image.

She held tight, though, pressed into me, and the musky smell of the sheep at my feet gave way to coconut shampoo and sweat and breast milk.

In the mirror, Max's long, messy copper hair framed my face, softened me up, and I saw my birth mom and all I wanted was to crawl as deep inside of Max as possible, grab the sharp angles of her while she braced against the mirror, pull myself in. I imagined four more limbs bursting from her sides, grasping at me, shoveling me inside what had turned into a gaping spider's mouth. I wanted her to gobble me down. I'd curl up, go to sleep.

What are you thinking? she said into my neck.

What you'd look like as a giant spider, I didn't say.

How I'd like to crawl inside your body, I didn't say

That I hate River, I didn't say.

What I said: How much I love you.

Pink midsummer twilight bloomed outside the casement windows. Inside, it was dim still. Max and River slept. I sat on the couch. The sheep stared at me.

I dialed my mom. We'd started talking more in the last couple months of Max's pregnancy. I hadn't been over to the house. Rick didn't want me there. I wanted to tell my mom I didn't think that was very godly, but it was something the old me would've said. I was trying.

Hello? she said.

We're home, Mom, I said.

I was thinking about you, she said.

Everyone's good, I said. River's sleeping.

She sounds like a good baby, she said.

I wondered what River would have to do to be called a bad baby. Tried to let it go but couldn't, so I asked, Was I?

Were you what? she said.

Good, I said. A good baby.

We were going through a lot then, she said. It's hard to remember. Penny was regressing. The day we brought you home she started sucking her thumb—she'd never done that before—and she refused to talk. And your father. I don't think when he agreed to the adoption that he thought it would actually happen. It took so long. We got on a list a year after Penny was born. I couldn't get pregnant. No one could tell me why. Some doctors thought it was the endometriosis, the fibroids.

She always called it *the* endometriosis, *the* fibroids, but didn't really talk much about it. She hadn't answered the question, not really, and we were quiet for a moment.

I wonder if I did the right thing sometimes, she said.

What? I said.

Oh, making excuses for him when the social worker would come, she said. She observed us, the three of us, and your father was never a get-down-on-the-floor-and-play type of dad—couldn't even suck it up in that moment and just play blocks with Penny—and the social worker said something about that on the side and I went on and on and on about what a good father he was: how attentive, how doting, how he was just distracted because of something at work.

Yeah, I said.

I wanted another baby so much, she said.

Yeah, I said. Listening to her, I was on autopilot. She did that kind of thing: took up space. Went on these tours of the past where she wanted me to tell her it was all okay, that she was a good mom, that she'd done a fine job.

Want isn't a good word, she said. I don't have a word for it. It felt . . . biological. Just know you won't ever understand that.

What's so hard to understand? I said. I hadn't expected that and it got me salty.

You can understand, Dean, but you can't really *understand*, she said.

I was there, I said.

She's a whole new person now, she said.

And I'm not? I said.

Honey, I wish it was the same, she said.

I knew on the other end of the phone she was shaking her head.

Men and women are just different, she said.

Tell that to Max, I said.

After we said our goodbyes, I snuck into the bedroom to grab some PT gear. The sheep followed. Max and River were asleep. I changed in the living room while the sheep watched.

Take a good fucking look, I said aloud, and bent over to give it the brown-eye while I pulled up my shorts.

Get the fuck out of here, I said. I tried to kick at it, but it was always just out of reach.

Motherfucker, I said. I would have torn it apart myself then. Barely remembered being so angry.

Nguyen, Crowe, and I were the only ones left from the first pump in the dismounted squad. Sergeant Moss made staff, and Command stuck him with another line company. Shit was like that—guys shifted around. Health of the Corps took precedence. Baptiste had gotten out. And Cobb had been separated with an other-than-honorable. Nguyen reenlisted in country, got promoted to sergeant. He stuck around—at least for the deployment. Stayed in the platoon and after Sergeant Moss left became squad leader.

At first, he tried it on like Sergeant Moss—no bullshit, distant, direct. Like, Sergeant Moss had been the fucking dad from just about every goddamned movie about growing up, right? But that wasn't Nguyen. He was too smart for it, too funny, too human. He'd say something to cut when one of the new guys did something fucking stupid and it'd go right over the guy's head. Over all our heads.

I skated through the second deployment—spent most of my time in the terp hut, did what I could to avoid extra duty. Sometimes it was unavoidable. It was a goddamned war after all. The new guys—Walker, Murillo, and Kubo—had come to us a month before we were supposed to deploy.

A month of a combat workup was enough time for you to know a dude so well you'd die for him—the Corps knew how to make you love someone. At the very least, after so much time with a guy you knew every last goddamned thing about him. But I didn't know the new guys. Didn't want to.

Since Ruiz, I had early-onset short-timer syndrome. Part of me was sorry for that, like I'd up and fucked off, dropped my pack. Felt like I'd set a standard and I wasn't living up to it.

After the seven-ton T-boned us, we rotated into rest and refit and Nguyen put Crowe and I in charge of skill-checking the new guys' CQB—how to enter a room and push in, how to pie a window from the outside, how to command a space. You know: speed, surprise, violence-of-action-type shit. And these fucking guys, they were floppy turds. Moved like old people fucked.

Crowe kept rubbing his face and asking me what we were doing wrong. He was losing his shit, which was funny, because Crowe had this Southern accent that made it sound like he was playing a kazoo when he spoke and he talked with his hands, too. So there he was, jumping up and down, red-faced, waving his arms around, giving commands and scenarios to these limp noodles, and then he finally told them they were fucking idiots.

Y'all are fucking idiots, he said.

You can't talk to me like that, said Walker. We're the same rank.

The kid wasn't wrong: Crowe was a lance corporal and this kid, he was a lance corporal, too.

The first three ranks in the Marine Corps come with time in grade. That means you can pretty much walk around with the thumb of one hand up your asshole and a finger of the other hand up your nose and you'll get promoted to PFC in six months and then lance corporal eight months after that.

So we usually got new joins as privates or PFCs and then we had time to smoke out the fuckups.

Sometimes, though, the new guys came with rank—maybe they'd been Eagle Scouts or platoon guides in boot camp or a squad leader at SOI. Or they'd gone broke dick, maybe dropped to the Porkchop Platoon for unsat body composition after failing a PFT in boot camp, or maybe SOI was backed up and they'd been put on camp guard. Anyway—no matter the case, they usually thought they were hot shit. But lance corporals were a dime a dozen. Everyone was a fucking lance corporal.

After lance corporal comes corporal, then sergeant—noncommissioned officers. To pick up corporal, you've got to have a high rifle qual, a decent PFT score, good proficiency and conduct marks, time in service, time in grade, and you have to show you're continuing your education—civilian or military.

Like, you could take community college classes in underwater basket weaving and the shit would count. Most guys order a couple Marine Corps Institute course booklets like *Fundamentals of Marine Corps Leadership* and *Personal Financial Management* and whatever their weapon specialty is—mortars, machine guns, TOW missiles, whatever—and then cheat on the test and send the fuckers in.

Anyway, all that gets added up into what the Corps calls a composite score. Once you meet or exceed the score for your occupational specialty and if that occupational specialty has room for more of that rank, then you get promoted.

Some occupational specialties have low scores. Some have high scores. It all depends on the needs of the Corps. If the Corps needs more corporals in one occupational specialty, then the score is probably lower. If they don't have need, the score might be high or the occupation might be closed for promotion.

So you might get a new join who's a TOW gunner who picks up corporal in less than two years because TOW gunner scores are the fucking base of the goddamned mountain, but then you might have a guy who's an assaultman—a demo specialist—who goes through his entire four years as a terminal lance corporal because the score is too high and no matter how many MCI booklets he does or how shit-hot his PFT score and rifle qual is, or even if someone wants to meritoriously promote them, it doesn't matter.

Crowe was an assaultman. He'd come in with me. I didn't like him, but the dude had a deployment under his belt; I'd been in the suck with him and knew what he was worth. He knew his shit and was good at his job. He should have been a corporal. Shit, maybe even a sergeant. But he was still a lance because he didn't have the points to pick up rank.

Higher-ups were always trying to say some shit about how we were all Marines and that there wasn't a difference between those who had deployed and those who hadn't, that we'd all earned the eagle, globe, and anchor. Every Marine was a rifleman.

But fucking not really.

On the level? That was bullshit. Riflemen were smart, well-trained killers, not POGs sitting behind a desk. And senior was senior.

So there we were, these three new guys looking like monkeys, trying to fuck a football, and Crowe said what he said, which was pretty fucking mild, considering, you know, some of the shit Sergeant Moss had done, and this wannabe-salty lance corporal fucking new guy said what he said.

Oh. And the other shit of being a terminal lance is that you've got nothing to lose. Most guys who spend their first four years as a lance don't re-up because . . . Jesus, would you? After four years of eating everyone else's shit and watching dumb motherfuckers around you get promoted based on a broken merit system? Fuck out of here.

Okay, so Crowe said what he said. Walker said what he said. And then you probably guessed it by this point: Crowe took him to the fucking ground and balled him up. He was calm about it, too, the way he did it. Like water filling a glass. All of a sudden or something. Kind of beautiful to watch. Crowe was into martial arts, jiujitsu and shit. Almost made me feel bad for the kid.

Tap, he said to Walker.

For a minute I had respect for Walker, thought he might take it to blackout, but then Crowe tensed and tweaked. Walker tapped. Crowe stood and brushed himself off, grabbed his rifle, and headed back to the Quonset hut where the platoon was berthed, swearing to himself in that Southern drawl the entire way.

Walker rubbed his neck and sucked wind. Kubo and Murillo shifted from foot to foot next to the outline of the house we'd made with some stakes and engineer's tape.

I felt for the kid. Like it was me, right? Goddamned choked-out in the PB on my first pump. There was part of me that wanted to run back into the arms of the Corps. This was how I'd do it. Take the kid in, mentor him, teach him to roll. The rest would follow: I'd re-up, deploy, realize my potential, become a fucking war hero.

Crowe's into martial arts, I said.

I crouched in front of Walker. He kept his head between his knees.

I don't think I could roll him up, I said. You know, I could teach you a bit if you wanted.

That was assault, said Walker.

The kid looked up, his face covered in snot and moon dust.

And you watched it happen, he said.

All those good feelings went out the window.

I have witnesses, he said. I'll go right to the lieutenant.

All I could think about was hurting the little shit. Wished Crowe had snapped an arm.

There are a lot of ways to eat shit out here, I said.

Are you threatening me? he said. In front of witnesses?

I am informing you, Lance Corporal Walker, I said, of the dangers surrounding you in a forward-deployed area. Just as Lance Corporal Crowe was informing you of various hand-to-hand combat methods. Isn't that what you saw, PFC Kubo? PFC Murillo?

Yes, Corporal, came the response in unison.

I didn't know they'd answer me like that. I felt like one of those fucking people in those churches who do the funky chicken and speak in tongues. I was feeling the goddamned spirit. Didn't know Walker from Adam. Guy could've been aces. I didn't give a shit. I could tell by Walker's face he knew he'd lost. That's all that mattered.

You must've forgotten where the fuck you are, Lance Corporal Walker, I said. Is that it? Your brain housing group made of rocks?

He didn't answer.

You two help Lance Corporal Walker find his brain, I said.

Corporal? said Kubo.

I think I saw it somewhere next to the tape house, I said. It's about the size of a coffee can. Looks like a fucking rock.

Walker and I stared at one another while Kubo and Murillo dug the rock out of the hardpan.

Your brain goes with you everywhere, I said.

No answer.

Good to go? I said.

Yes, Corporal, he said.

Oorah, devil dog, I said, patted Walker on the shoulder, went off to find the terps so I could get high and take a nap.

★

Indiana August heat stuck around in the dark—the humidity. It was like someone dumped melted butter all over me. Skin clogged up with it the minute I stepped outside. The moisture dampened everything. Under the streetlights while I ran, my shadow dropped behind, shortened, caught up, lengthened in front of me—each light was like an entire day.

Can't outrun your brain, dummy, said Ruiz. He was my shadow.

When we were sucking wind on long PT runs, Sergeant Moss would tell us that running made us good at fucking. We'd laugh and forget about the pain for a minute and then not long after start lagging again. He'd get annoyed and tell us it was nothing but a controlled fall. You can fall, can't you, monkeys?

And then the fucking lights started going out. Something was up behind me—I had that gut feeling—and when I turned my head, all of them, the lights, were going. Blinking out one after another. They were faster than me and I was in the dark and I fell over and over myself.

I sprinted, scared as hell, until something popped in my groin and I pancaked on the sidewalk, took the skin off a knee and my palms. When I got myself sitting on the curb, feet in the gutter, the lights were back and I lay on the sidewalk, heat pulsing over me. I took my phone out of the pocket on the back of my shorts and checked to see if I had any messages from Max. I didn't, so I tried to catch my breath and stretch and opened Insta.

I had a DM. I opened it.

Dear Corporal,

How are you? I am well. I am sure you do not remember me. I do not believe you knew my real name, which is Waleed Sherwani. Perhaps you remember that I was an interpreter that was called AJ? I am writing because thanks to the glory of Allah I am now living in Dearborn, Michigan, and I recalled that you lived in the state of Indiana (though I am sorry I could not recall the name of the city) and so I went searching for you. I have found many U.S.

Marines from my time as an interpreter. Some I have met in person. Perhaps you know them. The Marine Corps is a small world, yes?

In one month, I must travel for my work, which is the sales of machine parts, to Indianapolis, which is in the state of Indiana, and when my supervisor gives me this assignment, I think to myself that Corporal Pusey is from the state of Indiana. Just like that, a memory. The mind is strange, yes?

Corporal, I am wondering if your city is near Indianapolis, and if so, would you be wishing to meet?

I believe this is the correct person. I must confess to closely examining your photographs to be certain. Pleased to be expecting your reply.

Regards,
Waleed Sherwani (AJ)

AFTER A COUPLE weeks our bedroom, mine and Max's, became this shadowy den—the kind of place I imagined cavemen might live, grunting at each other and slapping dirty, charcoal-covered hands on the walls and breaking mammoth bones on rocks to suck at the marrow. Like having a kid had thrown us back in time.

All that dark made me think of the shark Court loved so much—alone down in the deep—or those cave animals with no eyes and see-through skin some goddamned scientist had discovered somewhere by accident. *Scientists Find Blind Translucent Albino Salamandercrabfish in Bumfuck Nowhere Cave*, or whatever.

An accident. That was me. I was the translucent albino salamandercrabfish. Felt like I was going to live the rest of my life in that room.

I was using FMLA and wasn't getting paid—didn't rate anything but a single paid sick day from UPS. At a year I'd get a week of paid vacation. In the Marines I got two and a half days each month. Paid. Instead of some asshole fighting a lava monster, they ought to put that shit in the recruiting commercials.

I wasn't sleeping. The switch to a regular schedule was a mind fuck and I couldn't really sleep during the day because the kid was up every few hours. Plus, Ruiz and the sheep crowded the room—a couple of turds who couldn't take a hint it was time to flush.

Rotting milk and sweet baby shit stink and body musk had seeped into our sheets and clothing and carpet and drywall. Ruiz ran his mouth constantly; the sheep crowded me. River slept in two-hour spurts and woke—fat, wide lips pulled back against purple gums mewling, keening, wailing. She wanted the boob. She was sucking all of Max's life.

Max still couldn't get up on her own. Kept talking about her pelvic wall and her perineum—used the word *tugging*, and every time she did, it made my teeth clench, and this swell of shame hit me like a fucking tidal wave. Like I'd done that to her.

One night she said, Jesus Christ, I just want to take a decent shit.

Like a prayer or something, and then we laughed about that. It felt good to laugh, but Max was impatient, and she didn't like to feel weak—didn't want to ask for help, didn't think she should have to. Like, she fucking *hated* it is what I mean, and every time she had to ask me for help, I think she hated me a little bit, too.

I've been on my own, she said. I'm not used to this.

What? I said.

Things needing me, she said.

I knew when she said *things* she was saying me and River. Maybe she was giving me an out. Like, *I don't want* things *to need me, but* a thing *is okay.* One thing. The baby. River.

When River finished eating, I changed her diaper, clothed her, swaddled her, rocked her, burped gas bubbles from her belly until her eyelids drooped, then laid her down in the automated rocker. I usually made it to some kind of twilight sleep next to Max, who slept like the dead, nursing gown open, a single swollen tit exposed like an unblinking eye.

That night I watched her sleep and wondered what kinds of things followed her around. What ghosts she had. If she had any. Everyone's got secrets, right? What was crowding her on the bed? Talking her ear off constantly?

I imagined her uterus flopping its jellied body across our sheets, pointing its tubes accusingly at her, and an angry, scarred taint. Maybe a kiddie-diddling priest from her childhood waiting around every corner with a smile and a Hail Mary.

Or maybe she was okay. Nguyen had said to me right before I'd gotten out, he'd said, It's okay to be okay. Nguyen figured you could go through terrible shit and come out clean. I wasn't so sure.

Max and I had been together for almost a year and I could tell you some things about her—I'd observed, right? Her favorite color and TV shows, why she didn't talk to her parents, how she'd been harassed by some pervy fucking physics professor at her community college. But then River came and the kid was like a magnifying glass showing me all the shit I didn't know.

I laid in bed, Ruiz talk-talk-talking, the sheep staring. I needed an Ativan but I was out. I'd tried everything else—melatonin, Advil PM, warm milk. I didn't want to call Court. I thought about the shark again, cruising the deep, dark water. We hadn't spoken since March.

Max wasn't upset about that. He's not a good person, she said. But she *was* upset that I couldn't sleep. Mostly because when I started tossing and turning every thirty seconds after the pillow got too hot or my legs started crawling, it woke her up, and because she felt so connected to River, she thought anything she felt, River must've felt, too.

It didn't help that whenever I held the kid, she fucking screamed and wailed. Max said it was no big deal, that lots of babies were like that, all the books said so. But I got the feeling she loved that the kid wanted her—made her feel like she was doing a good job. A better job than me.

When we were in the bedroom, because River was in there, sleeping with us, we texted each other. My phone screen lit up on the bedside table.

R u ok? she texted.

Can't sleep, I texted.

What r u thinking abt? she texted.

That you love River more than me, I didn't text.

That you're probably going to leave me, I didn't text.

That this bed is too fucking crowded with a sheep, a uterus, a taint, a dead man, and the two of us, I didn't text.

What I did text: *A Marine buddy texted me a while back and wants to meet up U should!*

I didn't think she'd give me up that easy. Kid was hard enough with us tag-teaming. It gave me the feeling she was trying to get rid of me, you know? Or maybe like she was planning on going unauthorized absence, deserting. Like, Spidey Sense blaring in my brain housing group like a goddamned car alarm: DESERTION DESERTION DESERTION. I'd come home afterward, and she and River would be gone. Cleared out of the entire goddamned apartment. UA. AWOL.

I wished we'd staggered our leave so we weren't together so much. Maybe she was feeling the same thing, trying to be kind when really she was thinking, *Get the fuck out of here, you fucking fuck.* Maybe it was some kind of trap to use against me later. I didn't know what I didn't fucking know. What if? What if? What if?

Trying to get rid of me lol, I texted.

River and I will be ok, she texted.

Okay. I texted it with a period because I was upset.

R u mad?? she texted.

No, I texted.

K, she texted.

A week later I was at this coffee shop in downtown Richfield. I'd never been. Swanky, hip. Lots of wood and bright light. Max suggested it. Wouldn't have thought places like that existed in Richfield. It was early morning—work rush—and the place was crowded.

I didn't know what anything was. Espresso, cappuccino, Americano— maybe that should have been part of the fucking TAP class. I imagined the fat former Marine with the EGA tat on his arm teaching us about the customs and courtesies of coffee shops: When ordering coffee in the civilian world you'll be faced with a number of options. Remember, it is never okay to resort to violence in a coffee shop.

Anyway, I ordered a coffee and the guy behind the counter got all fucking dramatic about it and rolled his eyes.

I'm not a mind reader, boss, he said. He was pale and twiggy under a rumpled V-neck and apron, arms covered in shitty stick-and-poke tats, wore a mustache.

I thought maybe he hadn't heard me so I said it again: Just a coffee.

The guy sighed and shook his head and I wanted to choke him with his fucking V-neck. I could feel the people in line behind me getting antsy, shifting their feet.

What *kind*? he said.

Regular, I said.

He laughed. Pour-over? Drip? Americano?

I went with the first thing he said because I figured it'd be the fastest way to get the fuck out of there.

There we go, he said. That'll be a five spot, boss.

I paid and waited for him to bring my coffee.

Anything else, boss? he said.

Just the coffee, I said.

It'll be up in a minute, he said.

I waited. He stared at me.

You. Can. Pick. It. Up. Over. There. He spoke slow and loud like I was a fucking idiot and pointed to the end of the counter.

My fists were clenched so tight, I thought the bones in my hand might explode, but I walked to the end of the counter and let it out in tiny little breaths like I'd learned. And was fucking proud of myself. When I turned, I saw the guy roll his eyes and shake his head and laugh with the woman who stepped forward. Then I watched him turn, grab a cup, and fill it from an airpot and the woman paid and left.

Couldn't even order a fucking coffee right.

I waited another five minutes for whatever I'd ordered and then turned to scan the place for Waleed until I saw him at a table in the back and my stomach flip-flopped and I spilled hot fucking coffee on my hand as I made my way to him. I knew the guy, but I knew him like I'd realized I knew other Marines—not really at all. We knew each other through a pinhole. That made me want to run. *Retreat? Hell, I just got here*, I thought. Ruiz would've gotten a kick out of that Chesty Puller–oorah bullshit, but he wasn't around.

Anyway, like I said, the place was crowded and I was dodging guys in blue plaid suits and brown loafers, women in pencil skirts and heels. They looked smart. Established. I tried to guess what they did for work. Lawyers, maybe—I wondered if Cooper and Hudson got coffee there—therapists, accountants, consultants, fucking dentists. They were the people who lived in those exposed-brick lofts and I knew then, seeing them all sharp and put together, how stupid the entire fantasy had been, how far away. Max and I would never have that; we'd live in a shitty fucking apartment complex forever or maybe we'd all end up in the bed of my truck, sleeping in a Walmart parking lot.

I hadn't had a haircut or shaved my beard in three months, and while I weaved in and out of the bodies and felt like a fucking kid, I kept waiting for one of them to offer me the loose change in their pockets. *Tiny little breaths, tiny little breaths*, I kept thinking.

Waleed stood when I made it to him, and he went to hug me, but I was holding the cup and covered in coffee. Instead, I dropped into a seat and he followed.

He looked older than I remembered: gray crept over his neat beard and eyebrows, spread up his sideburns like spilled ink. His body was thicker. Not fat but filled out. Less hollow. I looked around the coffee shop to keep myself from staring.

Should've been a fucking dentist, I said. I drank my coffee. It was more fruit than earth and left my mouth sour.

Waleed nodded like he knew what the hell I was talking about.

Salaam, Corporal, he said.

Shaku maku, I said.

That made him laugh.

What? I said.

You know what this means? he said.

Yeah: What's up, right? I said.

More complicated, he said.

He took a sip of his coffee.

Shaku maku, he said, means: What is everything? What is nothing?

I liked that. Fucking philosophical, not something a knuckle-dragging grunt would say. Made me feel like a college boy, like one of these guys walking around the coffee shop in their suits and starched fucking collars. I rolled it around in my head. *What is everything? What is nothing?* You could answer it however the fuck you wanted—a goddamned life story or nothing or what nothing was. What the fuck is nothing, right? The bottom of a quarry, grasshoppers with machine guns, fucking infinite choices.

Just like that, I was back in the terp hut. Warm and a little high. The pale, salamandercrabfish part of me burned away under the overhead, unshaded lights and the sun blaring through the floor-to-ceiling windows. No Ruiz. No sheep. No Max. No River. Light as air. I could've fucking slept right then and there in the middle of all those white-collars pounding away on phones and keyboards. But I didn't know what Waleed wanted and that was getting to me. Like, what the fuck man? I tried to change the subject and asked him why he was heading to Indianapolis.

I am, right now, he said, working as a sales representative for a steel manufacturer. We have clients there as I mentioned in my direct message.

Is it a good job? I said.

He seemed happy, comfortable. I wanted him to tell me how—how he got up every morning and went to work and smiled and came home and hugged his wife and played with his kids. What followed *him* around? I wondered if he knew how to get out whatever was inside of me.

Do you know what I did before the war, Corporal? he said.

You don't have to call me that, I said.

I was a teacher, he said. At a secondary school. I taught humanities. Literature.

He sipped his coffee.

That is why I was a good interpreter, you know? he said.

We drank our coffees and Waleed talked about Iraq—how an Army tank unit had taken over the AO not long after we'd left; how they'd started hasty stop and searches, tossing cars and roughing people up wholesale; how the violence had escalated. Classic Army.

Ali was killed not long before my wife, Fairuz, and I left, he said.

Ali? I said.

You might know him as BJ, he said.

In the middle of our second deployment, our mounted patrol dropped the six of us and BJ the terp on a block in downtown Fallujah. We were supposed to post up for the day and provide overwatch for the mounted section. We found the compound we'd scouted over a couple days. House was the tallest on the block, and after we cleared it, Nguyen paid the owner fifty dollars American to clear out.

In ten minutes, the man packed his wife, two toddlers, and a metric fuckton of personal shit into and on top of a beater—a white Opel. The younger kid slumped on the mother's lap in the back seat while the older stood on the upholstery and looked out the rear window at us while the man and BJ yelled Arabic at each other as he sped away toward the main thoroughfare.

Fucking guy, man, said BJ.

Who pissed in his Cheerios? I said.

That made him laugh.

I like this very much, he said, and took off his gear.

BJ was the tallest Iraqi I'd ever met, must've been, like, six foot five. But he looked young—peach fuzz above a pouty upper lip made me think of the teenager from the first deployment every time I looked at him; you didn't realize how tall he was until you were standing next to him. He was nineteen, he thought. He grew up homeless in Baghdad, didn't know what happened to his parents. Sometimes he told people they were dead, or that they'd sold him, or that Saddam had disappeared them. Had been working with Marines since two thousand six. Longer than any of us. He wanted to go to California. Be a movie star.

We barred the compound gate from the inside. Walls were six feet. House had two soft points on the first story. We locked and wired one with a hand grenade and posted up our mini command near the other. Sent the three new guys to the roof.

Can't believe you let them leave, said Crowe.

We inserted in the middle of the day, said Nguyen. This isn't a recon mission; it's a presence mission. LT wants everyone to know where we're at.

Nguyen radioed to the mounted patrol to let them know we were set and provide a sitrep to the LT.

This deployment's a fucking joke, said Crowe.

It *was* a goddamned joke. We all knew it. The war was over. We were nothing but cops—fucking rent-a-cops, even. Might as well have been the fucking Army. Still, I told Crowe to stow that shit and get a watch set up.

Everyone pulls two-hour shifts except BJ, I said. Pair the new guys with us.

Sergeant Moss wouldn't have let shit like this happen, said Crowe. Even fucking Ruiz would've kept them fucking people here.

You've got first watch, I said.

I slumped against the wall, opened my day pack for a bottle of water, and realized I'd forgotten one. Complacent as fuck. Worse than a goddamned new join. We'd checked the new guys' gear, but Nguyen hadn't checked mine. Make sure you got your shit was all he'd said. It was hot, pushing a hundred. My flak vest chafed my neck.

This isn't so bad, said Nguyen.

It's bullshit, I said.

No one's shooting at us, he said, or trying to blow us up; we're not filling sandbags. We getting a tax-free paycheck plus hazard pay. This is fucking paradise.

What do you think, BJ? I said.

The terp was already asleep.

Nguyen took off his gear, pounded water. I wanted to ask him for some, but I didn't. Didn't want him to give me shit, didn't want to set a bad example. Crowe was right about Sergeant Moss. Before we'd stepped off, he'd checked everyone's gear, even the salts like Ruiz. My tongue was tacky, thick spit crusted at the corners of my mouth.

You can drop your gear, Dean, Nguyen said.

I'm good, I said.

Kubo and Murillo came down the stairs, set up across the room from us.

The fuck you doing? said Nguyen.

Sergeant? said Kubo.

We're not going to fucking bite you, said Nguyen.

They stared at us for a minute.

Get the fuck over here, dummies, said Nguyen.

Yes, Sergeant, they both said.

You can drop your gear, said Nguyen.

They did. Goddamn, it was fucking hot. You moved and you sweated. You talked and you sweated. I looked over at BJ snoozing away and he looked cool as a fucking cucumber. There was a bottle of water in one of his pouches.

What was I saying? said Nguyen.

Bullshit deployment, I said.

Fuck no, he damn near yelled. It woke BJ.

Okay, Jesus, I said.

This is a good deployment, Dean, he said. This shit's ending. That's all. About fucking time. This isn't a war. No honor here. Maybe next time we'll deploy to Oki, Oz, the Philippines. Some place with bars and women. Or shit. Maybe there'll be a real war.

Fucking next time—I didn't give that the time of day. Nguyen was a lifer and I was getting out. I didn't know what the difference was between us—how he could stay in after we'd stood outside that barracks room. And this was Nguyen's third deployment to the same place in the same war in less than five years.

You're married, I said.

Eatin' ain't cheatin', he said.

You're so full of shit, I said. Couldn't tie your boots without Amber.

This made Kubo and Murillo laugh. BJ made a face.

You lick the pussy, Sergeant? said BJ.

Hell yeah, BJ, said Nguyen. Does a body good.

Nguyen held his fingers in a V up to his mouth and flicked out his tongue. It wasn't Nguyen; it was bluster. A bunch of bullshit to pass the time, get the new joins talking.

I don't eat pussy, Sergeant, said Kubo.

Why the fuck not, boot? said Nguyen.

Men aren't supposed to do that, said Kubo.

I do the work, bring home the money, said BJ.

What home? I said. Aren't you a fucking orphan?

It's for faggots, said Kubo.

We all laughed at that.

Eating pussy's for faggots? said Nguyen.

Murillo was cry-laughing.

I wished Ruiz were there.

We're all a bunch of faggots anyway, said Nguyen.

I ain't a fucking faggot, Sergeant, said Murillo.

Yes you are, boot, said Nguyen.

Murillo was heated, about to say something else, but I cut him off.

BOHICA, I said.

What's that, Corporal? said Kubo.

Bend over, here it comes again, I said.

The Big Green Weenie dry fucking you, right up your asshole, Murillo, said Nguyen. Welcome to the suck.

When I get to America, I will join the Marines, said BJ.

And then what? I said.

Then I will come back and fight, said BJ.

He took a swig of water, saw me staring, offered me the bottle, and I drank.

I didn't have to ask Waleed how Ali had died. I knew the fucking story. He'd been waiting on his visa paperwork or he couldn't get a letter of recommendation or he didn't have the necessary information because he'd been a fucking orphan and everything was tangled in red tape and all the shortcuts and fudged paperwork he'd done to become a terp—all those waivers the Corps was so happy to give out—were getting ironed out and they'd told him to stand by to stand by and then someone had decided they didn't like that he worked with the U.S. and figured out where he lived and that was fucking that.

My heart started going and the coffee in my gut boiled and Waleed was talking and I wanted to pound the table and rage and throw my coffee and reach inside of myself and pull that shadowy ghost out and rip it to shreds, slam my head against the wall until I couldn't remember a goddamned thing, pop benzos until I slipped into a fucking coma.

I regret we did not attend his funeral, said Waleed. The cemetery manager claimed angry ghosts were haunting the grounds. Fairuz is superstitious. Silly, yes?

I jolted at what he said about the ghosts and knocked over what was left of my goddamned coffee and it spilled over the table.

Motherfucker, I said, loud enough for people to turn and look.

I will get napkins, said Waleed. He smiled at the people staring.

Fuck the napkins, I was thinking, *tell me about the goddamned ghosts*, and then Waleed started to stand.

No, I said, catching him in mid-rise.

It came off rough. Everything was at the surface just then and I didn't know how to recognize that. Deal with it.

I got it, I said.

The barista leaned against the counter, talking to his two coworkers.

Napkins? I said.

Damn, said the barista. After all that trouble, you just spill it, boss?

He was smiling but my hackles went up. My body did quick math: This fucking guy, right? Like, who the fuck did he think he was? Not like he was a lawyer or a dentist—he was a goddamned barista. I was a fucking Marine, I fought in a war, I was a monster. Fuck this guy.

Fuck you, you fucking fuck, I didn't say.

I could kill you, I didn't say.

I'll burn this fucking place to the ground, I didn't say.

What I said: I'm a combat, battle-tested Marine.

I hated myself immediately. For a second he stared at me and it was like when you drop a rock into deep water, right before the water rushes back to fill the space. And then: splash. The dude lost it. Started laughing his ass off and I wanted to laugh, too, because what a stupid fucking thing to say to someone in the world, but he kept laughing and behind me I could feel everyone staring at me—the doctor in the hospital, Penny and Iris and Mom on Christmas, the Iraqi kid while Ruiz was flipping his safety on and off *click click click click*, the sheep, my birth mom. And I had this feeling like *Yeah so the fuck what? This is me, I guess.* And I took a step toward the guy. Wanted to hurt him. Was going to hurt. Wanted him to know who the fuck I was.

I'm a veteran, I said.

He wiped his eyes and smoothed his mustache.

Boss, who isn't? he said.

He raised his hand and said, Tenth Mountain Division, oh-three to oh-seven.

He pointed to a short blond woman at his left, said, One-Thirtieth Engineers, oh-five to oh-nine.

He pointed to a younger Black guy washing cups, said, One-Twenty-Second Fighter Wing, still in.

He turned back to me and shrugged. Air Guard, he said. No one's perfect.

Fuck you, said the young guy. He threw a rag at Tenth Mountain, who filled a paper cup from the airpot and put it on the counter between us.

This is my place, boss, he said. On the house.

I mumbled some thanks, and when I turned around, the place was empty: Waleed; some asshole writing a book, probably; three middle-aged cougars who looked like they'd come from the gym who were talking and making faces at the toddler and baby of another woman who was maybe in her twenties at a different table.

The woman with the kids was showered and clean, put together. The toddler scribbled with a crayon in a coloring book. The baby slept in the stroller. The woman read a magazine and drank her coffee. No one was watching me. No one gave a shit. And maybe that was worse than being watched and judged and shamed and feared. I cleaned up my mess. Sat down.

You look tired, Waleed said.

I blamed the kid.

The first few weeks are the easiest, I think. Later is much harder.

I nodded and made a face like *Uh-oh! Better hold on, I guess*, but it was salt ground into a wound. The woman and her family, Waleed and his. What the fuck was wrong with me?

You have just the one child, Corporal?

He kept calling me Corporal.

You don't have to call me that, I said. Yeah, just the one.

A boy or a girl? he said.

Girl, I said.

I have three girls now, Corporal, he said. Three! We had twins. Born here. They will be one years old next month. Let me say, the twins are a gift, but two at once? It is much harder than one.

I didn't know what the fuck to say to Waleed, and that made me itch, and I knew then, too, that he couldn't help me. Not the way I wanted him to. Like, the fucking guy wasn't a doctor, a psychologist, a priest—whatever the fuck I needed.

Did you want something? I said.

Want? he said.

Why'd you ask me here? I said.

That seemed to stop him up for a minute, and he fiddled with his cup.

You asked me here, Corporal, he said, and then smiled at me.

I slapped my hand on the table, cleared my throat, and looked around. The wannabe novelist had earphones in and the cougars and the mom with the kids were too far away to have heard or seen.

Don't call me that, I said.

He nodded that kind of nod you might imagine doing if you ran into a big wild animal in the forest. You know: *Okay. It's okay. You're okay. I'm okay. We're okay. I'm just going to get on out of here and go back the way I came.*

You want an apology? I said. That it?

An apology? he said.

For Ali, for the war, for Iraq—Jesus, I don't know, I said.

I wanted to see a friend, he said.

Tiny little breaths. Tiny little breaths. While my guts churned and rose and felt on fire, I spewed a bunch of shit about how I shouldn't have met him, that I was selfish to think he could help me, that I couldn't live two lives, that I had something wrong inside me something bad, that I owed something to Max and River, that I wanted to forget he and his country and the Marine Corps ever existed.

Selfish? he said.

I thought you could help me, I said.

Telling him all that, I couldn't look at him. Like I had something inside me that I expected Waleed to get rid of? To cut out? Like he was fucking Doc excising that BB from my head or some shit. Or maybe it was exorcise, like the dude was a goddamned holy man. Or a magician. Fucking magical Iraqi refugee. I stood to leave.

You know the response to shaku maku? said Waleed.

Maku shi, I said.

You know what this means? he said.

I shrugged.

There is nothing, said Waleed.

When I pushed open the door to leave, Tenth Mountain called after me, Welcome back to the world, boss.

In the truck on the way home, Ruiz ran his mouth about what a soft, brokedick, civvy piece of shit I'd become, letting some fucking Joe get one over on me.

Know what you are, dog? he said.

I didn't answer.

Motherfucking lamb chops, he said.

And then the sheep spoke.

Excuse me, it said.

I almost crashed the truck. Pulled it over to the shoulder.

I am not agreeing with him many of the time, but this time I am agreeing with him, said the sheep. It was Ali's voice.

And then, after a beat, I said, Much.

Much, said the sheep.

THREE WEEKS LATER River swiped at her toes on a floor play mat while I sat on our KIVIK and folded laundry and Max sorted through what I hadn't gotten to and shoved clothing into an overnight bag. Her six-week paid maternity leave had ended, and her boss was sending her to a two-day conference in Cincinnati. Good for advancement after you've taken so much time off, she'd said he'd said along with some other shit about how he respected her maternal instinct and how it looked like she was managing to take care of herself.

Max said what a motherfucker he was and how sexist what he'd said was and wondered whether or not she should report him to HR and didn't he fucking know that *this* was work? That she *was* working? She was pissed at me, too: she'd wanted to take unpaid time off, but even if I went back to work that day, we couldn't afford it. She made, like, three times what I did, and my Marines money was tapped.

Fuck, I hate this, she said.

It'll be fine, I didn't say.

At least you can take a decent shit now, I didn't say.

River won't even know you're gone, I didn't say.

What I said: Yeah.

The goddamned OODA loop in action. There was something about that *Yeah* that made me feel close to her. Like I knew she was blowing off steam, wanted an audience, wanted to be heard.

Domesticated, güey, said Ruiz.

The sheep slept on my feet, cemented me to the floor. It didn't talk much. Usually just to agree or disagree with Ruiz.

I was sleep deficient—that was how Sergeant Moss would've said it, like a fucking robot: *Marine, you must be sleep deficient to do something so grade-A-fucking-stupid.* Everything was fuzzy at the edges.

I'd gone two nights without sleep. A full forty-eight.

Sure, I'd gone without sleep in the Corps. The longest was maybe fifty hours—some bullshit screen operation during the second deployment. I remember thinking a headstone was Ruiz and refusing to go near it. Doc had said forty-eight hours without sleep was the same as being legally drunk. Said that your body would start shutting itself down to recharge and you wouldn't even know it. Microsleep.

I blamed it on the kid again—the lack of sleep. And since meeting Waleed I'd been having this dream where I was alone in the white vinyl Quonset hut where Command berthed us in Kuwait before making the flight to TQ. I'd been left behind. So I was panicked and rushing to pack my gear, and then Ruiz was there except his face was a baby's face and he had the sheep on a leash and then he and the sheep were on the cot next to me and the sheep's insides were spilling over me and Ruiz's hand was on my thigh and his head was in my lap and there was a hole in the back of his head the size of a fist and when I stood I fell and had that jolt thing like when you fall asleep at a desk or on an airplane or whatever and wake up and I couldn't go back to sleep.

And sometimes nothing, you know? Like some nights I didn't dream at all and slept like the dead and some days Ruiz and the sheep were nowhere and I went about my goddamned day.

They were the ringing at the base of my skull and the ringing was them—fucking interchangeable—and mostly all of it faded into the background and I lived with it because what the fuck else was I going to do? I'd heard all about the VA and what a black hole of bullshit it was. The thought of it made my ass twitch. All those malingering vets with their campaign ribbon hats complaining about tinnitus and back pain.

I knew I had health care from UPS, but I didn't know how to sign up or use it, and asking Grant with his youth pastor smile got my blood up—and, really, the thought of both of those things exhausted me. Like, no shit, made me tired. It felt like I was inventing all of it, making up problems. And that made me feel kind of good, too. That's what civilians did: made fucking problems out of nothing, right? I kept telling myself I was okay. Made me think of Nguyen again: It's okay to be okay.

I was tired; I was up with River, nagged by Ruiz, nervous about Max leaving. Yeah, I was fucking nervous to be alone with the kid. Scared shitless, more like. But I wasn't dying, wasn't a goddamned amputee, didn't have a sucking chest wound. At most, Doc would've told me to change my socks and drink water. I wasn't a malingerer. I didn't need to catch the fucking Log Train.

I folded a onesie—it had been decorated at the baby shower I hadn't been invited to. Penny's handwriting on the top read *Love Wins* and below that she'd painted a rainbow and it fucking bothered me. Because, like, love wins against fucking what? Lay down some enfilade fire with a fifty-cal on love and let me know who wins. Drop a MOAB on love and tell me what happens.

Hearts and minds, dog, said Ruiz.

Max said something about how six weeks wasn't enough and how capitalism was killing America and not just like a metaphor but that it was literally killing people—she said it like that, *literally killing people*—and how it didn't matter—and by that she meant capitalism—that it was all just made up, a concept, and how people cared about something made up more than they gave a shit about people, babies, her baby—which is what she called River: *her* baby—and how some countries got six *months* or more of parental leave. Paid, she said.

Leave it to Penny to get political on a fucking onesie, I didn't say.

Competition is good, I didn't say.

She's my baby, too, I didn't say.

What I said: Yeah.

I kept folding. Onesie after onesie. Left side behind, right side behind, fold in half, fold in half. *Fold fold fold fold.* It was mindless, repetitive. Like cleaning a rifle.

Once, at the armory when everyone was bitching about cleaning weapons Crowe's hillbilly ass had called it prayer, he'd said, When I clean this rifle, it's like how some people pray. We'd all laughed at that and called him a fucking psycho, but even Cooper and Hudson treated the range like it was church.

Max zipped her suitcase and sat behind me at the kitchen table, breast pump going, her laptop open. She clacked away at the keys, making instructions for me. Instructions. *Clack clack clack clack.* This is bullshit. *Fold fold fold fold. Clack clack clack clack.* So goddamned unfair. *Fold fold fold fold. Click click click click.* You lamb chops? *Fold fold fold fold. Knock knock knock knock.* Dean, are you all right? *Fold fold fold fold. Clack clack clack clack.* I've been on my own. *Fold fold fold fold. Click click click click.* Vaya con Dios, pinche puta. *Fold fold fold fold. Knock knock knock knock.* You deserve a nice girl. *Fold fold fold fold. Clack clack clack clack.* My baby. *Fold fold fold fold. Click click click click.* I could show you if you want. *Fold fold fold fold. Knock knock knock knock.* She sounds like a good baby. *Fold fold fold fold. Clack clack clack clack.* Maybe you should look for a better job. *Fold fold fold fold. Clack clack clack clack.* I should be with her. *Fold fold fold fold.*

You're doing that wrong, said Max.

She was standing next to me.

It saves space if you roll them, she said.

I don't want you to go, I didn't say.

I've been hallucinating a zombie sheep, I didn't say.

I'm sorry this is so hard, I didn't say.

What I said: We'll be fine, you know.

Ruiz sucked his teeth and laughed. The sheep shifted across my feet. I'd jumped out of the fucking loop. My own worst goddamned enemy. And then we were in a fight, of course.

I'm her mother, said Max.

I didn't say you weren't, I said.

Without you, she said, her arms wide like she was trying to show me something. Like she was about to be crucified.

That confused me and I just kind of looked at her like *What the fuck are you talking about?*

That's the end of the sentence, she said. We'll be fine . . . *without you.*

You're putting words in my mouth, I said.

I'm not going. I'm not. I'm going to quit, she said.

We need the money, I said.

It's too much, she said.

Part of me was, like, *Thank fucking Christ,* you know? Like, yeah, I wasn't sleeping well because of the kid and because of the weird fucking dreams, but I hadn't even closed my eyes the night before because I was terrified of Max leaving. And I knew it was crazy, but I kept thinking, like, *What if she doesn't come back? What if her plane crashes? What if there's an active shooter? What if? What if? What if?* And that part wanted to sit down with Max, figure it out. Talk money, talk jobs, talk future. The future. A future. Our future. Right?

But there was also the part of me—the fucking asshole part who kept ruining everything—that said, I'm not an idiot, Max. I can take care of our kid.

This isn't about you, she said.

I went back to folding clothes while Max waited for me to say something. But, like, what could I say? She was out here, doing calculus, and I was banging rocks together, trying to make fire. Got a feeling like she wanted me to ask her not to go, but I knew if I did that she'd lose it.

It's bath time, I said.

I picked up River from the floor and headed to the bathroom.

In August, a couple months after we got back from that second deployment, Nguyen invited the entire squad for a going-away barbecue at his place in Carlsbad.

The Five was wide-open on the way south from Camp Pendleton and I did ninety in the center lane. It felt like drag racing after the Humvee patrol speeds of seven to ten miles per hour on the deployment. I was a few months from getting out. My asshole puckered and my stomach flip-flopped whenever I zoomed by road trash or tire casings.

It was a good feeling. Made my heart open, my eyes sharpen. Put my head on a swivel. When traffic slowed a motorcycle split the lane on my passenger side, throaty roar ripping into the truck cab, I hoped it was an IED.

I thought about re-upping.

I hadn't been to Nguyen's new place—he and Amber had moved to a condo a few blocks from the beach. I texted him I'd just pulled up, and he told me to come around back. I was the first one there. Nguyen was at the grill, fucking with the starter knobs and the propane tank, his back to me, while his son toddled around the patio and played with a toy truck. The kid saw me, and I must've scared him, because he flipped shit.

Ba, ba, ba, ba, ba, he said, and started crying.

Nguyen turned around and scooped the kid into his arms. It was so natural, I felt like I didn't even know Nguyen and I thought of the car seat in Sergeant Moss's car and Ruiz offing himself and felt like the world was all in on something I wouldn't ever see.

Who's here, Raven? Nguyen said in that breathy baby voice parents use like they're talking to a fucking dog or something. Who is that, Ray-Ray? Is that Dean? That's Ba's friend, Dean, Ray-Ray. Say, Hi. Say, Hi, Dean.

Ray shoved his face into Nguyen's neck and moaned and grabbed on tight while Nguyen went on cajoling the kid fucking forever while I stood there smiling like an idiot until my mouth got sore. Finally, Nguyen distracted him with the truck he'd been playing with and I was old news.

Nguyen went back to fucking with the grill.

I took a seat in a deck chair.

I'm early? I said.

Fifteen minutes prior to fifteen minutes prior, Marine, said Nguyen. You're on time.

We laughed at that.

But, yeah, he said. A bit.

Where's Amber? I said.

Work, said Nguyen. Got a promotion a couple weeks ago and now she's got to go in Saturdays.

That's some shit, I said.

Money's good, said Nguyen. Hey, try to watch your language, yeah?

He pointed to Ray, who rammed the truck into one of the stanchions of the covered patio.

Little ears, he said.

That feeling of not knowing Nguyen only got stronger. Nguyen had held a guy's head like a football in a bar parking lot once so I could punt the guy in the teeth. I wished I wasn't there. I wished we were at a bar. I wished we were drunk. I wished I was back on the highway, jamming down on the gas pedal. I'd smash through the guardrail on the Five and nose into the ocean.

Nice place, I said.

I can smell gas, Nguyen said. I think the starter's busted. Come on, I'll give you the grand tour. Got to get a lighter anyway.

Nguyen offered me a beer and I took it. He didn't get one for himself. Ray crashed the truck into a marble-topped kitchen island. The condo was big, airy. Floors were clay, cold on my feet.

Going to make me drink alone? I said.

I've got orders, said Nguyen.

Turning into one of those lifers who calls his wife Home Six? I said— fucking lifers treated their entire families like they were in the Corps.

Nguyen laughed. No, Amber wouldn't go for that.

Oh, I said. Got it.

Orders meant he was fucking off out of the battalion, and I guess I assumed after he'd extended for the last deployment with us—and after Ruiz—that he'd just stick around for good, so I was surprised but didn't want to show it, so I asked as casually as I could where to.

Recruiter school, he said.

I hadn't known it was one of his choices. Tried to think of the list he gave us at Dave and Buster's a year ago. What the fuck *did* I know? Not much. I got that shrinking feeling again. The world growing up around me and I was me, but small. That's not right. It was like I was me but I was a shell and the real me was inside the shell, but in this hollow, echoing place, and everything outside was so big, I couldn't focus on anything but parts. Felt like I was pressed up against a theater screen. Like, there I was in this condo and I didn't fucking recognize anything. Couldn't dig the words out of my brain housing group for the simple things around me. *What's that yellow curved thing? What's that big silver cube? What's that thing making it bright over the table?*

I almost lost hold of the bottle that'd started to sweat and I downed half of it. Cold weight in my gut nailed me to the floor.

Didn't know it was on your list, I said.

It was a goddamned knife in the back. After all the bullshit. After Ruiz. It was one thing to stay in, do a lat move or even go officer. But here he was, headed off to throw a fancy uniform over the blood and peddle it to someone else. To someone else's *kid*, right?

After this last deployment I was close to just calling it quits, he said. Tried to get med-sepped—PTSD or whatever, felt all fucked-up—so I went and saw the Wizard.

Wizard was battalion psych. Lost your mind, go to the Wizard. You know, if I only had a brain. Get it? We all had to see him before and after deployments to bullshit our way through the pre- and post-deployment health assessments. Yeah, of course we were fucking tired and depressed and sick and angry and drank too much and had violent thoughts—who the fuck didn't, right?—but if we let on to that, the Wizard wouldn't let us deploy. So we gamed the game.

Anyway, if sick call at BAS was a quick way to get labeled a malingerer, and shunned until you proved otherwise, the Wizard was a surefire way to get deep-sixed out of the Corps—like fucking draftees trying to get sectioned out of Nam or whatever; at least, that's what we all thought. The Surge was over, and the Corps was cutting away the rot where they saw it—dudes getting tossed with OTHs and no bennies and all kinds of shit. Like an insurance company saying having a heart was a preexisting condition to a heart attack. It's what had happened to Ruiz.

Sergeant Moss had warned us from day one to stay the fuck away from the Wizard. When we asked him why, he told us first to shut the fuck up and follow orders and then he told us that going to see the Wizard was breaking the chain of command—that we dealt with our shit in-house and we should come talk to him first.

Command just wanted the power. But back then it sounded like Sergeant Moss cared, right? Like we were a family and he was a hardworking papa trying to keep his family together. Like, *Come here and talk to me, son. Let's have a heart-to-heart.* But Sergeant Moss's heart-to-hearts usually left you sweaty and shaking and puking or choked-the-fuck-out trying to figure what the hell had just happened.

Nguyen was going on and on about the Wizard. And the guy, he said, he's Navy. An officer. But not like most other officers. He's all right. And he told me this thing, like, the guy said, *It's okay to be okay.*

What's that mean? I said.

Like, that maybe there's nothing wrong with me, he said. That it's all in my head. That I think I'm supposed to be messed up because of all the people who think vets are supposed to be messed up.

Who sent you there? I said.

No one, he said.

Ray rammed the truck into the baseboards of the kitchen island and made engine noises. I drank the rest of my beer.

Amber mentioned a couple times she thought I should see someone, said Nguyen.

Nguyen had railed against the Wizard just like Sergeant Moss. Sat us down and told us ghost stories: Who here knows Corporal Bliss? he'd said. That's right, fucking none of you. Because he went to see the Wizard after our first pump because he couldn't sleep and the next day his shit was cleared out of the barracks.

You always told us to steer clear, I said.

It's no big deal, said Nguyen. Just talk. Mostly asked me how I felt about things. And it's not the same. Like I said, this guy, he wasn't trying to shrink my head or anything. Showed me that I'm fine.

He was about to go on when Ray slammed the grille of the truck into my ankle and I yelled, Fuck, and Nguyen got all bent out of shape and I started apologizing and Ray started crying and Nguyen rushed over to him and I stood there, brain buzzing, not knowing what to do, and Nguyen was saying how the kid liked me and just wanted to play and I kept saying I was sorry and then I stooped down and picked up the truck and zoomed it around the floor in front of Ray and rolled it up and over Nguyen's head and that made the tears stop and then I rolled it over Ray's legs and that made him laugh and he wiggled out of Nguyen's arms and kneeled in front of me and started making faces.

I picked up Ray, stood and Nguyen watched us for a second.

We're good, I said.

He nodded and went to the fridge.

Damn, he said. Out of buns.

Little ears, I said.

Store's right down the street, like, two blocks, he said. Think you can watch him?

Yeah, I said. We're good.

I'll be ten minutes, he said, and Crowe and the others should be here soon, and Ray's water bottle is outside on the table on the patio, and if he's hungry, you can give him a banana or something.

Bro, I said. We're good.

I don't think I knew I was going to leave when I said it. I didn't. Or maybe I did. Maybe I was pissed at Nguyen for trying to be someone new, for moving on with his life. For being okay.

Standing in Nguyen's inspection-ready condo holding Ray-Ray, I could've been cradling Ruiz's ruined head against my chest or that Iraqi mom rubbing her daughter's back or a shepherd running his hands through lambs' fleece or AJ and BJ holding hands in the terp hut or Sergeant Moss clinching my neck from behind.

There were different kinds of love. I didn't deserve any of them.

And then Ray was a hot pan and I dropped him on the couch in the living room and turned on the TV and the kid was Jell-O. Zombified by a cartoon with two guys in different-colored clothes watching a pride of lions from a concealed position. I got his water bottle and set it next to him and found some toys in cubbies under the TV and set them around him like sentries. Then I touched him on the head—I don't know why—and left.

River sat propped up in this little chair that went in the tub; she slapped the water, bouncing and jerking, not quite in charge of her muscles. Whenever a drop of water landed on her face, she looked like she'd discovered a new dimension. I didn't know how any part of me could've made her.

Like, if I was that fucked-up, then there must be something wrong with her, too, right? Maybe it was just something I couldn't see yet, something that would grow down deep inside her until one day she'd shoot poison into her veins or slice herself open or join the Marines or put a gun into her mouth. *What if? What if? What if?*

I imagined her without a head.

OD, dog, said Ruiz. *That's how women do it. Maybe that's what your birth moms did.*

After I lathered her up and rinsed her off, I let her splash away and I opened the Instagram page for that cheap-ass-looking adoption website I'd been cruising and clicked the link that led to their website.

There were tabs for unplanned pregnancies for how to adopt a baby for choosing an adoptive family for adoption forums for searching for your birth parents for searching for the baby you put up for adoption.

I got lost in the shit.

She could be looking for me right now, I thought. *Maybe she's on this website.* Maybe she had a profile built up and she was closing in. Locate, close with, and destroy the enemy by fire and maneuver and repel the enemy assault by fire and close combat—that's your mission every single time we step outside the wire, said Sergeant Moss. I dug my thumbs into my eyes until fireworks exploded in the blackness.

It gave me a headache, acid reflux, bubble guts.

Corporal, said the sheep.

When my vision cleared, the sheep was nose to nose with me and River was underwater. She'd slipped out of her chair.

I didn't move to grab her. I wasn't scared; she looked happy there under the surface—her features all distorted and widened out. *Moon face*—that was the thought that went through my head. I wanted to take a picture, post it to Instagram. I'd caption it *Drownproofing*, and all the Marines on my timeline would know what I meant. They'd laugh. Say, Pusey's doing the damn thing right.

Time split then.

Like, no shit, time stopped and branched like two mirrors reflecting one another: two long hallways headed off to infinity in different directions. In one River was limp and drowned, seal slick and blue in a puddle of soapy bathwater while Max blew air into her tiny lungs and there was a tiny coffin and a tiny hole in the ground, and in the other I pulled her up, toweled her off, rubbed lotion on her body, gave her a bottle, put her to bed, and life went on.

I pulled her up by her arm.

Think you're some kind of John Wayne? I said. It was something Gunny Bat said to us when he'd observe training and one of us broke SOP or when our hair was too long or when our boots were bloused around our ankles or our sleeves weren't tight enough around our biceps. Think you're some kind of John Wayne, Devil Dog?

She didn't say anything back.

My gunny used to say that, I said.

River didn't say anything.

A gunny is a gunnery sergeant, I said. It's a rank in the Marine Corps. Papa was a Marine. Papa was in the Marine Corps. Can you say, Marine Corps?

I was using that voice, the one Nguyen used with Ray, and I hated myself a little for it, but it felt good that she didn't say anything back. I liked how she watched my face, how she reached for my nose and lips. Grabbed any skin just a bit too hard. Her nails were sharp. They cut my chin. There was no blood, no marks, but she'd broken the skin. It stung if I smiled. That made me feel good, too. Like she'd chosen me. Marked me. Wanted me. Like this wasn't all some big fucking mistake and I wasn't just some placeholder treading water until the better thing came along.

That's what it felt like with Max most of the time. Like she'd stumbled and fallen onto my dick and everything after was just one big fucking mistake and that made me one hundred percent certain she wasn't coming back.

You don't want to leave me, do you? I said.

River didn't say anything.

You need me, don't you? I said.

River didn't say anything.

I wanted to show her the ocean then. The Pacific. Put her toes in the freezing water that crashed up to any of the beach towns along the southern coast. I would join back up. Take my pick of jobs, duty stations. I knew how it worked now. I could game the game. I'd negotiate a signing bonus. I knew they needed bodies.

I'd pick something non-deployable—some instructor of something on Camp Pendleton. School of Infantry or whatever. Shit, Division Schools. I could go teach MOUT. Heel toe heel toe heel toe, I'd say.

Slow is smooth; smooth is fast, I'd say. Speed, surprise, violence of action, I'd say.

We'd live in San Clemente or Dana Point. A little bungalow a couple blocks from the water. We could have a life there—in the sun and salt crust. Under palm trees. I'd teach River to surf. I didn't know how to surf, but I'd learn and I'd teach her. Max could go to school, get her degree. We'd wear nothing but sandals and our feet would be sandy from the beach, brown from the sun. At night we'd sit by a firepit after River was asleep and tell each other about our days and I'd talk about the new Marines and tell animated stories that made her laugh and when eventually I'd have to reenlist and go back to an infantry unit I'd cross-train and change my MOS and go Air Wing or something and make new stories, not just turn the page, but rewrite everything and then Max would tell me about school, her classes, what she was learning, and I'd listen to her and maybe I'd take online classes or night classes and we'd talk about school together and she'd help me pass math because I've always shit the bed when it comes to numbers. It was better than the downtown apartment. Felt more real.

Damn, dog, said Ruiz. *Got them motherfucking Marine Corps goggles on.*

I didn't say anything.

I like this plan very much, said the sheep. *Hollywood.*

Ruiz stood next to me, put his hand on my shoulder, his lips in my ear, and he pointed at River, who was on her back on a changing pad on the counter between our twin sinks.

So much for suicide watch, said Ruiz.

I don't know what you mean, I said. I said it out loud.

You know, said Ruiz.

I patted River dry.

Oh, fuck me, I guess, said Ruiz.

Still I stayed quiet.

Is that where we watch them finish the job, sir? Ruiz made himself sound like me.

She's a baby, I said.

Babies are smart, dog, he said.

Fuck do you know about babies? I said.

Six younger brothers and sisters and no pops, homie, said Ruiz.

I forgot he had a family. *Had* had. Corps made that shit hard to see, to remember. Like, dude could show up to the unit with dicks for fingers or some shit, but if he fit the mold, could do his job, you might not realize it until years down the line. Someone might say, *Hey, you remember that guy with dicks for fingers?* And you'd say, *No.* And they'd say, *Yeah, come on. Dude ran the fifty-cal like it was a motherfucking business.* And you'd be all *Oh, shit! Johnson! He was a good dude. He had dicks for fingers?* Then you'd make some joke about being old and forget all about his dicks for fingers.

Maybe she doesn't like ghosts, I said.

Dog, no one asks to be brought into this world, he said. *Least we can do is let people choose when they want to check the fuck out.*

River got fussy and I shushed her and Ruiz went on and on and I tried drowning him out with the shushing like when I'd put River down for a nap and it wasn't working so I closed my eyes and sang running cadence.

Little yellow birdie with a little yellow bill, I sang.

I put one hand on River's warm pear belly.

Landed on my windowsill, I sang.

She popped her lips and chirred at me.

I lured him in with a piece of bread, I sang.

Her jerky frog kicks and air punches vibrated through my body and she squealed.

And then I crushed his little fucking head, I sang.

When I opened my eyes, Ruiz and the sheep were gone. River smiled at me.

I could hear you talking to her in there, said Max. Singing, too.

She was on the couch in the living room when River and I came out of the bathroom and into the kitchen to get a bottle of milk. Max had pumped her supply. I took a bottle from the fridge and put it in the warmer. River clung to me, shoved her fist in her mouth.

Oh, yeah? I said.

I doubted she could have heard me talking to Ruiz over the fan, through the door. How loud had I been? I played it cool. Cool as a motherfucking cucumber. Cool as an ice cube. Cool as a corpse. I tried to think of other shit that started with *c* that was cool.

It's good, said Max. Talking to her.

I know, I said.

All the books say so, she said.

She was reaching out, maybe. Trying to make peace.

I've read them, I said.

She sounded like she liked the song you were singing, too.

Voice of an angel, I said.

Maybe you could teach it to me, she said. I couldn't really hear it. Didn't recognize the melody.

Maybe, I said. I walked away humming the cadence.

After I gave River her bottle and read her a book and put her in the rocker in our bedroom, I came back out to the living room. Sat on the couch next to Max and she collapsed into me. Her hair was greasy at the part. I didn't mind. I liked the smell coming off her. It was real. Filled my lungs. Felt heavy.

I don't want to leave you, she said.

You mean her, I said.

Plural *you*.

I think our kid is suicidal, I didn't say.

Please don't go. Please, please, please, I didn't say.

Do you want to take first watch? I didn't say.

What I said: We'll be fine.

Couldn't sleep again that night. Room was hot. White noise hissed and popped. Sheets scraped my skin like sandpaper. Max kept letting out these long, purring farts.

The sheep rested its head on my pillow, and I smelled rot and hot disease. It stuck in the back of my throat. And the sheep was being torn apart by the dogs and then I was the sheep and the dogs were my mom standing over me asking if I was all right and we were in the car on the way home from school and she told me she might not have given birth to me but that she was my mother and the car was the high-back and Ruiz's hand was on my thigh and he asked if I was nervous and then we were in the dark room at the OP and his arms were around me but the arms were Penny's and the OP was the Speed Rail and Penny's arms belonged to the bar hicks beating me in the bathroom and those arms were Max's blood-speckled thigh and the doctor was asking if I wanted this and I kept telling her, *Me zien,* and I was River being pulled by the jaw from between Max's legs and Max was my birth mom and I was me and I was bawling in someone's arms I couldn't see and then I was the dogs howling and barking and tearing into the sheep and when I took a bite it was a persimmon and Rith was telling me to slow down, that it wasn't crayons, and I couldn't stand it and I got the fuck out of bed threw on some PT gear and ran.

When I got back, sweaty and scraped out, I opened the internet on my phone and went to adoption dot com and made a profile. I didn't know the name of the hospital I was born at, the city I was born in—info the website wanted to make sure I got the most accurate match. They were on my birth certificate, which was in my mom's house, I was pretty sure, where I hadn't been in almost ten months, so I figured I'd fill it in later.

Like, maybe I'd call up my mom and tell her what I was up to and she would tell me to come over and when I got there she'd tell me she might not have given birth to me but she'd always be my mother and then I'd tell her that, yeah, I knew that and we'd hug it out and she'd get me my birth certificate and we'd hug again and tell each other we loved each other and I'd apologize to Penny and Iris and Rick and ask their forgiveness and I'd let Rick take me to church and I'd get saved—I knew guys who got saved and they seemed happier than pigs in shit.

Grant was saved. I'd go with him, forget all about my birth mom, and I'd just go on about our fucking lives singing hymns and doing good deeds, maybe digging wells in fucking Africa or something like nothing had happened.

And then I clicked *search* and on the next page there was a single match. It read: *Added by Birth-Mother, looking for Adoptee.*

Gender: Male

Birth date: fifteen Nov, nineteen eighty-nine

Ethnicity: White

Birthplace: Tacoma, WA

Adoption place: Olympia, WA

I clicked the fucking profile. There was a pop-up. *Upgrade to Premium to View Profile four-three-nine-zero-seven-six.* Of fucking course there was a pop-up. Of fucking course there was a premium membership. Everyone wants to get theirs. I memorized the profile like a rifle serial number. Four-three-nine-zero-seven-six. *This is my mother,* I thought. *There are many like her but this one is mine.* I could hear Ruiz's eyes roll. *Four-three-nine-zero-seven-six.* I laughed at myself. *Four-three-nine-zero-seven-six.* Wanted to click to pay for the premium account.

Fifteen bucks a month. That's all that stood between me and messaging four-three-nine-zero-seven-six. One tap, and fifteen fucking lousy bucks. *Four-three-nine-zero-seven-six.* Maybe I didn't need to know the hospital, the city. Maybe I was the only fucking kid adopted that day in Washington State. I wasn't even thinking that my birth mom might not have made a profile, that adoption dot com wasn't the end all be all, that I might share a birthdate with some other guy from the same state who was adopted, that I might not have been born in Tacoma, adopted in Olympia. I was thinking, *Four-three-nine-zero-seven-six.* I didn't want to click off the results page. *Four-three-nine-zero-seven-six.* Was worried that the profile would fall into some internet hole and I'd never find it again. In my head I drafted the message I'd send.

Dear Four-three-nine-zero-seven-six,

I might be the kid no *boy* no *child* no *baby you abandoned* no *surrendered* no *gave up twenty-three years ago . . .*

And then I thought about adoption dot com showing up on our bank transaction statement, having to explain that to Max, who had insisted a joint bank account made way more sense if we were going to live together if we were going to pay bills together if we were going to have a kid together.

Anything you don't lie about, güey? said Ruiz.

I ignored him. It was three in the morning. Max would be up in a couple hours to drive to Fort Wayne to catch her flight to Cincy. I was going on seventy-two hours without sleep. I didn't feel drunk like Doc said. Fucking corpsman. I tried to remember if I remembered what being drunk felt like, if I could tell I was drunk when I was drunk.

I went to shower the run off me, hoped the hot water might burn up whatever was in me keeping me awake, put me to sleep in the same way I'd hoped the run might.

My body ached and my head floated and my skin was greasy, gray. I had a potbelly and my chest was soft. My beard and hair made me fucking sick. Nasty. That was what our DIs always said. Come here, Nasty. Hello, Nasty. Stop picking your face, Nasty. Unsat. Unsatisfactory. A fucking civilian. That's what my problem was.

I did a set of squats and then dropped and did push-ups on the linoleum. Then sit-ups. The pump made me harder. I liked it. Missed it. I got my beard trimmer out from the drawer and ran it without a guard over my beard and the last four months of growth fell off. Did the same to my head, too. I lathered up and scraped my face, ran a finger over my skin looking for rough patches. Felt better. Like I was taking care of myself. Self-care.

Damp shower heat filled the bathroom and twisted around me, loosened my skin, wet my lungs. I disappeared into the mirror fog.

I rinsed the loose hair from my chest and shoulders, raked my skin and stubbled scalp with soap, watched it all circle the drain while the water scorched me raw until my bones felt rubbery. I closed my eyes. I took deep breaths. I cleared my head. Ruiz and the sheep were gone.

When I got out, I swiped my hand over the mirror, and it was River's face reflected back at me on my body, and I yelped and stepped back and almost fell through the fucking shower curtain.

Wittle baby got a chubby tummy? said the face.

I felt my face. It was mine.

Poor wittle baby can't sweep? said the face.

I knew then it was that fucking shadowy ghost inside of me. Eating me up, driving me fucking crazy, and I wanted to know when it had happened. When had it gotten to me? I still didn't know. I thought of the cemetery near the widow's house on the first deployment, the screening operation on the second, all the black nights at OPs and on patrols through the city, fallow fields, date groves, all those times in the terp hut. Maybe they had done this. Maybe Waleed had cursed me. For what? I didn't know. Doing nothing, maybe. It could've gotten me anytime. Country full of fucking ghosts.

Wittle baby sad? said the face.

You're a bad baby, I said.

I put my hands over my mouth—River's mouth.

No one wuvs wittle baby, said the face.

She made a pouty face and the voice was clear as day. I took my hands away. It didn't matter.

Hush, wittle baby, said the face.

I'm your father, I said. But I didn't believe that of course. It wasn't River. It wasn't me.

The face went on to sing a lullaby and something about the way it looked at me made my skin prickle at the back of my neck, my stomach drop, my breath catch. Like I was a meal or something.

I wanted Max. I wanted my mom and Penny and Nguyen and Sergeant Moss and my rifle. My rifle, right? I would get it and blow this fucking thing away, whatever it was. But I didn't have any rounds. I was rounds complete. No. I was round deficient. Sleep deficient. Lost in the sauce.

Court. His name popped into my head. I wanted Court right then. He could be as good as a rifle. And I damn near ran out of the bathroom to where I'd left my phone on the couch and stood in the living room steaming and naked and texted Court. I didn't expect a reply. It was four in the morning by then.

Hey man, I texted.

Know it's been a while, I texted.

Sorry, I texted.

Miss hanging out, I texted.

And then I regretted sending four texts right in a row and I was what-iffing it to death thinking about how it all came off when those three dots . . . showed up.

Party tomorrow nite, he texted.

Just need some downers, I didn't text.

Max wouldn't like that, I didn't text.

Do you know how to kill a ghost? I didn't text.

What I texted: *See you then*.

Period and all. Motherfucking serious.

River was still asleep, and the sun was coming up when Max woke up and came into the living room. She asked if I had slept at all, and I lied and said I had. I waited for her to notice my face, my hair. But instead she asked why I couldn't sleep in the bedroom. She asked if I was angry still. She said she didn't want to fight. That this was all too hard—leaving.

I feel like I'm being torn apart, she said.

And I thought that was dramatic but didn't say it, of course. I lied to her and told her I couldn't sleep because the room was too hot, which wasn't really a lie, not really. The room *had* been too hot. I kept waiting for her to say something about my hair, my face. Still she didn't. She hugged me. We kissed. I'd never done that with someone before—kissed them on the mouth, hoping they would come back. Wanting them to come back. She ran her hands over my head. Looked at me.

You look like River, she said.

That's it. Nothing else about it. She kissed me again and left. I watched her round the corner of the sidewalk that led to the parking lot of the apartment complex and then I went to get the rifle out of the utility closet.

I SET THE gun case on the coffee table and sanded my palms and fingers over the rough plastic, got worried about popping it open. Like I wouldn't remember how to handle it, like I'd fail it. Maybe it would reject me, send me away. *Bad baby.*

As much as I wasn't one of those fucking nutjobs who named their rifle, you *did* get to know your weapon. You could tell which one was yours when you held it. Someone else's didn't feel right—no two things are exactly alike. There are minute differences. You feel them in your bones.

I popped open the case.

Damn, dog, said Ruiz. *Pretty little peashooter right there.*

The sheep shifted on its rotting hooves.

Ruiz wasn't going to let up. I admired that, I guess. Maybe not admired but remembered. Ruiz was like that: fucking relentless. My mom would have said *obstinate* if she had met him, probably. It's what she said about Penny. Your sister is being obstinate again, she would say. I asked her what it meant the first time she said it and she told me it was a nice way of calling someone an ass.

I thought about Penny and Ruiz meeting. The world might've just imploded. Extinction-level event. That made me snort. I felt good.

I put the rifle in my lap, moved the case to the floor, spread a cleaning towel on the coffee table, put the rifle on top. I opened my cleaning kit and assembled the cleaning rods, screwed a bore brush on top, couldn't find the toothbrush I used to get the nooks and crannies, so I went to the bathroom and got River's. She didn't need it anyway. Didn't have any teeth. We used it for practice. Getting her used to the feeling. The books recommended it. Practice is preparedness. Had Sergeant Moss said that? Sounded like some shit he would say. Someone in the Corps had probably said it at some point. Gunny Bat got on us all the time about shit like that: *Proper prior planning prevents piss-poor performance, Marine.*

Same shit, right?

In boot camp our rifle cleaning gear came with a towel that had the outlines of each of the parts of the M-sixteen. Called it a Mickey Mouse cloth. Baby bullshit, you know? So you can break it down Barney-style, said our DIs.

Imagine a smiling purple dinosaur combat gliding into a room pumping bullets into bodies, enemy targets, people.

Upper receiver, firing pin retaining pin, bolt cam pin, extractor, extractor pin, charging handle, bolt, firing pin, bolt carrier, buffer, action spring, handguards, lower receiver. Even the sling got a space—coiled and neat in the lower middle of the cloth.

DIs didn't let us take apart the bolt, so we never dealt with the firing pin retaining pin or the extractor or the extractor pin—not until later on in the fleet at least. I closed my eyes and imagined the pieces, how they were arranged on the towel. How I would lay them out covered and aligned, in a grid, like a marching formation, like an Instagram page.

What's up, dog? Nervous? said Ruiz.

His hand was on my knee on my thigh on my crotch and my stomach wrapped around my throat and I kept my eyes closed tight and breathed not those tiny little breaths but like how my PMI showed me how to breathe when I was sighting in on a target at three hundred yards calm normal deep like I was trying to fall asleep and let my hands float over the rifle felt the stock and the receiver the rails on the handguard the barrel found the takedown pins by touch and popped the forward one.

No, I said. I'm not nervous.

I opened my eyes.

With only the pivot pin connecting the upper and lower receivers, the rifle looked broken. Mangled. The little girl's deformed legs. The high-back after the IED. My face the night of my last birthday after the fight in the bathroom. The space between Max's legs after River's birth. Ruiz's head.

Break it down shotgun-style, said Sergeant Moss. Like a double-barrel shotgun. Combat expedient. You could keep the thing clean and the pieces out of the dirt and on the off chance you were cleaning the goddamned thing and you started taking fire for whatever reason, all you had to do was reconnect the upper and lower receiver.

I finished breaking down the parts, cleaned the inside with gun oil. Time passed: a minute, an hour, a week, six months, a year, a goddamned decade.

When I was done, I reassembled the carrier and fit the charging handle and bolt carrier into the upper receiver; the parts slid home like polyurethane wheels on a roller rink.

I wished for the weight of a loaded magazine, the sound of round chambering, the heart skip of a bullet finding its target. I wanted to shoot. Another reason to go to Court's. I'd take the rifle. Court had rounds. We'd make up. It would be like old times.

I checked my watch. River would wake soon; it was like I was waiting for my day to start. I didn't want her to wake up. Was thinking about that face in the mirror: *Poor wittle baby.* I wanted to run again, pound the pavement until the muscles in my legs turned to jelly, the bones to dust. But you can't leave a kid alone. I knew that much.

I hadn't been alone with River up to that point. I mean, I'd given her baths, stayed with her for an hour or whatever while Max bugged out to the store. Other than that, for the last two months it'd been me and Max. And mostly Max. She took charge, you know? She was in the bar buying me a drink. She was asking me to move in with her. She was picking out our furniture and arranging it and making our schedule for the day. She'd left me a schedule.

It was like she'd known River for years. Like she'd been a parent her entire life. Like she was in River's brain. And maybe she was. Kid had grown inside her for nine months. Had to be a connection there. I wondered if my birth mom felt that with me. Wondered what it might feel like to sever that connection. Maybe it was just starry-eyed, head-in-the-clouds bullshit. Motherfucking recruiting myth.

Or maybe that's how she'd known I was a bad baby.

You look like River, Max had said. I opened my camera and took a selfie and then I opened an app and put that picture side by side with a shot of River and stared at what I'd made. She wasn't wrong. The kid had my face. I thought of the delivery nurse: That's your face, Dad, she'd said.

I got my computer and uploaded the original photo of River and started cutting and pasting River's face into old shots of me from the Marines. Found one of me, Ruiz, Crowe, Cobb, Baptiste, and Nguyen from the first pump and pasted River's face over Cobb's—both a couple of crybabies, so it made sense—and there we were, in the shit together. I laughed at that. Baby in the shit.

I pasted the picture of her into another so it looked like I was carrying her on patrol in my drop pouch. I pasted her face over mine so that she sat on a Humvee rooftop at sunset cleaning an M-two-forty. Put her in a watch post, put her on patrol, put her on a cot penning letters on Marine Corps note paper to Mom and Penny back home.

Might sound stupid, but I was close to crying—fucking lump in my throat, eyes misting up. Sheep was pressing up against me and I couldn't look at Ruiz. I got this future flash of me and River years from then and we were coming back from a run we were laughing together. We were sitting across the table and drinking glasses of cold water, and we were talking. Talking about everything: school, friends, movies, shooting, life. And then I posted the one picture I'd made of her in my drop pouch to Instagram with a caption that read, *Daddy-daughter weekend hashtag getsome hashtag operationinfantfreedom*.

And then River woke up and whatever I'd felt before about not wanting to get her, about the face in the mirror, was gone, and in its place was this feeling like *Fuck Max. River is mine.* I was excited. Jazzed up. Not ashamed of that. Like, here was this kid. My kid. I think I realized that then. *My* kid.

Like, Max might've felt that, like, at the minute River was born or maybe even before, but it took me close to two months and however many days, hours, minutes, seconds, or whatever. Instead of just rolling through the motions in neutral, taking care of this lump, I was moving through the gears. Something had clicked in the training. It was coming together and I damn near burst through the door shouting reveille like I was a DI or some shit and she squealed when she saw me and my heart was in my throat and I sang marching cadence to her while I undid her swaddle and changed her diaper.

C-one-thirty rolling down the strip! Daddy and River gonna take a little trip! I sang.

River smiled, kicked her frog legs.

Stand up, buckle up, shuffle to the door, I sang.

I wanted her to grow up knowing me. Like, I didn't know shit about my dad and I didn't know my birth parents at all, so it felt like a chance to balance the world out or something. Justice.

Jump right out and shout, Marine Corps! I sang.

River barked and yipped along.

I'd tell her everything—how I was adopted, growing up, going to war. We'd be honest with each other. She'd ask me for advice. I'd teach her about the rifle: safety rules, how to break the thing down, how to clear a room. How to protect herself. I'd be one of those motherfucking TV dads—the ones kids come to when the going gets tough. Fucking super dad.

If my chute don't open wide, I sang.

I bounced around like Richard fucking Simmons. Kid loved it—clucked and smiled, tried to sing back to me. Almost laughed, I think. I picked out a fresh onesie. *Uniform of the day*, I thought.

I got a reserve by my side, I sang.

In the kitchen I sat her in the IKEA high chair. The ANTILOP.

If that chute should fail me, too, I sang.

I got her milk from the refrigerator, added water to the warmer on the counter, slammed the lid, and started the timer.

Then look out, Satan, I'm coming after you! I sang.

River slapped the high chair tray. She kept time.

Ah-slashin'-and-ah-stabbin'! I sang.

Slapslapslap

Ah-stabbin'-and-ah-slashin'! I sang.

Goddamn, dog, said Ruiz. He shook his head.

My phone chimed and I ignored it. Knew it was Max asking about River. But we were doing our own thing. We didn't need her. She could go UA if she wanted.

The water inside the warmer seethed, and when the machine beeped its end, I flipped open the lid, diddy bopping like I was back on the block, feeling fucking good, and I grabbed the bottle with my fingertips by the threaded mouth and got scalded by steam from the machine. I yelled and dropped the bottle; half of the milk spilled across the countertop, streamed to the floor. River started to cry, wail, scream.

Just like that, the world I'd dreamed up exploded, rolled over an IED, took a nonstandard response to the chest. I searched for more cadence but she kept up the howling and Ruiz kept talking and the sheep wound itself through my legs.

I screwed the lid on the bottle and tested what was left of the milk on my wrist like Max had showed me. Licked the drip when it rolled over my skin.

Silk on my tongue. It tasted like honey. I hadn't been breastfed. My mom got up in arms about shit like that—people railing about breast is best or whatever whenever it cycled into the news. She'd say something about how I turned out fine and Penny would give some fucking one-liner and I'd beg to quit talking about mom's tits and they'd both tell me not to say *tits* and we'd all have a good laugh at each other. I missed them, really.

I turned to River. Screaming had stopped. She was down to a pouty whimper. I tipped the bottle toward her lips. A bead of milk formed on the nipple, but she wouldn't latch on, just clamped her mouth and thrashed her head. Went back to crying. I told her she had to eat. That she was upset because she was hungry. I shoved the nipple at her mouth. She blew raspberries and screeched at me. I got angry, frustrated; screeched back louder. Made things worse. Imagined River's tiny body in my hands, then her neck in the crook of my arm like my own neck in the crook of Sergeant Moss's.

River screamed on both the inhale and exhale of her breath. Something rhythmic about it—kind of calmed me down. Like the kid was meditating or something. Chanting. Some spotters in sniper teams did that shit—said *om* or whatever to center the shooter, help them keep time with their breathing. Made me think of my PMI: How does that feel?

Anyway, wasn't weird that River was crying. She was a goddamned baby, for fuck's sake. And besides, she didn't get a bottle normally. It was new. We'd tried once or twice in the last week to get her warmed up to it, but, like, she must've been all *Where the fuck is the goddamned tit? I got it.*

And I knew she was stuck in a feedback loop—crying because she was hungry, hungry because she couldn't stop crying. She would've been fucking five by five if Max had walked in the door right then and there. I didn't have a damned thing she wanted—nothing to barter with. Set up to fucking fail.

Yo, dog. That's what I'm saying, said Ruiz.

The fuck you saying? I said.

That we ain't made for this bullshit, said Ruiz. *This women's work.*

I took a breath. *Tiny little breaths. Tiny little breaths.* Couldn't blame River. Couldn't really blame Max, either. I thought about the fucked-up dolphin with the twisted spinal cord whose pod had fucked off and left it floundering in the ocean. I was that fucking dolphin all deformed and defective and River could tell. There was something about me she could sense. In my blood, maybe. In *our* blood.

I unlocked my phone, went to open Insta to find that dolphin. Was going to wait River out, you know? She'd eventually get tired. Give up. Max had patience for that. It was good for her to work it out, Max said. Good for her to get used to her emotions.

River screamed. I was hungry. River screamed. I opened the fridge. River screamed. Nothing in the fridge. River screamed. I closed the fridge. River screamed. I saw the list Max had made. River screamed. Fifth down the list—after *Wake up, Diaper change, Bottle (make sure to test on wrist!), Diaper change*—was *Grocery store.* River screamed. The store would need another list. Max hadn't left one. River screamed. Grocery store would require going out in the world. River screamed. Outside the wire. River screamed. Into the shit. River screamed. If I wanted to eat, we had to go to the store. If we were going to the store, River had to eat. Got to check your corners, your overhead. So, fuck it, I opened my photos and played River a slideshow of the most recent images: Max blowing raspberries on River's fat thighs, a series of River trying to nurse pretty much anything within reach, the doctored images of River at war that I had saved to my cloud. River in the gunner's turret of a Humvee, River filling sandbags for guard post reinforcement, River watching a mushroom cloud bloom in the distance after EOD exploded a cache of mortar and artillery rounds.

Max wasn't on board with screens. She thought they were nothing but a way to pacify. Fit people into boxes. She would've said River just needed to feel her feelings. That trying to distract her taught her to feel small or something, taught her that she was inconvenient. That I should let her cry so she could hear her voice. Feel it.

But, like, she got quiet and then distracted enough that I could slip the bottle to her lips and she drank it down. I just wouldn't tell Max. What was one more thing? And it was like she could hear me thinking a state away because my phone chimed and it was her again. I ignored it. She knew I was busy.

Anyway, what was the difference how I got the kid to eat? I was getting the job done. Work smarter, not harder, right? I only had an hour before she would go back to sleep. All I wanted to do was scroll pictures that weren't my life right then and stare at the adoption website, pay for a premium membership, find my birth mom, run away, start over. But the store was on the list and I was hungry and so was River and Marines get shit done.

In the parking lot of the apartment complex, blocky beige three-story buildings trimmed in white loomed over us like guard posts. I got River into her car seat and made sure the harness was snug at the correct height over her shoulders; I sat her favorite stuffed penguin in her lap. It was part of her personal protective equipment.

Step off in one mike, I said to River.

River trilled, kicked her legs.

Solid copy, I said.

I patted myself down for my keys, wallet, and phone, opened the driver's door—the sheep was curled on the floor and Ruiz sat bitch.

Motherfucker, I said.

River yawned.

Oorah! Yut! Kill! said Ruiz. He punched the dash of the truck, made a face like the Hulk.

Be advised, I said. We are Oscar Mike. One vic, four packs leaving the wire.

River and the sheep said nothing. Ruiz shook his head.

At least you part of the story you telling now, I guess.

What's that mean? I said.

Means you been trying to tell stories but you ain't in them because you been trying to forget it all—cut yourself out, make yourself different. I told you, dog, you a monster. Can't change who you are.

You're not really here, I said.

Whatever you got to tell yourself, said Ruiz.

We is real, said the sheep in Ali's voice.

Are, I said.

Are, said the sheep.

At the exit of the apartment complex I stopped, looked right and left for cross traffic. Early-October Indiana was overlapping shades of green and yellow. Hadn't frosted yet. Still warm. Breeze through the canopies of oaks and maples pushed branches and it made me think of seaweed in a current. Beams of sun sliced through shadows. It was like being under-water. Sperm whales dove through waxy leaves tailed by the crippled dolphin. My phone chimed again while I pulled the truck into the flow of traffic and my eyes caught the flash of a sign posted next to the entrance banner to the apartment complex and I read, in messy black spray paint: COMPLACENCY KILLS.

In the store, while the sheep followed and Ruiz called out danger posi-tions and targets, I combat glided: heel, toe, heel, toe, heel, toe, behind the shopping cart. River rode in the car seat set in the rear of the cart and watched me. I made faces to try and get her to laugh, smile. She wasn't having it. Tired, hungry. My time was ticking down. Probably thirty or forty-five minutes at the most before she lost it again.

I talked to River while we rolled through the store. Told her about boot camp about shooting about speed surprise and violence of action. I told her about the sheep and Ruiz and the dogs. Everything. She didn't say a word. The shoppers, mostly women, smiled at us and oohed and aahed when we made a stop near them to grab apples or bread or lunch meat or whatever. They were nothing but distractions, potential targets. I smiled at them. Thanked them. Talked about the unseasonal weather.

Be polite, be professional, but have a plan to kill everyone you meet, kid, I said to River.

She popped her lips.

Near the toy aisle, across from the bakery, an old man blocked our path with his cart. He was bent over the glass, looking at cakes. I stood in silence for a minute.

This a motherfucking choke point, dog, said Ruiz.

The sheep slipped on the polished concrete.

Ram this pinche puta, said Ruiz.

I white-knuckled the handlebar. Felt every single nick and gouge catch on my calluses. Then River grabbed her penguin and screeched. Shoved the thing in her mouth. The old man turned to us—his whole body, like, the guy couldn't use his neck, and at that weird bent-over angle it puffed him up like a fucking giant bird.

Howdy, he said. Stood with some trouble.

I gave the greeting of the day, cleared my throat, nodded at his cart, and the guy turned to me and went into this bullshit about his granddaughter's second birthday and how he'd volunteered to get the cake and the guy's words turned to mush in my ears and then Arabic and I smelled cooking meat and fresh bread and cigarette smoke and open sewer and the sheep wasn't the sheep but instead was Ali—BJ—and he was translating what the old man said about his granddaughter and not being sure if she'd rather have chocolate or strawberry and I told the old man that he couldn't block a patrol with his vehicle and that if he did that again he'd end up a stain on the street and BJ translated to the old man and the old man told me through BJ that he didn't know what I was talking about and then he took a few steps toward me and that thing growing inside me was all heat and blood and it swelled and pushed against my rib cage and I thought killing him might feel good might be a solution to all my problems. It would be justified: shout, show, shove, shoot. I was making my way through escalation of force and the old man was not complying and I was bottlenecked, at a choke point, ass hanging out in the breeze, and then the old man leaned over me and looked at River and I was back in the grocery store and Ruiz and the sheep were gone and I was surrounded by tables full of pastries and cupcakes.

How old? said the old man.

Two months, I said.

The old man made kissy noises and funny faces at River, who laughed.

Congratulations, he said. She's just perfect.

I nodded and picked at a divot in the cart handlebar with my trigger finger and River blew a raspberry. The old man hung around for a minute. Looked at me like he wanted to say something. *Say something, motherfucker,* I thought.

It's not safe to have the car seat in the back of the cart, he said, and then pushed his cart to the bakery cashier.

I doubled back to the toy aisle, put two small toy guns in the cart, then went to pay for the groceries.

Treat, never, keep, keep, I said to her back at the apartment.

River didn't say anything.

Treat every weapon as if it were loaded. Never point a weapon at anything you do not intend to shoot. Keep your finger straight and off the trigger until you are ready to fire. Keep your weapon on safe until you intend to fire.

River didn't say anything.

The range is two-dimensional, good to go? You shoot from one point to the other. You don't have to worry about anything aside from your target. But out in the shit, when you're clearing houses and killing bodies and eating babies and your geometries of fire start to overlap because you aren't on a doggone range, there's a fifth safety rule, good to go?

River didn't say anything.

Know your target and what lies beyond, I said.

While River's milk heated, I taught her how to handle the rifle. Held one of the toy guns in my palms in front of her and said things like Sight alignment, plus sight picture, plus trigger control, equals expert.

River was in her swing and frog-kicked her legs and reached for the colored plastic rifle. I showed her the different firing positions. Imagined her as she was in the photoshopped pictures I'd created. She looked happy—gurgling and smiling and panting while she reached for the toy rifle that without much thought I snapped another picture, the toy out of the frame, opened Instagram, and posted it.

River took the bottle without fussing and conked out on the changing table. I didn't bother to swaddle her. She was so relaxed, it was like her limbs were full of soup instead of bones. I wanted to sleep like that. It'd been seventy-two hours. I willed time to speed up so I could get to Court's.

★

While River slept, I drew Dog targets on computer paper with a black marker. Taped them to the walls of the apartment at different heights. Then, real rifle tucked into the pocket of my shoulder, cheek draped over the stock, I cleared the apartment, sighted in on the targets. I combat glided from room to room. Ruiz cleared the rooms with me, on my six, picked up the sectors of fire I couldn't cover on my own.

The world shifted back into place after months.

I took a break, sat on the couch, cradled the rifle like it was River. Wanted to load a magazine with live rounds. Wanted to insert the magazine into the magazine well. Wanted to rack the charging handle. And then I wanted to feel the cold metal in my mouth, wrap my lips around the barrel, pull the trigger.

I didn't know where the spark of that came from and I wondered if it was like that for Ruiz. Just a split second of want. A fucking lightning strike. Impulse.

I didn't have ammunition. Buying ammunition would've meant going to the store. And going to the store would've meant waking River. And changing River. And getting River into her car seat because I couldn't leave a baby alone in a house when it was napping, could I? No. I knew that. I could not. Not even if there was an emergency. Not even then. Not even if I hadn't slept in three days and my dead friend was standing in my kitchen, kicking at a dead sheep that talked with the voice of a dead interpreter.

Even if I managed to get to a gun shop and back before River woke, pulling the trigger would've meant waking her in the end anyhow. And you never—never never never—wake a sleeping baby. All the books said so.

My phone chimed again and Ruiz and the sheep were gone and I was sweaty and spent from moving and I wanted to shake the thought I'd just had so I finally checked my messages. Mostly from Max:

She up?

How's it going?

Send pics please?

I miss you both

Know ur busy. Txt/call when you can.

I texted her back. *Going good. Went to store. Played hard*

Those posts r cute, she texted.

Yeah, I texted.

Three dots blinked, hung on the screen, then disappeared, then hung again.

U upset? she texted.

No. Yup.

Ur being short, she texted.

Just tired. Busy like you said, I texted.

K, she texted.

How's the conference? Good to be back at work? I texted.

No one understands the concept of Q&A. Like sit down Louise from Dayton ur not a panelist and no one asked for comments [angry face emoji angry face emoji] she texted.

There are some things I want to tell you, I didn't text.

I taught our baby how to handle a firearm properly and perform basic raid operations, I didn't text.

[picture of the apartment covered in dog targets] I didn't text.

I want to find my birth mom, I didn't text.

I thought of those dots blinking on Max's screen, her worry about what I might write. Like, I knew she probably wanted me to send pictures of River, a steady stream of them. Mainline the kid right into her heart. But I figured, too, that it might be hard for her to see that. I knew it was hard for her. I knew that. And, like, I loved her. I didn't want to make shit harder.

What I did text: *Lol. Go home Louise*

The other handful of messages were from Mom and Penny. Penny was in town from West Lafayette. They invited me and River to dinner at Mom's. Mom and Rick had been asking for a few months. Rick wanted to bury the hatchet, I think.

I don't need a babysitter, I texted Max.

??? she texted.

My mom and Penny, I texted.

Thought they could lighten the load, she texted.

You don't trust me, I texted.

Dot dot dot. Gone. Dot dot dot. Gone. Dot dot dot.

Not about you. Then she was dropping periods at the end of her texts.

Dot dot dot.

You don't communicate.

Dot dot dot.

They're your family.

Dot dot dot.

River's family.

Dot dot dot.

That makes them my family.

Dot dot dot.

I thought I made that clear.

Something about that made my insides explode.

And I'm not your family? I texted.

Not fighting over txt, she texted.

Dot dot dot.

Let me know when she wakes up.

I stood and threw my phone into the couch and pulled a pillow to my face and screamed into it.

Yeah, dog, said Ruiz. *Let me hear that war cry.*

Then he and I worked out together like we were on a quarterdeck in boot camp, changed exercises every twenty seconds—high-intensity intervals. Mountain climbers, push-ups, Hello Dollies, flutter kicks, side-straddle hops, bicycle crunches, side arm circles, overhead arm circles, push-ups again, side-straddle hops again, high-knees, squats, mountain climbers again, toe crunches, then one last set of negative push-ups. Sweat burned my eyes, bile rose in my throat. I ran to the bathroom and popped in the sink.

I brushed my teeth. Took a shower. Wasn't worried about what I'd see in the mirror. I was electric. It was over with Max. That was it. I was okay with it. Fuck it, right? We weren't married. The shit wasn't working. I wasn't who she thought and I couldn't keep on being the fucking guy I'd made up, that I'd thought I'd wanted to be. So fuck it. Wasn't supposed to be this hard.

I'd go back to my old life. Back to being twenty-three with my entire goddamned future ahead of me. Back to the dives with Court. Back to house parties and titty bars and bonfires. I'd get back on twilight at UPS. I'd kept my nose clean. Grant would recommend me. Shit, maybe in a year or two I'd apply for a driver position, too. I could drive manual, didn't have a record, could make it look like driving a Humvee was good experience or whatever. I'd move out the second Max got home. Get my own place. Live alone. See River in the mornings. Or every other day or weekends or something. We'd figure it out. It'd be easy.

Or maybe all of that except I wouldn't go back to how it had been. No Court. No bars or house parties. No UPS. No Indiana. California. I'd join back up. Be a lifer. Send Max child support every month like ninety percent of the other lifers who saw their kids on weekends, then holidays, then between deployments, then—after their wives eventually got remarried—never.

Or maybe fucking none of that and I'd just disappear. Do everyone a favor.

Or. Washington. I'd go to Washington. Rain and forest and mountains and ocean. All those things I'd dreamed about. I'd find my birth mom. She'd want to be found. I'd forgive her.

I opened adoption dot com on my phone and signed into my profile. I paid for the premium account. I ran the search again with my info and four-three-nine-zero-seven-six appeared.

Added by Birth-Mother, looking for Adoptee.

Gender: Male

Birth date: fifteen Nov, nineteen eighty-nine

Ethnicity: White

Birthplace: Tacoma, WA

Adoption place: Olympia, WA

I clicked on the new View Profile button and held my fucking breath. Four-three-nine-zero-seven-six became Carole Brewer. The profile had been updated last in two thousand six, the year I turned eighteen. Carole Brewer. Carole Brewer. Carole Brewer. I said her name out loud. Carole Brewer was born in nineteen seventy-one. Carole Brewer. Carole Brewer. Carole Brewer. I was trying to summon her like Bloody fucking Mary or something. Carole Brewer was single. Carole Brewer. Carole Brewer. Carole Brewer. Hi, this is my mom, Carole Brewer. Carole Brewer had two years of college. Carole Brewer. Carole Brewer. Carole Brewer. I repeated the name to where it didn't mean anything anymore, to where I kept asking myself if I was saying it right. Carole Brewer was a registered nurse. CaroleBrewerCaroleBrewerCaroleBrewer wrote CT for religion. CaroleBrewerCaroleBrewerCaroleBrewer was white.

My mouth was full of sand. I couldn't swallow. There was an option to contact. To send a message. I would do it. I would.

But I needed to confirm my birth city. Like target confirmation. Like proper prior planning prevents piss-poor performance. I wasn't in the goddamned Army, for fuck's sake. Tomorrow. I would do it tomorrow morning. Court's first. Ativan. Sleep. Sweet unconscious deep dark slack-jawed motherfucking sleep. Then breakfast at Mom's to confirm my birth city.

I'd be sharp, fresh, ready for whatever bullshit they were ready to throw my way.

And then River woke crying and the muscle memory kicked in. Routine routine routine. The military, prison, parenthood. Maybe fucking everything. Do something more than once and it's a goddamned routine. I was good with routines. Told Max I thought I'd probably do all right in prison because of the routine but she told me that wasn't funny.

I tasked Ruiz to pack the diaper bag. I changed River. The sheep gave moral support. If Ruiz and I were door kickers the sheep was fucking Headquarters and Service. The sheep was the standard measure for the zany shit Ruiz and I did. So you knew when to laugh, when to cringe, when to cry. One man, two ghosts, and a baby. Maybe I was in a fucking television show and didn't know it. Some fucking idiot would watch that show and love it. Talk about it around the watercooler. I singsonged Carole Brewer's name the entire time. Sang it to different tunes like "Twinkle Twinkle Little Star" and "You Are My Sunshine" and "Rockabye Baby."

I went to text Max that River was awake and almost sent a string of Carole Brewer Carole Brewer Carole Brewer. I lined the squad up in the living room and delivered the warning order for our mission. I said, Carole Brewer Carole Brewer Carole Brewer. Carole Brewer Carole Brewer— Carole Brewer. Carole, Brewer Carole Brewer Carole Brewer: Carole Brewer Carole Brewer Carole Brewer. Carole Brewer Carole Brewer Carole Brewer; Carole Brewer Carole Brewer Carole Brewer. Carole Brewer Carole Brewer? Carole Brewer.

I texted Court I was on my way and off we fucking went. One vic four packs leaving the wire.

SO THEN THERE I was, driving to Court's. The sun was low. Time had passed. Microsleep. Doc said it would happen. I was on eighty-five hours without rack time. My heart was pumping mud. My truck was a Humvee. River was asleep in her car seat. The sheep took the turret. Ruiz was the VC. I slapped my face a few times, hyperventilated in through my nose, out through my mouth, cranked the air-conditioning.

Fuck, I said.

You know that kind of fuck, right? That same-shit, different-day kind of fuck. That waking-up-the-second-day-still-with-a-hangover kind of fuck. That asshole-behind-you-talking-too-loud-on-his-cell-phone-in-the-checkout-line kind of fuck. That hitting-every-red-light-when-you're-late kind of fuck.

What, thought you was getting rid of us, wedo? said Ruiz.

No, I said.

Yeah you did, he said. *Trying to go motherfucking UA and shit.*

No, Corporal, I said. I know the mission.

The night was dark and clear and cold. The corn had been harvested. Everything was flat and never-ending. It looked like a desert outside. Then it *was* a desert outside. Shadows in the moonlit fields were barns and farm equipment and then they were date palms, herds of sheep, wild dogs.

I reached over in the single cab and put my hand on River's chest, felt its gentle rise and fall.

Blacker shadows flitted and followed in the corner of my eye, and I thought of the gravedigger's ghost. Ghosts. I was nothing but a haunted house. How does a haunted house take care of a kid, you know?

The road was pockmarked and crumbling again, covered in trash. Not like before I left home, before the city annexed the land and leveled it all and covered it in concrete and built the out-of-place mansions, but like a different road altogether. I swerved to avoid the potholes, the trash and rubble.

You lost, dog? said Ruiz.

I know where I'm going, I said.

Lost in the sauce, said Ruiz.

I do not recognize much of these, said the sheep from the turret.

This, I said.

This, said the sheep.

Time to call the Wizard, said Ruiz.

I'm not crazy, I said.

The dog cannot make its tail straight, said the sheep.

What's that mean? I said.

Can't change who you are, güey, said Ruiz.

I don't want to change shit, I said. Just want to sleep.

For the first time since being home I felt like I was telling the truth.

How will your woman be feeling about this? said the sheep.

My woman? I said.

Oh, damn, said Ruiz. *Goat's a motherfucking blue falcon for sure.*

Sheep, I said.

What this means, blue falcon?

That you're a buddy fucker, I said.

I not fucking nobody, said the sheep. *Always with the fucking.*

A snitch, dog, said Ruiz.

The moon was gone, and we were at the bottom of the quarry, monsters cruising swift and silent through the blackness, right on our tail, coming to get us, drag us down down down. I drove without lights, blacked out, knew the road by its feel, by the sound of it under the tires.

Every grain of sand, clod of dirt, chunk of asphalt, I knew where it had come from, where it'd started in the goddamned universe. Knew where it would end up.

Court's driveway was lined nut to butt with cars on both sides. A goddamned quarter-mile-long gauntlet. Ruiz fidgeted next to me. I parked, turned off the car, sat in the dark.

I texted Penny and Mom that everything was good but that I was tired and that we should have breakfast tomorrow morning. That I had some things to talk about. Then I texted Max I was in for the night and River and I were doing great. I looked at River. She nursed in her sleep. Maybe she was missing Max. I didn't text that to her.

I went back to the mission at hand. Listen, you can't leave a kid in the car. That's not fucking safe. And besides, no Marine left behind.

Anyway, we'd be in and out. Fucking Ricky Recon. It was for her sake, really. For hers and Max's. The Ativan was the goddamned cure for the insomnia, the hallucinations. I'd be better. This was going to make me better. I told myself that. I believed it. Believed it enough to get me moving.

I slid on a BabyBjörn, unbuckled River from her seat, lifted her and pressed her against my chest, secured her to me, got out of the car, slung the diaper bag. Kid barely made a sound.

Come on, I said.

Walking into a motherfucking ambush, dog, said Ruiz.

I didn't give a flying shit if he was right. I was thinking of sleep. My head wasn't in the game. I was mindset white. Unaware and unprepared. I was thinking of profile four-three-nine-zero-seven-six—Carole Brewer.

My name sounded good with Brewer. Dean Brewer was better than Dean Pusey. I wondered if Carole Brewer named me when I was born— if, when she thought of me, she called me by that name in her head.

Do you think she named me? I said.

Gravel crunched under my feet. River warmed my chest.

Corps wanted you to have a mother, would've issued you one, said Ruiz.

Cut that shit, I said.

Nah, for real, though, he said. *It don't mean shit. Like* What if she named me? Oh, what if she's looking for me? What if she never cared a cunt hair about me? Mommy Mommy Mommy. *Get the fuck out, dog.*

Maybe she is death, said the sheep.

Dead, I said.

Dead, said the sheep.

You wouldn't want to know? I said.

Got plenty other problems is all, said Ruiz.

Fuck this, let's go, I said.

Ruiz shook his head.

What? I said. It was a challenge.

Can't go in there with you, dog, he said.

Nervous? I said.

He clicked his tongue and lifted his chin. I could see my breath.

Ain't no fucking joke, he said.

We'll be in and out, I said. Secret squirrel shit.

He shook his head.

Can't do it, Dean, he said.

You, too? I said to the sheep.

Goat's with me, said Ruiz.

Sheep, I said.

Proper prior planning prevents piss-poor performance, said Ruiz.

This is a goddamned mutiny, I said.

Duty to disobey, said Ruiz.

That meant that he thought I'd lost it.

Dead fucking weight, anyway, I said, and Ruiz looked hurt but I didn't give a shit and I turned right into Chubby Bunny, who was standing in the driveway alone, looking up at the sky. Chubby Bunny from El Dorado, from Court's party last year.

Her name hit me then: Lily Cruz. Like I'd touched her and there it all was. She'd had a sister older than us by a year, maybe two? Sister was smart, student council president. Lily got into X. Always smelled like VapoRub. Go-down-on-her-and-clear-your-sinuses-type shit was the joke.

I'd forgotten about it until I remembered her name, but her parents paid one of those rehab camp cults to kidnap her in the middle of the night our junior year and take her to the wilderness in Utah or wherever to straighten her out. You know, the kind of thing where they teach you how to tie knots and make a fire out of ass hair and an old contact lens all while starving you and telling you what a piece of shit you are.

Kind of like the Marines without the guns.

She asked me who I was talking to, and I said no one.

Fucking no one, I said over my shoulder into the darkness. Darkness as dark as a fucking moonless night in the windowless room of a PB outside Fallujah. I asked Lily what she was looking at and she said the sky and I told her no shit.

She looked at me. I could've been ten feet tall with a dick growing out of my forehead, she would've looked at me the same way.

My sister says people who use BabyBjörn carriers hate their babies, she said.

I didn't know what the fuck she was talking about.

Hip dysplasia, she said, and shrugged. Ergobaby is better, I guess.

Good seeing you again, I said.

I'm a fucking great aunt, she said.

I left her in the driveway and walked up to Court's front door with River. Stacked like we were about to hit it in a raid. The BabyBjörn was my Kevlar vest, my shield. Then the front door, it maybe looked like the widow's front door, and I blinked and it was Mom's, then the door to my barracks room, but when I looked back Lily was still in the driveway. I was still at Court's.

I didn't know what I was walking into. That didn't really matter. I wasn't doing it alone. I had ass. Backup. That's really all that matters in a fight: Do you got ass? Bad motherfuckers on your left and right? Shock and awe.

Prepare to breach, I said to River.

She didn't say anything.

Breaching, I said.

I opened the door and stepped inside and the entire goddamned scene stopped me in my tracks. Got caught in the fatal funnel. Voices and music overlapped like talking machine guns and cut us down. I was glad Ruiz wasn't there—never would've heard the end of it: *How's it feel to be fucking dead, boot?*

Sometimes, a small guerrilla force can overcome shock and awe through sheer force of will.

My heart started going and I got a twitchy feeling in my chest like I needed to clear my throat over and over like there were fluttering wings beating the insides of my lungs.

It was all the fucking same as it ever had been, like everyone in the fucking house had been paused in time for eleven months, and when I opened the door, they started up again. People stood in groups talking, people sat bumping lines of whatever off tabletops, people—goddamned teenagers, looked like—played King's Cup at the kitchen table, people donkey-laughed at shitty jokes, people touched other people's arms and hung off each other and swore this was the last time, people led people into dark back rooms.

Some people did double takes at the sight of River, reached for her, tried to touch her. I fucking dared them. Fucking sheep. Goddamned baaing fat-body civilians. Lamb chops. Every single last one of them. That got me going again.

I knew Court would be in the basement. I just had to get there.

When I took a step into the living room, the party disappeared. The house changed. There was a rifle in my hands. River faced outward in the BabyBjörn, carried a squad automatic weapon. We were in the shit then. Together.

We combat glided through the maze of rooms. Clear. Clear. Clear. Room after room. They were never-ending. I didn't need Ruiz or the sheep, their rotting stink choking me out, holding me down.

We were on a mission, River and me. One mind, any fucking weapon. One mind, like she was part of me and I was part of her. We moved together because we were the same. She saw everything inside my head then. Knew every single part of me.

The house kept shifting, changing. It was a barracks a semi-trailer a Humvee a hospital a beach a warehouse a bar a cornfield a car a living room an apartment complex a bathroom a truck bed. Corridor after corridor, room after room. A goddamned tangle of a maze.

It's going to be okay, I said, and River didn't respond because she didn't need to and that made me feel good, close to her. We were swift, silent, deadly.

Me and you, I said.

One, I said.

Two, I said.

The count on deck is two killers of men, sir! I said.

We dropped body after body in those rooms. Double tap. Dead-check. Mozambique. NSR. River let that SAW talk. We didn't leave anything up to chance.

Kill bodies, eat babies, I said.

Moms and dads and sisters and girlfriends and stepdads and kids and teachers and senior Marines and boot lieutenants and Iraqis and muj and interpreters and old men in grocery stores and loudmouthed wannabes and bar hicks and sleazy bartenders and lounge lizards and JLo and police officers and nurses and doctors and strip club bouncers and shift supervisors and warehouse managers and loading partners and and and. Fucking everyone. River and I laid waste to them all.

Get some, get some, get some, I said.

We kept moving.

I sang cadence while we moved: *Sight alignment, sight picture, put it right between the eyes! Slow steady squeeze and the motherfucker dies!*

Then, finally, we came to a barricaded room—door made of metal, all kinds of locks and chains and boards. I knew what was behind that door. The shadow. The fucking ghost inside of me. We'd kill it together. River and me.

I set a linear charge; River kept watch. I called out, Breaching! And popped the fuse, split the fucking door in half, and we cleared by fire, entered.

When the smoke dispersed, in the corner was the shadow, tall and shifting and sharp. Wounded and fucking angry. It looked like me, like Ruiz, the sheep, my birth mom, and it opened its gaping mouth and roared and charged and we lit it the fuck up.

And then I heard Court's voice: Dean? The fuck?

The house snapped back together. I was in Court's basement and I heard people laughing, music playing. It smelled like weed and sump pump mildew and Febreze and the muffled bass gave the house a heartbeat that became my heartbeat and I was sweating and cold and my mouth was dry and River was nowhere.

Pulled a goddamned Houdini. Kid couldn't even roll over yet.

Come on, kid, I said. Time to rally up.

Dean, you got to go, man, said Court. You're fucking up every-one's high.

River didn't rally. Nothing. And it was like, for a minute, was any of it real? Like, maybe I was back at Court's the night I'd choked that guy out, met up with Max—done one line too many, maybe packed my nose with something laced. It was all a fucking jumble in my head.

Then the BabyBjörn hanging from my waist bumped my knees; my Kevlar was gone. No more ass. I was alone, a fucking soft target. I started yelling River's name.

River! River! River! I yelled it loud and fast until it didn't make sense until it wasn't a word and I tried to push past Court and he grabbed my shoulders, and I screamed in his face and threw an elbow into his mouth, shoved him into a group of people, and came into the basement living room like some terrible Bible-type shit, you know?

We hadn't gotten the shadow. That was it. I was sure the shadow had River and I was sure everyone was the shadow. I'd fucking kill them all.

Their faces distorted and smirked; their fingers stretched and reached for me. Teeth sharpened and eyes sunk and everyone grew around me like weeds.

The shadow was the cause of everything. It was why I couldn't sleep. Almost four days. It would kill me. I was sure this was it. It had been in me for years, using me up, biding its time. I started swinging.

Jesus fucking Christ, Dean! said Court behind me somewhere.

I stepped into the weeds and they swirled and moved around me, slapped and clawed at my wrists and ankles. They laughed and screamed and I pushed them off, tried to fight through them until I couldn't anymore and I dropped in the middle of them all, let them take me down down down to the floor to the bottom of the quarry to the pitch-dark room at the PB to the inside of a bullet hole to the bottom of a grave.

And I heard someone say, I knew I seen that motherfucker! He's the one sucker punched me, fucked up my neck!

Then my nose exploded and my eyes were full of tears and my mouth clogged with snot and blood and I spit it on the ground between my hands and there was someone on my back, pressing me into the floor, and their arm jerked and choked my neck and everything got quiet.

I didn't try to fight back. I deserved it all then. I knew that.

In the atrium of the PB, Sergeant Moss was telling me to tap.

Tap, he said. He was calm as a motherfucker, those oak arms sure as shit about what they could do. And I didn't tap.

Couldn't.

Wouldn't.

And then Ruiz's face was next to mine, the sheep's, too. Penny's and Mom's. Rick's. Max's.

Tap, they said.

Fucking put me out of my misery, I said.

Tap, they said.

You don't want that, I said.

Tap, they said.

Better this way, I said. I was crying.

Tap, they said.

So, fucking finally, I did.

I tapped and the noise rushed back in. There was yelling and the weight was gone and air broke into my lungs and this fucking light exploded right in the middle of all the weeds and they shrank and withered and screamed and died.

Chubby Bunny stood in the center of that light, holding River to her chest. River, who was a burning, raging star. I never heard a sound like the one she made. Like, that sound erased every other sound that ever existed. It was terrible and beautiful. It broke glass and caused earthquakes on the other side of the world and traveled through time and somewhere standing on a roof looking out over a graveyard next to Ruiz I thought I heard someone scream.

Chubby Bunny held River out like she was toxic, arms thrust forward. *One arm's distance, motherfucker*, I thought.

I remember I reached out, took her. I remember she quieted down in my arms. Didn't cry. I remember Chubby Bunny said, I found this upstairs. I remember that. Like she'd found keys, a wallet. I remember walking, keys jangling, talking. I don't know if I said anything. I was in and out. Microsleep. Words got fuzzy and garbled, fucked-up comms. *How copy?* I thought. *Say again*, I thought. *Broken and unreadable*, I thought.

Taking you home, Court said. I remembered that, too.

Thank you, I didn't say.

I'm sorry, I didn't say.

Help, I didn't say.

I didn't say anything. Nothing smart left to say.

I remember River asleep in my lap. I remember cold window glass on my forehead. I remember farmland, not desert, in the headlights. I remember telephone poles zooming by in the dark. It all flickered like old home movies.

Then we were in front of a door. Court talked at me. Something about getting help. I couldn't keep up with what he was saying. It was like I was in the past, trying to catch up to the present. I wasn't synced up. Everything was all contrails and auras and the ends of words. I remember Court rang the doorbell and left.

I woke in my old bedroom at Mom and Rick's. The room was cool and bright. Penny sat on my bed, River in her arms.

Nice hair, said Penny.

What? I said.

Or lack thereof, she said.

I sat up. Blood rushed to my head. My face ached. I touched my nose, breathed in. Didn't think it was broken.

I found my phone in my pocket. It was nine. I had missed texts from Max.

I have to go, I said.

Penny stood with River, smiled at her, made kissy faces, started up that natural baby sway thing people do when they hold one. It was hypnotizing, that rhythm.

You're good at that, I said. I swung my legs out of bed.

Mom let me hold you a lot when you were little. It was my favorite thing. Holding you on that old sofa—remember that one with the weird pattern? So fucking nineties—it's like my first real memory.

Mom told me a while back I was a bad baby.

You were a crier, she said.

I'm your first memory? I said.

She swayed with River and watched me. I couldn't look back.

I've got to go, I said again. But I didn't move. I didn't know what to do with my hands if I wasn't holding River. I folded them in my lap and felt like a fucking kid, like some recruit sitting in the schoolhouse, waiting for a DI to give the order to move. Left hand, left knee. Right hand, right knee.

Mom came into the room and said good morning, said that breakfast would be ready in a few minutes, and then she left. Penny followed with River, and I was alone in my room that wasn't my room in a house that wasn't my house, wasn't my home, and Penny and Mom were trying to act like everything was all good and nothing had happened and with Mom I was kind of used to that but with Penny it felt like bad acting.

I stood up and started moving around, got my blood going, took a deep breath, slung the diaper bag onto my back, and followed Penny to the living room.

Mom asked from the kitchen if I wanted coffee and I didn't but I still said yes and I paced the room while Penny sat on the couch, River in her lap.

Where's Rick? I said.

Oh, he's at work, said Penny. Mom said it's just to open. He'll be back soon. He promoted a manager. I guess the shop's doing okay.

How about Iris? I asked.

She's sick, said Penny.

I nodded, knew it was bullshit. Felt bad about Christmas, then got angry that I felt bad, decided to drop it.

Listen, I said. That's what I said to her, Listen. I'm going to go.

I took a step toward her.

I'm sorry about all this, I said, and stepped closer.

Max will be home soon, I said, and stepped closer.

River needs to get home, I said, and stepped closer.

No, said Penny.

She didn't even look at me. Just kept on playing with River.

And I tried to say it all again, like maybe she hadn't heard, but she said no again.

Penny, I've got to go, I said.

She looked at me finally.

And just how are you going to get there? she said.

What I heard: And just how are you going to get there, you deadbeat, piece-of-shit, piss-poor excuse for a dad?

Drop the backpack and sit down, she said.

Drop my pack she told me. It was heavy. The weight of it cut into my shoulders. I slid it off, let it hit the floor. I fell onto the couch next to Penny.

You know, if you hadn't shown up last night, she said, we were coming to you today.

Max? I said.

Before Penny could answer, Mom came back into the living room and started saying, Here, here, here. Holding out her hands, slapping fingers to palms, beckoning, willing River into her arms.

They fussed over River. Finally, Mom glanced at me and said I looked terrible. Oh, honey, she said. You look terrible.

I thanked her. Like, Thanks, Mom, you make me feel so good. And I wished I hadn't said it, but Penny laughed and River trilled and Mom said she was sorry she was sorry, okay? And that she might not have given birth to me but she was my mother and couldn't she be concerned for her child, her baby? Her baby boy?

And then I shrank shrank shrank. Kept shrinking. I was a toddler I was a baby I was a fetus I was a pollywog I was two cells flopping on the couch like the first fish to beach itself and breathe air.

Maybe that was my earliest memory, you know? Maybe I could remember all the way back to when I was conceived. The point of impact. Maybe that moment was like an echo bouncing through my blood and bones forever. Or did I remember being in the womb? Being born? I could picture myself being delivered, pulled from between my birth mom's legs by a set of hands. Did I make that up? Was that a memory? Was I smashing together a memory of River being born and a story I was trying to tell myself? How was Penny so sure I was her first memory? What would be River's? What was my birth mom's?

I wanted to know where I was born. The birth city. I needed it.

Then Rick walked in and it was like one of those dreams where you're naked and that's not weird at all until someone shows up and points out how weird it is, draws everyone's attention to it. Like, I felt my face get red, I couldn't sit still, started clearing my throat. My chest tightened, breath sped, like something was squeezing my middle. I stood up to get air, took River back from my mom. Moving felt good. If I moved enough, I could move the entire world, speed up time. I was an animal. A monster Ruiz had said.

I don't know what I was expecting—a dressing down, a disappointed daddy talk, a sermon, a knife to slice the pound of flesh or gouge the fucking eye I owed. I was ready to gut myself to get what I wanted, and when I got it, I could disappear and never come back and I'd forget it all and they'd forget me, the mistake I was, the bad baby. Just a blip in time. What was twenty-three years? Nothing. Half a blink. Not even.

Dean, said Rick. I'm so sorry. I'm so, so sorry. And he walked toward me and I was ready to throw a haymaker right into his stupid fucking face but then he was holding me, wrapping me, and River was between us and it wasn't like he was crushing me, wasn't even holding me that tight, but I wanted him to be in that moment.

It was like whiplash the minute I felt his arms around me and I lost my footing. Like, I didn't want him to let go, didn't even know that I had wanted it, needed it.

The top of his head smelled like body odor and patchouli and I stopped clearing my throat, stopped feeling naked, stopped thinking about my birth mom and disappearing, and I breathed him in. Breathed not in tiny little breaths, not controlled like I was on the range, but wild and gulping. I breathed every ounce of oxygen in the atmosphere. Breathed like I imagined one of those fucking sperm whales breathing after it broke the surface. Took in so much air that whatever had been squeezing me, constricting me, broke, popped off, went flying right out of the fucking room.

I didn't go through a list of things I wanted to say and didn't then. All I said was I'm sorry. I'm sorry, I said. I meant it. I did. And I said it to everyone, to Mom and Penny and Iris, even though she wasn't there. I couldn't remember the last time I'd apologized for hurting someone and meant it.

We didn't apologize to targets, not to collateral damage.

We shot and exploded and destroyed and combat glided through the rubble. Slow is smooth; smooth is fast. And we did our jobs. To complete the mission, some breakage was acceptable.

It hit me then, like *hit me* hit me: I wasn't in the Marines anymore. I know, big fucking news flash, right? But it wasn't like before when I was trying to be someone new, be anyone or whatever, and it wasn't like with Ruiz where I was still trying to be in. It was like Oh, shit, this ain't that. This was different.

This was real.

All those infinite choices of who I could be and what my life could look like, all those choices had been spinning around and around, blurring on this big fucking wheel, and I couldn't get a look at anything because the wheel was constantly spinning and I was just waiting waiting waiting for it to stop and land on something, anything, to tell me what to do, who to be. And then it was like it'd stopped spinning through all those possibilities and everything got still and quiet—outside and in—and I knew who I was, who I was going to be.

Did you two want a room? said Penny.

Penelope Anne, said Mom. She was one of those parents who used our full first and middle names when she was mad or disgusted or excited or disappointed or anything really. I liked that I knew that.

I liked that when she said it, memories fucking freight-trained through my brain: Penny graduating high school, Penny caught smoking at fourteen, Penny publishing an op-ed advocating for sex education in the local paper at seventeen, Penny caught stealing earrings from Claire's at thirteen, Penny accepted to college, Penny covering me in makeup, Penny grounded for having a party while Mom was out of town at sixteen, Penny calling her sophomore history teacher a fascist and getting suspended for two days at fifteen, Penny getting caught making out with a boy at the quarry at thirteen, Penny tricking me into cleaning up her room at nine. Maybe that was my first memory. I held on to it.

We sat at the table for breakfast. Rick prayed and I didn't bow my head, but I didn't roll my eyes, either, and I held his hand when he offered it and I took Penny's hand, too, even though she made a face. Mom held River and fed her a bottle she'd found in the insulated pocket in the diaper bag. Kid barely made it through before she fell asleep. We ate and Rick talked about the store and Penny talked about the last year of her PhD and the dissertation she was finishing up writing, her relationship with her committee, jobs.

Just a waiting game now, she said. My committee is kind of over it because they know I'm going to get hired.

Mom talked about the new partner at the doctor's office where she worked—how young he seemed, how clueless.

Sometimes I wish I would've been a nurse or maybe even a doctor, said Mom.

There are tons of RN programs out there, Mom, said Penny.

Oh, I'm too old, said Mom.

I have lots of older students, said Penny.

Where would I find the time? said Mom.

She likes her job, said Rick.

Oh, I didn't realize your name was Gale, said Penny.

It went back and forth like that for a while and I was sitting there grinning like a fucking idiot, like a big fat baaing civilian, like lamb chops, and I didn't give one single fuck until Rick asked me how I was and I knew what that meant, but I was thinking still about where I was born; Carole Brewer's name bounced around inside my grape.

What do you mean how is he? said Mom.

I mean what I said, Gale, said Rick.

He just had a baby, said Mom, and—she made her eyes big and nodded at me like I couldn't see her—last night . . .

Aren't you going to stick up for Dean? said Rick to Penny.

Why? said Penny.

Your mother just answered for him, said Rick.

So? I don't like him that much right now, said Penny.

Rick laughed.

Penelope Anne, said Mom.

What? said Penny. We're all thinking it. It's just that sometimes I still wish we could return him.

Now Mom laughed.

You used to ask that all the time when you were little, she said.

I thought your favorite thing to do was hold me when I was a baby? I said.

What can I say, said Penny. I am large.

What's that mean? I said.

I contain multitudes, she said. Whitman, babe.

How much college debt do you have? I said.

She threw her napkin at me.

I threw it into the living room.

Hey, I said. Do you still have that vet's number? The one in your program?

She nodded. I nodded.

Then I cleared my throat and told them all the story about adoption dot com about four-three-nine-zero-seven-six about the deformed dolphin and the sperm whales about Carole Brewer and how she'd made the profile on my eighteenth birthday about how I just needed my birth city so that I could contact her. Rick nodded and shook his head and said wow over and over and Penny wiped some tears and Mom stood and rocked River and I sat at the table and waited for her to say something and when she didn't, I said, Mom?

She looked at me, eyebrows raised, and I looked at her, eyes wide, waiting for her to fill the silence.

What, sweetie? she said.

Where was I born? I said.

That's on your birth certificate, she said.

You don't remember? I said.

I gave you a file folder of all those important documents when you got home last year, she said.

I knew the folder she was talking about. It was at the apartment. I felt like an idiot. So much for proper prior planning preventing piss-poor performance. So much for situational awareness, I guess. I could hear Sergeant Moss's voice: *Fuck me, right?* I'd had the answer I needed all of twenty feet away from me.

Mom, just tell him, for Christ's sake, said Penny.

No need for that, said Rick.

Penny, do not raise your voice, said Mom. The baby.

I just need the city, Mom, I said.

You know, after Penny, when I couldn't get pregnant, no one could tell me why. Not a single doctor. Unexplained infertility. I heard it so many times. There were a few doctors who guessed but they never diagnosed. The endometriosis, the fibroids—they didn't have the technology there is today.

She walked between the living room and the dining room rocking River while the rest of us sat at the table.

You know what your father said after they tested his sperm?

Mom, said Penny.

This concerns you, said Mom.

Penny wanted to know how, and she and Mom went back and forth about why Penny should care about our father's sperm count and Rick tried to make peace and I said it was no big deal that I would just check the folder when I got home and I got itchy and checked my watch.

Rick sighed, stood, took plates to the kitchen.

You know, Joseph was a stepdad, said Mom.

We lived in Tacoma, right? said Penny.

My heart pounded: *Birthplace: Tacoma. Birthplace: Tacoma, Birthplace: Tacoma.*

Mom started listing all the places we had lived in Washington, talking about the coast, the mountains, how they never got to either as much as they wanted and wasn't that always the case when you lived someplace like that? She wanted to know how often people who lived in Arizona went to the Grand Canyon. She started talking about Mount Saint Helens and how it was only a matter of time before Mount Rainier blew and how glad she was to not have to worry about that all the way in Indiana and how important it was for us to be prepared that we should have water and blankets and dry food in our cars in case of some kind of disaster and finally I said, Mom, maybe a little louder than I meant to say it, maybe a little louder than I had the right to, and Penny said my name and took a step toward me and River woke and pouted and Rick stepped into the dining room and my mom started to say something but I interrupted her and apologized, cleared my throat, and said I was sorry, and then asked her to tell me.

She shushed River and rocked her and after a minute said, Vancouver.

I don't remember going to Vancouver, said Penny.

You didn't go, said Mom.

That's in Canada, I said.

There's a Vancouver in Washington, said Penny.

You were born in Vancouver, said Mom. I told you, it's on your birth certificate.

And that was the motherfucking end of four-three-nine-zero-seven-six, of Carole Brewer. My mom went on rocking River, Rick faded into the kitchen, Penny put her hand on my arm and wanted to know how I was doing, and all I could do was fucking laugh.

I laughed so hard I started to cry, and Penny asked me again if I was okay, this time a little more seriously, and I tried to answer and breathed in at the same time and choked on my spit so that I had to run to the bathroom to spew a fountain of phlegm and scrambled eggs and toast and bacon into the toilet.

Rick knocked on the door and asked if I was all right and I told him I was and that I'd be out in a minute and then sat on the cool tile and opened Insta. The two pictures I'd posted of River had a few dozen likes, some comments—the photoshopped one was mostly Marines. I read the missed texts from Max.

I miss u both, she'd texted.

[heart emoji heart emoji heart emoji]

Flight leaves here at early AM

Boarding

Landed

I'm home where r u???

I texted back that we were at my mom's.

On our way home, I texted.

I don't know what I did for Max to put so much stock in me, but I felt the weight of it then.

After I rinsed my mouth, I went back to the living room, hugged everyone, told them Max was home, that I had to leave, that I was sorry, that I would be okay, really I would, that I wanted to walk, that a couple miles wasn't too far, that I would text when I got home, that I knew we had to talk more, that I wanted to talk more, that we'd see each other soon.

OUTSIDE, SLOW WIND moved the trees. Leaves fell. Across the street, the white-hair who'd probably called the cops on me stared and pretended to rake a bare patch of grass. I raised my hand. He didn't wave back.

I walked.

On the corner of the neighborhood a boy sold gasoline in plastic jugs. Women in abayah and headscarves pushed kids along sidewalks. Out-of-work men smoked hookah in the alleyways I passed. I wove through runners and other parents pushing strollers and a guy waving a Domino's sign in front of a strip mall.

I sang "The Marines' Hymn" to River. Listed Marine Corps words: Go-fasters, I said. Papa is walking in his go-fasters. Crunchie, I said. Papa was a crunchie. Listed Arabic words and phrases: ogif, tafteesh, arfae yudik, aftah albob, shokran, inshallah, shaku maku, maku shi. Listed the things we would do when we got home: Eat, tummy time, books, nap.

At a red light I pushed the crosswalk button and pressed my lips to River's cornsilk hair.

How does that feel? I asked.

She smiled and smacked wet lips.

We're going to see Mama, I said. Can you say *Mama*?

When I looked up, moving through the intersection in a staggered column, was a foot patrol. Ruiz and the sheep took up tail-end Charlie.

I raised my hand. Ruiz raised his. I watched him until the patrol rounded a corner, moved out of sight, and then the future lay out in front of me.

★

In ten years I'll be sitting in a circle of eight veterans, telling this story. When I'm done talking the group therapist, a tall, waify brunette with a sharp jawline and feathery bangs will stand from her seat in the circle.

The meeting space is bright—early spring sun blasts through the open windows, bleaching the art and canvas signs printed with sayings like *It's Okay to Not Be Okay* and *Be Kind to Your Mind* that hang on the walls. I only think *What a load of bullshit* on occasion.

The therapist thanks me and the vets clap, nod, say thank you while I give them an almost smile, the one Max used to say was charming, and check my watch because I'm due to pick up River from Max's in twenty minutes.

I'm thinking about the student grades I need to enter because even though I don't teach science or engineering or robotics or whatever I've got students in the robotics club and there's a robotics competition coming up and failing students can't go and they're all on me about it and I need to email one student's parents about setting up the conference they asked for and another pair of students' parents about a book I assigned and I need to loop in the vice principal because things are escalating no matter what I do and the parents might be working together because both sets of parents' emails about the upcoming book assignment used the words *disappointed* and *inappropriate* and *offensive* and they had the same three-paragraph structure and whiny, holier-than-thou fucking tone and Jesus fucking Christ, what would they rather me teach instead? Fucking *Green Eggs and Ham*?

My heart pounds and the room is too bright and the ringing at the base of my skull itches like the goddamned clap, but I close my eyes and take a breath.

Not a tiny little breath: a big, deep breath.

I hold it for a couple seconds.

Let it out.

Hold at the bottom again.

Meanwhile, I tense and untense my body from feet to jaw.

I open my eyes.

The therapist tells us she'll see us soon and then she says our motto: Slow down to speed up, she says. And she asks us to repeat it and we do because it's how we end every session and because we're veterans and we still drop into following orders easily, and I think whenever I say the motto: Slow is smooth; smooth is fast—which is probably the therapist's intent. She knows her clients.

The group thins one by one. Disperses, I think. I think a lot more than I used to. React less. And then I think about Sergeant Moss and how he used to say, Dispersion, fuck-knuckles! when we bunched up while training patrol tactics in the Backyard. I smile at that. A big fucking grin.

At the door, the therapist puts a hand on my shoulder. What's got you smiling? she says.

Oh, I say. And I pause and think of all the things I could say instead of the truth, but I stop myself. Instead, I tell her the truth. I say, Everyone leaving made me think of the word *dispersion* and that made me think of patrolling and how my old sergeant used to call us fuck-knuckles when we were training.

The therapist laughs. *Fuck-knuckles* is a new one, she says.

And I say something about how Marines have a way with words because when I say things like that it makes people laugh and the therapist laughs again and I thank her and walk out of the meeting space and into the main hallway of the office suite.

All around me are open and closed doors, a T-shaped intersection, a stairwell to my rear leading to a second floor. And instead of thinking about how I might clear those spaces with a rifle, I'm thinking about what I'll teach next week and what I'll do with River during spring break the week after—I'm supposed to help Court gut and drywall his parents' garage because they're getting ready to sell their house and property and move to Florida. Mostly I'm thinking about what me and River will do over the weekend—Penny asked to FaceTime, Mom and Rick asked for help mulching the garden. Maybe we'll go for a hike at Ouabache State Park. Hiking for fun. What a fucking civilian. I think about dropping my pack and walk out into the sunshine.

Fifteen minutes before I need to get River. I'll send emails later.

On the drive I take the city route instead of the interstate because I know the interstate will be clogged. I let NPR drone in the background about whatever terrible bullshit is happening in the world because I'm the kind of guy who listens to NPR instead of music, and while I navigate the downtown grid I compose and revise those emails in my head. There's space in my head for more than ghosts now.

I think of alternative books to teach if the parents get their way and I think of how the year before a group of parents went after one of my colleagues when she assigned her freshmen some classic American novel the parents said promoted promiscuity and drug use and how the school board made my colleague stop teaching it. So I plan like the parents will get their way because I don't have rose-colored glasses about that after five years on the job. I think, *Proper prior planning prevents piss-poor performance.*

Penny calls from Oregon—she's on her lunch break—and I tell her about the parents and she tells me, like she always does, that I should go to grad school, get a PhD, move west, find a university gig with more freedom.

People are people, I say, because that's what I always say, and I know she knows the same goddamned thing is happening everywhere. I know she's mostly joking. I know she's not really asking me to move, to leave River, to abandon her. I know that she, Penny, didn't abandon me. I know it, but it's still an inventory I need to get a sight count of. And even then, I feel my heartbeat rising, feel that anger welling up, and I make up some excuse about pulling up to Max's so I can jump off the phone call, so I don't tear Penny a new one over the phone for no reason.

The therapist would call that progress.

Ten minutes until I need to get River. On the radio there's more terrible news.

The city streets are crowded but the cars move fast through the arteries. One of many things I've come to appreciate about Richfield.

The limestone and redbrick buildings cast the streets in shadow, cooling off the truck, which I still drive even though Max tells me to get with the times and buy something electric or at least hybrid. I pass what used to be the Speed Rail, now a family pint-and-slice joint River and I hit up sometimes on weekend afternoons, get food to go. We like to sit in the grass near the riverfront, which only a few years ago was nothing more than an embankment of retaining rock and tangles of bramble. Now there's a park, paved trails, boutique thrift shops where River likes to loudly declare her love for everything—oversized faux fur bucket hats and nineties acid-washed, elastic-waist jeans, fishnet gloves.

Above me the lofts I imagined living in with Max a decade ago loom. It's a memory that makes me squirm because of my stupidity or maybe my selfishness. It's almost easy to fall into the what-if trap: What if I'd asked Mom to watch River that night? What if I'd told Max what was going on when it first started happening? What if I would've gone to the VA sooner? Therapy sooner? Gotten the meds I needed? Grasshoppers and machine guns.

I'm quick to head off those thoughts, to be tender toward my younger self. I breathe and think of how the therapist tells me I'd just wanted to be whole. A whole person.

A real boy, I think. Just like Ruiz had said.

When I'm angry—if I get cut off in traffic or a student acts a fool in class—it's his voice in my head, quick and sharp. Or when I'm out pounding the pavement in the morning, he's singing cadence, keeping pace, making sure I don't fall behind. But I don't see him. On the anniversary of his death each year I go to a bar and have a vodka rocks like he used to. I'm a little sad. A little quiet. A little introspective. I know words like *introspective*. I use them.

Over the years the war has faded. At first I thought I was outpacing it, changing myself enough, leaving it behind. But the war was only blending in—camouflaging itself. The kids hawking gas and the abaya and headscarf women stand in the stark lines of electrical boxes and telephone poles. The out-of-work men smoking hookah crouch in the curves of hedges and car tires. Bakers make bread in the reflection flashes of store windows. In from the shadows. Less rough and demanding to be seen, but still there. Always there.

The sheep, though, paces in my periphery, still flitting along in shadows.

We've all got our ghosts.

Five minutes, I think, looking at the clock on the radio. More news. There's a new podcast about a cold-case murder I want to share with

River. She likes things like that. I have to run it by Max because we make decisions about River together.

I wasn't always good about that. I used to take shit like that—Max wanting me to run things by her—as needing permission, like she wanted me to get on my goddamned knees and beg for every little thing, but, really, she'd just wanted us to be thoughtful. It's taken me years to understand. *Petulant baby bullshit, so fucking stupid*, I think, and stop myself again. I shake off the shame and out loud I say, Let that shit go. Another canvas sign on the therapist's office wall. Let myself laugh at how I sound like some live, laugh, love Instagram influencer. Fuck it. It works.

When I told the therapist about being an asshole to Max, she'd just nodded, said, Where do you feel that in your body?

Everywhere, I'd said, annoyed as fuck by the line of questioning.

It doesn't mean you're a bad person, she'd said.

I'd burst into tears when she said that. Hadn't realized how far into mindset black I'd gotten.

Max and I tried to make it work in the months after her work trip, my break—that's what Mom calls it. When I got home with River the morning after Court's party, I told her everything. Told her about the war and Ruiz and the sheep and Court and the party and all the lies and deceptions and omissions. I asked her for help and she'd helped, but she couldn't trust me and I wasn't ready to do the work to earn it back.

Therapy, she'd said.

No way, I'd said. Fuck that. I don't need someone to tell me how I feel.

Even after everything that happened, I wasn't ready. Max ran out of patience.

We're friends now. Text, co-parent, spend holidays together. Max sends Mom and Rick birthday presents. But we've gone separate ways—want different things. She's dating a guy in his forties. His name is Paul. He's the HR director for a plastics manufacturer. Boring as all hell. Not a bad guy. Put together. Positive. Predictable. Good at small talk. Had been a bit of a prick when I first met him.

For a long time I kept thinking I deserved to be alone—some kind of penance for all the bullshit I put everyone through—but I've dated, too. A woman from my teaching program for a year until she moved to

Virginia for a job, a guy I met at a conference in Austin until the distance got too difficult, randoms on the apps. I came out before all that when I started therapy and told the therapist all about Ruiz and we figured it out together. Penny called me her big gay brother even though I'm younger and not gay and Rick hugged me and Mom said the thing she always says: I might not have given birth to you, but I am your mother.

I wanted to keep looking for my birth mom, but fucking life, right? VA appointments, River, trying to repair things with Max and Mom and Rick and Penny and Court, school, therapy, job interviews. But in the first summer of the pandemic, when all that shit hit a wall and life stopped and the stir-craziness set in, I sent away for my original, pre-adoption birth certificate. All it took was an application and twenty dollars to release the document. A month later I got a form letter telling me some bullshit about how there was a restriction placed on the release. Meaning one of my birth parents didn't want their name revealed. Stonewalled.

It's good I was in therapy then.

I turn onto Max's street and my heart jumps in my chest because it always does when I'm about to pick up River. Fucking excitement. I love the kid. But it's nerves too. Especially these days when it seems like she mostly wants to lose herself in a book or listen to music in her room while she draws—the kid's a goddamned artist. I don't know where it comes from but, goddamn, it's a hell of a thing to watch her make something. Sometimes she sits at the kitchen table and draws and I play music she doesn't know and she makes fun of me while I dance and tidy the house, do the dishes. I do shit like that. I'm comfortable doing shit like that. And sometimes we talk. Or she talks. I try not to ask questions, to correct, to react, because tweens scare easier than rabbits. I know that from teaching. I try to just let whatever roll off her tongue—thoughts, feelings, dreams.

I'm amazed by her. Frightened. What's amazement and fear combined? Awe. I'm in awe of her. I'd always thought me and Ruiz were hard. Big men ready to do violence. But we were nothing. Not nothing. Unsustainable. River's a goddamned rock. River rock. Rock, I call her.

I'd always thought power came from compartmentalization, control. Keeping emotions in check and then directing all that pent-up whatever in a single direction. Like I was some kind of claymore. Point front toward enemy. But for one, that shit's single-use. And all that cycling? All that letting things build up and build up and forcing them out through one little hole just stretched me out. Made it so all my emotions got tossed in the same place, mixed together until all I had was anger. One-trick pony. Must be hard not to know yourself, the therapist said when I told her that. Makes me feel like a newborn deer wobbling on matchstick legs. River's a goddamned mighty stag. Eleven and knows exactly what she feels, what she wants. Grabs the words and molds them so they're just for her. It's not radical to her, but to me? Awe. Shock and awe.

I pull into Max's driveway and watch River check her phone and smile and I wonder who she's texting. She stands and opens the front door and yells to Max probably, but I can't make out what she says even with the windows down.

When she gets in the truck, we'll say hello to each other and I'll ask her if she's all right because she looks tired. She always looks tired on Fridays. Same with my students. Week wipes them right the fuck out. She'll ask me about therapy because I'm honest with her about most everything and she knows I go to therapy, then we'll ride in silence for a bit, the radio filling the space, and I'll ask her about her classes, especially the science class she's been struggling with, but she'll interrupt me and ask me if I ever loved Max and I'll know she wasn't just tired and I'll think about her face when she checked her phone and know something else is up because I'm a good dad now, fat and happy, and all these possibilities will zip through my brain: a fight with Max or something with her friends or maybe a crush at school. And I'll say yes. She'll ask me how I knew.

You really want to hear that story? I'll say. A love story?

She'll nod.

Sure, I'll say. I'll tell you a love story.

ACKNOWLEDGMENTS

Contrary to popular belief, making a book isn't a lonely act—even if it feels like one sometimes. The ecology of a book is far reaching, and because of that I owe a ton of people huge thanks.

Monkey Bicycle and the *Cincinnati Review*: Thanks for publishing some early excerpts from this novel and making me feel like I might be doing something right.

Faculty and students in the MFA in creative writing at Pacific Lutheran University, otherwise known as the Rainier Writing Workshop: Thank you for your community, wisdom, and not-shitty feedback. Big shout-outs to Rick Barot for accepting me into the program, Marjorie Sandor for planting the seed in my head all the way back to my Oregon State undergrad days, and Renee Simms for weird (great) generative-writing assignments. Ultimate gratitude to Scott Nadelson and Kent Meyers for mentoring me, helping me to stop corralling this book with arbitrary constraints, asking questions I found difficult to answer, and giving head pats when I needed them. I am a person in need of many head pats.

Bloomsbury and my team there: Thank you for the time and attention and labor and patience, for believing in me as an author and in this book and for helping me make it better. I feel honored and lucky to keep getting to work with you all.

Anton Mueller: Thank you for being an incredibly close reader, genuinely caring about this book, helping me solve yet another ending, asking me to see my writing through a different lens, and challenging me to give Dean and Max depth and life.

Chris Clemans: I am lucky to have you on my side as an advocate and reader and friend. Thanks for reading slop while I figured out what I was doing, for getting hyped when I finally figured it out, and for writing a romantic war-comedy trailer to pitch it when it was done. I don't know how other agents do it, and I don't want to find out. You're awesome and I appreciate you. Onward.

Kaitlyn Andrews-Rice: I wouldn't have a book without you and our Mini Writing Group of Accountability. Truly. You're the best reader and always encouraging me to go full bore with whatever voice I'm writing in, and I deeply appreciate and need that (see above re: head pats). It's hard to come by someone who's smart, has tact, is fearless, and gets writing. You've been that person for this book. Can't wait to be that person for yours.

Susannah Breslin: Thank you for letting me annoy the hell out of you with my insecurity early on in the drafting process. Also, thanks for reminding me to write like myself. You helped me find some much-needed confidence.

Katie Flynn: Big thanks for the structural attention and the thoughtful reads and the extra writing-project distractions.

Bridget Gelms: Thank you for your support and excitement and feedback and movie-texting distractions.

Margaret Luongo: Thank you for being a continually great mentor and friend and for your generosity and time and guidance.

Curtis Dickerson, Michael Stonewright, and Maggie Waz: Thanks for reading the early mess of this and for being supportive of that mess and not laughing me out of our Zoom-room workshop.

Jenna: Thanks for being patient (mostly) and gentle (mostly) with my dramatic writer self, but also thanks for not enabling it. You gave your time and energy so that I could spend my time and energy on this thing, and that takes trust and faith and confidence, and I saw (and still see) that, and I'm going to try and remember it the next time that dramatic writer self tells me I'm stupid and I suck and no one likes or believes in my writing. Thanks for being my best friend and my favorite reluctant reader. Love you.

Maeve: When I started writing this book you were napping—sometimes on my chest—or crawling around my feet while I tried to finish my one-thousand-words-a-day goal, and we were together a lot. At first because I was at home taking care of you during the day, and then it was the early days of the pandemic, and for a while it was nothing but the three of us. And all that time with you made me think about being a parent and how joyous-scary-boring-hilarious-frustrating-beautiful-heartbreaking-humbling-and-and-and it is. So, I think, in a way, that this is your book, too. Thanks for helping me make it, kid. Love you most.

A NOTE ON THE AUTHOR

MATT YOUNG is a teacher and writer. His stories and essays have appeared in *Time* magazine, *Granta*, *Tin House*, *Catapult*, and the *Cincinnati Review*, among other publications. The recipient of fellowships from Words After War and the Carey Institute for Global Good, he teaches composition, literature, and creative writing at Centralia College in Washington. He is the author of the memoir *Eat the Apple* (Bloomsbury, 2018). This is his first novel.